ISBN 978-1-330-00717-4
PIBN 10002335

This book is a reproduction of an important historical work. Forgotten Books uses
state-of-the-art technology to digitally reconstruct the work, preserving the original format
whilst repairing imperfections present in the aged copy. In rare cases, an imperfection in
the original, such as a blemish or missing page, may be replicated in our edition. We do,
however, repair the vast majority of imperfections successfully; any imperfections that
remain are intentionally left to preserve the state of such historical works.

1 MONTH OF
FREE
READING

at
www.ForgottenBooks.com

By purchasing this book you are eligible for one month membership to ForgottenBooks.com, giving you unlimited access to our entire collection of over 700,000 titles via our web site and mobile apps.

To claim your free month visit:

www.forgottenbooks.com/free2335

Similar Books Are Available from
www.forgottenbooks.com

"'Which style is considered the more fashionable?' inquired Felicia, turning to Alfred, whose eyes having met hers, instantly dropped."—*Page 52.*

Lady Felicia.

A NOVEL.

By HENRY COCKTON.

" Mr. Wilkins and Fidele stopped to gather a variety of wild flowers, when Alfred and
Felicia—as if they really understood all about it—went in advance."—*Page* 248.

LONDON:
OFFICE OF THE NATIONAL ILLUSTRATED LIBRARY,
227 STRAND.

LADY FELICIA.

A NOVEL.

BY HENRY COCKTON,

AUTHOR OF ' VALENTINE VOX," "SYLVESTER SOUND," &c., &c.

LONDON:

OFFICE OF THE NATIONAL ILLUSTRATED LIBRARY,

227, STRAND.

MDCCCLII.

LONDON :

J. HADDON, PRINTER, CASTLE STREET, FINSBURY.

CONTENTS.

LADY FELICIA.

CHAPTER I.

INTRODUCTION.

In the celebrated borough of Sudbury, some years before the patriotic struggles of the enlightened freemen had won for it that political repose and parliamentary independence by which it is now so peculiarly distinguished, there was a glorious electioneering contest between Lord Charles Jocelyn and Captain Coleraine.

The immediate cause of this contest was not at the time held to be extraordinary: it was indeed simply this, that Sir William Wardle, whom the freemen had previously elected, had lost his seat merely in consequence of its having been proved before a Committee of the House of Commons that he had performed divers acts of generosity which, by virtue of a singular political fiction then in existence, were designated acts of bribery and corruption.

It may to some appear to be strange that a man's generosity should have involved the loss of that which it cost him forty thousand pounds to gain; but such, notwithstanding, was the fact, and the only consolation Sir William had was that of strongly recommending his friend Lord Charles to those by whom that generosity had been experienced.

Lord Charles was a Blue; the gallant Captain was a Yellow—colours which at that ennobling period of British history com-

B

prehended all the political virtues; but although in point of
colour the candidates were opposed, their aspirations were
equally pure and patriotic: they both aspired to the honour
of representing in Parliament the views and feelings of the
independent freemen; and as those views and feelings were
based upon the principle of bringing their votes to the best
market,' each' candidate naturally conceived himself to be
strictly, if not indeed peculiarly, eligible.

From this great principle of political economy those freemen
were never known to swerve. Nothing could ever induce them
to violate it. If not immaculate, they were, in this respect,
immutable. Having the privileges of freemen, they exercised
those privileges like freemen—they sold their votes to the
highest bidder, to be collectively sold again.

They had no bigoted predilection for this or that particular
faction—not they; they had no desire to keep this or that
party in power: on the contrary, the more frequently the reins
of government changed hands the more gratified they were,
provided always that every change involved a fresh election.

It will hence be perceived that the honour of representing
these highly enlightened freemen was sufficiently great to
warrant strong exertions; and as both the noble Lord and
the gallant Captain had been inspired with an exalted appreciation of that honour, they resolved on doing all in their
power to secure it.

The result of the petition against the return of Sir William
having been with confidence anticipated, arrangements were
made for the canvas before that result was absolutely known.
Agents were appointed, committees were formed, musicians
were secured, and blazing banners were displayed, while the
public-houses were all "open" houses, to which the philan-
thropic freemen daily flocked, with a view to the development
of their love of enlightened liberty, by eating, and drinking, and
singing, and shouting, and thus preparing themselves to fight

for that glorious colour to which the superior amount of pay might be attached.

There was, however, one freeman residing in the borough—and it may be held to be a marvellous fact that there was one—who had invariably kept aloof; who had, in the midst of temptations, maintained a position of perfect neutrality; whom no one had ever been able to bring to the poll; and who had never been induced even to "name his own terms!"

Of course, all his brother freemen held him in contempt; they pronounced him to be both a fool and a rogue—a fool to himself and a rogue to his family; and marvelled that he should thus refuse to exercise that privilege, the sale of which they conceived to be their indisputable and inalienable right.

His name was Murray. He was not a rich man; he had, on the contrary, barely sufficient capital to carry on his business, and as this was known, he was never given up: he was invariably importuned; and as the warm solicitations of highly influential men attached to both parties proved in this instance as usual unavailing, they combined to starve him into compliance—to force him to vote either one way or the other—not only by withholding their custom, but by pouring in their bills and demanding immediate payment.

Conceiving, however, that as the election was so near he should be able to stand against this, and that when the exciting contest was over the virulence of the combination would subside, he still adhered to his principle of neutrality, sustained by the conviction that the purity of his motives—for however impolitic they might have been considered, they really were pure—would never be permitted by Providence to involve him and his family in ruin.

Well, the day of nomination arrived, and the borough presented a series of scenes which in those days of civilization were held to be essential to success. The band of the Blues first paraded the town, playing patriotic airs with more power than precision,

and followed by a troop of dauntless freemen bearing aloft with
constitutional pride their flags and their banners which boldly
proclaimed their noble devotion to the altar and the throne,
and armed with bludgeons of every description from the rough
hedgestake to the lead-loaded cane.

The Blues, however, had not been out long when the equally
pure Yellow patriots appeared with their band, banners, and
bludgeons; and as they soon met the Blues in a narrow street,
each party prepared to walk into the other's ranks. Both
scorned to give way, and the battle commenced. Patriotic
blood flew about in all directions. Heads were broken, banners
were rent, and musical instruments were hurled into the air
amid shouts of "Britons never will be slaves!" "Yellow for
ever!" and "Blue to all eternity!"

As the Yellows were the stronger body, they very soon made
it appear; when the Blues, finding most of their best men
disabled, beat a retreat, and were pursued by the Yellow
patriots with the most enthusiastic shouts of victory.

At the end of the street, however, the Blues, who had sent
to head quarters for assistance, met a powerful reinforcement,
the leader of which called upon them to rally, and promptly sent
a detachment round for the purpose of attacking the enemy
in the rear. The formidable character of this reinforcement at
once caused the Yellows to halt; but they were still determined
to stand their ground, and they did so for some time valiantly;
but when they saw the detachment coming down upon their
rear with blue colours flying and Blue patriots cheering in a
state of wild rapture, they were seized with an universal panic,
and finding themselves thus completely hemmed in, they rushed
into the houses, barricaded the doors, and then flew to the
windows, from which they hurled upon the hot devoted heads
of the Blues every article of furniture they could find.

At this interesting juncture, a desperate and formidable body
of the Yellows rushed to the rescue with shouts of revenge;

when the Blues who had been harassed by the missiles from the windows—for not even a poker, a chair, or a pair of tongs could descend without doing *some* slight execution, while a bed-post, a table, or a small chest of drawers invariably laid a *few* low— retreated just in time to establish a barricade, with two waggons, a cart, and a showman's van—which happened to be passing at the time, and which contained a British lion, whose services they certainly would have solicited, had they been sure of his being a Blue—behind which barricade they formed themselves into line, and thus left the Yellows in possession of the field.

Broken heads had now to be mended, and beer had to be drunk in considerable quantities, in order to keep the spirits of the patriots up; and when these two grand desiderata had been accomplished, the eventful hour fixed for the nomination arrived.

This was the most imposing scene of the day—a scene in which the forces of both parties were concentrated—and when the candidates appeared upon the hustings, surrounded by their influential friends, a glorious chorus of yells, groans, and cheers burst forth with electric effect.

No time was now lost. In the midst of the din, the returning officer came forward and opened the proceedings, briefly, it is true, but with infinite tact; when the highly influential individuals who had the honour to propose and to second the " fit and proper persons" to represent the enlightened freemen of that independent borough, performed their parts with a fine sense of pantomimic propriety. They made a most eloquent display of their arms: their voices of course were not allowed to be heard, but they evidently felt that the eyes of all Europe were upon them, and hence deemed it highly correct to call to their aid the true poetry of motion, in order to strike conviction into the noble freemen's souls.

Nor were the freemen blind to these striking pantomimic appeals: they watched them narrowly, expecting every moment

to be called upon to show what effect those appeals had had upon
them; but when the show of hands had been called for, neither
that returning officer, nor any other returning officer in Europe
could have told on which side the majority stood.   This gentleman, however—being a strictly conscientious man—guessed at it:
he declared the result to be in favour of the Blues, when a poll
was demanded on behalf of the Yellows, amid terrific cheers on
the one hand, and maniacal yells on the other.

The band of the Blues now struck up enthusiastically, and
the Yellow band, inspired with the spirit of emulation, struck
up too.   It was strongly suspected that they played different
tunes; but the particular tune which either played was above
suspicion.   It was then, and has been ever since, questionable
whether the musicians themselves knew what they were playing.
Their object was to blow away as hard they *could* blow, and
certainly that object was attained.

Meanwhile a highly influential Blue, upon the hustings, was,
with unexampled energy, expatiating on the varied virtues and
purely patriotic principles of the party to whom he was devotedly
attached, and of whom he was one of the most conspicuous orna-
ments; but as it was very soon felt that on such an occasion he
was rather too long-winded, a detachment of the Yellows, with
the view of supporting their *own* eternal principles, brought a
fire engine, laden with liquid filth, and played upon him and all
around him, not only with spirit and precision, but with the
most refreshing impartiality.

To obtain possession of this engine, the Blues now directed
all their energies; and as the object of the Yellow party was to
retain it, a battle of course immediately commenced, and although
many sanguinary battles have been fought for objects of less
intrinsic value, there is not on record one in which more heat
was displayed, or of which the result more completely involved
the destruction of that for which both sides contended!   The
engine was utterly demolished; and when the patriots had

fought until they felt that they wanted a little more beer, they retired from the field, as if by mutual consent, while the bands played simultaneously—" *See the conquering heroes come !*"

During the two following days, drinking, voting, parading, and fighting, formed the chief constitutional amusements of the people. Every effort was made to buy and bring up the independent freemen : they were brought from all parts of the country, until both sides experienced some difficulty in polling even one man an hour, when, as the numbers were nearly equal, it was mutually agreed that the poll should finally close at four o'clock.

Now it was under these highly exciting circumstances that the Marquis of Kingsborough—the noble father of Lord Charles —walked gaily into Murray's establishment, ostensibly in order to have a little chat with him, albeit he had just been mysteriously informed that that gentleman was out at the time, endeavouring to borrow a little money to meet a bill.

" Good morning," said the Marquis, addressing Mrs. Murray, whom he found in the shop alone. " Mr. Murray within ?"

" No, my Lord," replied Mrs. Murray, with a feeling of embarrassment inspired by the presence of so great a man. " He is not in the way just now, my Lord; but I expect him in shortly."

" Oh! its a matter of no consequence. I merely called: nothing more. How is business ?"

" Dull, my Lord: exceedingly dull."

" Indeed! Dear me ; why how do you account for that ?"

" Mr. Murray doesn't vote, my Lord; and all our best customers have in consequence left us."

" Oh! that's it !—I see! But dear me he must be a very simple man to injure himself and family in that way! He certainly ought to vote on one side or the other! A neutral man in a town like this can never expect to get on. I am no advocate myself for exclusive dealing, but, as you know, men in general will not deal with those who refuse to oblige them. Besides, men who have the privileges of freemen, ought to exercise those privileges; if not, they become, of course, perfectly valueless."

"I wish, my Lord, that Mr. Murray was not a freeman."

"No doubt of it; but as he is, he ought not to abstain from acting like a freeman. But you fascinating daughters of Eve have so much influence over us! I suppose now that you have been persuading him not to vote?"

"No, indeed, my Lord; I wish him to vote; but his impression is, that if he doesn't vote at all, he cannot permanently offend either party."

"But surely a woman of your good sense cannot fail to perceive that he thus offends both! He has not, I presume, any very strong political predilections?"

"He never interferes, my Lord, with politics at all!"

"Then, let him vote which way he will, he cannot be charged with apostacy. Let him vote by all means. If I were you," continued the Marquis, with a smile, "I wouldn't let him rest until I had driven him to the poll! It isn't as if you wished him to do anything wrong! I'd *make* him go!—that is, I would use all my influence with a view of inducing him to go. It's folly—perfect folly—for a man thus to lose all his trade, when by the mere act of exercising his right he might be prosperous! Talk to him—the silly man—talk to him well! The idea of a respectable establishment like this having no trade is monstrous! But come, do some business: for goodness' sake do some business: send some goods up to the Hall: some sheetings and shirtings—you know what to send—say thirty pounds' worth to begin with."

"I feel indeed exceedingly obliged to you, my Lord."

"Not at all: not at all. Here, I'd better pay you now."

"That, my Lord, is perfectly unnecessary."

"It may be; but thirty pounds in hand shall be always worth as much as thirty pounds in the book."

"Your Lordship is very considerate. Shall I send the bill up with the goods, my Lord ?"

"No, write down now goods thirty pounds, and put paid to the bill."

Mrs. Murray now felt so exceedingly tremulous that she scarcely knew how to hold the pen : she did, however, manage to make out the bill, and the Marquis immediately paid the amount.

"Send the goods up," said he, "at your own convenience—any day will do—and mind that you talk to that silly man well. He ought, for the sake of his family. By the way, what family have you ?"

"Two children, my Lord."

"Oh! two; and another I perceive—very well—two. Are they boys or girls ?"

"Girls, my Lord."

"Ah; then the next child, of course, you expect will be a boy! Never mind me: I'm an old married man. You *do* expect a boy—I'm sure of it! Now, listen. Let your husband go at once to the poll, and if it *be* a boy I'll stand godfather to him! If it be a girl I'll not neglect her; but if it be a boy I'll make a man of him. Take no notice of this to any one but your husband. If you'll but persuade him to go to the poll, I'll do what I say. Good morning."

For some time after the Marquis had left, Mrs. Murray felt perfectly bewildered. The receipt of the thirty pounds, under the circumstances, had alone been sufficient to cause deep emotion ; but the thought of her boy—for a boy she felt sure that it would be—her own boy, being the godson of a Marquis, inspired her with rapture !

Feeling, however, that Murray had yet to be persuaded, she regained her self-possession, and calmly awaited his return ; and when he did return, he with an overhanging brow went at once to his desk without noticing her smile.

" Have you been successful, my dear ?" she inquired.

" No," he replied, angrily, " I have not. *You* may oblige people as long as you please : you may even impoverish yourself to oblige them; but when you want them to oblige *you*, they'll see you ruined rather than make an effort. The very men whom I have assisted now refuse to assist me. Even Johnson, whom I have constantly served—whose cheques I have cashed and kept week after week, when I conceived that he was short at the bank—even he—although I know that he has plenty of money now—couldn't make up the sum if I'd give him the world !"

" Well, well, my dear, their conduct is unkind, but we shall be able to manage without them."

" Louisa, how you talk: how can you speak so lightly of that which is to us of so much importance ? You know that my credit in London is at stake. I wouldn't let that bill go back."—

" My dear, we have more than sufficient to meet it ! You want twenty pounds to make up the amount, and while you were out I took thirty."

" Thirty pounds !" exclaimed Murray, with an expression of amazement. " Have the Palmers been here then to settle their bill ?"

" No, dear: no. I've received an order for goods to that amount, and the money you'll find in the desk."

In an instant Murray opened the desk, and the six five-pound notes met his wondering gaze.

" Why," said he, having convinced himself of their real presence, " who, my dear—who has been here ?"

" One who, when I told him that business was dull, gave me the order, and paid me at once."

" But who—who gave you the order ?"

" The Marquis; and a nice, kind, good-tempered creature he is."

Murray's countenance fell.

" The Marquis!" he exclaimed, "I see! This is intended for a bribe. Did you in my name promise him a vote?"

" No, my dear, I did not. He gave me the order, which, of course, I felt justified in taking; and when he insisted upon paying the amount, I was but too happy to receive it."

" I have a great mind—much as I want money—to send it back."

" Nay, dear, that would be very unwise. But come in, and then I'll explain all that passed."

With a thoughtful expression, Murray followed his wife, and when they were seated in the parlour behind the shop, she thus continued :—

" Now my dear, there can, of course, be no doubt that the object of the Marquis in calling here was to induce you to vote for Lord Charles."

" Then he'll not gain his object."

" But listen, dear; listen. I say that, notwithstanding this order was given without any direct reference being made to its having been given to induce you to vote, it is quite clear that that was his object in calling. But this is not all. Having, in the course of conversation, very justly ascribed the loss of our trade to the fact of your being neutral, he expressed a hope that instead of injuring yourself and family by keeping aloof, you would ensure prosperity by exercising the privilege you possess, and promised — mark! absolutely promised, that if our next dear child were a boy, he would, in the event of your going to the poll, stand godfather to him! ' If,' said he, ' it be a girl, I'll not neglect her; but if it be a boy, I'll make a man of him!' "

" And what said you to that?"

" He gave me no time to say a word. Having made this promise he moved to the door, bade me good morning, and hastily left."

A pause ensued, during which there was a struggle in Murray's mind between his principle of neutrality and his interest. His wife watched the development of this conflict anxiously; and, when she feared that neutrality would triumph, enforced her own views with all the eloquence at her command, portraying the most brilliant scenes of prosperity, and dwelling especially upon the bright prospects of her boy, until Murray, with a resolute air, rose to leave, when she cried with thrilling intensity, "William, dear! William! Where—where are you going?"

"My mind's made up," said he, thoughtfully.

"To what, dear William? Pray tell me."

"To vote."

"God bless you!" she exclaimed, and embraced him with rapture. "Oh," she added, "you have made me so happy! But fly, dear; speak to no one on the way; don't stop to talk to a soul; and when you have voted come back at once to me."

Murray kissed her and left to record his vote, and that vote secured the return of Lord Charles.

Of course, when they saw him go up to the poll, both the Blues and the Yellows were struck with amazement, and as they had no knowledge of his having been bribed, they conceived that in order to prove his independence he had absolutely given his vote away, which was held by them to be the most monstrous act of folly it was possible for any sane man to commit. The Blues, notwithstanding this, gave him three cheers; but the Yellows yelled and groaned with desperation. They moreover broke his windows in the course of the night; but in the morning he received anonymously sufficient to repair them.

From this time his business increased rapidly, and when a month had expired, Mrs. Murray was confined with her third child, which, to her inexpressible delight, *was* a boy! And oh! how brilliant, in her gentle judgment, was that dear boy's prospects! And such a sweet boy!—such a noble boy! Who could tell that the patronage of the Marquis would not enable him to become the First Minister of the Crown, the Archbishop of Canterbury, or the Lord High Chancellor of England? Why, even then to her the germs of greatness were perceptible!—to her he developed surpassing genius at the breast!—and often while he slept would she sit and gaze upon him with a true mother's feelings of pride, and then clasp him to her heart in the perfect conviction that he was absolutely born to be illustrious!

The Marquis—to whom the birth of his *protégé* had become known—shortly afterwards called and saw the child, and was really delighted with its appearance; and when the day appointed for its baptism arrived, he performed his promise, and expressed a hope that "his Alfred" would be well taken care of. And he was taken care of: indeed, in one sense, too much care was taken of him, and physical delicacy was the result. Having completed his seventh year, however, he was sent by the Marquis to a boarding school, at which his health improved, and he became a fine boy. He remained here until he was nearly fourteen, when he was about to be sent to Eton with a view to his being prepared for Oxford; but as at this period the noble Marquis died, the youth's brilliant prospects sank below the horizon.

He had by this time received a sound preliminary education; but as Murray was unable to bear the expense of its completion and equally unable to give him a profession, Alfred went home in order to learn his father's business, with the only prospect then in view of being eventually able to conduct it.

To this change — mortifying as it was to all concerned Alfred endeavoured to reconcile himself: he endeavoured to acquire tradesman-like habits, and to bring his mind to bear upon the one grand object, but with very equivocal success, for the talent which was in that sphere most applauded, appeared to him to resemble low cunning too closely, while the practices to which it was deemed necessary to have recourse did not accord with his notions of honour. He, notwithstanding, remained at home until he was twenty-one, when his father— conceiving that if he were to see how business was conducted in London, it would tend to enlarge his views and to render him more competent to commence on his own account—made arrangements with the proprietor of a celebrated establishment in the metropolis, to which Alfred was transferred, and in which he appeared under the immediate patronage of Mr. Bartholomew Wilkins—the principal assistant, and the most accomplished salesman of the day — who undertook, with feelings of pleasure and pride, to "polish him positively up."

CHAPTER II.

MR. WILKINS.

MR. WILKINS was an exquisite of the most exalted caste : his style of dress was *distingué*. An immense gold chain adorned his vest—which was either of white cassimere, crimson velvet, or emerald satin—and while his bosom was studded with brilliants, and his fingers were duly embellished with rings, his air was that of a milliner's pet, and his *tout ensemble* striking.

His toilet never occupied less than three hours : it might be said indeed to have occupied the whole of the day, for, as the shop was lined with glass, he was throughout the day engaged in admiring himself in every possible point of view, and really he sometimes appeared to be absolutely lost in admiration. There was not a man in Europe who entertained a higher opinion of his personal appearance, and had it not been for his hands, he, beyond all doubt, would have considered himself not only irresistible, but perfect.

Those hands of his were a source of great mental affliction : they were the only real trouble he had. They were large and red, and he could neither reduce the size of them, nor blanch them. Fancy soaps—of which he had a great variety—were ineffectual: cosmetics of every description failed; even poultices, applied in gloves, night after night, proved unavailing: they were still large and red, still calamitously ugly. Nor did his nails in the slightest degree redeem them; they were short, and stumpy, and shapeless, and flat, while by some mysterious process of nature, the skin made everlasting efforts to conceal

them. He rubbed it down, and trimmed it up, and tried to
check its progress by all the means in his power; but as it
would grow, and that in the most ragged manner possible, he
had as much trouble to keep it back, as the spirit of supersti-
tion has to keep back intelligence.

It will hence be perceived, why he could not—with any
degree of justice to his discernment, or by virtue of any stretch
of the imagination—consider himself perfect; but with the
exception of his inelegant hands, he certainly held his appearance
to be faultless. And who could attend to a lady with more
grace ? who could address her more eloquently, or in language
more suasive and deferential ?   What could surpass in beauty
his style of showing a shawl? It was great—truly great.
With what consummate tact would he display its peculiar
excellences! With what masterly effect, while throwing it
out for inspection, would he strike a stately histrionic attitude!
He was, in this department, the first man of the age, and, in
consequence commanded the highest salary on record.

His genius, however, was not confined to style: he was
highly—nay, magnificently imaginative. He was the author of
the history of every valuable shawl in stock—a history embellished with romances of sterling interest. He was, moreover, a
student of Indian warfare. He read with avidity all the public
despatches and *would* have a shawl—of course nominally—from
the glorious scene of action, wherever that glorious scene might
be, and, as the intrinsic value could not be defined, he would
set a price upon it, exactly in proportion to the splendour and
importance of the achievement.

At first, while listening to these interesting romances,
Alfred regarded them as lessons got by rote, to be repeated
whenever an opportunity offered, and fancied that he should
very soon discover a sameness in them calculated to weaken, if
not to destroy their effect; but when he found that the imagination of his mentor was illimitable, that he was never at a

loss for something novel, and that his versatility was
striking as the style in which it was displayed, he
that *his* Pegasus was but a screw, and felt anxious t
thing up.

"I quite despair," said he, on one occ
Wilkins had sold a cashmere shawl for a hund⌐⌐⌐⌐⌐⌐⌐⌐⌐⌐y
virtue of representing it to have been taken from ⌐⌐⌐⌐ Saib,
at the storming of Seringapatam—"I quite despair of ever
being able to compete with, or even to approach, you."

"Despair, sir!" exclaimed Mr. Wilkins. "Despair! Folly,
Mr. Murray, sir!—absolute folly. Can the eaglet soar like the
parent bird? Can a man reach the top of the tree without
climbing? Did Rubens, Handel, Shakespeare, Burke, Demos-
thenes, or Alexander? They all excelled in their respective
spheres, as I excel in mine; but was this excellence attained
all at once? Most unequivocally not! Before a man reaches
the top of the tree he must of necessity surmount the lower
branches. Emulation, Mr. Murray, emulation and hope are
the best half-and-half any student can drink, and beats all the
grog he can take to inspire him. Despair! Had Milton or
Correggio despaired, would they ever have been what they
were?"

"Perhaps not," replied Alfred, "but they were great men!"

"Great men! Every man is great who can do something
better than every other man. I can't write like Milton, it is
true!—nor can I paint with Correggio; but could either of
them sell a shawl with me? They had genius sufficient, no
doubt! Milton might have been taught to show a shawl:
Correggio might have been instructed how to sell one; but that
was not their mission: each stuck to his own sphere, and they
both achieved greatness, but neither was greater in *his* sphere
than I am in mine!"

Alfred smiled, and was about to draw a line between the
greatness of Mr. Wilkins and that of Correggio; but as a

customer happened to enter at the time, the subject dropped
without receiving any additional illustration. He nevertheless
felt that the "mission" of Mr. Wilkins was, in his estimation,
a high one, although he could not but think that it was far
more honourable to grind the colours for a man like Correggio,
than to invent with a view to deception, even so brilliant a
romance as that which had reference to Tippo Saib's loss at
the storming of Seringapatam.

The next morning, while the great Mr. Wilkins and his
"principal" were engaged in conversation, Alfred had an
opportunity of distinguishing himself in that particular
"sphere" in which his mentor shone with so much effulgence.
A lady entered, and expressed a wish to look at a certain
scarf, which was then displayed in one of the windows. She
spoke to Alfred, who immediately placed it before her, and
as she did not appear to approve of it much, he submitted
several to her notice, and although much embarrassed, said a
few words occasionally in their favour, while Mr. Wilkins
hovered near him, with the view of interposing, in the event of
his being unable to effect a sale. At length he showed her
one with which she appeared to be quite delighted, and Alfred
in consequence, became eloquent in its praise. The lady
looked at him earnestly while he was speaking, and seemed to
linger at every pause, as if she wished him to proceed, until
he blushed and became more embarrassed than ever, when
perceiving this, she said, "Yes—it is—*very* beautiful. I'll
take it."

"Allow me, sir," said Mr. Wilkins, coming forward. And
having seized the scarf, he folded it up on the instant, while
the lady produced a brilliant purse.

"Where will you permit me to send it?" inquired Alfred.

"Our carriage is at the door," replied the lady, who rose
and bowed to Alfred with an elegance the most refined.

Having received the parcel from Mr. Wilkins, Alfred followed, and gracefully handed the lady into the carriage, in which sat an elderly gentleman, who took no notice either of her or of him, and as the carriage drove off, she bowed again, and Alfred returned to the shop.

"Bravo!" exclaimed Mr. Wilkins, as he grasped Alfred's hand in a state of enthusiasm. "Well done, sir!—Excellent! —elegant!—good!"

"You did it very well, Mr. Murray," observed the principal; "very well—very well indeed."

"I wonder who she is," said Mr. Wilkins. "As the carriage didn't drive up until she was about to leave, I hadn't time to examine it minutely, but I'm sure I saw a coronet upon it. However, Mr. Murray has made an excellent beginning, and I have not the slightest doubt of his success."

These words of encouragement were pleasing, of course, and Alfred acknowledged them mechanically; but his thoughts were engaged in reviewing that scene in which he had played so conspicuous a part. An analysis of the feelings with which he had been inspired was perfectly impracticable then: the more he dwelt upon them the more embarrassed he became; and yet what, after all, had occurred? She had spoken to him; but then that voice!—so soft, so silvery, so sweet!—in imagination he heard it still, and it sounded like celestial music! She had smiled. Well? Oh! but what a smile! In that smile her whole soul seemed centred; and as she gazed at him as if enrapt, what eloquence beamed from her beautiful eyes! But what could have been the cause of that electric sensation which ran thrilling through his veins? Could it have been her exquisite loveliness? He had seen lovely women before! *They* had never inspired him with feelings at all comparable with those which he experienced then! But had he ever before seen one *so* lovely? He fancied he saw her still, and felt enchanted: that fascinating smile of the soul re-inspired him with ecstasy! But while she appeared to gaze with rapture upon him, Mr. Wilkins broke the spell.

. "Mr. Murray," said he; and on the instant Alfred started as if from a dream,—"we have a beastly thing here, the intrinsic value of which is infinitesimally small, but which it strikes me you'll be able to make a tidy price of."

Alfred approached, and found that the "beastly thing" referred to was a dingy-coloured, ill-looking shawl, which appeared to be worth about eighteenpence.

"It's a Frenchman," continued Mr. Wilkins, "and its unrivalled ugliness has been hitherto its sole recommendation. Hence no one has fallen in love with it; and as it will never be sold on its own merits, some extrinsic virtue must be attached to it in order to make it move off these premises, to which it has stuck from time immemorial, and to which it will otherwise still stick to all eternity. The man who designed it is, I hope, in heaven; but I wish that he had been there before he had compassed his design; indeed, he had no business to be on earth at all, for his mind must have been in a frantic state of infelicity. If, therefore, you wish to immortalize yourself, sell it."

"At what price?" inquired Alfred.

"Why," replied Mr. Wilkins, "there is a legend that it originally cost three guineas!—and this may have been the veritable golden legend,—but I don't feel that I have the power to stretch my credulity to that extent. It is, however, worthy of belief that it originally cost something, notwithstanding it was all that something too much; and as it will not go off at any sacrifice, however tremendous or alarming, we must put a value upon it commensurate with its idiocratic character. Its price has been marked down year after year until it has reached the lowest depths of degradation. We must snatch it from this abyss. It must rise like the phœnix from its ashes, to which it ought long ago to have been literally

reduced; and as it is a species of phœnix—for it may with
perfect safety be affirmed that it is the only one of the sort
in creation—its single existence at a striking price will offer
a temptation which cannot long be resisted. Now, let me see.
Being a Frenchman it must, of course, be attached to the
history of France, and have reference to some stirring period.
The revolution! That will do. The unhappy Queen of
Louis the Sixteenth was beheaded. Very good. This was
her shawl—her favourite shawl—the shawl which, just before
she was dragged to the guillotine, she gave to one of her
maids of honour, who, having taken refuge in England, became
short of money and sold it to us. Eh? What do you think
of that? Don't you think it will do?"

"No doubt of it," said Alfred, "but you'll be able to
manage it better than I shall."

"I don't know so much about that, Mr. Murray. Try at
all events what you can do. If you succeed in selling the
extraordinary work of art, no matter by what means the sale
may be effected, you will prove, sir, to my satisfaction at least,
that you are able to sell anything upon earth."

Well! Alfred, of course, promised to do what he could; but
immediately after that promise had been given his thoughts
again reverted to *her* whose mysterious influence had been so
irresistible. He tried to take a common sense view of the
matter—to seduce himself into the belief that there was
nothing extraordinary in what had occurred—that her fascinating manners were the mere result of social refinement, and
that even her smile, of which the effect had been so thrilling,
was a purely conventional smile! Still there was something
which he could not define; some species of magic which defied
common sense; some mystery which he was utterly unable
to solve.

But, then, who and what was she? Was she an aristocratic
coquette? Did she lavish upon all such smiles as those by

which *he* had been enchanted? It might be so! And yet how could he believe it? What could be her motive? "The gratification of vanity! The thought of her being vain was no sooner conceived than repudiated. *She* vain! Impossible! No; his heart told him that she was not only beautiful, but good, amiable, gentle, intellectual, and pure—an angel of beneficence and love.

Upon her all his thoughts were throughout the day centred; and when the evening came, instead of going with his friend he repaired to his room to enjoy the sweets of solitude. Here fancy held a festival and revelled unrestrained: she created bright visions of hope, love, and joy; she led him through her realms, in which every sense was dazzled, and united him to her in whose honour the festival had been held; and even when he had retired to rest she opened before him a series of scenes illustrative of illimitable felicity.

In the morning he felt languid and looked somewhat pale, and Mr. Wilkins, who noticed this immediately after he had completed his toilet, looked at him with an expression of anxiety.

"Have you," said he, "been taking a black draught this morning?"

"No," replied Alfred.

"Then you want one. You don't look the thing; and there's nothing in Nature to beat a black draught: it purifies the blood, polishes up the imagination, and sweeps away the cobwebs from every corner of the soul. You must have one, my boy, by all means. But what were you doing with yourself all last evening? Reading, I suppose. Well! there's nothing like it to begin with; but when a man has laid a solid foundation, if he be anything of an architect at all, he may build for himself an observatory upon his books, and take a practical survey of all around: he may then study man as he finds him, with some chance of mastering his subject, and acquire that sound substantial knowledge of the world which books alone never can impart. You should have been with *me*, my boy, last night! You would then have had a practical illustration of this. We had a glorious evening!—Greek meeting Greek; intellect clashing with intellect; genius eclipsing genius, and wit darting from soul to soul. That's the style of thing, sir!—that's what I call intellectual recreation!—that's the way to prepare a man for the duties of the morrow!—I only wish, Mr. Murray, that you had been there."

Alfred could not respond to that wish: he felt, that in imagination at least, he had been throughout the night in far more enchanting society: still his mind was filled with anxiety the most intense; his eye was upon every carriage that passed, and he panted with impatience for the approach of that, into which he had the previous day handed her who had acquired so much influence over him.

"Am I never," thought he, having watched in vain for hours—"Am I never to see her again? My heart prompts me to believe that I shall; and yet she does not appear."

At length a carriage dashed up to the door; but not *the* carriage: no; it had a more aristocratic appearance, and Mr. Wilkins prepared for a triumph; but although it was not *the* carriage, the lady who alighted from it was *the* lady; and as Mr. Wilkins saw this at a glance, he courteously called Alfred forward.

Alfred instantly turned pale as death. Her presence at once checked the action of his heart, and he became so exceedingly tremulous, that he felt scarcely able to appear before her. He did, however, manage to approach, and having bowed, seemed to inspire a vague notion that she had asked to look at something, but what he was utterly unable to tell. Perceiving his embarrassment, Mr. Wilkins immediately came to his aid. " French cambrics, Mr. Murray?" said he. "The last

consignment are of the most superb texture. Allow me to
point them out to you."

Alfred blushed deeply, and followed Mr. Wilkins—who
added, in a whisper, " Courage, sir—courage!—nothing on
earth can be done without courage!"—and having received
the French cambrics at his hands, returned to her before
whom all his courage had fled

She looked at them for a moment, and then looked at him.
She appeared to be endeavouring to recall something to her
mind, and, although Alfred did not pretend to understand it,
he could not but think that her manners were extraordinary.

At length, she said, with some slight degree of hesitation,
" Mr. Murray, I think, I just now understood your name to
be ?"

Alfred bowed, and his face became crimson again.

" Have you," she added, " been living here long ?"

" Scarcely a week," replied Alfred.

" Indeed! You came from the country, I presume ?"

" From Sudbury, in Suffolk."

" Sudbury ! We have an estate near Sudbury!—Murray,"
she added, thoughtfully. " Are you the young gentleman in
whom the late Marquis of Kingsborough took so great an
interest ?"

" The late Marquis was indeed extremely kind to me."

" Aye! You were one of the Mr. Montague's pupils.

" I was with him seven years," returned Alfred.

" Exactly! Oh, I perfectly well remember you now! It
struck me yesterday that I had seen you before somewhere,
but I couldn't at all recollect where. I also fancied that you
recognized me!—But in that, of course, I may be mistaken.—
I will, if you please, take this piece."

Alfred bowed, and then said, with an expression of intense
earnestness, " *Will* you allow me to know whom I have the
honour of addressing ?"

The lady smiled, and slightly blushed, as she opened her card-case, and having presented her card, smiled again.

Not another word was said on the subject. Alfred glanced at the card, and almost unconsciously placed it in his bosom; and when the cambric had been packed up and paid for, he handed her into the carriage as before.

"Very fair, Mr. Murray, very fair," said Mr. Wilkins, as Alfred re-entered the shop. "I only wish you had a little more confidence. What made you so tremulous? What had you to fear? I saw your colour come and go, like that of a regular virgin. Modesty is all very well in a woman, but it's out of its natural element in a man. That which tends to elevate her, depresses him. It is to him a peculiarly sinking virtue: it drags him below the surface of society, to which he never can rise again until he shakes it off. Modesty always keeps a man back, whereas confidence carries him forward; modesty lingers about the fortress—confidence walks up and takes it by storm. Your retiring men are of no use in *this* world!—they do but retire from such opportunities as those which they ought to embrace, and thus make way for others to seize them. Women don't like modest men: they like a rattle: they tolerate them only when they are known to have talent, without a tithe of which, others possessing confidence shine. Go into society. What is a modest man there? The very incarnation of insipidity, while he who has confidence blazes away. There are some men who act like buffoons in society, and what is the consequence? Why laughing eyes encourage and reward them. Men, in general, have too much self-respect, too much pride to be so ridiculously vain, and it is, of course, correct that they should have: I don't recommend the cultivation of such an accomplishment; but I hold it to be incumbent upon every man to acquire confidence, which is absolutely essential to success, and in no place is it more essential than in an establishment like this. But you'll gain it by and by,

I've no doubt;" he added. "You have but to appreciate its importance; a little experience will do all the rest. Now that lady gave you every opportunity. I saw her chatting to you in the most familiar style."

"She knows me," said Alfred.

"Indeed! Who is she?"

Alfred gave him her card.

"The Lady Felicia Jocelyn!" he exclaimed, with an expression of the most intense amazement. "Well, but—how came she to know you?"

"The late Marquis was my godfather."

"What! Your godfather! The late Marquis?—What Marquis?"

"The Marquis of Kingsborough"

"The Marquis of Kingsborough!—Your godfather!"—*Your* godfather!" reiterated Mr. Wilkins, who really looked as if he felt bewildered. "Do you mean to say—God bless my soul— the Marquis of Kingsborough!—Stop: let's have a look at the Peerage."

The peerage was referred to, and there it was found that the Marquis of Kingsborough had three daughters, of whom Lady Felicia was the youngest.

"Well," resumed Mr. Wilkins, having satisfied himself on this point, "you have to an almost inconceivable extent amazed me. But, having such brilliant connections—being as you are spiritually related to one of the first families in England—how is it that you are here? Why don't they give you a commission in the army, place you in the treasury, attach you to an embassy, or send you to Parliament? They certainly ought to do *something*!"

"I have no claim upon them," said Alfred.

"No claim! I consider that you have a strong claim, as the godson of him from whom they descended, and whose memory of course they revere."

"I am afraid," said Alfred, "that you are not doing justice to your practical knowledge of the world. But we'll talk this matter over together quietly, this evening; and then we can enter fully into the matter without the slightest chance of being disturbed."

This was agreed to with pleasure by Mr. Wilkins, who, having a deep veneration for the aristocracy, began to regard Alfred as one of the "order," and consequently as a superior being.

On the other hand, Alfred's spirit was depressed: his vivid imagination had been checked in full career; his fancy had been supplanted by matters of fact which were death to all the hopes he had inspired. Nor can this change be deemed, under the circumstances, extraordinary. The occurrence of anything for which we are unable to account prompts us at once to give the reins to imagination; but when that which we hold to be a mystery is solved, we "pull up" to contemplate reality. Alfred could now account for all that had occurred between him and Lady Felicia; he could account for her manner the preceding day, which had struck him as being so mysterious, and viewed as the natural effect of curiosity that which he had fondly ascribed to love. Everything appeared to be clear to him then. She had seen him before; and being unable to recollect where, she had looked at him with the view of refreshing her memory. Could anything be more natural? But, then, while looking she smiled! What then? Was there anything extraordinary in that? But why should her smile have had so thrilling an effect? Simply because while she looked at him so earnestly he couldn't understand the real object she had in view. Thus he sobered down his rapture, thus he cooled his warmest hopes, and thus eclipsed those visions of joy by which he had been so enchanted. But could he ever forget that smile, or cease to remember its effect? What feelings were those which that smile had n   ? Were they not in reality those of love? They must have been! But if even they were, ought he to encourage those feelings? Had she fallen in love with *him*, there might have been some ground for hope; but he felt that to cherish a love for her, she being indifferent, would be madness. But was she indifferent? He was quite disposed to believe that she was not; but feared that that belief would have vanity for its basis. She had, it was true, been exceedingly polite; but was not her recognition of him alone sufficient to account for that politeness? He dwelt upon this throughout the day, and viewed it in every possible light; but the gulf fixed between her position and his own convinced him that he ought to repudiate an object, the attainment of which he could *not* but deem hopeless.

In the evening, having repaired to a tavern with his friend, he felt somewhat more reconciled to that which he had, by a popular process of reasoning, transferred to fate. He ate a chop and enjoyed it, and so did his friend; but neither said a syllable having reference to the subject under consideration until the brandy had been brought, when Mr. Wilkins thoughtfully filled his glass and proposed as a toast, with due solemnity of expression, "May the prospect which now brightly opens before you, and of which the effulgence is glorious, be realized beyond your most brilliant expectations, and lead to an illustrious career!"

"I thank you," said Alfred, with a smile, "but I really have no particularly brilliant expectations!"

Mr. Wilkins looked at him intently for a moment, and then exclaimed, "What! Why, if I were as you are, the godson of a Marquis, I wouldn't give *that*, sir, to call the King my uncle!" And Mr. Wilkins snapped his middle finger emphatically.

"But," said Alfred, "what have I any right to expect?"

"Patronage, power, high consideration, and a lucrative berth to begin with."

" But the present Marquis doesn't even know me!"

" Of what importance is that! The very fact of his illustrious father having been your illustrious godfather will alone be sufficient to prompt him to give you a fair, if not indeed a magnificent, start. See what a variety of brilliant berths there are, with salaries ranging from one to five thousand a year, either of which he could procure for you with all the ease imaginable! See with what facility the thing may be done! He goes to the Minister and says—with that elegant *sang froid* which so peculiarly characterises our glorious aristocracy—'I want an appointment for a young friend of mine, a gentleman in whose welfare the late Marquis took considerable interest, and who is indeed, in a spiritual sense, related to our family. Have you anything at all good on hand? What can you give him?' 'Why,' says the Minister, 'I've so and so; but that's only worth about a thousand a year!' 'Well,' says the Marquis, 'give him that — give him that : let him begin low—give him that.' The thing is done; and there's an immediate end of the matter."

" Well," said Alfred, " but assuming that it might be thus easily accomplished, how would it be possible for either the Marquis or the Minister to know that I am competent to fill the vacant office?"

" Competent! They wouldn't trouble their heads about that. They would take it for granted, of course, that you were competent, and so in reality you are : you *must* be competent to look at the subordinates while they are doing the work!"

" And yet my salary would be considerably higher than theirs!"

" Of course! That's legitimate! Work and pay, almost universally, keep pace with each other—in an inverse ratio : maximum work?—minimum pay : minimum work?—maximum pay. That's the system—a system of which some may

complain, but with which, good or bad, you have nothing
to do; you are not responsible for it; it was not established
by you; there it is, and that's enough. Without, therefore,
presuming to enter into the abstract merits of a system which
has worked so well, and which is, moreover, sanctioned by the
highest authorities, let us go at once to the primary point;
that is to say, the first step to be taken. You are not known
to the Marquis. Well, your first object will therefore be to
make yourself known to him. But how? By what means?"

"Why, if at all," replied Alfred, who was anything but
sanguine on the subject, "it had better be done, perhaps, by
letter."

"I think not,"—said Mr. Wilkins—"I decidedly think not:
I submit, sir, that that would not be the better plan: it strikes
me that the simple course which I shall suggest will have more
effect than ten thousand letters. You are known to the Lady
Felicia: very well. The familiar style in which she conversed
with you this morning prompts me to believe that she is well
affected towards you. What follows? Enlist *her!*—solicit
her advocacy!—get *her* to speak to the Marquis; and if your
cause be *not* triumphant I'll die! I'll stake my existence
upon the result. A single word from her will be amply
sufficient to start you on the high road to wealth and distinction. Speak, therefore, to her!—secure *her* interest—and
there you are!—*all* right—placed in a position to pursue a
magnificent career."

"Well," said Alfred, "certainly, the course you suggest is
the one most likely to be successful; but it is at the same
time one which I feel I should be utterly unable to adopt."

"But why? What possible objection can be raised? Can
the mind of man conceive the slightest degree of impropriety
in the pursuit of such a course? She knows you: she has
known you from boyhood; and, while from her manner I infer
that she respects you, I feel that she would do all in her power

to serve you. What more can you want? Can any man breathing be placed in a better position to solicit a favour?"

" Perhaps not," replied Alfred. " I do believe that I could ask such a favour of any one else, but I feel quite sure that I couldn't ask her."

" Well, but why not? That's the point which puzzles me? Why not?"

" I don't know, and therefore can't explain."

" You have, I presume, a high respect for her?"

" I have."

" And were it in your power to promote her happiness, you would exercise that power?"

" I would by all the means at my command."

" Very good: then exercise it now. You possess it!—the opportunity of promoting your interests would delight her!"

" It might; but if her efforts should fail, she would be in at least a corresponding degree mortified."

" Fail! She would not fail. There wouldn't be the most remote chance of her failing. The Marquis couldn't refuse her!—at her request he'd go to work at once."

" He'd consider it, I apprehend, strange that she should take so much interest in me."

" He might at first; but when she had explained to him that you were the godson of the late Marquis; that she knew you when you were a boy, and that she had recognized you here, he'd no longer consider it strange, but perfectly natural, and therefore correct. Now I'll tell you how I'd go to work, if I were fortunate enough to have your chance. The very next time she called, I'd delicately intimate in the course of conversation, that had the late Marquis lived he would have placed me in a position very different from that which I occupy now; and if I found that this hint had no effect, I should at once express a wish that the present Marquis had some knowledge of me, seeing that if he had, and I could prevail upon some friend to speak for me, he might be induced to exercise his influence in my favour. This would be sufficient: she'd take it at once!— she'd say, 'I'll do myself the pleasure of naming you to the Marquis,' and the thing would be done. Don't you see?"

"Oh! I understand what you mean, perfectly, and as you appear to be so sanguine on the subject, I'll think about it."

"Think about it!—do it sir!—do it at once. Never dream of allowing so splendid an opportunity to slip. There's not a man in a million who has such a chance, and if you fail to embrace it, you may never have another, if you live a thousand years! What says Shakespeare — the greatest plagiarist Nature ever had—what does *he* say on the subject?—

> ' There is a tide in the affairs of men
> Which, taken at the flood, leads on to fortune :
> Omitted, all the voyage of their life
> Is bound in shallows and in miseries.'

Had those lines been written expressly for you, they could not have been more to the purpose."

" Well," said Alfred, there's of course no necessity for being precipitate! When I have seen and conversed with her again, I shall know, perhaps, better how to act."

In the judgment of Mr. Wilkins it was perfectly impossible for Alfred to know better how to act then he ought to have known then: he continued to urge the necessity for *immediate* action, to show the facility with which patronage can enable a man to achieve greatness, to portray in glowing colours the various phases which in his view, characterised the transition from obscurity to immortality, and to contend for the influence of the Marquis being limitless; and as the more brandy and water he imbibed the more enthusiastic he became, it at length appeared abundantly clear to him, that there was scarcely an office under government to which Alfred was not eligible, or which he could not procure with the most perfect ease.

As a matter of courtesy Alfred listened until the hour prescribed for their departure had arrived; but his thoughts had reference less to the prospects portrayed by his eloquent friend, than to Lady Felicia herself. It is true, facts tended to dispel the bright visions he conceived, but as the realms of fancy were to him realms of bliss, he continued to revel in them still.

In the morning the head of Mr. Wilkins troubled him even more than his hands. This he ascribed solely to the energy with which he had enforced his views the previous evening. He was, however, still enthusiastic in the cause, and embraced every possible opportunity of reverting to that which he conceived to be Alfred's grand object. But Alfred—although he wished it to appear that he appreciated his friend's solicitude—panted for the re-appearance of Lady Felicia without reference to those ulterior views which had alone excited the imagination of Mr. Wilkins. He watched for her with impatience the most intense; but he watched throughout the morning in vain. Why would she not come? Why should she come? Her curiosity had been gratified! She knew then that she had seen him before!—she also knew where she had seen him. What more could she want to know? Nothing! Then why *should* she come, unless indeed, with the view of making a purchase? Having recognized him, she had treated him with courtesy and would do so again, if she ever had occasion to call again; but weeks, or even months, might elapse before she re-appeared there! —she might indeed never call again: she was not confined to that particular establishment! Why then should her absence be deemed strange? It was true he expected her. But why did he expect her?—for what purpose did he wish her to come? It was not his intention to pursue the course suggested by Mr. Wilkins. The prospects which he had portrayed had not dazzled him. He in reality cared nothing about them. All he cared for was to see her—and why? He knew not: he only knew that he anxiously wished her to come.

The day passed; and but for the hope—the blessed hope— of seeing her on the morrow his thoughts would have been as gloomy as the night. Her card he looked at a thousand times, and while pressing it passionately to his lips, he resolved on having it framed in gold and wearing it as an amulet.

The morrow came: but what to him was the morrow? Felicia came not with it. Felicia! Aye! Felicia: the title he abhorred.

The third day came, and his spirit sank. Felicia still absented herself; and hope ceased to sustain him. Oh! that she had moved in a sphere less exalted.

His friend, Mr. Wilkins, who had become most sincerely attached to him, and who felt deeply interested in his welfare, perceiving his depression, and ascribing it to the assumed fact of his advancement being delayed, did every thing which *he* thought calculated to cheer him, and suggested the expediency of writing to Lady Felicia, with the view of inducing her to speak to the Marquis at once; but Alfred—to whom his friend's enthusiasm on this subject had become painful—courteously opposed the pursuit of such a course, by contending that it would be considered presumptuous. No! he would never write to *her* on such a subject: he would never apply to her to promote his advancement; although he *was* nothing to her— although she *did* regard him with perfect indifference—she was the last in the world to whom it should appear that he was actuated by any selfish feeling.

Alfred, however, in thus assuming that she regarded him with indifference, was mistaken; he was not indifferent to her; but in order to explain the nature of the feelings she had inspired, it will be necessary to introduce her formally.

CHAPTER III.

FELICIA.

LADY FELICIA was a beautiful blonde: her figure was petite, yet perfect; and while her countenance had a peculiar sweetness of expression, her skin was as fine and clear as that of an infant. She was amiable, elegant, ingenuous, and gentle; her manners were of the most refined caste: she possessed a true and trusting heart, full of the purest sympathy, and seemed to have been created to be universally beloved.

And yet her sisters, Lady Florence and Lady Augusta never loved her. Being fine, bold, commanding girls, haughty and imperious, they regarded the gentle spirit of Felicia with contempt, and proudly assumed an authority over her, which tended to alienate her from them. Even when they were children, they never loved her; for being a special favourite of the old Marquis, who invariably called her his " own little angel," while he took but slight notice of them, jealousy prompted them to conceive a dislike to her which proved to be perfectly invincible.

Nor had the Marquis, her father, any deep affection for her: for as her birth and the death of the Marchioness occurred simultaneously, and as by that death he lost a splendid estate, strange as it may seem, he never could look at Felicia without wishing that she had never been born.

Being thus virtually excluded from all affectionate intercourse with her immediate relatives, it will not be deemed marvellous that Felicia should have attached herself to one whose devotion she knew to be ardent and pure, notwithstand-

ing the social position of that one was inferior to her own.
Fidèle had been her companion for years; she knew that
Fidèle loved her passionately, and that although she was then
but her maid, she was not only affectionate and highly accomplished, but descended from one of the first families in France
—a family whose wealth and influence excited the brutal
vengeance of the sanguinary Robespierre. In Fidèle she
confided—they were, indeed, like sisters—and to her she communicated the fact of her having recognized Alfred.

"Fidèle," she observed, "I have again seen him whom I
yesterday told you I fancied I knew."

"Indeed!" said Fidèle. "Well, and do you really know
him?"

"I knew him when he was a boy: and such a sweet boy!—
so intelligent, so handsome, and so affectionate!"

"And is he much altered?"

"He has grown amazingly!—but there are the features still.
Oh, what a favourite I used to be of his!—how delighted he
always was to see me! The moment the carriage stopped, out
Alfred would run, clapping his hands enthusiastically, while
his beautiful eyes danced for joy! I remember being very
wicked once: I hid myself in a corner of the carriage; and
as he could not see me, he mournfully said, 'She's not well,'
and wept. Oh! how sorry I was; I sprang from my hiding-
place instantly, and kissed the tears away."

Fidèle looked at her archly, for a moment, and then said,
"You did?"

"Oh, yes!" replied Felicia, "but we were children then!"

"How many tears would he have to shed now, before you
would check them with a kiss?"

"You are a wicked girl, Fidèle," said Felicia, playfully; "he
is now a man!"

"And is he still enthusiastic?"

"He was very much embarrassed!"

"Ah"—said Fidèle, thoughtfully—"embarrassed. And is he really *very* handsome?"

"If you were to see him," replied Felicia, with a blush, "I *think* that you would say so!"

"Oh, I *must* see him!—When can I go?"

"When you please!—Go at once. Take a coach; you will not be gone long."

"But how shall I know him from the rest?"

"By his brilliant complexion, and—I need not say more: you cannot possibly make a mistake.".

Delighted with this opportunity of seeing him whom Felicia had loved when a child, and inspired with a somewhat romantic idea of his personal attractions, Fidèle prepared to start immediately, and having sent for a coach, proceeded to the establishment in question, ostensibly in order to make some trifling purchase.

On her arrival, the appearance of Alfred struck her at once; but Mr. Wilkins came forward: and while he was attending to her with all his characteristic politeness, she had an excellent opportunity of noticing Alfred, who stood as if enrapt. She watched his countenance narrowly, and admired him much, and marvelled that features so pleasing should be so rigid; but although she could scarcely perceive a muscle move, his eyes proclaimed the existence of rapturous emotions.

Having effected a purchase—in doing which it was by no means apparent to Mr. Wilkins that she was in any particular haste, while in his gentle judgment she did not sufficiently appreciate the importance of his original observations—she bowed to Mr. Wilkins, with an elegance which pleased him, and hastened home to communicate her impressions to Felicia.

"Oh!" she exclaimed, "what a love of a man!—so elegant, so handsome, and has *such* eyes!—he is in my view the very perfection of manly beauty. But dear me," she added, "how thoughtful he appeared; What *could* he have been thinking about so intently? Have *you* no idea?"

"How *should* I have?" returned Felicia. "But was he *very* thoughtful?"

"He stood all the time I was there as if lost in admiration of some beautiful vision; and if it *were* a vision," she added, archly, "I *think* that I can tell who presided!—Can't you?"

"How is it possible, dear, for me to tell?".

"Can you not guess?"

"Why *should* I guess?"

"Poor fellow. I feel for him. Don't you?"

"What *do* you mean?"

"Shall I explain? Do you wish me to explain? I think not. Besides, there is no necessity for it. What a pity it is that he is not in a somewhat higher social position; is it not? But how came you, even as children, to associate?"

"The late Marquis," replied Felicia, was his godfather, and used to take me with him, whenever he went to see his little *protégé.*

"The late Marquis his godfather! Oh! then his family is *distingué?*"

"Respectable," said Felicia.

"And rich?"

"I really don't know; I should say, that if his family were wealthy, he would not be in business."

"Oh, that does not, I apprehend, by any means follow—at least not in England. You have merchant princes—men, who, notwithstanding they have amassed millions, are in business still!"

"True," said Felicia, "but he is not a millionaire."

"Then I wish he was. However, he is a very charming person; and would, I have no doubt, make a most delightful husband."

Felicia now felt more strongly than ever, that she still loved him whom she had loved when a child. She could ascribe her emotions to nothing but love. Even the preceding day—when unable to recognize him — her sensations had been peculiarly thrilling; but when she had ascertained who he was, she had re-inspired all those beautiful feelings which had formerly given her so much delight. Nor could she for a moment doubt that he still loved her. She felt sure that he loved her!—if not, why should he have been so much embarrassed? — why so tremulous? Why should he have begged so earnestly to know who she was? and above all why, when she gave him her card, should he have placed it so promptly in his bosom? He *did* love her! — fondly! — she knew that he loved her! But then, alas! how hopelessly! Had he been highly connected: had he been in the army or the navy, or the church: had he been a physician, a judge, or a banker, or even a mere member of Parliament, he might have ventured to solicit her hand; but occupying the plebeian position he did, without influential friends, without wealth or distinction — the son of a tradesman, and the servant of a tradesman, without the prospect of being anything but a tradesman himself — how could he attempt to make the slightest advance without its being considered in the highest degree presumptuous! What would the Marquis—Florence—Augusta—what would the whole world say if such a proposal were made? Why, ridicule the most caustic, and contempt the most galling, would follow as a matter of course! No! the idea appeared to be monstrous! She loved him it was true; and he loved her; but never again must they meet on earth! Oblivion was essential to the happiness of both.

Having arrived at this conclusion, Felicia endeavoured to wean her thoughts from him: she "made up her mind" to see him no more: she "made up her mind" to forget him; and with that view associated more with her sisters, notwithstanding their haughty bearing pained her; but, although she held oblivion to be essential to happiness, oblivion was not at her command!—do what she might, go where she might, see or converse with whom she might, Alfred was ever present to her imagination: Alfred engrossed all her thoughts.

For three weary days and nights she struggled with her feelings, and made every effort in her power to crush them: she had recourse to ridicule; she summoned all her pride, and sought to inspire her heart with contempt; but ridicule, contempt, and pride combined, were unavailing: Love proudly triumphed over all, and Felicia became pale and spiritless.

Fidèle, who watched her anxiously, perceived this change with grief; and, prompted by the purest and most affectionate solicitude, made every possible effort to cheer her. She guessed the cause—the real cause—but feared to breathe a word having reference to it. Nor did Felicia revert to the subject until the morning of the fourth day, when, in mournful tones, she inquired of Fidèle—who could not conceal her tears—why she wept?

"I weep," replied Fidèle, "because your sadness grieves me. If you were to smile, I should not weep!"

"Fidèle," said Felicia, "I am indeed unhappy. You may have divined the cause—you doubtless have—but oh! how I have struggled to forget him!"

"Forget whom?" inquired Fidèle.

"Forget whom? The only one on earth whom I care to forget. Have you *not* then discovered the cause of my unhappiness?—Fidèle, you have ever been dear to me: in you I have ever confided, and will confide still: to you, I will, therefore, entrust this secret—that the only one whom I am anxious to forget, my heart tells me I love."

"I perceive," said Fidèle, who now resolved on diverting her thoughts if possible, "and he whom you love—or rather fancy you love—is the man for whom you had an affection when a child. But why should that make you unhappy? Why are you so anxious—why struggle to forget him? You may as

well strive to forget that you live. Repudiate at once a task
so utterly hopeless. Strive rather to subdue this anxiety; to
conquer these feelings which you now ascribe to love, and to
smile at the thought of your having condescended to entertain
them for one who is of course beneath your notice."

",Teach me to do this, Fidèle—I have endeavoured to teach
myself in vain—teach me how to treat him with contempt:
prove that he *is* beneath my notice; prove that he is unworthy
of my love: awaken my pride; stir up the soul of dignity;
fill my heart with scorn, excite my ambition: inspire me with
feelings of any description sufficiently powerful to conquer
those of love, and you will render me a service indeed."

"Do you really wish me to do this?"

"I do."

"To embody the objections that may be urged with the
view of inducing you to repudiate the idea of loving such a
man?"

"State them all: omit none: let me have the whole list,
that their combined weight may at once crush those feelings
which are unhappily now in the ascendant."

"Well, then, in the first place look at your position. You
are the daughter of one of the first peers of the realm: you are
living in a style of magnificence—moving in a most distinguished
sphere, and able to command the devotion of the highest nobles
in the land. To be a Princess, a Duchess, a Marchioness, or a
Countess, appears to be your destiny. Who but a man of high
rank would aspire to your hand? Who without a coronet
would be considered eligible? Surrounded by splendour, you
have power at your command, with all the collateral advantages
of which rank is the germ. This is your position. Now look
at that of the man whom you fancy you love. He is the
servant of a tradesman — trained to servility— the obsequious slave of every one who calls to make a purchase—
excluded from all refined society — hopeless of emerging

from his grovelling state, powerless, spiritless, low-born
contemned"—

"Fidèle," exclaimed Felicia, with an expression of indignation,
"if you proceed thus I shall hate you."

"You will remember," said Fidèle, "that you engaged me
as an advocate, and that it was therefore incumbent upon me
to paint him in the very darkest colours, and to make him
appear as contemptible as possible, with the view of striking
down his pretensions. It is the practice—the usual practice.
Custom prescribes it, and the highest authorities not only
sanction but encourage it. It is, in fact, termed the, sacred
duty, of an advocate to do all in his power to wither the hopes
and to ruin the reputation of him against whom he appears.
But as this practice is displeasing to you—and I am sure that
it is not very pleasing to me, for I believe him to be at least
respectable—I'll pursue another course which will be less
offensive, seeing that I shall simply state that as you occupy
one of the highest social positions, while he occupies one of
the lowest, it would be considered madness on your part to
descend from your position to his, and thus to exchange wealth
and magnificence for poverty and contempt."

"Why poverty and contempt?" exclaimed Felicia. "They
would not, I apprehend, necessarily follow?"

"Comparative poverty must," replied Fidèle: "the contempt
of your brilliant connections would."

"But what are brilliant connections to one, who in the very
midst of them cannot be happy?"

"Do not believe that you cannot be happy in the circle to
which you have been ever accustomed. To those who have
not been accustomed to it, that circle appears to be a perfect
Elysium: thousands upon thousands struggle through life to
secure the privilege of moving within it; and although it is to
you of course familiar, and therefore less attractive, you must
not even dream of descending from it, for it is indeed exceedingly

questionable whether the recollection of what you were, and the thought of what you might have been, would not destroy your happiness for ever. Why should you not be happy, surrounded as you are by all the luxuries and elegancies of life—why should you not hope to be happier still as the adored wife of some illustrious man, whose name and fame would be immortal? Besides, it does not follow that because you admire this person you really love him. The passion you have inspired may indeed be but transient It was quickly conceived, and may be quickly subdued. Call reason to your aid. Think of the unexampled sacrifices you would of necessity have to make in the event of your allowing this passion to supersede reason. All would have to be given up—family connections, state splendour—all."

"And I feel," said Felicia, with an intensity of expression, " that I *could* give up all for him!"

"You may have that feeling now," returned Fidèle, " but an appeal to your judgment would soon prove its weakness."

"Its weakness!" exclaimed Felicia. "Its strength is unrivalled! It surpasses that of all the other feelings combined!"

"Its strength may appear to be incomparable at present because it happens to be now in the ascendant. The other feelings have allowed it to reign for a time, but they will not allow it to be permanently despotic ; they will not allow it to trample upon them!"

"But it *does* trample upon them!"

"Then its reign will be short."

A pause ensued, during which the expression of Felicia's countenance was intensely contemplative, while Fidèle displayed the utmost anxiety to read her thoughts. At length she said, "Fidèle, I understood you to say just now that the circle in which I move being familiar to me, was therefore the less attractive. Do you think that if I were familiar with him that he would appear to *me* to be less attractive?"

"No doubt of it," replied Fidèle, who now conceived that she should be able to carry her point triumphantly. "*Such* familiarity would, indeed, create contempt! You could *not* associate long with such a man. The more you knew of him the less you would like him."

"Then I'll bring it to the test," said Felicia. "I have the utmost confidence in your judgment, and therefore I'll bring this point to the test. I'll see him frequently; I'll converse with him familiarly; I'll accustom myself to him; and then, if indeed there be any truth in your doctrine, his attractions will fade"

"But," said Fidèle, in a state of alarm, for she did not at all expect this, "would not that be rushing into danger?"

"The only danger to be apprehended, according to your view, is that of his incurring my dislike, which you would not hold to be any very great calamity."

"But why not abandon the thought of seeing him again? Why not keep aloof entirely from him?"

"Because I have discovered it to be of no use. I have tried it for three days, and found it to be even worse than useless; absence tends but to strengthen that feeling which I am so anxious to subdue. No; I'll act upon your suggestion; I'll try your plan; and if it *should* be successful, I shall have more faith in the soundness of your judgment than ever."

"Well," said Fidèle, somewhat hopelessly, for it really was *not* in her judgment the best course to pursue; "but it will look so strange if you call there frequently."

"I do not intend to call at all," returned Felicia, "I mean to have him here."

"Have him here!" echoed Fidèle, with an expression of amazement—"Have him here!

"It will I think be better; because we shall be able to converse here without the slightest fear of interruption."

"But surely you do not mean to send for him?"

"I do, Fidèle; and I want you to be my ambassadress."

"Well, but what earthly excuse can you make?—what can you possibly say?—how can you explain to him why he was sent for?"

"No explanation will be needed. He is, as you say, but the servant of a tradesman—"

"Forgive me!" exclaimed Fidèle, earnestly. "Do not be angry with me for that: I had no idea of hurting your feelings, which you know I would not willingly wound for the world. It is true that I said this; but why did I say it?—what was my motive?—can you not appreciate it?"

"I can, and do—I am not angry!—I am, on the contrary, gay! I was merely saying that as he is the servant of a tradesman, he ought to attend to his *master's* customers; and that as I am one of those customers, he ought to attend to me. I mean to have him here on business! and all I wish you to do is, to call and select a few pieces of silk for him to bring here. You understand me?"

"I do; but *had* it not better be deferred?"

"I never was in a better humour to receive him. You perceive I am not unhappy now! I feel quite inclined to be playful! I have not been in such high spirits for days."

"But have not those high spirits been induced by the prospect of seeing him again?"

"How can you entertain such an idea? Go, Fidèle, and you shall see how grandly I'll receive him! Don't let him bring many for me to select from. Two or three will be quite sufficient. Don't overload the poor man! And Fidèle —you can—if you like—just notice his countenance when you tell him that they are for *me* to select from. You, of course, understand."

"I fear," said Fidèle, "that I understand too much; but for Heaven's sake remember the immense disparity which exists between your position and his."

"I shall not forget it," returned Felicia, and smiled as Fidèle left the room.

Now Alfred that morning felt more depressed than ever; he despaired of ever seeing Felicia again: the bright visions by which he had been charmed, had disappeared, and it seemed to be abundantly clear to him, that he was no more to her than the most perfect stranger. Nor was Mr. Wilkins in particularly high spirits that morning; he had discovered that Alfred's estimate of the value of his advice was not even remotely comparable with his own. *He* knew—that is to say he fancied, which to him was precisely the same thing—that Alfred ought to write to Lady Felicia, in order to get upon that glorious line of which obscurity and immortality are the termini, and to commence at once that brilliant career which his vivid imagination had portrayed; but as Alfred could not see so far as Mr. Wilkins, as he had not had the vast experience of Mr. Wilkins, as he knew not the influence of a Marquis so well as Mr. Wilkins, and repudiated the idea of writing in opposition to the advice of Mr. Wilkins, Mr. Wilkins felt— and very naturally—that that advice had been thrown away, and in consequence lost that sublime equanimity for which he had been theretofore distinguished

But this was not all! When Fidèle arrived—notwithstanding he bowed with all the grace he had in him—notwithstanding he actually placed himself before her—notwithstanding it could not fail to live in her memory, that he and no one else had attended to her before — she absolutely passed Mr. Wilkins, and went direct to Alfred! Gods! what could be the meaning of this extraordinary procedure! He turned and looked with an expression of amazement the most intense! Could such a thing

"be,
And overcome him like a summer's cloud
Without his special wonder?"

What had he done? what "ignorant sin" committed? He looked back with all the serenity at his command, with the view of recollecting whether anything occurred, when she previously honoured the establishment, calculated to render him in the slightest degree obnoxious; but no!—the only thing which could be held to be at all remarkable, was the fact of her not appearing to be particularly tied to time!—beyond that, his memory contained no record having reference to her previous visit. What on earth then could be the cause of this mysterious manifestation of contempt! He couldn't tell: he couldn't even conjecture! He only knew that during the whole course of his experience a case of the kind had never occurred to him before, and hence it was indeed a "heavy blow," and a very "great discouragement."

"Meanwhile Alfred was attending to Fidèle, and as she was exceedingly affable, he got on remarkably well, until, having chosen two pieces of silk, she said, "*Will* you do me the favour to send these to Kingsborough House, in order that my lady may decide upon one of them?"—when in an instant the colour left his cheeks, and he was seized with an universal tremour. "They are both so very beautiful," continued Fidèle, without appearing to notice his embarrassment, "that I really do not know which to choose; Lady Felicia must therefore decide for herself. Will you be so obliging as to send them about four?"

"I will"—replied Alfred tremulously—"I will do so, with pleasure."

Fidèle rose, and having bowed gracefully to Alfred, left; she also bowed, as she passed, to Mr. Wilkins!—which was something!—it caused him to feel a *little* better:—he accepted it as a slight composition, but by no means in full of all demands.

"Have you not effected a sale?" he inquired, as Alfred stood and looked as if bewildered.

"Not yet," replied Alfred, confusedly.—"Not yet. Not yet—no—not yet. Just let me have a word with you," he added, and Mr. Wilkins as a natural matter of courtesy approached him. "Now," resumed Alfred, "these two pieces are to be sent, about four o'clock, to Kingsborough House, for"—

"Kingsborough House!" exclaimed Mr. Wilkins, "Kingsborough House! What, the house of the Marquis of Kingsborough?"

"Yes, in order that Lady Felicia"—

"*Give* me your hand," cried Mr. Wilkins, in a state of wild rapture. "*Give* me your hand. Why this accounts for all! That conduct—that marvellous conduct—which I considered incomprehensible, can now be distinctly understood! I see it all! The lady passed me in that extraordinary fashion, because, and solely because, she had been deputed to address *you;* and that which I painfully ascribed to contempt, was but an act of strict obedience to orders. I congratulate you—fervently!—I give you joy with all my heart! But now," he added, with an effort to subdue his enthusiasm, "let's look at the matter serenely; don't let's make a mess of it now. You have to go at four o'clock "—

"They have to be *sent* at four o'clock!"

"Sent! What do you mean? You'll go yourself, of course."

"No, she said, *send* them, not *bring* them."

"And have you eaten so many tons of country pudding that you can't understand that when she said send, she meant bring? Why did that lady pass me to get to you? Was it because she conceived that I wasn't old enough, or fat enough, or tall enough, to attend to her? or because she had been instructed—distinctly instructed—to address you?"

" She might have been instructed to *address* me as a matter of courtesy," said Alfred, " but does it therefore follow, that she wished me to attend there. myself ?"

" Why, what in the name of all the pantheonic gods, is the matter with you, Mr. Murray ? There has been during the last few days some spider spinning his web in your brain, to catch your brightest intellects for slaughter. You have not been yourself; you've been nothing like yourself: what is the meaning of this mighty change ? In spirit and appearance you have been altered for days, and now you are going to allow the same influence to annihilate your judgment! You have one of the finest chances man ever yet had—no man under Heaven ever had a finer chance—and yet you refuse to seize it: you have been sent for—absolutely sent for—to have the foundation of your fortune laid, and yet you hesitate to go! *Is* there a man out of St. Luke's like you ? Go by all means; don't hesitate a moment: go boldly; go with all the confidence of a man. What have you to fear ? Nothing; but all to hope for. Never allow a chance like *this* to slip ! It is manifest—it must be, even to you, manifest—that that young lady—whoever she is—would not have come here if she hadn't been sent. Is it likely that she would—is it anything like likely—does it appear to *you* to be anything like likely ?"

" No," replied Alfred, " doubtless she was sent !"

" And by whom ?—that's the point !—by whom was she sent ?"

" By Lady Felicia, of course !"

" Very well then ! Of course she was sent by Lady Felicia; but why ?—for what purpoes ?"

" To look at the silks !"

" *Have* you no soul ?" inquired Mr. Wilkins, as if doubtful whether Alfred really had one or not. " Of course she was sent to look at the silks—ostensibly !—but what was the *latent* object ? Why, to get you up there ! Lady Felicia says in effect—of course I don't pretend for one moment to give the very words, but she says in effect—to this young lady—she didn't say who she was, did she?"

"No," replied Alfred, "but as she said, 'my lady,' I thought she might be Lady Felicia's maid!"

"Very likely: come that isn't *half* a bad guess; but no matter: she says to her, I know the young man whom you saw in that shop the other day"—

"Whom *she* saw?"

"Yes! she was here about three days ago; I waited upon her, and I'll bet ten to one she was sent then; for, now I recollect, she kept her eyes almost constantly upon you. Well!—she says to her, 'I *know* that young man—she might say that gentleman, but that's of no importance—I knew him when he was but a child; the late Marquis was his godfather, consequently, he is spiritually related to our family, and, therefore, I should like to have a little conversation with him, in order to ascertain how his interests can best be promoted; but as I find that I cannot converse with him in the shop, without being interrupted, or exciting the notice of those around, I have been thinking, that I had better have him here, that he may calmly explain his present views, and thus enable me to exalt his future prospects. Go, therefore, and look at some silks—go straight up to him; don't let any other soul attend to you: if he should be engaged, say you'll wait— and when you have selected two or three pieces, tell him that you wish to have them sent for me to choose from. Don't ask him to come himself, because that would appear to be somewhat too pointed: tell him to send them; he's certain to bring them, and thus the object I have in view will be attained, as a perfectly natural matter, of course.' Now, what do you think of that? Isn't it feasible?"

"Certainly, much of it appears to be so!" replied Alfred.

"It *is* so!—its all so!—mark my words, its neither more

nor less than the true state of the case. She wants to give you an opportunity of stating your views, and soliciting her interest with the Marquis, and if you fail to embrace so glorious an opportunity, I shall begin to think that you really are about the most verdant goose in creation. Go at once : go with all the confidence in nature: Heaven and earth! never allow a chance like *this* to slip! There, say no more about it : the idea is too monstrous to be dwelt upon. Go, sir, and be assured of this, that I wish you—warmly and most sincerely wish you—all the success you can wish yoursèlf."

This Alfred believed; and, certainly, some of the observations of Mr. Wilkins appeared to be perfectly correct. It seemed clear that Felicia *had* sent this young lady, and that, with the view of enabling him to make his appearance at Kingsborough House; and, although it was not so clear that her object was that which Mr. Wilkins had suggested, it was manifest that·she had *some* object, the nature of which he panted to ascertain, and yet he felt disinclined to go!

The time drew near; and Mr. Wilkins, perceiving that Alfred was still irresolute, pulled out his watch, and said, " Now, Mr. Murray: punctuality's the life and soul of business ; time's getting on."

" Do you *still* think," said Alfred; " that Lady Felicia really wished me to go ?"

" Most decidedly !" replied Mr. Wilkins. " Nothing can be more abundantly plain. But, even if she did *not*, what possible objection can you have to attend to her ? But she did!—she sent that lady expressly for the purpose of inducing you to go!—therefore, say no more about it : go boldly, and at once."

Well! if Alfred could have·invented any excuse in the slightest degree calculated to satisfy·Mr. Wilkins, he would not have gone even then ; but as he found it impossible to do this, and as he did not wish to make it appear that he had not sufficient courage to go, he resolutely made up his mind at once, and with a feeling of actual desperation started.

Fidèle, on her return to Lady Felicia — not wishing to attach any importance to the fact of Alfred having been tremulous—merely stated, without reference to his embarrass- ment, that she had selected the silks, and requested them to be brought at four o'clock. This, however, failed to satisfy Felicia: she wished to know how he looked, how he appeared to feel, and how he acted; to which Fidèle briefly replied, that like most other inexperienced persons, he appeared to be "exceedingly diffident."

Anxiously, and with a throbbing heart, did Felicia watch for his arrival, and when he had arrived, she felt scarcely equal to the task of meeting him. Summoning, however, all the courage at her command, she desired the servant, by whom he had been announced, to show him up, and requested Fidèle to assist her in making the purchase, which Fidèle at once discovered to be necessary, seeing that he had no sooner entered the room, than Felicia became quite unable to speak.

" Oh: you have brought the silks," said Fidèle, and Alfred mechanically opened the parcel. " These are the two," she added, turning to Felicia. " They are both very beautiful, are they not?

" They are," replied Felicia, faintly. — " Which do you prefer?"

" Upon my word, I don't know."

"Which style is considered the more fashionable?" in- quired Felicia, turning to Alfred, whose eyes, having met hers, instantly dropped.

" I really am unable to say," returned Alfred.·

" Which do you think is the more quiet?"

Alfred again ventured to raise his eyes and said, tremu- lously, "I think—this."

" Exactly," said Felicia, making a strong effort to regain
her self-possession. "Then upon that I'll decide.—Your
friends, I hope, are well, Mr. Murray?"

" I thank you," replied Alfred, blushing deeply, "quite
well."

" I knew Mr. Murray," said Felicia, addressing Fidèle,
"when he was but a youth!"

" Indeed!" said Fidèle archly.

" Oh, I used to see him frequently when he was at school."

" You were, I hope, a good boy at school?" said Fidèle,
with a playful expression.

"I was at least happy," returned Alfred, with a sigh.

" And are you not happy now?" inquired Felicia.

" I cannot expect to be so now. I thought of no social
distinctions then."

" Well," interposed Fidèle promptly, " it is, I believe, the
happiest time : but we must not be unhappy because we
cannot all be kings and queens."

" It is not, I apprehend, necessary to be either," suggested
Alfred, " in order to ensure happiness."

" Certainly not!" returned Fidèle. " But," she added,
with the view of changing the subject, "there is, I presume,
quite sufficient here for a dress."

Alfred bowed, and Fidèle paid him; but he said no more;
nor did Felicia utter another word; she kept her eyes fixed
upon him earnestly until he had retired, when she sank
into a reverie, from which Fidèle, perceiving that she had no
desire to be disturbed, did not disturb her.

CHAPTER IV.

THE CONSULTATION.

DURING the absence of Alfred, Mr. Wilkins gave the reins to his imagination, which·took him at once to the Treasury, leaped over a variety of lucrative appointments, flew to Sudbury, where Alfred was elected without the slightest opposition, brought him back to town, and went with him into the House to see his friend take his seat, ·and to hear him deliver his maiden speech, amidst thunders of applause, which had scarcely subsided· when the flight of his steed ·was checked by. the Honourable Member's return to the shop.

"Well," he exclaimed, rubbing his hands joyfully, "how did you get on ?—how did you get on ?—All right ?"

"Yes," replied Alfred," I have sold one of the dresses."

Sold one of the dresses !—*Do* I want to know about your selling one of the dresses ! I'm all on fire to ascertain what has been done to enable you ·to commence an illustrious career, and you tell me that you have sold one of the dresses. Of course you saw her ?"

"Oh yes, I saw her."

"Well ! and what did she say ?"

"Nothing on the subject to which you allude."

"Nothing ! But of course you said something ?"

'"Not on that subject."

"No ! Heaven and earth ! why, what *could* you have been about ! Not a word ?—not a hint ?—not the ghost of an allusion ?"

"No. If even I had felt inclined "—

"*If* even you had felt inclined! Did you not then feel inclined?"

"I was about to say, that if I had felt inclined to do so I had no opportunity."

"Why not?"

"That lady was there."

"What a pity. That was awkward—very awkward. But was she there the whole of the time?"

".Yes: she was there when I entered, and there she remained."

"Then she ought to have known better: she ought to have retired. But it's just like these ladies' maids—blister them!—they assume more than their mistresses, twenty to one, and give themselves five hundred times as many airs."

"I don't *know* that she is the lady's maid," said Alfred.

"I'll bet ten to one of it!" rejoined Mr. Wilkins. "It's just how they act! Still I think you might have got in a word or two *somehow:* you might have introduced the *small* end of the wedge!"

"That I think I *have* done."

"Bravo! Bravo!"

"I am not quite sure; but I think that I have—as you say—introduced the small end of the wedge."

"And yet you told me that nothing had been said on the subject!"

"Nor was there on the subject to which you referred. That which *I* wish to open, and to which I think the wedge has been slightly applied, is one of far more importance than that which you contemplate."

"Indeed!" cried Mr. Wilkins, with an expression of wonder. "One of far more importance! What—what do you mean to say?—*more* important?—more important than—why, what on earth is it?—*more* important?"

"Aye!—Far more important."

"Well, but what can it be?"

"You shall know all," said Alfred, "by and bye; we can't conveniently enter into the whole matter here. When we close we'll go to the house we went to the other evening, and then I'll explain all. I wish to consult you: I want your advice. The subject is one of extreme delicacy, but I feel that in you I may confide."

"My dear boy, 'Honour calls me to the field' when a man reposes confidence in me. But—just by the way of keeping me off the rack of conjecture—can't you give me a notion—the spectre of a hint—the merest and most impalpable apparition of an idea—of what it is, *now?*"

"I *could*," replied Alfred with a smile; "but if I were to do so without explaining all the circumstances, you would, I am sure, be unable to appreciate its importance. It had therefore much better be deferred until the evening: we shall then be able to enter into the whole matter calmly, and without the chance of being interrupted."

Well! Mr. Wilkins could not, he conceived, with anything bearing the semblance of courtesy, *press* the point—although he felt, and strongly too, that the slightest intimation would have been a relief. But what on earth could it possibly be? Something more important than that which he had contemplated! Gods! had he not in imagination planted him in the Treasury?—had he not taken him from the Treasury, to make him a Member of Parliament?—and was he not about to bring him back to the Treasury in order to make him First Lord? More important! To what heights did ambition prompt men to aspire! Did he want to be a duke? *more* important!— Well! he supposed that he should know all about it in the evening; but when he looked at the position of the First Lord of the Treasury; when he looked at the salary, the patronage, and the power attached to that distinguished position, he really thought it was high enough for any man to aim at.

Being utterly unable to guess the point of Alfred's ambition, and having a high opinion of his own power to control his thoughts, Mr. Wilkins at once set himself to work, with the view of banishing suspense; and although he was not in this particularly successful, it, in some degree, relieved him until it was time to close, when he and his friend repaired to the tavern.

" Now," said Alfred, having ordered a pint of wine, " in the first place let it be distinctly understood, that whatever may pass between us this evening, must be held to be strictly confidential."

" Most decidedly," returned Mr. Wilkins, " here's my hand and here's my heart."

" Very good. Now during the last few days you have observed that my spirits have been somewhat depressed."

" I have not only observed it, I have told you of it."

" You have, and you shall now know the cause.—When Lady Felicia first called I thought her manners most extraordinary; she looked at me with an expression of curiosity the most intense, and seemed to listen with rapture to every syllable I uttered. This, of course, I thought strange!—inexplicable! —but what appeared to me to be more extraordinary still, was the fact of her inspiring me with feelings which I never experienced before. Well! she left; but her vision remained; and upon that delightful vision I dwelt, giving free scope to fancy, which being thus encouraged, created scenes of enchantment which need not be described. The next day, however, her expression of curiosity was accounted for; she had felt that she had seen me before, but was then quite unable to recollect where. So far, therefore, the peculiar intensity with which she regarded me the preceding day was explained! —Still there was something which I could not fathom—some mystery which I could not solve: the feelings with which she had inspired me gained strength, and forced upon me the conviction that I loved her."

"Well!" said Mr. Wilkins, having listened with great attention, "all you have to do is, to make her believe it. Do that, and you'll make yourself as safe as the bank. She'll do anything on earth for you then; she'll promote your interests by all the means in her power, and never know when she's done enough. If you want a woman to serve you, make her believe that 'you love her. It's about the best game on the board. Women like to be loved: it gratifies their vanity; it enhances their own estimate of the influence they possess, and makes them feel as well again. There can't be a safer speculation. It's perfectly sure to succeed. Make her believe that you love her—*no* matter whether you do or do not—and whatever you want through her you'll have, if it be within the pale of possibility. It's a good scheme of yours; I like it much: it proves that you know a thing or *two ;* and now that we have settled this point, let's go to that which *you* say is far more important than any which I have at present conceived. Now what is it?"

"You have taken such a strange view of the subject," said Alfred, "that I scarcely know how to proceed. When I told you that I loved lady Felicia, I thought you would have understood all; instead of which you regard it merely as the means of inducing her to promote my interests in the manner you have suggested."

"Well! and it will be the means of inducing her to do so, i. you can but induce her to *believe* that you love her!"

"But I have no thought of inducing her to promote my interests in the way *you* contemplate! In loving her, I hav a higher object in view!"

"But when you talk of loving her, you don't mean to say, *suppose*, that you love her as you would one whom you though of making your wife?"

"I do, indeed," replied Alfred, with a sigh.

"Pooh, pooh, pooh! Mr. Murray: pooh, pooh, pooh! Th

thing's absurd! You mustn't dream of anything half so irrational. What! Do you mean to say that you think of making *her* your wife?"

"I do."

"What, the Lady Felicia!—the daughter of the Marquis of Kingsborough!—one of the first peers of the realm!"

"Yes."

"Then let me advise you, as a friend, not to utter a syllable on the subject to any other soul upon earth! Why you perfectly astonish me! You!—a man of sense and education—you, who are capable of reasoning with a philosopher—*you* entertain an idea so preposterous!"

"Well," said Alfred, calmly; "it may appear to be preposterous—nay, it may be so in reality—still it is an idea which I *do* entertain, whether its realisation be practicable or not."

"Practicable!" echoed Mr. Wilkins, "Practicable! Don't dream of it!—don't allow yourself even to dream of it! You might just as well have fallen in love with one of the daughters of the Emperor of China. It's all very well to love her—to love her as I love her—that is to say, as I love every beautiful woman—but to love her with the view of making her your wife, is far beyond the scope of consistency."

"But suppose she loves me?" suggested Alfred.

"To suppose that," returned Mr. Wilkins, "were to suppose what I should call a social impossibility."

"Why so?" inquired Alfred.

"Oh! I don't at all allude to your personal appearance—which is perfectly unexceptionable; nor do I speak with reference to your intellectual attributes, which are, in my judgment, of a high order; but I really don't believe that these aristocratic creatures *ever* love! Coronets, wealth, and magnificence are the objects of their affection—not men! What are men to them without rank?"

" Well, but suppose—I put it hypothetically—suppose that she is an exception to the rule—assuming it tò be the rule—and that, being an exception, she really loves *me* ?"

" Well, we'll take it so, if you like; but even in that case, you'd be as far off as ever! She'd never be allowed to form an alliance with you! She might love you fondly—passionately—but would they care a straw about that? If she wept, she might weep — what care they for tears? If she broke her heart, she might break her heart — what do they care about hearts? Had she five hundred hearts, full of love, and all. pure, they'd infinitely rather the whole of them were broken, than see her give her hand to a man like you."

" But suppose she felt perfectly convinced that by such a marriage only could her happiness be secured."

" Why, they'd say she knew nothing about it. They wouldn't let her know. ' What,' the Marquis would say, for one, ' would you disgrace the whole family? Happiness! Look for a coronet, girl!—one which will reflect additional lustre upon our race. Love!—fiddlesticks!—*don't* talk to me about love; if you do, I'll lock you up in a lunatic asylum!"

" Very good: I anticipate all this," said Alfred; " but suppose she were to act independently of all considerations having reference to her family?"

" Is it conceivable that, in a case of this description, she *would* do so? That's the point. Is it conceivable that she would leave a princely home, surrounded by all the wealth, rank, splendour, and magnificence, for which the British Peerage is peculiarly distinguished—that she would give up the whole of her brilliant connections, abandon the unrivalled glories of the court, and repudiate all those scenes of enchantment which ravish every feeling, and dazzle every sense—is it, I ask, conceivable that she would make all these gorgeous sacrifices, merely for the purpose of living with you?"

" She might, it is not impossible! I do not say that

she would; but she might do so; and if she did, what then."

"My theory of the stars is this, that every star is a separate world;' and whenever I see a star shoot — that is, whenever I see it attracted from its sphere by another star — I say, ' There goes the destruction of both.' Do you understand? :—Very well, then! I hold this to be an analogous case. If *she* were to shoot—if she were to be attracted by you from her *own* sphere—that is, the sphere to which she has always been accustomed—I should say the same thing: I say, ' There goes the destruction of both !' "

" But, why should it be so ?"

" You marry. Very good. One of her friends calls you out; he shoots you through the head, and she dies broken hearted. That's about the quickest way to settle the matter. But, suppose he did *not* do so — suppose you were both allowed to live—could you ever be happy? Could you be happy if she were not? — and is it likely that she would be happy, deprived as she would necessarily be of those luxuries by which she has ever been surrounded? Say that the luxuries to which I refer have a tendency to create a distaste —to cloy, to pall upon those who have them—what of that? It is when they can't get them they feel their loss!—then it is that their appetite returns, and that too considerably keener than ever. But we are talking now precisely as if she loved you, and that with sufficient desperation to make all these sacrifices for you. You have, I suppose, no grounds for believing that she is in so frantic a state of mind — have you ?"

" I don't believe that she is particularly frantic," replied Alfred; " but I do believe that I am not indifferent to her."

" Indifferent! No! It would be, indeed, strange if you were! She knew you when you were a child: her grandfather was your godfather; and as you have done nothing to forfeit her respect, she respects you. But respect and love are opposite feelings! — they are, indeed, so opposed that they cannot co-exist!—you must not, therefore, take it into your head, that because she respects you she loves you. If she were to give you any reason for believing that she absolutely loves you, it would be a different thing, but"—

" She *has* given me reason to believe that she does. I feel convinced that she does."

" Very good! So you may! But what has induced that conviction ?"

" Her general manner towards me. Her eyes tell me that she loves me, and her smiles confirm the fact."

" But we must not imagine that every girl who looks at us, and smiles, is in love!"

" I do not imagine anything so absurd; but there are eyes and smiles which are eloquent indeed! Besides, why should she feel so embarrassed ? To-day, when I went, she could scarcely speak, and when she did, every word was faint and tremulous."

" She might not have been well! That might have been the cause of her not coming herself! But look here, my dear fellow; the human imagination is a vagabondizing attribute; there's no stability about the human imagination; it's here, there, and everywhere, supplying men with reasons for believing whatever they wish to believe. It has been at work in this case; it has pandered to your wishes; it has veiled reality, and caused you to ascribe every look, word, and action to love. That's it! But if even it were not so; if even she did in reality love you — the thing would be hopeless; she'd never make the sacrifices we have contemplated; and as to your love for *her*, you'd be better without it than with it. Stick to her by all means — stick to her — with the view of inducing her to promote your advancement; but don't allow love and his legions to annoy you; if you do, mark my words, you'll be lost. You've a good chance now, a capital chance, a chance of a million, a glorious chance; embrace that; and make the most of it! leave no stone unturned, and—who knows?—you might in a few years get up to such a pitch, that the world wouldn't know you to be the same man. Make your way!—there's nothing like it—why not work up to the peerage itself? If you were to do so, *that* would be the time to talk about loving Lady Felicia."

" I wish that she had no title."

" No doubt. But she has—that's the point—it's of no use to wish, we *must* take things as we find them. *I* know a girl—a beautiful girl—I only wish that she had ten thousand pounds; I'd marry her to-morrow if she had, but she hasn't, and therefore we are as we are."

" I should not care for money in that case," said Alfred.

" Ah," said Mr. Wilkins, with a smile of great significance, " when you are about *ten* years older you'll be a better judge of its value. But come," he added, " let's have a chop. We shall talk about love till it's time to go."

The chops were ordered; and as Alfred, who was not in high spirits—made no attempt to re-open the subject, Mr. Wilkins felt that it had been quite exhausted. He therefore started another topic, on which he had it *all* his own way, and when they had supped and drunk a glass of grog, they with opposite feelings and thoughts returned home.

CHAPTER V.

THE AMBASSADRESS.

ANXIOUS to divert her thoughts from Alfred, Felicia that
evening went to a ball. It was one of the most brilliant of the
season, and if countenances faithfully portrayed real feelings,
all present must have experienced the delights of Elysium.
Even Felicia looked happy—the joyous glance and conventional
smile having nothing whatever to do with the heart—but she
felt indeed wretched. She danced, she conversed, she joined
the promenade, she did all in her power to enter into the spirit
of the brilliant scene around her—society having enjoined a
look of delight even though the heart bleed—but the absence
of one threw a gloom over all. She looked calmly round; she
resolved on forming an impartial judgment; she would *not* be
prejudiced in his favour. Well, was there in all that gorgeous
assembly one at all comparable with him ? No; not one: to
her they appeared as so many automata, ticketed with titles,
and dressed up for show. Her sisters, Florence and Augusta,
were in their glory. They took but slight notice of her: nor
did the Marquis trouble himself at all about her; her principal
companion throughout the evening was Alice Hardwicke, a fine
high-spirited, light-hearted girl, who having no fortune, was not
much annoyed by those who dealt in undying affection, and
with her she chiefly conversed until *ordered* by her sisters to
accompany them home.

Florence felt sure that she had made a conquest: it was
perfectly impossible, in her judgment, for the young Earl of
Elfin to resist her last *coup*, and forty thousand a year was not

despicable; while Augusta, although she had "secured" Lord Loraine, had heard that his estates were dreadfully encumbered, and hence resolved on ascertaining the truth or falsehood of the statement before she took any farther steps.

On these interesting "affairs of the heart" they conversed with each other until they reached home; but not a word was addressed to Felicia. Being neglected, she was silent until she retired to her room, when she gave free vent to her tears.

"What has happened?" inquired Fidèle, anxiously. "What has occurred to distress you thus —you are not well?"

"I am not happy," replied Felicia.

"Nothing, I hope, occurred at the ball to annoy you?"

"No, Fidèle—no."

"Was it very magnificent?"

"Yes; but I never felt more lonely."

"Indeed! Did you not dance?"

"Oh, yes; but I felt as if in solitude, Fidèle, notwithstanding. I have no taste for such entertainments: they impart no pleasure to me now: I have a contempt for the brilliant surface when I look at the hypocrisy and heartlessness beneath. To the heartless such scenes may be pleasing—as evil deeds are to the evil disposed; but to those who seek pure and tranquil happiness they are abhorrent."

"But why should this have thus distressed you? You knew it all before!"

"I never felt it so deeply before! Oh, Fidèle," she added with a sigh, "if I could but exchange this dazzling sphere for one of peace and tranquil joy, I should be indeed the happiest of the happy. Ah, me!"

Fidèle understood all this perfectly; but not a syllable having reference to the real cause escaped her: she did what was necessary almost in silence, and, having done so, retired for the night.

In the morning Felicia felt more wretched than ever. She

F

had had a dream—a dream in which the purest love and the most heartless tyranny 'were mingled—a dream in' which it appeared that she and Alfred were united; that their union had been early blessed with several sweet children, and that they lived most happily in a delightful little cottage, when the Marquis came, purchased the estate on which it stood, and immediately razed it to the ground.

This, although but a dream, had a painful effect; she viewed it as the harbinger of oppression, and dwelt upon it bitterly, though silently, until her friend, Alice Hardwicke, was announced.

Alice Hardwicke! Alice! Should she reveal the secret to her? Would it be safe? Had she sufficient stability to conceal it? Was she not too light-hearted?—somewhat too much of a rattle? She had not time to answer these questions before Alice appeared.

"I am delighted to see you," said Felicia, as they embraced. "This is indeed kind."

"I told you," said Alice, with a playful expression, "that I would call and have five minutes' chat. Well! how did you enjoy yourself last evening?"

"Not much," replied Felicia, "except, indeed, while I was with you."

"Why that is the very compliment that *I* was about to pay, and that with the most perfect sincerity; for with the exception of the time I was with you, I did not enjoy myself at all. That, however, is nothing unusual: I very—very seldom indeed derive much pleasure from assemblies of that description: in fact, I don't believe that I really ought to go to such assemblies at all; nor would I go, were it not to smile at the gilded wings of folly, and to notice how they flutter. I have no business in the 'best' society—I speak in a purely mercantile sense—I have really no *business* there, for it is but a mart—a marriage mart—in which beauty is bartered for gold."

"Are you not too severe?"

"Not at all, my love! I believe that you *know* that I am not. What business *have* I there? What am I? The daughter of a general officer. Well! but what am I not? An heiress. Should I not have more homage paid me were I the daughter of a sweep with half a million? Not that I want their homage! I know its value too well. But were I a paragon of perfection—were I celebrated above all others for beauty, wit, intelligence, and sweetness of disposition—I should stand no chance in this, the 'best' society, with an idiotic girl worth two or three hundred thousand pounds."

"I believe that you are correct," said Felicia. "Wealth is, indeed, the great idol."

"And the only one, I fear, sincerely worshipped. Look at that Julia Lollard, for example. There's a fright! Can any one be more tasteless or inelegant? *Did* you ever notice her eyes? I never beheld so inveterate a cast. It is really quite an optical illusion. When she is looking at you she appears to be directing her attention to something over her left shoulder. She cannot help that, poor thing; but what a host of admirers she has! And why? She is the only child of a man who is said to be worth a million! The men are, however, in this respect, by no means the worst. Lady Hawke last night was in a desperate pet; I really thought that she would have slapped her daughter Flora for being civil to Lieutenant Wright. 'Have I not,' she exclaimed, 'told you again and again that he is a beggar! Let me see no more of it, I desire. Devote your attention to Sir William Blazon, Miss!' 'Well, ma, I do,' said the poor girl, 'but he's so *excessively* odious!' 'Odious!' retorted the enraged mamma, 'I've no patience with you! Look at his wealth!' Thus, my dear, are girls bought and sold; thus are their natural feelings outraged. They are sacrificed at the shrine of splendour; and Cupid, once the King of Hearts, is now but the Knave of Diamonds."

"Splendour," said Felicia, "instead of being essential to happiness, appears to have a tendency to destroy it."

"It has that tendency when hearts are not left really free. They may say what they please about the influence of splendour, but freedom of choice is the only true source of happiness. Look at Louisa Delisle and Charles Livingstone; they were devotedly attached. I do not believe that there were ever two persons who loved each other more fervently; but their friends interfered; there was not sufficient wealth on either side to enable them to live in splendour, and the match was broken off. Their feelings were not consulted; their hearts were not considered; their happiness was not for a moment studied. No; the match was broken off: she was married to a wealthy fool, he was tied to the daughter of a rich banker, and now they are all living in a state of splendid misery. Give me happiness — sweet, enduring, tranquil happiness! I care not who has the splendour."

"But how is this tranquil happiness to be secured?"

"I don't know—mind! I don't pretend to *know*—but I believe that pure happiness is to be secured by being united to him whom you love."

"Were you ever in love, dear?"

"What—really in love—absolutely in love—with a man?— Well, I never had that question put to me before. Do you mean really—truly—sincerely in love?"

"Yes."

"Well, upon my word, I don't know. I don't *think* that I ever was; but I'm sure that I should like to be: it must be so sweet. Oh! I should like it dearly!—I know that I should— it must be so nice, so delightful! But then whom is one to fall in love with? It might be practicable if one were morally blind; but the idea of falling in love with ones eyes wide open, with any one of the set whom *we* meet, is absurd. They are all so selfish—so glaringly selfish—we must look a little below the sphere in which *they* move, if we think of inspiring pure love."

"But would you be content to look below your own sphere?"

"Most certainly! If I loved a gentleman—he must be a gentleman; but that is of course understood, for if he had not the feelings of a gentleman, I could'nt love him—if, I say, I loved a gentleman, and he loved me, and I felt that our mutual happiness depended upon our marriage, I'd consent without the slightest hesitation, if even we had but sufficient to live in a quiet and moderate style."

"But would you not wish to return to the sphere in which you had been in the habit of moving?"

"Why should I? why should I wish to return to scenes from which I derive no pleasure? If I had a brilliant fortune; if I could go blazing with diamonds, and were thus in a position to command the adoration of the satellites of wealth and splendour, my vanity might prompt me to return; but I should be absolutely mad to wish to return to scenes in which I knew that I should experience nothing but humiliation. How many poor girls are rendered unhappy by being doomed to move in circles in which they are but ciphers! Give me, as I said before, happiness, the great object proposed, the grand aim of our existence, and I should no more think of returning to scenes of heartlessness and hypocrisy, than I should think of undervaluing the blessings of Heaven."

"Unfortunately," said Felicia, "this happiness is so vulnerable: we are so susceptible of vagrant thoughts and ephemeral feelings, that it is capable of being wounded by a breath. The grand point is, *could* you, in a lower sphere, be happy?"

"Yes!—in a cottage! with him whom I loved."

This Felicia held to be conclusive; and as the subject was

not pursued, Alice proceeded to give a graphic description of what she termed, "a funny amour" between the Dowager Lady Dewlap and an octogenarian Peer, which ended in his running away with her ladyship's daughter; and having succeeded in painting their portraits to perfection, she left Felicia, with many expressions of affectionate esteem.

For some time after the departure of Alice, Felicia dwelt upon all that had passed, recapitulating emphatically every point which had a tendency to strengthen the resolution she had formed. But then, how was that resolution to be carried into effect?—In what manner was she to proceed? She could not send for Alfred, in order to declare her views and feelings: nor, if even she did send, would he declare his. What then was to be done? That she loved him fervently, she knew: that he loved her with corresponding warmth, she believed; and that their mutual happiness depended upon their union, she had far less reason than ever to doubt. But how was he to know all this? Should she write to him?— How could she write on such a subject?—What would he think if she were to do so?—what *could* he think? No: she could not write: nor could she enter into any verbal explanation. He ought to have known that she loved him: she knew that he loved her! But perhaps he did know an omitted to declare himself, solely on account of that "socia distinction" to which he had referred. It might be so—nay she felt that it was so!—but how was she to communicate t him the fact that such a declaration would not be displeasing He might linger in a state of unhappiness for years: h might, indeed, never declare his love: he might pine and die— and all because she omitted to give him sufficient confidenc to declare that which she panted to hear him declare. Ho —how was she to act?—Perhaps Fidèle could assist her perhaps *she* could suggest to her the means by which thi primary object could be with delicacy accomplished. In Fidèl she *must* confide, and could with safety. She therefore rang for Fidèle, and while doing so made up her mind to reveal all.

"You rang, I believe," said Fidèle, as she entered, and found Felicia deep in thought.

"Oh—yes," returned Felicia. "Come and sit down, Fidèle; I wish to consult you on a subject of some importance."

Fidèle, who felt that she knew the nature of that subject, approached, and sat beside her.

"Fidèle," continued Felicia cautiously, "when Mr. Murray stated yesterday that he could not expect to be so happy as he was when at school, because he then thought of no 'social distinctions,' what did you imagine he meant?"

"Merely, I presume," replied Fidèle, "that he considered childhood to be the happiest period of existence."

"Because," added Felicia, "he thought of no 'social distinctions'—that is to say, because he could then freely love without the fear of any 'social distinction' forming a barrier tween him and the object of his love. Was not that what he meant?"

"It might have been."

"It was, Fidele! I feel sure that it was: but I am not more convinced of the fact, Fidèle, than you are! You know that he loves me: you must have perceived it—you did perceive it!—for when he sighed you were anxious to change the subject on which you feared he might dwell. Fidèle," she added, with an expression of intensity, "I know that you have an affectionate heart: I know that you are sincerely attached to me, and would be, indeed, delighted to see me happy: I can, therefore, appreciate the motive which has prompted you to say what you have said, in order to induce me to repudiate the idea of having *him*, in whom all my hopes of earthly happiness are centred: you do not believe that my happiness depends solely upon him: you do not believe that I cannot be happy without him: you, on the contrary, fear, that the loss of that splendour to which I have been accustomed would cause me to be wretched—that I should long to return to that brilliant sphere in which so many ignorantly aspire to move—that, in fact, I should be unable to reconcile myself to a life of pure tranquillity: but be assured, Fidèle, that a tranquil life is the highest point of my ambition—that the sacrifices of which you have spoken would not be regarded as sacrifices by me—and that, if even I valued my social position, I would give it up freely for him, so convinced do I feel, that I should but exchange empty splendour for love, peace, and joy. Seek not, therefore, to turn my heart from him, for that no power on earth can do!—seek rather to aid me in accomplishing that, by which alone my happiness can be secured."

"You know," said Fidèle, "that I am entirely devoted to you: you know that if I can promote your happiness, I will do so most willingly: you also know that when I appeared to speak in disparagement of him it was done at your request: do not therefore be under the slightest apprehension that I shall either say a word to wound your feelings, or urge anything in opposition to your views: if you believe that the pursuit of the course you contemplate will secure your happiness, hope will prompt me to believe so too; and if you think that I can in any way promote the attainment of the object proposed, you may command me."

"But I want you to see," said Felicia, "as clearly as I see, that happiness *will* be the result. He loves me, and I love him: he will be devoted to me, and I shall be devoted to him can anything but happiness spring from such an alliance? Say that we shall not live in splendour: what then? Is splendour essential to happiness?"

"No," replied Fidèle, "we well know that it is *not*, but splendour is not, I would submit, the only sacrifice that you would have to make; you would have to repudiate your family and connections."

"Say rather, Fidèle, that they would repudiate me. But let us look at that serious point calmly. I have a father whom I am bound to honour; but does my father really love me? I have never, I hope, been disobedient: I have never, to my knowledge, done aught to offend him; but is he an affectionate father to me? I leave you, Fidèle," she added, bursting into tears, "I leave you to answer these questions. And then my sisters," she continued, "are *they* kind to me? Have they ever behaved to me like dear sisters? Do they not seek to humiliate me by all the means at their command, to tyrannize over me and treat me like a slave?"

"They are not so kind," replied Fidèle, "as sisters generally are; but then their whole souls are centred in society."

"Yes, Fidèle, and such society as that which I could, with great pleasure, give up. What is such society to me? Its charms are confined to the designing and the thoughtless; pride and insincerity form its chief characteristics, and therefore I do not see that I should make any very great sacrifice were I to exchange it for the purer and more tranquil society of him whom I love. Do you not perceive, Fidèle, that I must sacrifice either the one or the other?—that I must either give up this hollow-hearted society or sacrifice my happiness for ever?—and can you for a moment hesitate to say which sacrifice you think I ought to make?"

'Happiness, certainly," returned Fidèle, "is the one grand object proposed. But how is Mr. Murray—you will pardon me for putting the question—how is he situated—I mean in a pecuniary sense?"

"I know not," replied Felicia, "I do not believe that he is rich, nor is it necessary to my happiness that he should be."

"No; that I understand! Still it would not be so well if he were desperately poor!"

"If he were, my feelings towards him would be unchanged; but he is not: besides, were it found to be necessary, I could always procure for him *some* lucrative appointment! I know all the Ministers well; I was conversing with two of them last evening, and I am sure that either of them would do anything to oblige me."

"Would it not be as well," suggested Fidèle, "to procure for him some such appointment at once?"

"I am not at all aware of its being necessary. If I find that it is, it can very soon be done. But how am I to ascertain whether it is or not?"

"You might easily inquire if such an appointment would be acceptable."

"But how? Can I send for him in order to make this inquiry?"

"Well, I don't see how you can send for him expressly for that purpose. It might, in the course of conversation, be named."

"But how am I to have this conversation with him?"

"I understand," said Fidèle, smiling archly. "You mean how are you to communicate to him the fact of your being anxious to have some conversation with him."

"I'll not attempt to conceal it," said Felicia. "That *is* what I mean. It is clear that the first step must be made, either directly or indirectly, by me; he has manifestly not sufficient confidence to declare his love in the first instance; and it is, Fidèle, on this very point that I am anxious for your advice and assistance."

"You wish him, in the first place, to know that a declaration of love would not be offensive?"

"Exactly. Now do suggest something, there's a dear."

"Well; it must, of course, be done indirectly: any direct intimation of the kind would amount to a declaration on *your* part. Have you any friend whom you could depute to manage the matter delicately for you?"

"I have one," replied Felicia.

" Miss Hardwicke ? '

" No : one in whom I repose the utmost confidence, and upon whose devotion, judgment, and delicacy I can rely : I mean you, Fidèle ; you are the only friend in whom I can, in such a case, with safety confide."

" I feel proud of the possession of your confidence," said Fidèle, " and will, conditionally, undertake the task."

" Conditionally ? " echoed Felicia.

" Yes ; I will not see you sacrificed without making an effort to save you. If I find that he is unworthy of you ; if I find that he does not really love you ; if I find that he is selfish and unamiable, or discover anything tending to convince me that unhappiness *must* be the result of your union, I will not promote it ; but if, on the other hand, I find that he loves you, and that he is in reality the dear, kind, devoted soul I trust that he is, there is nothing within the scope of my ability that I will *not* do to bring your hopes to a happy issue."

" I accept your conditions," said Felicia, with a smile of confidence. " I willingly subscribe to them all. Exercise your judgment ; study him well. I have not the slightest fear of the result. Will you see him to-day ? "

" Shall I ? "

" Will it not be kind of you to do so ? Will you not thereby relieve him ? Be assured that you will."

" Then I'll see him to-day."

" There's a dear, good girl. Go at once. You must not distinctly tell him.—But I'll leave all to you. Use your own discretion, and I shall be content."

Having no very exalted opinion of rank and splendour as sources of pure happiness, and believing that Alfred loved Felicia as fondly as Felicia loved him, Fidèle had no disinclination to perform the task she had undertaken, and therefore prepared for her departure at once. But how was she to commence ? How was the subject to be opened ? This point now occupied all her thoughts, and continued to occupy them until she reached the shop, when she decided upon letting chance prescribe the commencement.

As she entered, Alfred—who, without being able to tell why, had been expecting her all the morning—approached, and bowing tremulously, handed a chair. She wished to see some lawn, and Alfred showed her some lawn, while Mr. Wilkins, although engaged in completing one of his triumphs, watched him anxiously.

"Do you feel more happy to-day, Mr. Murray?" inquired Fidèle, with a smile.

Alfred smiled too, but very slightly, and blushed as he replied, "I spoke, I believe, comparatively."

"You did; but Lady Felicia feared that you were not happy at all!"

"Lady Felicia is very considerate," returned Alfred. "She was when a child. She is also," he added with an earnest expression, "very beautiful."

"And as amiable as she is beautiful," responded Fidèle. "She has a heart, Mr. Murray—as pure a heart as ever beat in human breast."

"I believe it," said Alfred, in tremulous accents, and with an expression of the most intense earnestness. "She cannot *but* be pure."

"He who secures Lady Felicia, Mr. Murray, will be a happy man."

"He must be, if indeed he be able to appreciate her goodness; for she *is* good; I feel that she is."

"You do not overrate her. *You* were enamoured of her once, were you not?"

Alfred moved his head mournfully and sighed.

"I mean," added Fidèle, "when you were a youth!"

"Ah," said Alfred, "as I yesterday observed, I thought of no social distinctions then."

"To what social distinctions do you allude?"

"To those, for example, which exist between Lady Felicia and myself."

"Why need *they* distress you?'

"I have of late held titles in abhorrence."

"You are not a republican, I hope, Mr. Murray?"

"No," replied Alfred mournfully, "I am not a republican."

"Then why abhor titles? You do not wish that Lady Felicia had no title?"

"I do indeed."

"But why?"

"I dare not explain."

"You dare not explain?"

"If I were to do so I should be deemed one of he most presumptuous men upon earth."

"Why presumptuous? What *do* you mean?"

"If I were an Earl I should be justified in explaining."

"Then you wish you were an Earl?"

"For that purpose I do."

"You are a very funny man," retorted Fidèle, playfully. "You hold titles in abhorrence. and yet you would have one. But if Lady Felicia had no title, what possible difference *could* it make to you? I perceive," she added smiling, "you mean that if she had no title, *you* would propose for her! Well! none could blame you! But why should the *title* make all this difference? Why not do so as it is?"

"Because I would not incur her displeasure for the world."

"Are you quite sure that by pursuing such a course you *would* incur her displeasure?"

"I fear that I should; but if even I did not, with what chance of success could *I* propose? A proposal from me would at least be laughed at."

"You do not know Lady Felicia," said Fidèle. "You do not know the natural sweetness of her disposition. Such a proposal,

sincerely made, would meet with neither ridicule nor displeasure."

"Do you really *believe*," said Alfred earnestly, "that I should
not offend her ?"

"I do : I feel convinced that you would not."

"If I were *sure* of that !"—

"*Be* sure of it !"

"It would be a great relief if I did but explain to her the
feelings with which she has inspired me : if she did but know
the nature of those feelings, I should regard it as *some* consolation !"

"Then let her know at once. You are not a stranger to her !
You were friends in childhood—playfellows !—let her know at
once."

"But how ?" inquired Alfred—"how is this to be done ? By
letter ?"

"Yes, write to her. You can mention my name, if you
please : you can even say that I encouraged you to write "

"You have imparted new life to me," said Alfred. "You
have filled my heart with joy !—But the Marquis !"

"It will be as well not to consider him at present. If you
conjure up all the difficulties at once, they may appear too
great to be surmounted. Your first task is to write to Lady
Felicia. Enclose the letter in an envelope addressed to me,
and I'll undertake to deliver it to her."

"I know not how to thank you," said Alfred.

"Then make no attempt."

"But I *do* thank you, with all my heart !"

"Here is my card. And now about this lawn. Your
people will wonder what we have been chatting about so long.
This piece, I think, will do."

"Shall I send it ?" inquired Alfred.

"No : I'll take it with me ; I have a coach outside."

Alfred packed up the lawn with alacrity, and when he had

handed her into the coach, he said, " Allow me again to thank you."

" Mr. Murray," returned Fidèle, " I feel interested in your success, and will do what I can to promote it."

Alfred bowed, and the coach drove off.

" Well," said Mr. Wilkins, before Alfred had fairly re-entered the shop, "anything up ?—anything new ?—anything fresh ?"

"Yes," replied Alfred, "something of great importance."

"You *don't* mean that!" said Mr. Wilkins, with a singular expression of doubt mingled with amazement, "You don't mean to say that you've got a brilliant berth to begin with ?"

" No," replied Alfred, "but I feel more than ever convinced that Lady Felicia loves me."

"It'll spoil it," said Mr. Wilkins, shaking his head doubt-fully, " I fear it'll spoil it !"

"I hope not," said Alfred.

"Very good! So do I! But give me something substantial. There's nothing substantial about love : there's nothing at all palpable in it! A lucrative berth is full of meaning!—it means a position in society : it means a splendid establishment : it means an interest in our glorious constitution : it means a full purse, and a balance at the banker's ; but love means nothing but sighs and simplicity : it is but a ghost in an armour of muslin—a mere bubble, blown in the sun, but to burst and resolve itself into its original soapsuds. Love is all very well after business ; but do business first. Get a splendid appoint-ment—make *that* secure—and then you may talk about love, if you like. I wouldn't be pestered with it if I were you; because it can *come* to nothing !—if you loved her like life, you couldn't have her !"

" I am not sure of that," said Alfred calmly.

" Not sure ! but is it likely ?"

" *I* think that it is. I am at all events going to make an effort to secure her. I shall write to her to-night and explain all."

" What ! explain how you love her, and that sort of thing ?
Do you mean that ?"

" Yes."

" Then you'll cut the throat of the finest chance a young
man ever had of becoming illustrious. You write to her; you
declare your passion; you tell her she's the idol of your soul,
and so on; well!—what will be the consequence ? This !—
eternal estrangement from that very hour! You are sure to
offend her!—safe as death!—and if you do you'll for ever be
done."

" I have been led to believe," said Alfred, " that such a
declaration will not be displeasing !"

" Who has led you to believe it ?"

" The lady with whom I have been conversing. She, in fact,
advised me to write."

" Did you tell *her* then that you loved Lady Felicia ?"

She appeared to me to know it !"

" Stop a bit. A thought strikes me. I think I see a move.
She *advised* you to write."

" Yes; and told me that if I enclosed a letter to her, she
would deliver it : she, moreover, said that I might, if I pleased,
state that she had encouraged me to write."

" Very good," said Mr. Wilkins, with an expression of deep
thought. "Then I'll bet ten to one that she was sent by Lady
Felicia, expressly, in order to induce you to write. Now look here.
To love Lady Felicia—or Lady Anybody else—hopelessly—that
is to say, without half a chance of having her—were to put
yourself into a state of moral perspiration to no purpose; but
if she is so desperately enamoured of you, that she is willing to
make a mob of sacrifices for you, that's a shawl of another
pattern, and one too in which you'd be a natural idiot not to
speculate. When I, last night, set my face dead against love,
I'd no conception of its being at all likely that she would
dream of making the sacrifices which *she* will have to make;

but now that it appears she *has* an idea of making these sacrifices, love not only enters into the speculation, but becomes absolutely the leading article. Write, therefore, by all means. I'll be bound to say she has a mint of money; in which case you'll not want an appointment at all. But mind *how* you write : a great deal depends upon style ! I don't know whether you are much of a hand at it; but magnanimity and poetic ardour are indispensable."

" I fear," said Alfred, " that my style of composition is not particularly striking; but, perhaps you'll be kind enough to assist me."

" By all means; certainly; I'll do so with pleasure! *I'll* think of a thing or two worth the money, and when we shut up we'll go at it. But, heaven and earth! what a fortunate dog! Why, you have absolutely the luck of a legion.—Well ! fortune may be blind; but she has a fine nose."

The composition of this letter now engrossed all their thoughts; and when the time for closing had arrived, they repaired to a private room, and went to work.

Under ordinary circumstances Alfred was a somewhat rapid writer, having commenced, he would go on without waiting to enrich his sentences with new thoughts ; but so deeply impressed was he with the importance of this epistle, that he was for some time unable to write at all. The same, however, cannot be said of Mr. Wilkins : *he* allowed nothing to check his career: he went away triumphantly, and flourished with so much enthusiasm, that three sides of foolscap were filled before he permitted his pen to rest for a moment ! But when he reviewed what he had written, he found that his task was by no means complete : indeed, he made so many erasures and interlineations, that but little of the original remained. This, however, he held to be a matter of no importance : he resolved at once on making a fair copy, and did so with consummate tact.

" Now," said he, having completed his task, "just let me know what you think of this. Here, I'll read it to you.—Now : are you ready ?"

" I'm all attention," replied Alfred ; and Mr. Wilkins, having effected the clearance of his throat, read as follows :—

" BRIGHT ANGEL !

" Vouchsafe to receive, with all that benignity which constitutes one of the sweetest characteristics of your illustrious nature, the fervent declaration of one whose devotion is unrivalled, whose whole soul is centred in your smiles, and who, to secure the supreme felicity of basking in your effulgence, would make any sacrifice, however alarming.

" As Jacob loved Rachel—or, to come down to our own times—as Romeo loved Juliet—even so, delicious Felicia, do I love you. In infancy I loved you ; in manhood I adore you : and had I the wealth of worlds to lay at your feet, I'd deposit the lot, and revere you.

" You are my idol ! Without you, the world to me would be an incomprehensible chaos. You *are* my world — my atmosphere !—I must breathe that or die.

" When, after seven or eight weary years, I beheld again your incomparable loveliness ; when I heard the celestial music of your voice—saw the seraphic expression of your eyes, and gazed upon the smile which danced divinely round your angelic lips, I felt enchanted !—no tongue can express, no pen can describe the ecstatic ardour of the love which you inspired ! —neither Ætna, nor Vesuvius, burns so fiercely as the flame which your surpassing beauty kindled. I felt at once ravished and racked ! — ravished by the wonderful combination of matchless elegance and unexampled loveliness, and racked by the reflection that I was not a monarch.

" Oh ! that I were an Emperor, that I might place you on the throne to be the envy of surrounding nations, and the glory of the world! And yet, after all, what are rank and magnificence, compared with the pure and devoted love of him who, to secure to you unbounded joy, would sacrifice his life? What are pride, pomp, and splendour, when compared with connubial felicity, and inexhaustible affection! Life without love, is the body without the soul, the crown without the head, the violet without the perfume, the moon without the sun.

" Deign, therefore, dear one, to grant me an interview, in order that I may pour out my soul in streams of rapture, and lay my fond and faithful heart bare. Of that heart you are supremely the mistress. You have the power to wither it utterly, or to fill it with the purest conceivable joy. It throbs but for you. Day and night it pants to develop itself to you. Do not—oh! do not—permit it to pant in vain. Relieve it from the tartaric acid of suspense: change its contents from anxiety to rapture. One delicious hour—dear divinity of earth—will be sufficient for its perfect analysis. Name that hour—that blessed hour—and I will fly with the wings of immortal love to register my vows of eternal fidelity.

" With a pulse beating quickly to urge on the time, and a soul full of thrilling impatience to behold you,

" I have the honour,
" Sweet Lady Felicia,
" To be,
" With the highest admiration
" And esteem,
" Your Ladyship's
" Most devoted Adorer,
" ALFRED MURRAY."

" There sir!" exclaimed Mr. Wilkins, with an air of triumph, " What do you think of that?—That's the style of thing to create a sensation! Here, you see, you have the two grand principles—magnanimity and poetic ardour—conspicuously developed. You offer to sacrifice everything for her, from the wealth of worlds even to your life, and having thus proved yourself magnanimous enough for anything, you do the ardent by comparing the flame of your love with the blazes of Ætna and Vesuvius."

"I perceive;" said Alfred—"oh! I perceive: but the flight is, I fear, too high: I can't sustain it."

"Not sustain it?—Why I could keep it up for a month!"

"No doubt of it! But I should break down in a moment. The effect of this would be to induce her to regard it as a mere *sample* of what she might expect in the event of an interview, when, in fact, as far as I am concerned, it is the bulk! I could add nothing! You have said all that *I* could say, and more than I should ever have thought of saying. It is not only the title, but the book; not only the text, but the whole sermon! *My* object has been, to say as little as possible, in order that I may have the more to say when I *see* her."

"Well, then, let's have a look at what you *have* said."

"Shall I read it?"

"Aye, do. Now, then, let's have a specimen of *your* style."

Alfred took up the paper on which he had been writing, and read *his* epistle, which ran briefly as follows:

"DEAR LADY FELICIA!

"Pardon me for thus presuming to address you. Miss Legrange knows why I have not done so before; and how delighted I was to hear that if I did so, it might not be displeasing.

"I dare not venture to express to you the warmth of those feelings of love and admiration with which you have inspired me; but believe me to be,

"Dear Lady Felicia,
"Ever yours,
"ALFRED MURRAY."

" Cold enough," said Mr. Wilkins—" quite. And yet I think I see the move. You mean this to be a mere intro-duction?"

" Nothing more," replied Alfred.

" I understand: so that you can bring in *my* points when you see her! Well—they might then have more effect. I don't at all dislike the idea: on the contrary, I think it rather good! Your first object is to obtain an interview; and *then* you can go in to any extent. *I* see!—Well, it only affords another proof that two heads are better than one."

Alfred was quite pleased that he had not offended Mr. Wilkins; and when he had thanked him for the trouble he had taken, he copied the note in his neatest hand, and sent it enclosed to Fidèle.

CHAPTER VI.

THE DISCOVERY.

WHEN Fidèle had explained the substance of all that occurred during her interview with Alfred, Felicia expected an immediate communication; and although the conviction expressed by Fidèle, that he was all that she could wish him to be, gave her joy, she notwithstanding felt painfully anxious when she found that no communication would arrive that night.

In the morning, however, the arrival of the note repaid her for all the anxiety she had endured. Having received it from Fidèle, she passionately kissed it again and again, and then proceeded to read it with rapture.

She had *not* been mistaken: he did indeed love her! The note was brief!—very brief!—she *wished* that it had not been so *brief!* Had it extended to fifty—or even a hundred and fifty—pages, it would not have been too long!—She would have read and rehearsed it diligently, until she had committed every word of it to memory—it *could* not have been too *long!*—Still, brief as it was, it contained sufficient to prove that he dearly loved her.

" But," she observed, having several times perused it, " he does not solicit an interview!"

" No," said Fidèle, " but that he seeks one is of course understood!"

" How then are we *now* to proceed?"

" That depends upon you," replied Fidèle, with a smile. " Do you feel inclined to grant him an interview?—or will you reply to his note, and tell him that his temerity and presumption have amazed you? The pursuit of the latter course would only kill him!"

"Then, having no desire to compass his death, I decidedly prefer the pursuit of the former. But how is it to be managed?"

"Will you allow him to be *my* lover for a time? I'll not altogether deprive you of him; but if you'll transfer him for an hour or so, I'll invite him to come and see me."

"Excellent, Fidèle," exclaimed Felicia, "And then"—

"Why, when he has sufficiently made love to me, I must, I suppose, quietly give him up to you.

"But when can this be done?"

"You are anxious, I presume, to see him as soon as possible?"

"Need I confess that I am?"

"Well, the Marquis goes down to the House about four, and Lady Florence will be, of course, with Lady Augusta in the Park: shall I appoint four, or half-past, to-day?"

"Do, there's a dear girl."

"Very good, then I'll write a note at once. We can then arrange about his reception."

The following note was accordingly written :—

"Miss Fidèle Legrange presents her compliments to Mr. Murray, and begs to inform him that she will be happy to see him at Kingsborough House, about half-past four.

"Mr. Murray will, of course, inquire for Miss Legrange."

"Now, how shall I send it?" inquired Fidèle.

"Send one of the servants," replied Felicia—"send James."

"Had it not be better sent by the post?"

"As you please. But a note from you sent to a house of business *can* excite no suspicion. Besides, if it be sent by the post he *may* not receive it in time."

"Well, then, we'll send it by James," returned Fidèle; and when James had been summoned, she despatched him at once.

James, however, did not like this job; there were, indeed, very few jobs that he *did* like, but this—he having lost at dominoes three pints of half-and-half, and being in the midst of a winning game when summoned—was peculiarly unpleasant; still, ascribing it in a philosophic spirit to fate, he proceeded with the note, and having arrived at the shop, near the door of which stood Mr. Wilkins, he delivered it into the hands of that gentleman, with an air of the most superb hauteur, and said in a pseudo-aristocratic drawl, " Ah, note or-r for Mr. Morray."

" Does it require an answer ?" inquired Mr. Wilkins.

" Don't know."

Mr. Wilkins handed the note to Alfred, who opened it tremulously and turned pale as death and having read it, he made an effort to compose himself, and said, addressing James, " Very good."

" Oh ! " said James, who had watched him with an expression of curiosity, " no ansor—oh ! Good morning," he added with a patronising air; and throwing rigid dignity into his calves, he —by virtue of setting in motion the extensive machinery of his hips—very dexterously wriggled away.

Alfred then submitted the note to Mr. Wilkins, who had no sooner read it than he exclaimed, " Bravo ! Excellent ! Out and out ! *Nothing* could be better. Here you have what you want in a style of extreme delicacy—a positive appointment— but, as a precaution, ' Mr. Murray will, of course, inquire for Miss Legrange.' You certainly are, without any exception, the luckiest fellow alive. Half past four. Well, there are my waistcoats; wear which you please; there are also my rings, studs, and pins, take your choice: you are welcome to any- thing I have."

" I thank you," said Alfred, " but I shall not require anything of the sort. I shall go as I am."

" Go as you are ! You must do no such thing; you must go,

sir, in style, and the higher the style you go in the better. Your object is to excite admiration."

"But not of rings, waistcoats, and pins!"

"They are the legitimate germs of admiration. Being, as it were, engrafted on the man, they become part and parcel of the man, and attract admiration to the man. You don't attach sufficient importance to dress, notwithstanding its importance is held to be paramount. Its effect upon *men* is great; but its effect upon women is infinitely greater. We cannot dress too well for them; nor can they dress too well for us. They make their remarks upon us, as well as we make our remarks upon them; and as nothing attracts our admiration so much as a well-dressed woman, so nothing attracts *their* admiration so much as a well-dressed man. What do we think of women who dress in a tasteless and slovenly manner?—and what do you imagine they think of men who display a corresponding want of taste and attention?"

"But," said Alfred, "there is a medium between dressing as you say in a slovenly manner, and coming out in the highest style of fashion!"

"True; but he whose style is the most attractive, is, by virtue of that style, the most attractive man. Society expects every man to dress in the best style he can, and if he doesn't dress well, it is, in the judgment of society, because he can't."

"But a man may dress well without being an exquisite! Simplicity, as well in dress as in manners, forms the general characteristic of a well-bred man."

"But simplicity will not tell with women: they want something more than simplicity. Why do they admire peacocks?"

"Because they are beautiful!"

"They admire their plumage; and as dress is our plumage, the more attractive it is the more they admire *us*. Therefore take my advice, and put on something striking: that embroidered emerald waistcoat, for instance, looks slap!"

"Well," said Alfred, with the view of compromising the matter, for he would not have worn the waistcoat for fifty times its value, "I'll try it on; and as I shall not return to business this evening, I'll go to the old place and wait till you come!"

This met the approbation of Mr. Wilkins, who promised to be there immediately after they had closed; and when Alfred had obtained leave of absence, he prepared for that interview of which the result he felt certain would either secure or wither his happiness for ever.

Now, when James had returned to the servant's hall, he called the elite together, and having laughed for a few moments merrily, with the view of preparing them to receive some humorous communication, said—"Well! of *all* the queer goes in natural philosophy, the go I've jest witnessed and experienced, is beyond all human comprehension, about the queerest of the queer."

"What is it?—What is it?" inquired the elite eagerly. "Oh! *do* tell us what it is!"

"Then bring your comprehension to a focus," said James, "and I'll expostulate. Miss Legrange says to me, says she, 'James'—I knew in a moment she wanted me to go somewhere for her—'James,' says she, 'be kind enough to take this,' and gives me a note, which I subsekently found was addressed to a fellowe named Morray. Well, I goes; and when the fellowe took the note, *if* we'd bin a going to have a hailstorm of stars, if an earthquake had been about to swallow him whole, if all the horrid ghosts in immortal creation had come in a body to take him away and skin him, he couldn't have trembled more. I *never* saw a fellowe so desperately dished, or one which looked so dead and diabolically doubled up. He was ready to sink into the earth! His eyes seemed fit to fall out of his head; his joints was disordered, his blood left his cheeks, and he looked altogether the image of one who had jest bin and done some excruciating murder."

"I wonder what he's bin up to," cried one of the elite.

"No good," said another, "I'll warrant."

"Did you ever see him before?" inquired a third.

"Yos," replied James. "It's the fellowe which brought some silks heor the other day. He's bin doing some dirty swindle, doubtless. But to see the fellow shake! That was fun if you like! You'd a split your sides a laughing. I thought drop he must. Look here: here he stood: just look here," he added, and gave a variety of ingenious imitations, which, by exciting the mirth of his friends, enlivened the sphere of their usefulness.

When, therefore, Alfred arrived, and James had informed them of the interesting fact, they all felt exceedingly anxious to see him; but as he had not only been announced to Fidèle, but shown into the room in which she sat working apparently with praiseworthy diligence, the gratification of their natural curiosity was unavoidably deferred.

On entering this room Alfred felt very nervous, but as Fidèle received him with an air of cheerfulness, he to some extent recovered his self-possession.

"Well, Mr. Murray," said Fidèle, with a smile; "then you adopted the course I suggested."

"I did venture to do so," returned Alfred, "but I fervently hope that I have given no offence."

"Well, Mr. Murray, the *offence* which you have given is not, I apprehend, very great: you will know the *extent* to which you have offended when you have apologized to Lady Felicia; but if you hope to be forgiven you will explain to her ingenuously the feelings by which you were prompted. Recollect, Mr. Murray, that she whom you seek is no ordinary prize: I speak not with reference to her social position: I allude to those qualities of heart and mind which are the sources, not only of admiration, but of the most intense affection. Let me, therefore, beg of you to

be ingenuous. If the hope you have inspired *be* realized, the
result will depend upon you, and you alone; your devotion
will secure the most perfect felicity; but unkindness or
neglect will plunge into utter misery one of the most
amiable creatures upon earth."

"I beg of you," said Alfred, "to believe"—

"Pardon me," interrupted Fidèle, "I feel so much inclined
to believe all you would say, that it is really quite unnecessary
for me to hear it. Besides, *I* require no confession! That
you must reserve for Lady Felicia!"

"But when may I hope to have the happiness of seeing
her?"

"Why," replied Fidèle, smiling archly, "I *could* introduce
you even now!—and *will*—if indeed you really wish me to
do so."

"Need I say that the introduction would give me great
pleasure?"

"Well, perhaps that is not absolutely necessary: I'll
therefore introduce you at once. Will you do me the favour
to step this way?"

Anxiously and with considerable embarrassment, Alfred
rose and followed Fidèle, who, having opened a door which
led into a splendid apartment in which Felicia sat apparently
reading, said, "I have the pleasure, Lady Felicia, to present
to you one who is anxious to make some apology."

Felicia, who looked extremely pale, rose and gracefully
extended her hand, which Alfred took tremulously, and not
only held, but, scarcely knowing what he was about at the
time, kissed it!

In an instant Felicia's blushes mounted, but she made no
attempt to withdraw her hand, which he still held and pressed
as he gazed at her in silence, but with an expression o
rapture, until Fidèle had politely placed a chair by his side,
and retreated to one of the windows with a book.

"I have ventured," said he, at length, with great intensity of feeling—"I have ventured to address you; and in that venture I have embarked every earthly hope I have. I knew that I was presumptuous, and therefore feared that I might offend you: I was painfully apprehensive of incurring your displeasure; but this kind reception tends to banish my fears, to prove that I was not altogether mistaken, to convince me that I am not wholly indifferent to you, and thus to inspire me with joy! Lady Felicia, my position is not unknown to you: it is, compared with yours, obscure. I have neither rank, influence, nor wealth; but if through the eyes soul communicates with soul, I may, I think, reasonably infer that you do not therefore despise me. I *have* but a heart to offer—a heart which, whether it be rejected or not, must for ever be devoted to you."

"I know not how it is," said Felicia, in tones which to Alfred were musical indeed, "I am perfectly unable to account for it; but when I saw you the other morning, I felt—notwithstanding the lapse of years—as if some sweet sensation had been revived. I knew not what it was, but some youthful feeling appeared to be re-awakened—some chord was struck which had vibrated before—and the effect was like that of the holy influence of a hymn, which we remember to have heard in infancy. We were but children when we knew each other first, and yet the feelings then created still live."

"Such words from you," said Alfred, "re-animate all my hopes. The feelings then created still live! You *loved* me when a child?"

"*As* a child," replied Felicia.

"And that is one of the feelings which happily still live. May I not draw that sweet inference?"

Felicia was silent, but that silence was sufficiently eloquent.

"I am aware," continued Alfred, "I cannot but be aware, that the course which I would prompt you to pursue involves

the sacrifice of that splendour by which you are surrounded ;
but I need not suggest to you that splendour is not essential
to pure happiness."

"I do not *believe* that it is," said Felicia.

"Nor need I remind you that happiness is the one grand
object at which we all aim, and to secure which no sacrifice can
be too great. If then, this sacrifice were made for me, what
on earth would I not do to make you happy ? My whole life
would be devoted to the grateful task of rendering your happiness complete, and that this is a task which I *could* perform,
your amiable spirit and gentle bearing, the purity of your mind
and the natural sweetness of your disposition, forbid me to
entertain a doubt."

"I will not ask you," said Felicia, " if you are sincere, because
that would imply a want of faith, when faith itself is in the
ascendant ; but you give me credit for the possession of qualities
which in me you have not yet had time to discover."

"My heart tells me that you are all that I have intimated,
and more ; if you were not gentle, amiable, and kind, you
would not have received me as you have done to-day ;
independently of which, my heart's impressions have been
confirmed by one whose opportunities of forming a correct
judgment, have been ample."

"You allude to Fidèle. She is a good girl and worthy of all
confidence, but her attachment to me has prompted her,
perhaps, to say more than an impartial judgment might
warrant."

Alfred smiled, and again took her hand, and gazed with
an expression of the utmost tenderness, and continued to
contemplate her beauty in silence, until Fidèle, conceiving that
it would not be wise to allow their interview to be prolonged,
came forward, and said, " I am sorry to disturb you, but you
really know not how the time flies."

This was held to be *very* premature. Both Felicia and

Alfred, indeed, marvelled at it! To them it did not appear
that they had been with each other two minutes! still—giving
Fidèle credit for knowing more about the flight of time than
they knew—they rose, but were even then in no haste to part.

"Now," said Fidèle, " do you quite understand each
other?"

"I hope so," replied Alfred, smiling. "But," he added,
addressing Felicia, "when shall I have the *pleasure* of seeing
you again?"

"That," returned Felicia, "I must leave to Fidèle."

"Yes, I'll arrange that," interposed Fidèle, "but discretion
now enjoins haste. Now, take leave of each other, and part."

"Felicia!" said Alfred: and having looked at her rapturously
for a moment, he embraced her! "God bless you! "You
have filled my heart with joy! God bless you!"

Felicia fervently bade him farewell, and he followed Fidèle,
who, having promised that she would very soon write to him,
playfully hurried him away.

While descending the stairs, he met some of the servants,
who looked at him in a somewhat peculiar manner, and smiled;
but he neither understood this, nor cared to understand it:
he reached the hall door, which the gouty porter managed,
by dint of great exertion, to open, and left the house in a
reverie of rapture.

He had however, no sooner left, than the servants assem-
bled, and felt quite indignant with James for placing him in
so ridiculous a light. He was such a nice young man!—so
handsome!—so excessively handsome!—so young, and yet so
manly!—*He* shake, and feel fit to drop! It was their unani-
mous opinion, that if he knew what master James had said
about him, he would quickly make *him* shake and feel fit to
drop! He was dressed so nicely, and looked so happy, and
had such a lovely head of hair! They never in their lives
saw a more delicious man; and when James appeared, they

told him so flatly, and wondered he wasn't ashamed of himself! But he wasn't! Not he, indeed!—not a bit of it!—*he* ashamed? No! He knew who *ought* to be ashamed!—he knew who ought to *sink* with shame!—and, what was more, he could tell if he liked; but he didn't like, and wouldn't tell, and nobody could make him tell.

" Why, what on earth do you mean?" they inquired.

" No matter," replied James. " What I know, I know; and what I've seen, I've seen; what I tells, I tells; but what I means to *keep*, flesh don't get out of *me!* I've seen, within the last few minutes more than I ever saw in *my* born days before."

" Good heavens!" they exclaimed; " why, what have you seen?"

" Seen! What have I seen! I've seen enough to make a man's hair stand up like the squills of a prickly porkipine I could hardly believe my own eyes. That she—so modest, so meek, and so mild—that she should ever have done such a thing"—

" She! What, Miss Legrange? Oh! do tell us—do, James —there's a good soul."

" I expected as much," said one of the housemaids; " I never *thought* she was a mite too good."

" You never *thought*," said James, contemptuously—" You don't know what you're a-talking about! I never said nothing about Miss Legrange!—Miss Legrange, I dare say, is as good as *some* people!—as it happens, I don't mean Miss Legrange at all!"

" Whom, then, *do* you mean, James?" inquired the rest, soothingly; for, as the housemaid who had spoken was no favourite of James, her observations had displeased him. " Whom, then, *do* you mean?"

" I mean Lady Felicia."

" Indeed! Well—well, James!—well! What of her?"

"That's locked up *here*," said James, striking his breast; "and the key's locked itself up."

"Oh, but you may as well tell *us*, you know;—it won't go any further."

"No, I know it won't—oh, dear me, no!—it would be all over Europe in the course of ten minutes"

"No, indeed, James; indeed, we'll not say a word about it · we'll not breathe a syllable to any living soul."

"Keep as you are, and then you can't," said James. "It'll be just as good for your health, and less trouble."

"But, surely," said one of his favourites,—" you might tell us in confidence."

"*May* I trust you? That's the point. May I trust you?"

"What! not when we pledge you our honour?"

"That's another thing. If you pledge me your honour, that alters the case. But, look here!—if I have any specie of interruption—however inconceivable—I shut up at once and for ever."

"You shall not be interrupted, James: now, then."

"Well, having an ideor that all was not right—conceiving that something uncommon was wrong—fancying that what was up was made too much of a mystery of—imagining that whatever it was, it ought not to be kept so much in the dark —knowing that the fellowe had trembled as if he'd been doing a crime—supposing that he'd been sent for here to clear himself if he could, and thinking that he and Miss Legrange had been together long enough, I listened at the door of the room in which I'd left them, and—to my unbounded astonishment—I heard—nothing!—not a word!—not a whisper!— not a breath!—all was as still as the silent grave. Ask me not what I thought—don't inquire of me what I imagined: question me not about the horrid ideas which flitted across my indignant brain!—form your own judgment: judge yourselves: judge of the thoughts that rushed into my mind

H

—judge of the feelings that stuck in my throat. I felt horrid! What! thought I.—But just as I was going to follow this thought, a great idea came up and struck me. In an instant—in the twinkling of an eye—like a flash of forked lightning it struck me, that as I couldn't hear them, they mightn't be there! and recollecting that there was a door in that room which opened right into the next, I made no more to do, but progressed to the next and listened there, and presently peeped through the key-hole, when, what should I see—what should I behold—but Lady Felicia—Heaven and earth!—a hugging that fellowe like life!"

"What!" exclaimed his favourite, "a hugging him?"

"A hugging him."

"What! right down *hugging* him?"

"What means this illiteration, woman?—as the black man said the other night at the play—I tell you that Lady Felicia was a hugging him!—aint that plain English?"

"Well, but look here, James, you *don't* mean to say"—

"I mean to say neither more nor less than what I *do* say, and that is that she was a hugging of that fellowe!'

"Well, but surely, James, you're joking!"

"Are you a unbelieving Jew?—are you a Turk, or a Greek, or a Hottentot, or what are you? I'll show you how she did it!—*then*, perhaps, you'll believe me. Look here. You're that fellowe, and I'm Lady Felicia. Now then," he added, embracing her warmly,—"*now* will you believe me?"

"James!" she exclaimed, having very correctly struggled, "*Don't* be so silly: ha! done—now, *do!*"

"I was only a showing you how it was managed, there's nothing like placing a fact before your eyes."

"Well, but where was Miss Legrange?"

"She was at that critical junction a making her way to her own room door."

"Then she did not see this?"

" Didn't she !   Was a woman's eyes made to shut at such a time ?   Could they shut ?   Would the lids come down ?   It aint in nature.   *She* saw it all : it aint likely she didn't. although she pretended, of course, not to see."

" I won't believe a word of it," said one.

" Nor will I," said another.

" Nor I neither," said a third.   It's a fib on the very face of it—a right down scandalous falsity !—and it's shameful to take a lady's character away so."

" Who's a taking away a lady's character ?" demanded James.   "When I say she was kissed, do I take away her character ?   Don't you all like to be kissed ?   Does your character go when you're kissed ?   If so, you haven't got a mite to bless yourselves with !—not one of you !"

" But we won't believe she was kissed at all !"

" You may believe, or believe me not, I aint a going to undertake to find you all in belief ; but if I didn't see them a kissing *and* a hugging, I'll go for a soldier, and fight till I drop !"

" But is it," said one, " likely that she would bemean herself so much as to take up with one like him ?   Is it natural ? Look at their different situations !"

" Nature," returned James, " don't trouble her head about difference of situations.   She didn't make the difference.   That aint her work.   She made them both flesh and blood, and that's quite enough for nature."

" Aye, but I mean in the nature of things !"

Well, in the nature of things they may love each other : in the nature of things they may kiss each other ; in the nature of things they may marry each other !—they may do all this in the nature of things."

" Marry ! ridiculous.   She marry him !"

" Is there the ghost of a law to prevent it ?"

" Don't be so innocent, pray.   The idea is stupid.   She

marry him, indeed! There, don't say another word about it. It's my belief that it's all made up, and the rights of it ought to be known!"

"So *I* say!" cried one of her immediate friends.

" And I agree with *you*," said another.

" You'd better go and ask her," interposed James.

" I don't know I shan't."

" If you do, you don't ought to die a natural death!"

" Oh, I aint one to get fellow servants into scrapes; but I mean to say that such barefaced stories are disgraceful to any sex."

" It isn't a story!"

" We know better!—we all know better! Lady Felicia to do such a thing!—she above all other ladies in the world! The idea's too monstrous to be swallowed. We won't have it!—so the less you say about it the better!"

Well! James had no desire to say much more about it! He knew what he had seen, and had told them what he knew, and if they wouldn't believe him, why he couldn't help it: he couldn't absolutely compel them to believe!—still he did think it hard that they should be so incredulous, and he told them so pointedly, and that too in tones which could not be mistaken; but they again declared that they would *not* believe him, and he, having a contempt for their scepticism, left them.

But although this strong declaration was made, and, before him, subscribed to unanimously, the majority of them *did* believe him, and immediately held a privy council. They had no desire to injure James. They all declared they'd "scorn the action." They wouldn't tell Lady Felicia for the world! They knew themselves better than that, they *hoped*. But they —of course confidentially—told Lady Augusta's maid, who in confidence communicated the fact to Lady Augusta, who, although she thought the secret worth knowing, did not at the same time consider it worth keeping, and, therefore, revealed it at once to Lady Florence, by whom it was hailed with malicious delight!

" Discovered at last!" she exclaimed, with an air of triumph, " I *knew* that there was something beneath the surface of that meekness; I knew that that soft, smooth tongue was but the organ of rank hypocrisy. The sly, insidious, artful creature!"

" But," said Lady Augusta, " you do not imagine that she has really disgraced herself?"

" Why, what else can I imagine? You say that they embraced each other! What is the rational inference?—what can any one infer from it, but that instead of being all gentleness and purity, she is forward and vicious, if not utterly abandoned. I am glad that the mask has been removed— exceedingly glad that her vice has been discovered."

"But she may not be vicious!" urged Lady Augusta. "She may have conceived a pure affection for this person!"

"Augusta, how you talk! A *pure* affection! She has an affection for him, doubtless; but, for Heaven's sake, say nothing of its purity."

" Well, how are we to act? Shall we speak to her on the subject?"

" Certainly not. Why should we?"

" I think we ought to put her on her guard!"

" What, and thus spoil all? No: that will never do. Put her on her guard, and she'll deprive us of that amusement, of which I anticipate her *pure* affection will be the source. Let us appear to know nothing whatever about it! We shall then be able to watch her actions, without creating the slightest suspicion. By whom do you say it was discovered?"

" By James."

" Oh, he it was who witnessed the affectionate scene. I must speak to him privately on the subject."

" Why you just now suggested the propriety of appearing to know nothing about it."

" Of appearing to *her* to know nothing about it. I want *his* version of the affair, and must have it."

" But when he knows that the fact has been communicated to you, he will quarrel with those whom he told in confidence, and thus cause the affair to be known to all !"

" You need not be at all apprehensive on that point: I'll lock up his lips securely. He shall not say a syllable to them on the subject, I know how to manage *him*."

Being somewhat less malicious than her sister, Lady Augusta suggested the expediency of explaining the matter to the Marquis, in order that *he* might check Felicia's assumed vicious career; but this course was strongly opposed by Lady Florence, who was anxious to *prove* the degradation of Felicia, and then to denounce her; and in order that she might proceed on sure grounds, she embraced the earliest opportunity of summoning James, that he might not only explain what he had seen, but assist in the achievement of the object she had in view.

" James," she commenced, calmly, when that confiding victim appeared before her unconscious of the treachery of those in whom he *had* confided, " I wish to speak with you on a subject of some importance. I may, I presume, trust you ?"

" Oh yes," my lady, replied the betrayed, with a comic expression of solemnity—" with anything."

" Aye, if even it be a secret ?"

" Certainly : by all means."

" Well, in the first place, I wish you to explain to me distinctly, what occurred this morning between Lady Felicia and the person by whom she was visited."

Had an earthquake angrily rumbled at that moment, its effect upon James would not have been more powerful than that which this tranquil announcement produced. It checked at once the natural action of his ˙ heart, and made him feel particularly ill.

"My lady," said he, at length, tremulously — "do you mean—what occurred?"

"Yes. I have heard *something* of it; but I wish you to explain the particulars."

"The particulars, my lady?—What particulars?"

"The particulars of what transpired at their interview— the particulars of what you saw!—you understand what I mean!"

"I saw no particulars, my lady," said James, who still trembled with great violence! "Who has been telling you, my lady, that I did?"

"Let it be sufficient for you to know, that I was not told by either of the servants."

"But it must have come from one of them, my lady!"

"Indirectly it might; but that is immaterial. Tell me at once what you saw."

"But I hope you'll not name it to Lady Felicia. I shall get into horrid disgrace, if you do!"

"It is not my intention to name it to her."

"I hope not, my lady. I'm sure, if I'd known that it would have gone further, I wouldn't have said a word about it for the world."

"Well, it is useless to talk of that now: therefore, let me know at once what occurred. You were, I believe, at the door."

"I was, my lady—unfortunately."

"Why unfortunately? I hold the circumstance to be extremely fortunate! But, proceed! You looked into the room, of course."

"I did, my lady."

"Well, what did you see?"

"I saw Lady Felicia, and this Mr. Murray."

" Well, they were embracing each other, were they not ?"

" Yes, my lady, I believe they were."

" You believe they were!   Why are you so reluctant to state what you know ?"

" I'm not reluctant, my lady : I only wish I had'nt got to do it."

" Absurd!   It is your duty to explain all.   You saw them embrace.   Well : what else did you see ?"

" Nothing else, my lady."

" You saw them kiss each other, I presume ?"

" Yes, my lady ; I certingly did."

" Was Miss Legrange in the room at the time ?"

" Oh yes, my lady : oh! she was in the room ; but while they were kissing, she turned her head of course !"

" Of course!—as a matter of delicacy!   Is that person frequently here ?"

" He never was here but once before, and that was when he brought some silks."

" About what time was it when he called then ?"

" About the same time, my lady : four or half-past."

" Aye! the time at which we are usually from home!   Well, now I'll explain what I wish you to do, and what you *must* do if you wish to save your character.   When next he calls— which will be I've no doubt in a day or two, in all probability to-morrow—let me know—privately—I'll be at home—let me know immediately after his arrival, that I may take the respon- sibility off your hands.   Do you quite understand me ?"

" Oh yes, my lady, I quite understand."

" Very well.   Then act up to my instructions.   You must neither take the slightest notice of this, nor say a syllable having reference to my knowledge of what has occurred.   If you *do* I'll procure your discharge with this character—that you not only peep through key-holes, but prate about all that you happen to see—a character which, you are as well aware as I am, would effectually exclude you from every family of distinction."

"My lady," said James in a tremulous voice—this severe intimation having touched him nearly—"I know that that would be a horrid character indeed—one which would ruin my prospects for ever—but I hope that by paying attention, my lady, and doing all that you wish me to do, to avoid having such a fatal character given me as that. This is the first time I ever peeped, my lady, and therefore I hope you'll forgive me. Whatever you tell me to do shall be done: I'll do all in my power to give satisfaction."

"Very well. At present I have nothing more to say. I'll give you some additional instructions in the morning."

With an air of deep humility James bowed and withdrew. His bosom swelled with conflicting emotions. His heart had been torn: he experienced the most acute sense of humiliation, and with all the finer feelings of his nature deeply wounded, he shut himself up in a state of misery the most intense, in order to call the roll of his afflictions. In his eclipsed judgment all was dark: his views, which were formerly brilliant, were now wrapped in gloom, and while his hopes appeared clad in the most dismal mourning to follow his murdered prospects to the grave, he contemplated with suicidal horror the clinching clear-headed but cruelly cold-blooded intimation of Lady Florence, in which the annihilation of every hope was involved. He had *no* consolation!—not even that of relieving his overburdened heart by a strong, indignant, withering declaration of what he *thought* of those whose perfidy he panted to proclaim.

"If," said he, confidentially to himself—and he really then appeared to be the only living creature in whom he could with safety confide—"if I could but explain to them exactly what I think of their utterly un-fellow-servant-like conduct, I should feel in my soul a little happy. But—as the warlike ghost says on the stage—this eternal blazon *must* not be to ears of flesh and blood! I must not breathe a breath on the subject to mortal! If I *do*—as Lady Florence said, when she told my fortune — if I do, I'm doomed. I can neither say a word, nor move a peg!—I'm bound hand and foot, soul and bones! I can neither put Lady Felicia on her guard, nor save that fellow from having his neck broke—for if it should come to the ears of the Marquis, out of the window, of course, he goes!—I might just as well have been born, demme, dumb!— And *wouldn't* Lady Florence keep her promise? Look at her eyes!—they'll tell you. Feeling!—she has about as much as a rattlesnake. Look at her, when she *knew* that she had me in her power, as tight as if she'd screwed me up in a vice!— why that thing which strikes people dead with its eyes, don't belong to a more varment specie! *She'd* do it!—safe. *She'd* give me a character! — send I may live. *I* should get another sitivation! — in a hurry. But, ought I as a man to submit to all this? Ought I *not*, as a man, to put Lady Felicia — which has always been very kind to me — on her guard? *That's* the point, the whole point, and nothing but the point.—Well," he added, "You're a free born Briton!— and Britons never will be slaves! There are two roads before you! — choose which you please! — one of them leads to a butler's place, and the other to a soldier's sitivation — you've only to choose! But, *must* the other force me to 'list? Can't I in private put Lady Felicia up to it? Can't I secretly tell her it won't answer her purpose to have that fellow here? I *might* do-so; and yet, if that basilisk *should* bowl me out.— But how could she? I'm not the only one which knows that he was here!—nor am I the only one which knows that she knows it! Why, then, should I alone be suspected? I must turn this point seriously over in my mind. I mustn't altogether forget number one; but, if I *can* save Lady Felicia from disgrace, without bringing disgrace upon myself, my heart tells me plump that I ought to do it; and if I can do it, I will!"

Having arrived at this manly conclusion, he felt a little better, and eventually rejoined those perfidious fellow-servants with whom he could no longer associate with pleasure, because he could no longer regard them as friends.

CHAPTER VII.

ILLIBERAL VIEWS.

DELIGHTED with his reception—which was indeed far more gratifying than his brightest hopes could have led him to anticipate—Alfred having wandered about the Park in a delirium of rapture, kept his appointment with Mr. Wilkins, whom he found in a state of intense anxiety, and who, grasping his hand, cried, "*Is* it all right?"

"It is," replied Alfred.

"That's glorious!—Gods! what a state of suspense I've been in. But sit down, and let's hear all about it."

With a heart filled with joy, and a countenance brightly proclaiming its existence, Alfred proceeded to describe the happy interview, giving the substance of all that had passed, and dwelling minutely upon various points, which he conceived to be of the most thrilling interest.

At first, Mr. Wilkins, making an effort to be tranquil, listened with the most profound attention; but he soon became excited, and that excitement increased gradually, until he heard that Lady Felicia had actually permitted Alfred to embrace her, when his enthusiasm reached the highest possible pitch, and he called for a bottle of champagne.

"In nothing *less*," said he, with an expression of delight, "will I drink to her glorious health! She's a stunner!—an angel!—a trump of the first water! Bravo, my boy!" he added, rubbing his hands joyously. "Bravo! I'm as glad as if the chance had been mine. You *lucky* dog! But do I envy you? No!—not in the mean sordid sense of the term envy!

—you are worthy of her, and she's worthy of you. That's the style of girl!—a girl after one's own heart!—repudiating 'pride, pomp, and circumstance,' for love, and sacrificing splendour for tranquil joy!"

"I believe that we shall be very happy," said Alfred.

"Happy! Gods! you must be happy. Now then," he added, when the waiter had placed the champagne before him, "I'll give you health, wealth, long life, happiness, joy, and every other conceivable blessing, to the amiable and strong minded Lady Felicia!"

"I drink it," said Alfred, "with all my heart!—God bless her."

"Amen!" responded Mr. Wilkins. "But now to business. In the first place, you haven't got her yet. That's a fact which should ever be present until it absolutely ceases to be a fact. Now, there are various popular apothegms bearing directly upon this very point; such as, 'The course of true love never did run smooth'—'There's many a slip 'twixt the cup and the lip'—'We're all born, but we're not all buried'—'Don't play with a mouse till you lose it'—and so on; but my motto is, 'Strike the iron while it's hot!'— which, in reality, comprehends all. Strike the iron while it's hot!—Don't allow it to cool! in other words, don't dilly dally, and thus give time for the intervention of friends who may cause her to weigh one thing against another, until your dearest hopes kick the beam. It's clear that this *must* be a clandestine marriage, and therefore the sooner it takes place the better. If you were to wait till you both became grey, you'd never obtain the consent of the Marquis, and there- fore you've nothing to wait for at all. What then is the next move? What do you conceive the next move ought to be?"

"That, I apprehend," replied Alfred, "must depend upon the nature of Miss Legrange's communication!"

" Not at all: not at all. The next move is to Doctors'
Commons !—to get the licence !"

" What, before I have gained her consent ?"

" Decidedly ! Can you not gain her consent as easily with
the licence, as without it ?"

" Oh, but that will look so precipitate !"

" It will look as if you really *meant* business, and that will
be one grand point gained. You take my advice: go to
Doctors' Commons in the morning ; get the licence, and keep
it in your pocket."

" Well ! I need not *show* it to her directly."

" Certainly not: you need not even hint that you have
it, until you've made sure that the sight of it will be
pleasing."

" But suppose they should know who she really is !"

" Make your mind easy on that point. You'll find them
men of business—pounds, shillings, and pence men: *they'll*
not go into her pedigree: all you'll have to do is to give in the
names and swear that you are both of age, which you can do—
for you see by the Peerage she's three months over—and all
they'll care about is your money."

" But if they *should* by any chance know her ?"

" It isn't in the slightest degree likely that they know her,
or ever heard of her ; and even if they should have heard the
name before, they'll write it, of course, as a matter of business,
and think no more of Felicia Jocelyn, than they would if her
name were Caroline Clerk. Therefore don't be at all apprehensive on that point. Go boldly, and state what you want,
and if the next communication you receive be as favourable as
I anticipate it *will* be, you can at least show it to Miss
Legrange. Take my advice, my boy, and go to-morrow
morning !"

" Well," said Alfred, " I will do so. And now there is
another point upon which I am anxious to have your opinion.

It has reference to the governor. Do you not think that I had better now explain all to him?"

For a moment Mr. Wilkins pressed his lips and knit his brows, and thus proclaimed the existence of thought the most profound; and having, by virtue of this process, screwed up a conclusion, he replied, "Well, look here: he's all right where he takes, although it's only by fits and starts that he *does* take; he's a perfect man of business: I've no fault whatever to find with him as a governor; he has always behaved very well indeed to *me;* but he's a Scotchman."

"A Scotchman," echoed Alfred, smiling, "Well?"

"Never trust a Scotchman. Have that sentiment engraved upon your heart of hearts! Never trust a Scotchman."

"I believe," said Alfred, "that I am, remotely"—

"So you may be," interrupted Mr. Wilkins, "but you are no more a Scotchman—not what I call a Scotchman—than I am a Welshman. I know what Scotchmen are; I have studied them deeply, and having analyzed their chief characteristics, I find that they are not to be trusted."

"But why not?"

"Simply because they can't stand the test of civilization."

"Because they can't stand the test of civilization?"

"Civilization spoils them. Take them in the rough—in their wild or native state—and they'll do! They are bold, manly, generous, high-spirited, and erect! But bring them here—let them associate with civilized beings—and their boldness changes to sycophancy, their generosity to the most sordid meanness; their high spirit sinks into servility, and, instead of standing like men erect, they are the most obsequious slaves."

"But I have known Scotchmen," said Alfred, "to be as proud as Englishmen *can* be!"

"Yes!"—when they have crawled up to eminence. That's when they change again! They then become haughty, overbearing, tyrannical! You can no more depend upon the friendship of a Scotchman than you can upon the colour of a cameleon."

"I must say," rejoined Alfred, "that this is a very illiberal view to take of the general character of Scotchmen; indeed, as far as it has reference to the effects of civilization, it is quite a Tory's view!"

"It *is* a Tory's view," said Mr. Wilkins, with an air of triumph, "and I am proud of being a Tory! Toryism is the only correct system upon earth! Look at the map—the map of the world—look at one as large as this table, and England will occupy the space of this spoon; and yet this speck, this atom, this almost imperceptible little spot, is the mightiest of the most mighty nations upon earth! What has brought this about? To what do you ascribe it?"

"Chiefly to the genius of the people," replied Alfred.

"The genius of the people! No such thing, sir! It is solely ascribable to the genius of Toryism!"

"But Toryism has ever been opposed to progress!"

"It has ever been opposed to innovation!"

"Which proves that our present position has been achieved, not *by* it, but in spite of it."

"Why, it is the foundation of England's glory!"

Alfred smiled.

"Would you," continued Mr. Wilkins—"would you strike at the very root of society?"

"No," replied Alfred; "but I'd lop off the useless branches."

"Would you lop off Toryism?"

"The tree would be far more healthy without it."

"Then you deem it useless?"

"It is happily harmless."

"But useless—that's the point—you deem it useless?"

"I do."

"Why look at its glorious struggles for ages!"

"It's struggles have not been particularly glorious: it has always been *eventually* defeated. Those struggles have been invariably to keep the nation back, and were useful only in so far as they tended to check precipitation. But we shall have, I hope, plenty of opportunities of discussing this subject; the point to which I am anxious to return is that which has reference to my explaining all to the governor. You intimate that I cannot depend upon his friendship. I have no wish at present to bring his friendship to the test. I should name it as a mere matter of courtesy!"

"I know. But take my advice, and don't name it at all. I'll tell you why. He might—I don't say that he would, but he *might*—wither all your hopes."

"But how? It's a matter of no consequence to me what *his* views may be on the subject! I should not think of asking *him* what course I ought to pursue! *His* opposition would have no effect!"

"You don't look at the matter in the right light," said Mr. Wilkins. "You don't understand what I mean. I'll explain. He's a Scotchman; and, as I said before, *never* trust a Scotchman. Now, suppose when you had told him all, he were to go and explain the matter to the Marquis?"

"Well, but what could be his object in doing so?"

"The patronage of the family, and through that family higher patronage; say the patronage of royalty. I merely say suppose—I put it hypothetically—*suppose* he were to do this, where would you be then?"

"There is something in that," said Alfred, thoughtfully. "There is, certainly, something in that."

"Mind! I don't mean to say that he would, but he could! —you give him the power to do it!—and I don't see any necessity for placing that power in his hands!"

"You are quite right," said Alfred, "quite right."

"It's unsafe, sir," continued Mr. Wilkins, who, having been

on one occasion, by virtue of treachery, supplanted by a
Scotchman, had cherished a mortal hatred of Scotchmen ever
since,—"it's unsafe, sir, to trust any man with a secret, when,
by revealing it, he may feather his own nest; but, to trust
a dirty Scotchman, who will stoop to any species of meanness
—a sweep who will sell his benefactor when he has used him
up, for sixpence—a crafty, crawling, servile viper, who will
cringe, and fawn, and lick the dust, until you invest him with
the power to sting you—to trust *him* with a secret, when its
betrayal might enrich him, would be an act of absolute
madness."

"You have said quite sufficient," said Alfred, "to convince
me that it *would* be unwise thus to make the matter known;
and, as there is no necessity for running the risk involved, I
shall certainly follow your advice."

This decision was highly satisfactory to Mr. Wilkins; but
he wished to achieve another triumph that evening: he was
anxious to prove that the principles of Toryism comprehended
all the virtues, and that every man was a Tory at heart; and
as Alfred—to whom the subject was not interesting then—
listened, or appeared to listen to his eloquence without
disputing his points, he held them, of course, to be perfectly
indisputable, and the consequence was, that when he retired
for the night, he did so on excellent terms with himself.

In the morning, Alfred dressed himself with somewhat
unusual care, and immediately after breakfast, repaired to
Doctors' Commons, where he found that Mr. Wilkins was
quite correct, in stating that he would experience no difficulty
in obtaining what he wanted. It was, *indeed*, a mere matter
of business. Felicia and Fanny, Jocelyn and Johnson, were
all the same to them: they wasted no thought upon either:
the document was prepared, they received the money, and
Alfred returned with the licence to Mr. Wilkins, who, on
hearing that all was right, expressed his satisfaction warmly.

The promised communication from Fidèle, now occupied all Alfred's thoughts, and he looked for it with the most intense anxiety. Business with him was quite out of the question: he had conceived an utter distaste for business: he couldn't reconcile himself at all to it—he had, in fact, suddenly inspired a contempt for it.

"I have been thinking," said he, in the course of the morning, "that I'd better speak to the governor, and leave."

"What, leave entirely?" inquired Mr. Wilkins.

"Yes," replied Alfred; "I can do no good here. *I* can't attend to business."

"No; I don't suppose you *can* pay much attention to it; but you'd better not leave!"

"Of what use am I here?"

"But little, it's true; still, you'd better not leave. If you say a word to him about leaving, you must give some reason for wishing to leave, and I know that he'll put all sorts of searching questions, which you'll find it very difficult to evade. No: instead of leaving, I'll tell you what I'd do: if, when you receive Miss Legrange's communication, you find you're all right, I'd tell him that certain circumstances have occurred which render your absence for a few days imperative."

"But he'll want to know the nature of those circumstances."

"That you need not explain. You can easily get over that. They are circumstances of a strictly private nature—which is perfectly correct—and those circumstances render your absence from business necessary. That will be quite sufficient. I don't anticipate anything like a failure: if I did I should urge the adoption of this course on the ground that, if you did fail, you could at once return; but I know what you want: you want to be continually meeting; therefore, take private lodgings for a week, and let Miss Legrange know where you are."

"Well, I think that that would be much better," said Alfred. "But when I engage the lodgings, to whom can I refer?"

"Refer to me. That will be sufficient. Refer to me."

Well! that point was settled, and Mr. Wilkins had in consequence another cause for congratulating .himself on the
correctness of his judgment; but while they were conversing, a
scene which would have alarmed them was being enacted by
Fidèle and the truly unhappy James, just outside.

Fidèle had been commissioned by Felicia to make arrangements with Alfred for the next interview, and James had been
commanded by Lady Florence to watch her, which he did until
he *could* have no doubt that she was about to enter that which
he termed the "fatal shop," when he approached her in a state
of excessive trepidation.

"Miss Legrange—I beg pardon"—said he—"but don't go."

Fidèle very naturally looked at him with an expression of
the most perfect amazement!

"Pray don't go in," he continued, "I've something on my
mind, and I'll ease it if you'll hear me."

"Why, what is the meaning of this?"

"Every thing's known," replied James, "and through me;
and now I've been sent out to watch you!"

"To *watch* me?" exclaimed Fidèle, indignantly. "To watch
me? By whom were you sent, sir?"

"I was sent by Lady Florence; but don't be angry with
me—only listen: through my wooden-headed stupidity, she
knows that Lady Felicia and Mr. Murray embraced each other
yesterday morning. I saw them—it is with shame I confess
it!—and told the other servants, who betrayed me to her."

"Good heavens!" exclaimed Fidèle. "Well! Proceed!"

"Well, she had me on the carpet and made me confess, and
with a horrid promise to ruin my character if I dared to say
she knew a word about it to a soul; she bound me to her hand
and foot, and now she has sent me to watch you. But I am so
unhappy, I can't bear it. I felt that I must come up and tell
you. So pray don't go in. If you do, and I tell her you did'nt,

her eyes will be sure to find me out. If you do want to see Mr. Murray, Miss, go into this confectioner's shop, and I'll let him know you're there."

"May I *trust* you, James?" inquired Fidèle severely.

"You may, Miss: indeed, indeed you may. I am so horrid *savage* with myself, that if I lose fifty characters I'll not say a word."

"Very well," said Fidèle. "Then I'll go in here, and you can say that I wish to see him."

Without any of his characteristic dignity of deportment, James rushed to "the fatal shop," and having entered in a highly excited state, called Alfred aside, and said in a tremulous whisper—"Mr. Murray, sir—come to the pastry-cook's—something—something wrong, sir—horrid discovery—fit to knock my head off—Miss Legrange—sir—come at once."

Without waiting one moment for the solution of the mystery involved in this fitful communication, Alfred, who felt sufficiently alarmed, ran for his hat, and on his return was accosted by Mr. Wilkins.

"What's the matter?" inquired that gentleman anxiously.

"Something wrong, I fear," replied Alfred.

"Gods!—I *hope* not!" exclaimed Mr. Wilkins; but before that exclamation had been fairly exploded, Alfred had quitted the shop with James.

"In there, sir," said James, having arrived at the confectioner's; and Alfred, as he entered, saw Fidèle in the soup room.

"My dear Miss Legrange," said Alfred, earnestly, as he approached her, "what is the meaning of this?"

"All has been discovered," replied Fidèle. "The servant James, who came for you, and who has been sent by Lady Florence, for the purpose of watching me, has just informed me that she, at least, knows all. He yesterday saw you take leave of Lady Felicia, and told the other servants, through whom it came to the ears of Lady Florence."

" The scoundrel !" cried Alfred, indignantly.

" He is heartily sorry for it, now," said Fidèle, " and wishes to make all the reparation in his power."

" Reparation !—the wretch! What reparation can *he* make?"

"If we are calm, Mr. Murray, we may make him useful yet."

" I understood you to say that he has been sent to watch you !"

" Yes; but being thoroughly ashamed of his conduct, he addressed me, in order to put me on my guard."

" What then is to be done ?"

" I know not. I tremble to think of the consequences. I came here in order to appoint another interview, but that is of course utterly out of the question now."

" Is Lady Florence an amiable person ?" inquired Alfred.

" Unfortunately," replied Fidèle, she is not."

" Then she will at once communicate the fact to the Marquis ?"

" No ; my impression is, that instead of telling him, she will exercise the power which this secret gives her of tyrannizing over her more gentle sister, and trampling upon her feelings."

Alfred, with an expression of rage which he struggled in vain to conceal, turned pale, and breathed violently.

" I know her so well," continued Fidèle, " that the fact of her having taken this affair into her own hands, convinces me that she intends to humiliate Lady Felicia by all the means at her command."

" *Something* must be done to prevent this," said Alfred, in tones of the most thrilling intensity, " *Something* must be done !—That wretch is outside still," he added, as James passed the window.

" Oh, yes," said Fidèle, " he'll of course remain until I leave here. I wish him to do so."

" But he had better not wait there ! He may be seen by some part of the family, to whom he will have to explain why he *is* there. Allow me to send him to the tavern just above. I have yet much to say to you. Let him wait there."

"As you please," returned Fidèle." "But do not speak harshly to him. I know that he is exceedingly sorry for what he has done. Besides, it will not be politic, under the circumstances, to speak harshly."

Duly appreciating this observation, Alfred went out to James, and said, as calmly as he could, "Go to that tavern, and wait till I come. You had better not walk about here. I'll let you know when Miss Legrange is about to leave. Here's a crown: go and have a glass of wine."

"I'm ashamed to *see* you, sir," said James, "I could *hit* myself to atoms."

"We'll not talk about that now," said Alfred. "We must make the best we can of it."

"Anything in life that I can do, to undo what I've done, or in any earthly way to make up for it, I'll do. I'm so *wild* with myself, I feel fit to swallow pison!"

"A glass of wine will suit you better," said Alfred. "Go and get one."

James looked at him for a moment, and burst into tears; for hearts whether rough or refined, are wounded more deeply by undeserved kindness, than by severity, however just. Eternal nature will be triumphant, let us struggle against her as we may. Had Alfred spoken harshly to him, he might have felt that it was, perhaps, a *little* more than he deserved; but as he not only spoke kindly, but gave him a crown, he couldn't stand it.

"Now," said Alfred, on his return to Fidèle, "as I was saying, *something* must be done. But what? How can that pure and gentle creature be saved from the galling indignities you contemplate? *Can* you suggest any course, the pursuit of which will destroy that power which you have with so much force described, and the exercise of which upon *her* I dread?"

"I cannot indeed," replied Fidèle. "I know not what to suggest."

"Miss Legrange," said Alfred, calmly, but with the most intense earnestness, "that you have a pure affection for Lady Felicia, I feel convinced; I believe that you would do all in your power to promote her happiness, and that if you conceive that her happiness could be secured by the adoption of even a course which under any other circumstances might fairly be deemed precipitate, your assistance would not be solicited in vain."

"You do me but justice," replied Fidèle. "I have indeed a pure affection for her. I regard her as a dear, dear sister, and *would* do anything by which I conceived her happiness might be secured."

"Do you believe that *I* have the power to secure her happiness?"

"I do. I'll no longer attempt to conceal the fact that you, and you alone, have that power. She loves you devotedly; she would make every possible sacrifice for you; and if I had not believed that you were worthy of her love, I should not have taken the part which I *have* taken with a view to the realization of your hopes."

"I feel indebted to you—deeply indebted to you—and yet I seek to be even to a greater extent your debtor! You have kindly thrown off all restraint, and so will I: feeling that a crisis is at hand, and being painfully apprehensive of losing her for ever, I'll at once propose a course of which the adoption will secure the grand object I have in view, and save her from all humiliation. This morning," he continued, having opened his pocket-book, "I obtained this at Doctors' Commons: it is, as you will perceive, a marriage licence. I should not have shown, nor should I at present have named it, had it not been for this discovery; but seeing the necessity for immediate action, I do not hesitate to hand it to you.

Could you not prevail upon her," he added, after a pause, during which she perused the license with an expression of the most pleasing curiosity—"could you not prevail upon her to consent to that document being at once used?"

"You have lost no time!" said Fidèle, with a smile. " This is one of the most powerful arguments I ever knew to be advanced. Shall I take it with me?"

"Do," replied Alfred. " I need not explain to you what I would say: I need not prompt you to argue the expediency of avoiding those indignities which I cannot bear to think of: I will leave all to you. But," he added earnestly, "do you not *think* that you shall be able to prevail upon her?"

" I'll *endeavour* to do so, be assured; and in order to prove that I do not despair, I'll lend you this ring; it *was* hers, and—fits her!"

" I know not how to thank you," said Alfred.

"Then pray do not make the attempt. Defer it, at all events, until I have been successful."

" Heaven grant that you may be successful!"

"I believe that I shall be. This licence will aid me. It is one of the most delightfully suggestive documents I ever perused! But it does not state when it is available!"

"Oh, it is available immediately!" said Alfred. " The ceremony *might* take place to-morrow morning!"

"But you do not, of course, *dream* of its taking place to-morrow morning?"

" I need not say"—

" I'm aware of it; nor do I wait for you to say that you would like it all the better. But to-morrow morning!—I shall scarcely have time even to *name* the subject, and having a serious task to perform, I must of course proceed with all possible caution. I have, in the first place, to communicate to her the knowledge of this discovery, and *then* to explain how its consequences may be averted. I have to place the bane and antidote both before her, and therefore I cannot see how it will be possible for your hopes to be realized *to-morrow* morning. To-morrow being Saturday, you *may* entertain the thought of Sunday morning, and as Sunday is *not* the day for marriages in 'high life,' the expediency under the circumstances of naming that day will be sufficiently obvious."

"But suppose Lady Florence should in the interim explain all to the Marquis?"

"I'm not at all apprehensive of that; but if she *should*, why then we must do the best we can. Lady Felicia, although gentle, is not without spirit; and the spirit with which *too* much oppression will inspire her, will be that of resistance. All this however, I hope, will be avoided."

"I hope so too. But when shall I hear from you?"

"This evening."

"Pray, let it be as early as possible."

"By seven o'clock I'll let you know what progress I have made. And now I must return. Will you be kind enough to let James know that I am going?"

Alfred took her hand and pressed it warmly, and having told her that her kindness would be ever remembered, he left her to look after James.

He had however no sooner entered the Tavern than he found that young gentleman's sonorous nasal organ in full play, and having aroused him could not fail to perceive that he was in a most mysterious state of intoxication.

"James," he exclaimed, "Why how is this? You are tipsy."

"Not tic'lr tips'," replied James, as well as he could, for his tongue was by no means glib. "Your're spec'bl gen'lm an' I'm sorry for it—can't say *more*—no man say more—cut'm throat—hic—can't say more—transport me, hang—hic—pison me—hic—can't say more!—I'm sorry for it."

"Well, but you cannot go home in *this* state," said Alfred;

and James appeared to entertain precisely the same opinion, for he immediately dropped off again to sleep.

"What has he had?" inquired Alfred, of the waiter.

"Two pints of wine, sir."

"*Two* pints?"

"Yes, sir. But he appeared to be very much excited when he came in."

"Should you, knowing this, have allowed him to have so much?"

"Oh it wasn't with drinking that he was excited; it wasn't by any means with drink. He appeared to have something very heavy on his mind."

"Well, he's in a nice state to go home with a lady, certainly; I'll be in again directly," he added, and immediately returned to Fidèle.

"Why that fellow," said he, having re-entered the shop, "is perfectly tipsy."

"Is it possible?" exclaimed Fidèle."

"I told him, certainly, to have a glass of wine, but he has been drinking two pints."

"Dear me! Why, what is to be done?"

"He cannot go home in his present state. If he were to do so he'd spoil all. I must get him to bed and let him sleep a few hours; he may be all right again then."

"Will you see him when he awakes, and impress upon him the necessity for keeping our interview a secret?"

"Certainly."

"Very well; then I'll return."

"You will not forget seven?"

"I will not, be assured," replied Fidèle. And when Alfred had taken leave of her, with many warm expressions of esteem, he returned to that interesting object of his solicitude, who was still in a state of oblivion the most profound.

"Can we get him to bed?" he inquired of the waiter. "A few hours' sleep will bring him round again."

"I dont know how we're to get him up *stairs*," replied the waiter, who looked as if he were endeavouring to solve a difficult problem. "But there's a sofa in the next room; we might get him on that."

"That will do very well," returned Alfred. "Now, James," he added, shaking that model of a spy with considerable violence, "James!"

"What-sh—lock?" inquired James, with remarkable indistinctness.

"Never mind the clock," said Alfred, "get up—come."

James had no desire to move. *He* was perfectly content to remain where he was. But Alfred and the waiter carried him into the other room, and having placed him on the sofa, left him.

"I'll look in again by-and-by," said Alfred. "Don't allow him to leave here until I have seen him."

The waiter promised that he would not, and Alfred returned to Mr. Wilkins.

"Gods! what a state of suspense I've been in," exclaimed that gentleman earnestly. "What was it?"

"Why," replied Alfred, "the servant who came for me, it appears, saw me yesterday embrace Lady Felicia"—

"And made it known?"

"Yes."

"The vagabond!—the crawling, sneaking, servile wretch —I'll bet ten to one he's a dirty Scotchman—the sweep! Did you kick him?"

"No, I think—I'm not sure—you shall know all about it by-and-by—but I think that I shall yet have to thank him for his interference."

"Well, but what did you *say* to the vagabond?"

"I told him to go and get a glass of wine.

"Wine!" exclaimed Mr. Wilkins indignantly, "give *him* wine! Give a donkey oats! or a Hottentot tight pantaloons But you don't mean to say that you gave him wine?"

" I gave him a crown to get a glass of wine, while I was conversing with Miss Legrange—whom he had been sent by Lady Florence to watch—and when I went to tell him that she was about to leave, I found him in a state of the most helpless intoxication."

" Bravo! Excellent! Where is he now?"

" At the tavern just below—fast asleep on the sofa."

" Glorious!—But here comes the governor; he has been in a desperate way about you."

The "governor" approached, and, addressing Alfred with an expression of severity, said, " You appear to be very *unsettled,·* Mr. Murray! I have noticed it during the last few days—very, *very* unsettled."

" I *am* unsettled," replied Alfred, calmly, " and shall be unsettled for the *next* few days. Indeed, circumstances of a strictly private nature have occurred, which render my absence for a few days necessary!"

" You had, perhaps, better leave altogether, Mr. Murray. This is a house of business; and business-like habits, sir, must be observed. The inattention and the irregularities which I have lately noticed, *no* man of business can sanction. You have been out this morning—not on business!—and you are unsettled still. I am sorry to make these observations, Mr. Murray, because I respect your father. I have known him for years, and respect him highly: but I must not, sir, on *that* account, have my business neglected."

Alfred made no reply: he left the shop, and having packed up his things, returned with the view of taking leave of the governor; but as the governor was then from home, he left a message with Mr. Wilkins, to the effect, that he hoped the next time they met they should meet in a more friendly spirit.

" Well," said Mr. Wilkins, " it's fortunate under the circumstances that he said what he did; but I know that he doesn't mean you to *go!*"

"If that be the case," said Alfred, "I'd better be off at once!—At seven o'clock," he added earnestly, "I shall have a most important communication from Miss Legrange: *pray* send it to me the moment it arrives."

"I will do so certainly. Where will you be?"

"At the tavern just here. Let me see you as soon as you have closed. I have *much* to say to you. Good bye."

On his return to the tavern, Alfred, having ascertained that his interesting charge was still soundly asleep—ordered dinner, which was served with remarkable promptitude, and which, although alone, he enjoyed highly, and settled himself down with a pint of wine before him, to contemplate *seriatim* the brilliant prospects of happiness with which his imagination teemed.

He had, however, scarcely conjured up the first vision—that of leading the amiable Lady Felicia to the altar—when, notwithstanding the truly delightful character of the scene—notwithstanding its natural tendency to engross his whole soul to the utter exclusion of every other thought—a great idea struck him, and with so much force, that his heart *sank* within him.

In an instant, as if by magic, his purse was before him, wherein he found—three pounds ten! He looked at it with an expression of bewilderment—he felt, indeed, faint! Three pounds ten! *He*, about to be allied to a lady of rank—to take her from scenes of surpassing splendour—when he had in his possession but three pounds ten! The thought appalled him: it *never* occurred to him before. Three pounds ten! Of what use was that truly *ridiculous* sum of money?—Three pounds—Why, what was to be done? That day was Friday. If he were to write home by that night's post, he could not receive a remittance the *next* day, and on Sunday no letters were delivered in town! And yet he hoped—fervently hoped—to lead Lady Felicia to the altar on Sunday. He began to perspire—freely!—and the wine became perfectly tasteless. Where could he *obtain* the money required? Of whom could he borrow it?—Of his friend Mr. Wilkins? How could he tell that Mr. Wilkins had any considerable sum at his command?—He might have a pound or two—but what was that? —and to whom else *could* he apply? It was true, he might go down that night by the mail: but then, look at the importance of his remaining in town! Still, as the promised communication from Miss Legrange would arrive at seven, and as the mail did not leave till past eight, he *might* go;—might! —he *must* go! *if* he could not obtain the amount required of Mr. Wilkins. He therefore immediately wrote the following note:—

"DEAR WILKINS,

"Come to me at once—for a moment! I have but to ask you *one* question—but one!—I shall be on the rack till I see you.

"A. M."

This he at once despatched by the waiter, who had not been absent more than two minutes, when Mr. Wilkins—without his hat—rushed into the room in a state of alarm

"Why," said he, "what on earth is the matter?"

"*Have* you any money?" inquired Alfred.

"Yes!—what do you want?"

"Have you any considerable sum?"

"I've not more than fifty pounds in my desk, but —

"That will be sufficient," said Alfred, who was greatly relieved. "Sit down for a moment, I feel quite faint."

"Well—but is that *all* you want me for?"

"All?—I've been torturing myself. It never struck me till just now, that money would be required, and unless I go down by the mail to-night, I can't get any from home until Monday."

"I've enough in my *pocket* to last you till then."

" But I hope to be married on Sunday morning !''

" On *Sunday* morning ?   What ! next Sunday morning ?''

" Yes!   I told you that I had much to say to you, and I
will, when you come in the evening, explain all; but let it be
sufficient at present for you to know, that I have reason—
ample reason—for believing, that on Sunday morning Felicia
will be mine !''

" Gods ! I'm right glad to hear that !   And *Sunday*, too !
Why I can be with you ''—

" You *must* be with us !''

" But I mean without having to ask leave of absence.
Nothing could be better.   Was this *your* suggestion ?''

" No, it was suggested by Miss Legrange, seeing that as
Sunday was not the day for fashionable marriages ''—

" I see, I see !   A very clever girl that Miss Legrange.   I
must have a little talk with her—she's no fool.   But Gods !
On Sunday morning !—and next Sunday too !   I don't wonder
now, at your feeling alarmed when you found that you had not
enough money to carry on with !   How much have you got ?''

" Here it is !'' replied Alfred.   " Three pounds ten.''

Mr. Wilkins on the instant burst into a roar.   He laughed
convulsively, and rolled about his chair, and held his sides, and
shook his head in a perfect paroxysm of merriment.   " Three
pound ten !'' he exclaimed, as soon as he could.   " Gods ! what
a job it would have been if you had'nt thought of it until the
very morning !   Three pound ten !   Why, the parson alone
would swallow that little lot !   and would'nt be satisfied then,
for I suppose its a five-pound pill *he'll* want to take !   And
yet—no : as you don't go as a brace of the aristocracy, such a
dose would excite suspicion.   A guinea, or a couple, will be
considered handsome; but even then, when you consider the
congregation—I mean the congregation of mortal cormorants
by whom you are surrounded, and whom you can't satisfy at
all—your three pound ten would'nt get you out of the church !

What sort of a dinner 'did you mean to give us on 'that auspicious occasion ? Bread and cheese with onions, and a pot of half-and-half?"

"The fact is, I never gave it a thought."

"Never mind, old fellow: you shall not want for money: *you* shall not be at a loss for that. You can have what I've got in my desk to begin with, and next week I'll sell out as much as you want."

"Oh that will be quite unnecessary," said Alfred. "I can easily get some from home."

"Do nothing of the kind! Astonish them thoroughly! *Never* dream of going to old people for money when you want to delight them! It takes the edge off! You leave it to me. But where's that sweep?"

"He's still in the next room."

"Let's have a look at him."

Alfred rose, and conducted Mr. Wilkins to the sofa on which the model spy was profoundly reclining.

"Fast as a church"—observed Mr. Wilkins—"the very picture of vigilance!—He's a beauty! and I *could* say exactly what I think of him, but as you tell me you may yet have cause to thank him, I abstain. And now, old fellow, I must be off. The governor's in an out-and-out rage : I never saw him in half such a way as he was when he heard that you had left. But that's nothing. At seven, my boy, I'll see you again. I feel just as anxious about it as you are"

He then left ; and Alfred, whose mind was now at ease—on that point, at least, which had so much alarmed him—resumed his seat, with the view of dwelling again on the vision which the fact of his having but three pounds ten had so suddenly dispelled.

This vision had, however, scarcely re-appeared before him, when the door of the next room slowly opened, and James, in a state of extreme anxiety to know where he was, peeped mysteriously in.

K

" Oh! sir," said he, faintly, having recognized Alfred, "what *have* I been about."

" Getting tipsy," replied Alfred. " How do you feel now?"

" Horrid, sir—horrid."

" Well, you must have some soda water."

" I wish, sir, I'd had some instead of the wine, for that, and my savageness, upset me wholly. I felt fit to gnaw the very flesh off my bones!"

Soda water was ordered; and when James had drunk one bottle, he felt in some slight degree refreshed, and went to the glass, with the view of restoring the characteristic respectability of his appearance, and having accomplished this, as far as he was able there, he said, "I'm ashamed, sir, to look you in the face."

" Go up and have a wash," said Alfred, without replying to this remarkable observation of the penitent. " You'll feel better then."

Appreciating at once the propriety of this suggestion, James applied to the waiter, who took him up stairs, and when he had put himself somewhat in order, he slowly returned to his friend.

" However I shall get over this," said he, " I've no more notion than an unborn babe. Lady Florence will fly at me like a wild tigress."

" Is she, then, a violent person?" inquired Alfred.

" Violent, sir! She's a rattlesnake. I can't compare her to anything else. She's got a pair of eyes that flash like lightning, and a tongue that'll tell you exactly what she means. What I can say to her, I can't think: whatever excuse I can make, I don't know."

" You'd better say that you were taken very suddenly unwell, which—as far as it goes—will be the truth. You'll, of course, not intimate to her that Miss Legrange has seen *me !*"

" I'd rather have my tongue torn out than do it! No, sir!
—I've done enough mischief as it is. She shall not hear a
word of it, either from me, or through me, and all that I can
do, sir, to make things right again, shall be done with all the
pleasure in life."

' Very good: then we understand each other, as far, at least,
as my interview this morning with Miss Legrange is concerned.
—And now, have another bottle of soda water, with a litle
brandy in it."

" I'll take another bottle of the water, sir; but—if you
please—without the brandy."

He accordingly had another bottle, without the brandy;
and, having again and again expressed his sorrow for what had
occurred, he left, with an exalted opinion of Alfred's generosity,
and, at the same time, the most perfect dread of again
encountering the flashing eyes of Lady Florence.

From this time, until seven o'clock, Alfred's suspense
increased gradually; but, precisely at that hour, Mr. Wilkins
rushed in with a note, which was opened with the utmost
eagerness.

" All right?" cried Mr. Wilkins, with an expression of
anxious hope—" *Not* all right?" he added, still more anxiously,
on perceiving that Alfred's countenance fell.

" Read it," replied Alfred; and Mr. Wilkins read as
follows:—

" DEAR SIR,—

" Having promised to write, I perform that promise; but
I have not yet seen Lady Felicia.

" On my return I ascertained that she had left home,
accompanied by the Marquis, Lady Florence, and Lady
Augusta; but where she is gone, or at what hour she will
return, I know not.

" Let not this, however, alarm you. If practicable, she shall know all to-night; but you shall, in *any* case, hear from me in the morning.

> "I remain,
>
> > "Dear sir,
> >
> > > "Yours truly,
> > >
> > > > "F. LEGRANGE."

"Well!" said Mr. Wilkins, having read the note attentively, "I see nothing very disheartening in this!"

"The Marquis knows all," said Alfred, mournfully. "They have taken her away in order to conceal her."

"Pooh, pooh, pooh, nonsense—choo, choo—absurd! She's gone with them, doubtless, to visit some friend: I see nothing in that!"

"Depend upon it they have taken her from home in order that I may see her no more."

"Don't you be ridiculous, old fellow, and torture yourself with these baseless fancies, for that they are baseless I feel quite convinced. She's out with them. Well! What on earth is there in that? She'll come home with them; and when she *does* come home, Miss Legrange will—if practicable, as she observes—explain all, and let you know the result. *I* see nothing in it! It appears to *me* to be a mere commonplace occurrence! If Lady Felicia, having had all explained, had refused to consent to the course proposed, you might then indeed feel *justified* in conceiving that all was lost; but the mere fact of her having gone out for a few hours with her father and her sisters affords *no* justification for excitement or alarm. For my part, I see nothing in it at *all*. Let me, however, hear what passed this morning between you and Miss Legrange: I shall then, perhaps, be able to form a more correct judgment. Don't fidget yourself. Explain all calmly."

Alfred did so; but instead of thereby changing the views of Mr. Wilkins, he confirmed them.

"You perceive," said that gentleman, having listened most

attentively to Alfred's recital, "that Miss Legrange herself feels convinced that Lady Florence will not at present tell the Marquis!"

"Yet, in spite of that conviction, Lady Florence *may* have told him!"

"Granted," returned Mr. Wilkins. "Granted! She *may* have told him; but depend upon it she has not done so. I feel that we really ought to have the utmost confidence in the judgment of that Miss Legrange! She knows the lady much better than we do, and as *she* feels convinced that the Marquis has not been told, we ought, by all means, to adopt that conviction."

"I wish that I *could* do so," said Alfred, with an air of sadness; "but I cannot: I feel sure that all has been explained, and, if *so*—why then for ever farewell hope!"

"But why?" said Mr. Wilkins. "Why, even in *that* case, bid farewell to hope?"

"Suppose he were to take her to some remote place and"—

"Well!—we'll put it so! Say to some enchanted castle, guarded by genii duly disguised as fiery dragons, prepared to swallow all who approach; or to some capacious cavern established somewhere about half-way between us and our antipodes, to which admission can be obtained only though the influence of a close corporation of griffins; or to some frightful phantom ship, manned with immortals and armed with the mortars of Jove! Pooh, pooh—*where* can he take her, to cut off effectually all communication between you? *Have* you any faith in her affection?"

"I have," replied Alfred, "faith the most unbounded!"

"Very well then; let him take her where he may, she'll manage, at least, to let you know where she is! Don't fidget yourself about any such nonsense. Mark my words.—She'll be home to-night, and in the morning you'll laugh at your fears."

Alfred, notwithstanding every effort was made by his friend

to re-inspire him with hope, felt wretched, and continued to feel wretched throughout the evening: nothing could rouse him: his imagination teemed with the most painful apprehensions, and when at length Mr. Wilkins had bade him adieu, he retired to his room with a heavy heart indeed.

CHAPTER VIII.

THE RESOLUTION.

MR. WILKINS was perfectly correct in his conjecture: Felicia *did* return that night. She had been to Richmond on a visit to her aunt, Lady Loftus, and returned about half-past eleven.

Fidèle, whose apprehensions had been as painful as those of Alfred—hailed her arrival with feelings of delight, and, having as usual accompanied her to her room—to which she as soon as possible retired—prepared to impart to her all that had occurred.

"Did you see him?" inquired Felicia, the very moment they were alone.

"I did," replied Fidèle. "But I have," she added with startling deliberation—"I have to communicate to you something which I fear will not only astonish but alarm you."

"Good heavens!" exclaimed Felicia. "Is he not well?"

"He is—as well at least as he can be expected to be—but listen:—Lady Florence knows more than you imagine: she knows that the last time you parted he embraced you! James saw you; and through him it came to her knowledge. This morning she sent him to watch me!"

"Is it possible!" exclaimed Felicia, with an expression of terror. "He *saw* us?"

"He did."

"Then all is lost."

"No! All is *not* lost, if you be but firm. She will not tell the Marquis! She has another object in view. Her object is to keep you in her power!—to trample upon your feelings—to subject you to every species of humiliation!"

"Indeed!" said Felicia, assuming an air of dignity—"indeed. She sent him to *watch* you this morning?"

"She did."

"How did you ascertain that?"

Fidèle explained what had passed between her and James, while Felicia listened with a look of contempt.

A pause ensued, during which Felicia's eyes expressed wandering thoughts, while her curled lip proclaimed the existence of indignant feelings.

"I perceive," she said at length—"I perceive. Her object is first to accumulate proofs, and then to descend with her whole weight upon me.—But proofs of what?" she added with the most intense expression of earnestness. "Proofs of what? —of pure affection? No: these are *not* the proofs she would have! This, then, accounts for that extraordinary change which I have noticed in her conduct to me during the day: this accounts for her anxious solicitude—her affectionate attention—her gracious smiles—her wonderful beneficence!— Does Alfred know of this?"

"He does. I told him all; and when I had explained to him my fears that the object of Lady Florence was to wound your feelings, his manly bosom swelled with indignation. 'Something must be done,' said he, 'to prevent this: *something* mus be done to save that pure and gentle creature from the indig nities you contemplate'—and then he proceeded with mingle feelings of hope and fear to suggest what *might* be done."

What did he suggest," inquired Felicia anxiously. "Wha did he propose?"

"As if in anticipation of what was about to occur, he ha procured this document which he intended to wear—at leas for some time—as an amulet; and suggested the propriety o prevailing upon you to consent to its being immediately used."

"What is it?"

"The marriage licence," replied Fidèle, and on the instant Felicia's eyes sparkled with delight.

"The marriage licence!" she exclaimed—"What, *our* marriage licence?"

"Yes; and an interesting document it is."

Felicia perused it, with an expression of rapture; but felt somewhat tremulous nevertheless.

"He would not have shown it at present," resumed Fidèle; "nor would he have even intimated that he had it in his possession, being apprehensive that he might be deemed precipitate; but feeling that, under the circumstances, it would save you from tyranny—the thought of which appalled him!—he begged of me at once to submit it to you. He *spoke*," she continued, as Felicia's eyes wandered over the licence still:—"he *spoke* of to-morrow morning! But, as I told him, if even you did consent, it could not take place before *Sunday*"—

"And did he urge it warmly?"

"*Hush!*" cried Fidèle, in a thrilling whisper—"What was that?—I heard something!"

She went to the door, softly, and having opened it, discovered Lady Florence!

"Oh!" said that lady, addressing Felicia with one of her most bewitching smiles, "*Good* night, dear! Perceiving a light, I thought you might have been reading. *Good* night."

"Have you been *listening*, Florence?" inquired Felicia, with a look of severity.

In an instant the blood of Lady Florence was up, and her dark eyes flashed with fury—"Listening!" she exclaimed. imperiously—"listening! How dare you accuse me of an act *so* mean!—and that, too, even in the presence of your maid! Listening!—I *could*, if I felt disposed, sink you to the earth!"

"No, Florence, no!" replied Felicia, firmly; "you may,

indeed, *wound* my spirit, but you have not the power to crush it."

Fearing that if she said more, she might defeat the object she had in view, Lady Florence looked at her haughtily for a moment, and then, with a sneer of contempt, withdrew.

" Is it possible !" said Felicia, when the door had been closed —" Is it possible that she could have heard us ? "

" I hope not—I think not;" replied Fidèle, who trembled violently. " I feel quite sure that she *could* not : if even she heard our voices, it must have been indistinctly. But oh ! what a terrible look she gave you !"

" Her looks," said Felicia calmly, " have no terrors for me.—With regard to this suggestion I'll reflect upon it ; and do you reflect upon it too. Let me know your impressions in the morning : let me know how you would advise me to act. As Alfred says, something *must* be done ! And now leave me, Fidèle ; I wish to be alone. Good night—good night."

Inspired with the spirit of resistance by the fears expressed by Fidèle, that the object of Lady Florence was to humiliate her—fears, which the imperious conduct of her sister that night had proved were but too well founded—Felicia, on being left alone, soon made up her mind to adopt Alfred's suggestion. It was clear, that the fact of his having embraced her could not much longer remain a secret : it was clear that an explanation would soon be demanded, and that when that explanation had been given, every possible barrier would be placed between her and the consummation of her hopes ; and as the consent of the Marquis could never be obtained—as it must necessarily be a clandestine marriage—she firmly resolved on the pursuit of that course which she felt would at once save her from the tyranny of Lady Florence, and render her happiness secure.

But oh ! how earnestly she wished that Alfred *then* knew that this resolution had been formed, that he might be relieved from those tortures of suspense which she could not but feel that he endured. The thought, however, of the rapture in store for him—the delight he would experience when the intelligence reached him—tended to diminish her sorrow for what he endured then, and she dwelt upon visions of peace, love, and joy, until—having, as usual, prayed for protection from on High—she calmly retired to rest.

In the morning Lady Florence re-assumed her lofty bearing, but said nothing having reference to the preceding night; and when Felicia, who was also, of course, silent on the subject, had been through the ceremony of breakfast—for with her it was but a mere ceremony then—she returned to Fidèle, to whom she had previously declared her resolution, and who had been most eloquent in Alfred's praise; and after a long conversation, in which every point was satisfactorily discussed, Fidèle was deputed to communicate the intelligence to him who was absolutely panting to receive it.

Having obtained this commission with an expression of the most perfect confidence that she would execute it with all possible delicacy, Fidèle hastened to impart the joyful news to Alfred, and indulged, during her progress towards the shop, in the most delightful anticipations.

On her arrival, however, Alfred was not to be seen. She looked round anxiously but he was not there, nor was Mr. Wilkins.

"Is Mr. Murray within?" she inquired of the proprietor, by whom she was addressed with due promptitude and tact.

"Mr. Murray has left us," replied that gentleman.

"Left?" said Fidèle, with a look of amazement. "Left entirely?"

"Yes, he left yesterday morning."

"Indeed! Will you be kind enough to tell me where he is to be found?"

"Upon my word I have no conception,—I don't know at all."

" He is, I presume, still in town ? "

" He *may* be—I really don't know. He may be in town or he may have returned to Sudbury—indeed I think it most likely that he is gone there, for he told me, that circumstances of a strictly private nature—some family matter, in all probability—demanded his immediate attention. If, however, he *should* call here I shall be most happy to hand him your card."

" I thank you ; but that will be unnecessary. By-the-by I sent a note here for him last evening, perhaps you will do me the favour to let me have it again ? "

" I'm not aware that any note came for him last evening."

" It was sent about seven o'clock."

" It hasn't *yet* been delivered. If it had been I must of course have seen it."

" Very extraordinary," observed Fidèle. " However, I beg to apologize for the trouble I have given you," she added, and having bowed left the shop.

" What news for poor Felicia !" thought Fidèle. " What a state of anxiety *she* will be in. How *very* unfortunate—nay, how very *wrong*. He ought *not* to have left town without informing me."

At that moment Mr. Wilkins, who had been to see Alfred for about the twentieth time that morning, to tell him that no communication had yet arrived, approached without his hat. He might have passed and she would not have noticed him, but he recognized her on the instant, and without the slightest ceremony addressed her.

" I'm *so* glad to see you," said he, in a state of rapture. " He's pretty well dead with suspense."

Fidèle *looked* at him—she didn't know him.

" Miss Legrange, I believe," he added hastily, " Mr. Murray"—

" Yes, yes," said Fidèle, " *Where* is he ? "

"Just here—just below."

"Oh! I'm so *glad* that you recognized me," said Fidèle, as she walked by the side of Mr. Wilkins, "I feared that he had left town."

"Oh dear me, no; he is here," said Mr. Wilkins, having by this time reached the tavern. "Will you step in, or shall I go in and tell him? He's quite alone."

"In that case I'll go in," replied Fidèle; and they entered the room in which Alfred was sitting.

In an instant he rose and, grasping her hand, surveyed her countenance anxiously. "But one word," said he; "*has* she returned?"

"Oh, yes," replied Fidèle. "She returned last night."

He led her to a chair, and was about to seat himself, when Mr. Wilkins beckoned him out of the room, and said "Look here old fellow, I can't come out again for the next *quarter* of an hour; *if* it's all right let me know before I leave; I'll remain here—I am so anxious."

Alfred promised that he would, and returned to Fidèle, who, in order to *startle* him with delight, announced to him at once that Felicia had consented.

As she had anticipated, he was indeed startled; he seized her hand, and pressed it warmly, and felt for a moment overpowered.

"Let me," said he, in a voice tremulous with emotion, "let me communicate this to my friend, that he may share the delight I experience now."

He left the room, and grasping the hand of Mr. Wilkins, exclaimed, "*All* right! Felicia has consented."

"Gods!" cried Mr. Wilkins. "That's glorious indeed! I give you joy," he added, shaking his hand heartily—"I give you *joy*, my boy! I give you joy! I give you joy!" when as he absolutely felt that the tears were about to start, he turned and left him.

Alfred now endeavoured to compose himself, and to some extent succeeded. He returned to Fidèle, and felt much more calm, and listened with the most intense earnestness to all that she had to impart.

"And now," she added, having explained to him minutely the feelings, expressions, and hopes of Felicia, and dwelt upon her virtues in a touching strain of eloquence—"how are we to act in the morning?"

"I have promised," replied Alfred, "to leave the entire management of the affair to my friend Mr. Wilkins, who has taken the deepest interest in my success, who has towards me, in fact, the true feelings of a brother, and who, I know, will do all in his power to promote our comfort."

"Do you mean the gentleman who came here with me?"

"Yes, that is Mr. Wilkins, and a warm-hearted creature he is. Somewhat too enthusiastic, perhaps; but true."

"That's the great point," observed Fidèle. "He appeared when he fortunately recognized me, to have your interest deeply at heart. But how are we to *meet* in the morning?"

"Can we do better than meet at the church? Shall we send for Mr. Wilkins, and hear what he suggests?"

"It will be, I think, as well," replied Fidèle.

Alfred wrote a note, and despatched it by the waiter; and Mr. Wilkins very soon made his appearance.

"We wish to consult you," said Alfred, "on the subject of our proceedings in the morning. In the first place, how are we to meet?"

"Well," replied Mr. Wilkins, "according to the arrangements which *I* have conceived, I call for you here, at half-past seven; and we enter the church at eight, precisely!"

"And meet there?"

"Much better meet there, because no suspicion can then be excited. When we leave the church, a carriage, of course, will be in attendance. We then proceed to a beautiful spot, which

I have in my eye, to breakfast, and thence to another delightful place, about ten miles farther, where, having spent a glorious and truly happy day, I mean to leave you. I presume," he added, addressing Fidèle, "that we shall have the additional charm of your society ?"

"I hope to be with you," replied Fidèle.

"But do you *leave* Kingsborough House ?"

"Of course !"

"But, I mean, leave entirely !"

"Oh yes ; my presence *there* would not, of course, be very agreeable, after this."

"I understand. Now will you allow me to offer a suggestion ?"

"I shall be, indeed, happy to hear it."

"I know what you ladies are. I have sisters at home, and when they go out—if it be only for two or three days—they are loaded with every variety of box, and trunk, filled with things which they tell *me* they cannot by any conceivable possibility, do without. I don't pretend to know to the contrary, and, therefore, am bound to believe them; and as I imagine that you and Lady Felicia may require, at least, *one* trunk, filled with this indispensable machinery, whatever it may be, and as you cannot, with any degree of convenience, bring it with you in the morning, I would suggest the expediency of packing one up, and sending it by one of the coaches, to-night, directed to me, to be left till called for, at the Booking-office, Greenwich, Kent."

"A very excellent suggestion, indeed," said Fidèle, "and one which can be very easily adopted! I have been at a loss to conceive how we could manage, but this removes the difficulty at once !"

"But," said Alfred, "will the adoption of this course be wise? The very moment Felicia's absence is discovered, the most searching inquiries, of course, will be made; and when they have ascertained that a box has been sent to Greenwich, they'll pursue us in that direction, and we may be annoyed!"

"Exactly," replied Mr. Wilkins; "very true. But we are not going in that direction! When they have ascertained that the box has been sent to Greenwich, they will naturally infer that we have gone into Kent, and *will* pursue us doubtless; but we shall not be there! I shall send a man over for it early in the morning, who will bring it to town, and despatch it to where we *shall* be!"

"Very good!" said Alfred, "very good indeed!"

"Really," Mr. Wilkins, observed Fidèle, "I cannot wonder at the fact of Mr. Murray having left the entire management of this affair to you! Have you any other suggestion to make?"

"One more,"—replied Mr. Wilkins—"but one. I would suggest the propriety of—I may say, the necessity for—Lady Felicia keeping up her spirits! Tell her to fear nothing!—for there is in reality nothing to fear. Let her but keep up her glorious spirits, and then we shall all be as happy as birds. I anticipate a day of days!—with *your* assistance, our happiness will be enthusiastic! And now, my boy," he added, "just order some wine, for I want to drink the health—the glorious health, of the lovely and strong-minded Lady Felicia!"

The wine was ordered; and when the toast had been proposed, and responded to, Mr. Wilkins poured forth a flood of eloquence, which ran and sparkled through a variety of subjects — including those of love, hope, felicity, and fear— until Fidèle, who was perfectly delighted with him, reluctantly intimated that she must return.

"Miss Legrange," said Alfred, as he pressed her hand warmly, "with all my heart, I thank you! Tell dear Felicia— God bless her! — that she has made me beyond conception happy, and that my devotion shall prove the purity and strength of my affection."

" I will tell her all this, and much more," said Fidèle. " You need not expect to hear from me again ; but, if anything *should* occur."—

" Pray, write in any case !"

" Well, then I will."

" Where's the licence ?" inquired Mr. Wilkins.

" Dear me !" exclaimed Fidèle, " what a fortunate thought ! I certainly should have taken it back with me. What we should do without you, Mr. Wilkins, I really don't know !"

The licence was at once returned to Alfred, and when Fidèle had shaken hands with them both cordially, she with a light heart and joyous spirits left them.

" A spicy girl, that," observed Mr. Wilkins. " Ladylike, clever, intelligent !—I must have a little *more* talk with her !— And now, my boy," he added, " I must leave you. The governor will frown like a thunder cloud when I go back ; but that's nothing. We'll have a glorious evening ! I need not tell you now to keep up your spirits ! *Go*, and get the ring, and then run to the parson. Eight o'clock, mind !—precisely ! —Good bye."

He then returned to the " governor," who, being indeed enraged, at once gave him notice to leave, declaring that he would *not* stand such perfectly un-business-like irregularities to please the most highly accomplished salesman in the realm !

CHAPTER IX.

THE ELOPEMENT.

FIRMLY adhering to the resolution she had formed, Felicia—having had but little sleep during the night—rose early in the morning, and with the assistance of Fidèle, prepared to leave her magnificent home.

She was tranquil: pensive, indeed, but not sad; her countenance proclaimed neither levity nor gloom. Fidèle, by the exercise of the most pleasing arts, endeavoured to inspire her with gaiety, portraying the brightest prospects of happiness, and speaking continually in Alfred's praise; but Felicia was still calm, and thoughtful, and pale, as if her heart had summoned all the blood in her veins, within its own immediate region, to sustain it.

The hour appointed approached; and Fidèle informed one of the servants that they were about to take advantage of that delightful morning by going for a walk—which, although unusual, excited no surprise—and when the time for their departure had arrived, Felicia rang the bell for the servants to let her out, and left the house firmly, accompanied by Fidèle.

At first, they proceeded in the direction of the Park; but turning to the right, they went round towards the church, near which not a soul was to be seen. Finding the door open, however, they entered; and on the instant Alfred and his friend approached.

"Noble girl!" said Alfred fervently, as he pressed her hand, and gazed with an expression of rapture.

"Alfred," said Felicia, somewhat faintly, "I have followed

the dictates of my heart; not upon impulse, Alfred, but reflection."

"My dear, my own Felicia!" he exclaimed, and pressed her hand still more fervently, and drew her arm gently within his own; and, having briefly introduced Mr. Wilkins, who had already begun to chat gaily with Fidèle, they proceeded to the vestry, where the minister received them, and then led the way to the altar.

During the ceremony — which was most impressively performed—Felicia's firmness never forsook her: indeed the very points which under ordinary circumstances would have affected her to tears, tended to impart to her additional strength, and 'while she knelt before the altar, with true humility, the spirit of prayer subdued all her worldly thoughts, and rendered them subservient to its holy influence.

The ceremony ended, they returned to the vestry; and there, for the first time, Felicia wept; and while Alfred, with the most affectionate solicitude, embraced her, and wiped away her tears, Mr. Wilkins did all that was necessary, and more, with the view of giving satisfaction to those whom the manifestation of his generosity concerned; and having taken leave of the minister, who had been extremely courteous throughout, they left the church, and immediately entered the carriage, which at that very moment drew up.

The blinds were down in an instant: for, although there were but very few persons about, it was held to be advisable to defy even the possibility of recognition; and Mr. Wilkins, having Fidèle by his side, began to inspire them with gaiety.

The route had been changed the previous evening: Brighton was now the point proposed; and in less than an hour, which did not appear to be half an hour, they stopped at Croydon. Here breakfast was ordered, and shortly afterwards the man whom Mr. Wilkins had despatched with a horse and gig to Greenwich, arrived with Felicia's trunk.

"Dear me!" exclaimed Fidèle, whom this arrival not only delighted, but amazed. "How very kind!—and with what admirable promptitude!"

"*Promptitude*," observed Mr. Wilkins, who had staked his reputation upon his arrangements—"Promptitude in an affair of this character is absolutely essential to perfect enjoyment: without it, doubts and fears arise, which are, of course, inimical to happiness. You would have thought of this trunk all day: you might even have been apprehensive that it was lost. Now, here it is! and by its presence, apprehension is defied. When I marry," he added, with a look of peculiar significance—"if I ever *should*—but we'll talk about that another time."

"Talk about that another time!" thought Fidèle.—"How very odd!"

He said no more: indeed, he left the room with the view of giving some additional instructions; but, certainly, the idea of his talking about that another time, struck her as being remarkable.

Breakfast was now announced; and considering the shortness of the notice, it was, on a small scale, a splendid set-out; which quite astonished Mr. Wilkins, because so many apologies had been offered, and he had heard so many expressions of an earnest wish, that he had *only* sent them word that he was coming, that they might have provided something delicious! Really, everything appeard to be sufficiently delicious! It is true, neither Felicia nor Alfred ate *much*, but Fidèle and Mr. Wilkins!—Well! It will be, perhaps, sufficient to state, that they were worthy of all belief when they declared that they never before ate *such* a breakfast."

Having enjoyed their repast, during which the facetiæ of Mr. Wilkins had been very agreeable, the expediency of "moving on a little farther" was suggested, and when the necessary instructions had been given, and Mr. Wilkins had had a private interview with the landlord, to whom the highest satisfaction was expressed, and by whom the *highest* satisfaction was received, they re-entered the carriage and were off.

Now, leaving them for the present to pursue their journey under more cheerful influences then they were when they commenced it—for even Felicia, although still calm, had had her spirits somewhat raised—it will be quite correct at once to return to Kingsborough House, inasmuch as their departure from Croydon and the startling discovery of Felicia's flight occurred simultaneously.

Lady Florence, and her sister Lady Augusta, were dressed for church, which they seldom, during the season, omitted to attend, seeing that that which they patronized was, at that period, one of the most aristocratic churches in town, and therefore a church which, though consecrated to the worship of the Most High, was virtually a Temple of Fashion, in which everything said and done *appeared* to be an absolute mockery of the spirit of true religion. From the actor in the pulpit, who went in state to preach humility to those who went in state to hear him—to the brilliant devotees—the gorgeously apparelled actors and actresses who represented the congregation—all seemed to be engaged in a purely histrionic display of which they themselves formed the very centre of attraction. They appeared to be, moreover, devoted to irony,—not only when they craved Divine mercy as "miserable sinners"— prayed to be delivered "from all blindness of heart, from pride, vain glory, and hypocrisy; from envy, hatred, and malice, and all uncharitableness"—and invoked the Holy Spirit to incline their hearts to keep the fourth commandment, when all their arrangements had been made for the day in which their man- servants and their maid-servants, and their cattle would be engaged—but throughout the whole service, which smacked of Rome and rendered the road to it easy. The very sermon seemed to be ironical—for exhortations to purity, simplicity, devotion, prostration of spirit and humility of heart, were delivered in the midst of an impious pantomime, in which some of the most conspicuous performers were pantaloons with painted faces, gloating upon the Columbines, who in the exercise of all the arts of fascination at their command, seemed to regard the brilliant scene as Christianity's Masquerade.

To this Temple of Fashion, or Fashionable Church, in which all this *appeared*—God alone knew the hearts of the gorgeous congregation—Lady Florence and Lady Augusta were dressed to go when the intelligence reached them, that Felicia went out for an early morning walk and had not yet returned.

" Out ! " exclaimed Lady Florence, " and not *yet* returned."

Both she and her sister were struck with amazement, and rushing to the room, in which the Marquis was, as usual, having his breakfast alone, and reading the most facetious of the Sunday papers, communicated the fact to him at once.

" Well :" said the Marquis coolly, " what of that ? She'll return, I dare say, when she's tired of walking ! "

" I fear," said Lady Augusta, " that she'll *never* return."

" What do you mean ?" demanded the Marquis.

" I feel quite convinced that she is gone expressly to meet that person whose object is to disgrace her ?"

" That person !   What person ?"

" He whom, the last time he came, she embraced "

" Embraced !" echoed the Marquis, with a look of alarm. " Embraced !"

" If I had done that which I ought to have done, *this* would not have occurred. "

" Who saw her embrace him ?"

" One of the servants."

" And did you know of it ?"

" I did."

" Then why not tell me ?"

" I should have done so, but Florence would not allow me."

"Why not?"

"She wanted, she said, to enjoy the sport!"

"The sport!" exclaimed the Marquis. "The sport! The sport of seeing your sister disgraced! Why, you infamous creature! *what* do you mean?"

"I said that I wanted additional *proof*," said Lady Florence, darting a look of fury at her sister.

"You said sport."

"It is false!"

"*Out* of my sight!" cried the Marquis fiercely, and Lady Florence, with a haughty expression, left the room. "Who is this villain?" he demanded of Lady Augusta.

"His name, I believe, is Murray!"

"What is he?"

"A mercer, I believe."

"A mercer!" cried the Marquis, with a look of disgust.

"I believe so: he came here with silks!"

"How often has the wretch been here?"

"Twice, I understand."

"Where does he live?"

"Upon my word, I don't know. James knows much more about him than I do."

"Ring, then, for James."

Lady Augusta did so; and the Marquis rose and paced the room with an aspect of ferocity.

"Send James up," said he, when a servant appeared.

"James, my lord?" said the servant. "He's just gone to church with Lady Florence!"

"Run and bring him back, then, *immediately*. You ought to be ashamed of yourselves," he added, when the servant had left the room, "both of you! You are just as bad as Florence. You *ought* to have told me, in order that I might have put a stop to it at once."

"I should have done so had it not been for Florence."

"Don't talk to me about Florence!   How could she prevent you?"

"You don't know how imperious she is!"

"Curse her imperiousness!" exclaimed the Marquis, who continued to pace the room violently until James, in a state of alarm, appeared.

"Now, sir," said the Marquis, "do you mean to say that you saw Lady Felicia and that fellow who was here embracing each other? If you tell me a falsehood I'll strangle you. Did you, or did you not, see them?"

"I did, my lord."

"You are quite sure?"

"I am, my lord, quite."

"Did you let her out this morning?"

"No, my lord; but I saw them go."

"You saw *them* go?"

"Yes, my lord; I mean Lady Felicia and Miss Legrange."

"Had they anything with them?"

"Nothing but what they had on, my lord; but a trunk was sent away last night by Miss Legrange."

"A trunk, do you say?"

"Yes, my lord, a large trunk; I saw the direction; it went by the coach to Greenwich."

"To whom was it directed?"

"To a Mr. Wilkins, to be left at the coach-office till called for."

"Order post horses—quick—four—*immediately!*—Don't lose a moment—away!—I'll spoil the *sport* of the scoundrel now."

"Shall I go with you?" inquired Lady Augusta.

"Do you *know* him?"

"No."

"Then keep at home."

He summoned his valet and went up to dress, while Lady

Augusta, whose only fear was that the "family" might be disgraced, imagined Felicia sitting at breakfast with Alfred and Fidèle, and the utter consternation that would be created by the sudden appearance of the Marquis.

As the utmost possible haste had been enjoined, the carriage was soon at the door, when the Marquis, armed with a loaded cane and attended by James and a powerful groom, who was also armed, started for Greenwich.

Having reached the Marsh Gate, which has since disappeared, he ascertained that a carriage and four had passed through about nine that morning; and feeling now convinced that he was on the right track, he urged the postillions forward.

On reaching, however, the Kent Road Gate, no information whatever could be obtained; nor had they at either of the other gates seen a carriage and four pass through: he, nevertheless, conceiving that there might be two roads, dashed on to Greenwich, and stopped at the first coach-office he came to.

"Have you a trunk here directed to Mr. Wilkins?" he inquired.

"We had," replied the book-keeper; "but a man came and took it away this morning."

"Do you know the man?"

"No."

"Do you deliver trunks to men of whom you know nothing?"

"Oh, yes; especially when they bring their cards. This man brought the card of Mr. Wilkins!"

"Does he live in the town, think you?"

"The man, or Mr. Wilkins?"

"The man."

"I don't know: he may: very likely he does. I don't know either of them myself."

"Have you seen a carriage and four pass through here this morning?

"No, not this morning."

One of the postillions here intimated to his lordship, that if they were ahead he should be sure to hear of them at the top of Blackheath Hill, and as the Marquis thought this very probable, they at once dashed up to the hotel on Blackheath.

Here, however, the people declared positively that no carriage and four *had* passed there that morning; and the Marquis, on being assured that if it had they must have seen it, ordered the post-boys to drive back to Greenwich, conceiving that they must have put up there, and went round to every house at which they *could* have put up—there were not many of that kind there then—and feeling at length convinced that they had not been there at all, he told the men to drive back as fast as they came.

That they had passed the Marsh Gate, the Marquis felt assured, and it was at the gate in the Kent Road, that he had missed them. He therefore thought—and very naturally—that they must have turned off at the Elephant and Castle and on his return to the Elephant and Castle, he turned up the Camberwell Road, and inquired at the Walworth Gate, but no carriage and four had passed through there. He then came back, and went round to the Kennington Gate, through which they really *had* passed; but fortunately—for the reputation of Mr. Wilkins, at least!—the man in attendance had not been there an hour, and, therefore, of course, knew nothing about it. He did not by any means *explain* to the Marquis, that he had not been there an hour! No: having seen no carriage and four pass, he felt justified in stating distinctly, that nothing of the kind *had* passed, and that if it had, he must have seen it!— he wasn't blind!

Well! What was to be done? They might have passed the Marsh Gate, merely for the purpose of putting him on the wrong scent, and, returning by one the of other bridges, proceeded in another direction! This struck the Marquis as being the course, which, in all probability, they *had* pursued, and, there-fore, he gave the word, "Home."

On his way home, however, he called on Lord Thurleigh, with whom he was on terms of the closest intimacy, and to whom he communicated all that had occurred.

"Is she of age?" inquired his lordship, calmly.

"Yes," replied the Marquis.

"Well, then, they have not gone to Gretna. They are married by this time."

"Married!" exclaimed the Marquis, with a countenance strongly expressive of a desire for *anything* rather than that! "Why the scoundrel is but a mere mercer!"

"Well! there is no law to prohibit such a marriage!"

"No law! but is it likely!"

"*I* think that it is!—*very* likely indeed! If a marriage had not been contemplated, she would not have left home."

"Well, but where could they get married?"

"Either in your own parish, or that in which *he* has been residing."

"Good God! But I cannot believe in anything so monstrous!"

"You had better go at once, and ascertain! I'll go with you. But, in any case, keep the affair close."

The church of the parish, in which the Marquis resided, being at hand, they went directly there, and at once ascertained that Felicia *was* married that morning.

"The minx!" exclaimed the Marquis, having looked at the register. "She who appeared to be so gentle, so calm!—the wanton, base, deceitful minx!—Oh, curse her!"

"Hush!"—said Lord Thurleigh. "Kingsborough!—Be cool.—Come, come: let us leave. It's a bad job—a *bad* job—but let us consider what's best to be done."

"What *can* be done!" exclaimed the Marquis.

"Nothing, to undo what *has* been done; but something may

suggest itself, calculated to subdue the most galling features of the case. Come!—let us return."

"If," said the Marquis, having re-entered the carriage,—"if the vagabond had been but a *gentleman*, I shouldn't have cared so much ; but the idea of being the father-in-law of a *mercer*, is monstrous !"

" Do you know him at all ?"

" *Not* I."

" You don't know whether he's intelligent, or not ?"

" I know nothing whatever about the vagabond!"

" My object in asking you, is to suggest, that if he be not a fool—and I don't believe he is—you might get him some appointment abroad."

" *I* get the scoundrel an appointment ! If he dare to come near me, I'll knock out his brains !—I'll do *that* for him, the villain !"

" There is no necessity for him to come near you ! The farther he is from you the better. I would *therefore* get him some appointment abroad. Keep this affair a secret—which you easily can do—until he is gone, and then proclaim that your daughter is allied to an *attaché*, to such an embassy, and so on."

" If they alone were concerned," said the Marquis, " I'd let the wretches starve—I'd let them *starve!*—but as such a vulgar, detestable alliance must, if known, reflect disgrace upon the family, I'll think of your suggestion—I'll think of it."

" Keep the affair to *yourself!*" urged Lord Thurleigh. " Don't let even the members of your family know of it ! Treat the matter lightly : you know all about it !—her absence has been accounted for, and there's an end of it"

Having left Lord Thurleigh at his residence, and stated by way of precaution to James, that his fears had been groundless, that his noble friend had ascertained that Lady Felicia had left town for a few days, and that all had been accounted for, the Marquis proceeded home, and was immediately accosted by Lady Augusta.

"*Have* you been successful?" she inquired, earnestly.

"Yes," replied the Marquis; "I have succeeded in ascertaining that she has been driven from home!"

"*Driven* from home!"

"Aye!—by you and Florence."

"Nay, do not say by me! Florence, I know, has not treated her kindly : the night before last, she was *very* severe."

"She'll endure no more of it! She's now beyond the reach of *your* tyranny, at least!"

"Believe me, *I* have not been tyrannous! But, where is she gone?"

"What! Do you want to continue your annoyances in an epistolary form?"

"No! indeed, indeed, I do not. I will not annoy her! Where is she?"

"I know all about it, and that's sufficient. Leave me : I wish to be alone."

This, although unsatisfactory, *per se*, was quite enough to convince Lady Augusta that "the family" had not been disgraced, and in less than five minutes it was understood distinctly by every member of the establishment, that Felicia had left to escape the tyranny of Lady Florence—and no one blamed her.

It was now two o'clock, and the happy marriage party—for even Felicia, although calm and thoughtful, felt happy with Alfred, while Fidèle and Mr. Wilkins were supremely so!—were within about six miles of Brighton, which they reached precisely at half-past two, and proceeded to an hotel on the East Cliff, to which Mr. Wilkins had been strongly recommended, and which he at once pronounced to be superb!

The ladies, immediately after their arrival, retired to change their dresses, and the gentlemen went for a short stroll on the

beach; but they were not absent long: they very soon
returned; and, as Alfred pressed Felicia to his heart, and
thought that she had never before looked so lovely, the
appearance of Fidèle quite enchanted Mr. Wilkins.

They went to the window to gaze upon the sea; but to
them its attractions were transient: they turned from the sea
to look into each other's eyes; and, while Alfred pressed the sweet
lips of Felicia, Mr. Wilkins absolutely kissed the hand of Fidèle!

They were silent:—it must as a remarkable fact be recorded,
that even Mr. Wilkins was silent!—but their eyes were
eloquent!—darting love's electric light from soul to soul, and
thrilling their hearts with rapture.

The silence, however, of Mr. Wilkins, could not be expected
to be of long duration: nor was it: he soon began again, and
—without interfering with the happy occupants of the other
bay-window—directed Fidèle's attention to every visible object,
from the distant horizon to the boy catching shrimps.

"There," said he, at length, enthusiastically, "there's a
sea!—a sea of which England—glorious little England—is the
mistress!—a sea, on which Britannia bids defiance to the
world!—and yet the rascally French dream of wresting it
from her!"

"Nay," said Fidèle, smiling archly as she spoke, "*that* is
not at *all* like you!"

"What's the matter?" inquired Mr. Wilkins, who thought
his remarks rather telling than not.

"Oh! that is not complimentary at all!"

"Complimentary! What not to the frog-eating French?"

"You surely do not *know* that I am a French woman!"

"*You* a French woman!" exclaimed Mr. Wilkins, who really
began to feel warm!—*You*!—Oh, you are jesting!"

"No, indeed, I am not, replied Fidèle; "I was born in
France, and educated in France!"

"You perfectly amaze me!" returned Mr. Wilkins, who

now absolutely *perspired!* "You do not *speak* like a French woman!—I cannot discover anything in your accent to justify the slightest suspicion of your being one!"

"Now you are *yourself* again!" exclaimed Fidèle, archly, "this is complimentary indeed!"

"If you view it as a compliment, you may be sure that, in passing it, I am sincere; for if I had had the remotest conception of your not being à thorough-bred English woman, I should not have got into *this* scrape! It may be all prejudice—doubtless it is!—but we Englishmen are taught to view the French with contempt, and I dare say that the French return the compliment!"

"England and France," replied Fidèle, "are two great nations, between whom peace will remove all prejudices eventually. They will know each other better by and by, and live, as it were, in each other's hearts."

"I hope so," returned Mr. Wilkins; "but as far as you are concerned, I'll appeal to any mortal—I'll appeal to Mr. Murray"—

"What's that?" inquired Alfred, on hearing his name mentioned.

"Why look here," replied Mr. Wilkins, "I was speaking of the French"—

"And *so* severely!" interposed Fidèle.

"Fie, Mr. Wilkins!" said Felicia, with a smile.

"Well, but who alive upon earth could *tell* that English was not her native tongue!"

"Her English is certainly pure;" said Felicia.

"Pure!—I'll defy all the linguists living to discover the slightest French accent or tone! Why, didn't you tell me, you villain!" he added, addressing Alfred, who was laughing very merrily,—"Why didn't you tell me that Miss Legrange was not English?"

"Why did you not tell me," said Alfred, "that you were

about to speak severely of the French!—But," he added, turning to Fidèle, "I was not aware myself that you were a French lady until this morning; and as I am quite sure that if *he* had known it, or even suspected it, he would not have been quite so severe, you must, I think, forgive him."

"Must I?—Well, then, I will;" said Fidèle, and gave him her hand with a smile.

This was satisfactory, as far as it went, but Mr. Wilkins couldn't forget it; he knew by her playful manner that Fidèle was not in the slightest degree offended; but there was the fact before him still!—he *couldn't* get it out of his mind: every word that he spoke, and every look which he gave, denoted the recollection of that "grand scrape," until dinner was announced, when the weight of the responsibility he had undertaken pressed upon him, and sank it for a time in oblivion.

The dinner was splendid; elegantly served, and deliciously varied, it was all that even Mr. Wilkins could wish; and was, throughout, highly enjoyed. The only drawback he experienced, was when he assisted Fidèle to a glass of wine: his hands, which were then unusually red, became, as he grasped the bottle, conspicuous. This, however, caused but a momentary pang: he was at once happily relieved by the thought, that if even his hands were noticed—of which he was not sure—they might imagine that he was an amateur sculler, and every one knew that the hands of a sculler *would* spread and become full of blood when warm. This, therefore, could scarcely be deemed a drawback: it was but a speck on the sun of delight, which imparted its influence to all.

When the dessert had been spread, and the waiters had left the room, Mr. Wilkins, with an expression of thought, filled his glass, and with a most profound sense of the responsibility attached to him, rose to propose "Health, peace, long life, and unmingled joy, to the beautiful, strong-minded, noble-hearted bride!"

"I feel," said he, "at a loss for words to express my profound admiration of one who has proved that she belongs not only to the gorgeous nobility of the land, but to the perfect nobility of nature. Nature, whose grand and glorious scheme embraces the heavens and the earth; which guides the course of the glittering stars, and lights up the love of the glow-worm; which hurls the thunder-bolts of Jove, and whispers to the afflicted heart the words of hope, and peace, and joy; which governs the universal world, and elaborates the delicate machinery of the insect; which forms the stupendous cloud-capped mountains, and paints the beautiful butterfly's wing; which raises the storm and calms the soul; makes Ætna boil and beauty blush; and, while convulsing the fathomless sea, hushes the innocent babe to sleep.—Nature has prompted the heart of the bride to obey her pure and perfect laws. Some may contend that in doing this the bride has made an awful sacrifice : but what is empty pomp compared with sound substantial happiness, which is, in whatever sphere we move, the grand and glorious aim of existence? She possesses a soul above tinselled splendour, preferring a life of tranquil joy. She might have married a coronet!—She has married a man!—a man in every sense of the term: amiable, honourable, generous, and true, he may stand erect as a man should stand, without a blush, in the presence of the greatest! If the amiable be united to the amiable, the intelligent to the intelligent, the pure and noble-hearted to the pure and noble-hearted, the union must be blessed: and as this is such a union—as it is essentially a union of hearts—a union from which I feel convinced every possible blessing will spring, I give you, with all my heart and soul, Health and long life to the beautiful bride; or, as they are perfectly worthy of each other, and, as the minister said this morning, 'Those whom God hath joined together let no man put asunder,' I'll couple them in this case, and drink—Health, happiness, peace, and pure joy to the bride and the bride-groom—God bless them!''

Fidèle was delighted: she openly declared that she never heard anything more beautiful; and when she had lavished a series of elegant and well-directed compliments upon Mr. Wilkins—who felt within himself that what he had said was not amiss—Alfred calmly rose to acknowledge the toast on behalf of Felicia and himself, and having eloquently dwelt upon the prospect of happiness which then brightly opened before them, he concluded by proposing the health of Mr. Wilkins, whom he eulogized highly.

Having got over this, the enjoyment of the evening was all that Mr. Wilkins had to think of, seeing that it had been arranged between him and his "governor"—whom he some-what softened before he left—that, instead of returning to town that night, he should start by the earliest coach in the morning. His mind was, therefore, perfectly at ease, and, being susceptible of the most joyous influences, he never before felt so happy.

But they were all happy. Felicia and Alfred were compara-tively silent; but they were not, therefore, less happy. They gazed on the tranquil scene before them: the sea was calm, the air serene, the spray was scarcely visible; and as they viewed the vast expanse, their souls partook of its repose.

They had coffee; but sat at the window still, and watched the western horizon, with its brilliant tints, its glittering peaks, and its gorgeous lakes of ethereal gold, until the peaceful moon appeared, serenely reflecting the glory of her God.

Having viewed this truly magnificent scene with feelings of pure adoration, Mr. Wilkins suggested the expediency of having lights, conceiving that on an occasion like that, they ought not to be *too* contemplative, and when lights had been brought, they withdrew from the window, and all was gaiety again.

The time flew fast, but at twelve o'clock Fidèle disappeared with the bride; and, as soon after this Mr. Wilkins retired, the bridegroom sat in a reverie alone, until aroused by the mysterious re-appearance of Fidèle, who smiling archly, said

"Good night."

CHAPTER X.

NOTWITHSTANDING the precautions of the Marquis—notwithstanding the belief, with which he had inspired the whole establishment, that the flight of Felicia was ascribable solely to the tyranny of her imperious sister, Florence, the first thing which attracted his attention in the morning, when he opened the fashionable paper of that period, was the following paragraph conspicuously displayed :—

"ELOPEMENT IN HIGH LIFE.—Yesterday morning a noble family, residing not *more* than a hundred miles from *   *   * Square, was thrown into a state of the most afflicting consternation, by the sudden and somewhat mysterious disappearance of one of its most lovely branches.   We do not pretend to know at present the particulars ; but the beautiful and highly accomplished fugitive is Lady ————, the second daughter of a noble Marquis, and "the gallant, gay Lothario" is connected, if not with the government of India, at least with the Indian empire's shawls."

With an oath, which startled the servant in attendance, the Marquis rose and paced the room trembling with passion.

"The Indian empire's *shawls*," he exclaimed, furiously. "*Leave* the room ;" he added, turning fiercely to the servant, who appeared on the instant to wither away, so magical was his disappearance.   "Had a thunder-bolt fallen and *crushed* her on the road—The Indian empire's shawls!"

Parched with rage he rang the bell, and the sprite who had just before vanished re-appeared.

"The *carriage!*—send Lady Augusta here!"—cried the Marquis, who continued to pace the room groaning with fury.

"Look at *this!*" he exclaimed, as Lady Augusta entered. "For this curse I have to thank *you!* One word from you, and *all* would have been averted."

Lady Augusta glanced over the paragraph eagerly, and started with a well-defined expression of horror. "The *second* daughter!" she wildly exclaimed. "The wretches have made a mistake!—they mean *me!*" and tottering towards a couch, she sank upon it and fainted.

The Marquis took no notice of this; he left the room, and proceeded to dress, and when the carriage had been announced he started to call on his friend Lord Thurleigh.

"Thurleigh," said he, as he entered the room, in which he found his noble friend at breakfast; "this cursed affair will drive me mad."

"Pooh, pooh," said Lord Thurleigh. "Mad! Make the best of it."

"*Have* you seen this?" inquired the Marquis, pointing to the paragraph in question.

His lordship coolly put on his spectacles, and having read the paragraph as coolly took them off.

"Well," said he, "it only shows that nothing can be kept from these fellows. How they manage to get their information God knows. Now who could have told them of this?"

"It matters not now who told them," said the Marquis. "There the thing is!—Now what's to be done?"

"What *can* be done? The fact can't be denied! By the way they say your *second* daughter. She is the youngest, is she not?"

"Yes, the wretch, the idiot, the fool!"

"Well, that's so far good. You may, even now, get over it.

Tell them that they have been misinformed, and insist upon
having the statement contradicted. And yet, as they don't
like to contradict themselves, and never will, however wrong,
unless they are absolutely forced to do so, they'll soon ascertain
that instead of the second daughter, it's the third, and then
another statement will appear in their own vindication. No ;
the better plan will be to let it rest as it is. Know nothing of
it. Your name is not mentioned. The appearance of your
second daughter, as usual, will prove that they are, at least on
that point, wrong: therefore, take no notice of it; let it die
away."

"It's easy to say, Thurleigh, 'let it die away;' but an affair
of this character is never forgotten."

"Oh, that will rub off. All you have to. do is to send him
abroad, and the sooner you do so the better. You can then
announce the marriage, formally, with whatever embellishments
you please."

"If the other girls were settled, I shouldn't care so much
but this you see will seriously interfere with *their* prospects !"

"I don't see why it should !"

"It must ! Who of any importance would marry a girl
whose sister eloped with a fellow like that! It *must* blast their
prospects, necessarily: we shall be the laughing-stock of th
whole town !"

"I don't see it :" returned his noble friend. I can't see it
That'll blow over. Make *no* stir about it: keep quiet. I
will soon wear away, and be thought nothing of. Do the
know of this at home ?"

"I have shown it to one of them."

"Tell them, when you return, to know nothing about it. I
will be perhaps, as well too to get them out of town. They'l
be better away, for the present, at least. Pack them off: b
next season all will be forgotten, or pretty nearly so; pac
them off."

This appeared to the Marquis to be about the best thing he *could* do ; and as his noble friend had no farther advice to offer, he shortly afterwards left him, with the view of ascertaining how he could most conveniently adopt the suggestion.

During his absence, however, instead of keeping the thing quiet, Lady Augusta—whose fainting fit was not of long duration—did all in her power to let the "world" know, that the newspaper people had made a mistake—that instead of the second daughter, they ought to have said the third—that it was her sister Felicia who had eloped—and that *she* would rather be burnt alive, than form such a vulgar connection ; while Lady Florence, having ascertained from James, that the Marquis and Lord Thurleigh had been to the church, had her suspicions, and went there too, and saw the register, and thus discovered all.

Meanwhile, Mr. Wilkins—who, in order to be home in time for business, had started from Brighton at six—returned, much to the satisfaction of the "governor," to whom he at once proceeded to explain the substance of all that had occurred.

At first, the "governor" felt incredulous, he openly declared that he could not believe it ; but when Mr. Wilkins had assured him, with due solemnity of expression, that every word of it was gospel, his scepticism vanished.

"This then," said he, "accounts for his being so unsettled ! But why not tell me! Surely he might have told me ! A lady of title, do you say ?—absolutely the daughter of a peer ?"

"Yes!" replied Mr. Wilkins, with feelings of pride "Lady Felicia—you'll find it all in the peerage—third daughter of the most noble the Marquis of Kingsborough !—worth a mint, and *such* an angel !—*I* had the honour of giving her away !"

"Then it was a clandestine affair ?"

"Of course ! But what of that ? There she is !—as lovely as life, and as happy as all the birds in Paradise ! Heaven and earth ! what a glorious day we had of it ! Magnificent!"

"No doubt," observed the governor, as a bright and purely business-like thought flashed upon him. "No doubt. But being a clandestine marriage, how did the bride get her ward-robe away?"

"How *could* she? She could'nt bring it with her!—nor could her companion bring hers! They have but one trunk between them."

"Dear me; why that must be very inconvenient?"

"It will be, of course, for a time; but they'll very soon get a new stock."

"Had we not better supply them?"

"Well," replied Mr. Wilkins, "it will be as well!"

"I *think* so! It must be peculiarly inconvenient for a lady of title to be without a wardrobe!—and I'm sure that if I could in any way promote the interest or the happiness of Mr. Murray, or save his lady from the slightest inconvenience, I should feel the greatest pleasure in doing so. Let us make up a parcel, and send it at once. Let's see: what things will they most require? A shawl or two—a few dresses of course!—a few pieces of lawn—some French cambric.—Just select what you fancy most likely to suit."   ;

Mr. Wilkins, with the assistance of the governor, did so. They selected a variety of things, and made up "a hundred and twenty pound parcel," which the governor would have doubled "with infinite pleasure" had not Mr. Wilkins suggested the propriety of not overloading them at once.

"You'll not have the money just yet, I dare say," observed Mr. Wilkins confidentially.

"Never mind the money," replied the governor. "I respect him too highly to think about that. Let him pay when it suits him. If he wants goods to treble the amount he shall have them. But I'll write to him myself. I *must* congratulate him on his good fortune. He's an elegant, gentlemanly fellow, and I feel quite delighted with his brilliant success."

In a state of mind bordering on enthusiasm, the "governor" went to the desk with the view of pouring forth upon paper the *ink* of his warmest and most profound congratulations. He had however scarcely commenced, when a carriage drew up—the very carriage in which Felicia had called—and the Marquis having alighted, addressed Mr. Wilkins.

" Are you the proprietor?" he haughtily inquired.

" No, my lord," replied Mr. Wilkins.

" Do you know me ?"

" The carriage, my lord, induces the belief that your lordship is the Marquis of Kingsborough."

" Oh!—I wish to speak to the proprietor—in private."

Mr. Wilkins, having shown his lordship into a private room, rushed back to deliver the message to the "governor," who immediately obeyed the summons, bowing most profoundly.

" You have," said the Marquis, " or had, a person named Murray, living here."

" I had, my lord," replied the governor; " but he has left."

" Why did he leave ?"

" To get married, my lord."

" Do you know to whom ?"

" I have just been informed."

" By whom ?"

" By Mr. Wilkins, whom your lordship first addressed."

" What does he know about it ?"

" He tells me, my lord, that he had the honour of giving the bride away !"

Groaning forth an oath which made the governor tremble, the Marquis convulsively clenched his hands, and stamped with indignation.

" Who is this person ?"—he demanded—" this Murray ?"

" He is the son, my lord, of an old friend of mine, and a highly respectable young man he is."

" Respectable !" echoed the Marquis, contemptuously.

" Well, my lord, he certainly *is* respectable; and, moreover, very intelligent !"

" Artful, you mean," said the Marquis. " Artful! But not quite artful enough. I suppose that he conceives her to be *wealthy*, does he not ?"

" I don't know, indeed, my lord: but I *presume* that her ladyship is, or *will* be rich ?"

" She hasn't a shilling!" returned the Marquis. " Nor shall she ever have one from me! Has *he* any property ?"

" I believe not, my lord."

" Then starvation stares them in the face !"

" But your lordship's influence will be sufficient, I apprehend, to promote"—

" What influence I have," interrupted the Marquis, " may be exercised; but, certainly, not in their *favour!* Let them starve !"

" Your lordship, on reflection, will not be so harsh "

" Harsh! Just, you mean!—Just! They shall not be saved from beggary by me! Do you know where they are ?"

" At Brighton, my lord."

" At some fine hotel, I suppose ?"

" I believe so."

" Ah! What little money he may have will there be spent, and then they'll have to face the world naked. But where did this incipient beggar come from ?"

" Sudbury, my lord."

" Sudbury! Then, I suppose, this hateful connection was first formed there ?"

" I really don't know. It may have been: he never said a word on the subject to me. If I had known it—if I had had even the slightest conception of what was about to take place, I should have deemed it my duty to put your lordship on your guard; but I knew nothing of it; and, therefore, all I can say is, that I feel extremely sorry that any one connected, or in any way identified with my establishment should have been so presumptuous."

" Presumptuous indeed!" exclaimed the Marquis.

" Still," resumed the governor, " knowing his father so well, I cannot but express a hope that, notwithstanding the young man has incurred your lordship's just displeasure, the influence of your lordship will not be used to crush him."

" Crush him! He has crushed himself! They are both crushed—effectually! If a look of mine could raise them from the depths of degradation, I'd close my eyes! They have chosen their *own* course, and let them pursue it!— Loaded with contumely, let them *grovel* through the world!"

Having obtained all the information he required, the Marquis abruptly took his leave, and, as he passed through the shop, cast a look of contempt at Mr. Wilkins, which that gentleman thought very discourteous.

" He doesn't look particularly joyful!" said Mr. Wilkins, when the governor, bowing with profound humility, had attended the Marquis to his carriage. " He doesn't like it much, I presume!"

" Not much," replied the governor, who, having no inclination to be communicative, thoughtfully returned to his desk.

Well! It was, of course, clear to Mr. Wilkins, that if the governor wished to keep it all to himself, he couldn't make him reveal it; still he did think it strange that, under all the circumstances, "not much" should have been the only reply vouchsafed. He, therefore, began to *imagine* what had passed, and drew a series of deductions from the haughty and contemptuous bearing of the Marquis, and the somewhat extraordinary taciturnity of the governor, who had been just before so remarkably enthusiastic; but as all these deductions, based, as they were necessarily, upon apocryphal evidence, failed to impart the full amount of satisfaction required, he resolved, having duly considered the matter, on making another effort to draw the governor out.

"I find," said he, having approached the desk, "that a coach starts at four, so that, if you have finished your letter, the parcel had better be sent off at once!"

"Well," said the governor, with a look of indecision, notwithstanding his mind had been fully made up; "I have been thinking that, after all, it had better not be sent! He may imagine that my object is to thrust the goods upon him."

"*He'll* not imagine that," said Mr. Wilkins. "He'll view it as an act of considerate friendship!"

"I fear not," returned the governor; "and I have too much respect for him to cause him, for one moment, to believe that I am actuated by the slightest desire to make a market of him."

"I am quite sure that no such belief will be induced by the adoption of the course you proposed. Instead of thrusting the goods upon him, you merely submit them: if they are not required, all he has to do is to send them back."

"*He'd* not return them: he'd feel, as it were, bound to keep them, whether they were really required or not. No· they'd better not be sent. They say second thoughts are best: they had better not go."

"Well! As you please, of course! But I think it's a pity, after having selected the goods, not to send them."

"It's the trouble we have taken that *he'll* think of! He'll say at once, 'These goods have been selected with great care, and, therefore, whether they suit or not, I must keep them: they must not have all this trouble for nothing!' Besides, the inconvenience that struck me will not be so great as I imagined! Brighton's a large place — a fashionable place: they can easily get supplied there! And, moreover, select for *themselves*, which, with ladies, is always a great consideration. I therefore think that, under all the circumstances, we —had better not send the goods at all."

"Very *good*," said Mr. Wilkins. "But if you have the slightest doubt about the money, *I'll* be responsible for the amount."

" *You'll* be responsible ?"

"Willingly; and would if the amount were double."

"You *have*, I believe, a little money in the funds ?"

"You know that I have."

"Then *keep* it there! Take my advice, Mr. Wilkins:— what you have *keep !* You are, I know, good for treble the amount, and, under ordinary circumstances, I shouldn't for a moment hesitate about accepting your responsibility; but these are not ordinary circumstances : I know somewhat more than you imagine."

"Indeed !" said Mr. Wilkins. "What is it you mean ?"

"Well," replied the governor, "I'll *tell* you because it appears, from what you have said, that you might otherwise have reason, and ample reason, to complain of my silence. The fact is, Mr. Murray has made a mistake !—a grand mistake !—an alarming mistake !—The speculation into which he has entered is a failure !—a dead failure !—a miserable failure !—Lady Felicia hasn't a shilling."

"Indeed !"-

"Not a shilling ! nor will she *ever* have ! The Marquis has just explained all.

Mr. Wilkins was thoughtful for a moment; but at length he said, "Well! it can't be helped! they must do the best they can !"

"But what can they *do !*" cried the governor. "She has a title; but what's a title ? a title won't pay rent and taxes !— nor will it feed and clothe them. A title will *do* with plenty of money, but what is the use of a title without ? She is highly connected; she has friends—influential friends—if friends they may be called—but what's the use of having friends, if they'll do nothing for you ? *I* don't see how they're to get along at all !"

" I have not the slightest fear of them," observed Mr. Wilkins.

" Well, but what are they to do! *She's* fit for nothing! and he's above his business now! What *can* they do? There they are, comparatively naked in the world, with a title to live upon—nothing but a title!—which is, of itself, utterly value-less—repudiated by her family, friends, and connexions, not one of whom will make the slightest effort to serve them."

" But how is it possible for us to know that?"

" The Marquis declared to me distinctly, that if a look of his could raise them from the depths of degradation, he'd close his eyes!"

" He's a beauty!" observed Mr. Wilkins. "But the Marquis isn't everybody!"

" Look at his influence! And what did he say to me when I mentioned it to him? ' What influence I have,' said he, ' may be exercised, but certainly not in their *favour*,' which, being interpreted, clearly means, that what influence he has will be used against them!—That's what I look at: they'd better have no influential friends at all, than have to contend against their influence!—In fact, instead of having influential friends, they have a lot of influential enemies. How then *are* they to get along? He has no property: she has no property: *her* friends won't aid them, and his friends can't. There they are."

" Then you think there's *no* hope for them?"

" Not the slightest."

" Are his friends poor?"

" Poor! no, they're not poor; but they haven't got more than they know what to do with. Besides, just look for a moment at the *style* to which this Lady Felicia has been accustomed. Lapped in luxury—brought up in splendour—surrounded by magnificence—and dressed like a Queen, with all the delicacies and elegancies of life at her command—it were madness to suppose that a tranquil existence—if even sufficient to support it could be ensured—would have any permanent charms for *her*. A creature petted and pampered as she has been never can be reconciled to mere respectability. Hence, assuming that he had sufficient to enable them to move in a respectable sphere the speculation would be a bad one; but when we come to look at the absence of *all* means, the prospect is frightful to contemplate. Had he married a tradesman's daughter he might, and I dare say would, have got on; but to marry the daughter of a peer without a penny! *Poor* fellow, it's all up with *him*—as the Marquis said, starvation stares them in the face."

A slight smile played round the mouth of Mr. Wilkins, which the governor observed, and at once resumed.

"Look at her!" said he, "What *can* you expect? Can a creature like that be kept for nothing? Can a trifle. support her? Can any business stand against it? Will she be content with plain clothing and food? No; all will be dissatisfaction and disgust. When she rises she will miss her maid; when she wants to go out she'll miss her carriage—when her finger aches she'll miss her physician; when she dines she'll miss her delicacies —her jellies and creams, and her sparkling champagne; when its warm she'll miss her delicious ices; when its cold she'll miss her delicious soups: when the evening comes she'll miss her entertainments—her conversaziones, soirées, operas, and balls— and when she goes to bed she'll miss her gold fringes, her blue satin curtains, and rich damask quilts. Here's a creature who'll miss all the luxuries of life, and who'll hence be from morning till night disgusted, day after day, and year after year —and yet although she's the wife of a friend—you *smile* at the frightful prospect."

"I smile," said Mr. Wilkins, "not at the prospect, because —although sufficiently frightful, no doubt—I can't see it. It is not at the prospect of seeing our friend and his beautiful wife reduced to misery, that I smile. I smile because you really *know* neither the one nor the other. Why he's a fine high-spirited fellow! while she"—

"Why don't you"—interrupted the governor — why *don't* you . take a man-of-the-world's view of the matter? High spirited! The spirits of a man are in his pocket. If his pocket's .full, he's full of spirits: as the money dwindles his spirits dwindle, and when its gone his spirits follow. Spirit's the soul of society, and society's the soul of civilization, but money's the soul of spirit! Look at that!—I say the soul of spirit!"

"I know you do," said Mr. Wilkins; "I perfectly well understand what you say; but what I mean by his being high-spirited is, that he is not a man to be easily crushed! When he finds that her family will render no assistance, his pride will prompt him to *prove* to them that he can do without it. I have no fear of *him!* He is not a man to despair! He has too much energy—too much intelligence!—he'll make every effort to work his way up, and she'll aid him!—if not with her hands, with her smiles, which are frequently far more efficient."

"It's all very well," said the governor, "to talk; but it isn't so easy to do. When a man has no money his spirit leads off, and his energies *must* follow suit."

"I don't see that," observed Mr. Wilkins. "We find that they frequently *do* follow suit; but I don't see that they of necessity *must.* Besides! your remarks apply to a state of destitution! Now, he is not destitute: he's *not* without money; nor will he be in *any* case just yet! He'll at all events have time to turn himself round, and to ascertain what can be done. As I said before, I've no *fear* of him! *He'll* do something, and promptly too!—He'll not wait till the wolf's at the door."

"Well," said the governor. "We shall see! But mark my words :—it's an awful speculation."

The parcel intended for Alfred was unpacked, and the goods were duly restored to stock: no letter of congratulation was written by the governor; but Mr. Wilkins sent one by that night's post, in which—after playfully hinting the expediency of not going "too fast" at first, and stating, that when he saw him on Sunday, he should have to communicate something "worth while"—he sent his—four asterisks, thus * * * * to Fidèle, and enclosed a half of a hundred pound note.

CHAPTER XI.

"Louisa! — Louisa!" exclaimed Alfred's father, rushing with a letter into the room behind his shop, immediately after the post came in on the Tuesday morning.

"Gracious, dear!" cried Mrs. Murray, feeling somewhat alarmed. "What has happened?"

"What has happened?" he echoed, with an expression of rapture. "What has happened? Joy has happened!—fortune has happened!—wealth, honour, distinction, everything has happened! Give me a kiss: *give* me a kiss: a good one!—Now then," he added—"But don't put yourself at all out!—don't be in the slightest degree excited! Be calm, and cool—and—read it yourself."

Mrs. Murray took the letter eagerly, and perceiving at once that it came from Alfred, her anxiety became still more intense; but when she had read the announcement of his marriage with Felicia, she instantly burst into tears.

"My boy!"—she exclaimed, with thrilling fervour—"my dear, my own, my soul's sweet boy! My proud heart told me that he would be great!—I always felt that he was *born* to be illustrious!"

"Illustrious!" cried Mr. Murray. "There he is! It's all over! The point's achieved! My life and soul, though, here's a job! Isn't it' glorious! *Where* are the girls? Julia!" he shouted, having opened the door. "Come down—all of you—quick—come along. Bob! run for your uncle Cy! Tell him to come like a flash of lightning!* Soul and body! here's news to be sure."

Down came the girls, and away ran Bob for uncle Cy; and while Mrs. Murray, with feelings of pride, was announcing the happy event to her daughters, Murray rushed to his friend the chemist next door, in whose shop he found some of the magnates of the town.

"I've just heard from Alfred," said he, as he entered.

"How does he get on?" inquired the chemist.

"He's married!"

"What, already?"

"Yes, and whom do you think *to?*"

"Can't imagine."

"To one of the daughters of our Marquis: the Lady Felicia!"

"What! Why, you don't mean that!"

"It's a positive fact. They were married in London"

"What's that? what's that?" inquired those around.

"Why," replied the chemist, "young Alfred Murray is married to one of our Marquis's daughters."

"And ducks!" said Mr. Chubb, who, although a coarse person, held nearly half the mortgages in the borough.

"It's true," said Mr. Murray.

"And ducks, I tell you!"

"Well, but I pledge you my word that it *is* so."

"I'll bet a five pound note of it!"

"I'll not rob you: I tell you it's a fact."

"Well, but which of them? Come now: what's her name?"

"Felicia."

---

* It will here be highly correct to explain that Mr. Murray did not mean this strictly, seeing that as Cyrus weighed two and thirty stone, it was physically impracticable. Mr. Murray merely meant that uncle Cyrus should be urged to come quickly, which if he did—considering the extremely slow rate at which he usually travelled—*would* be, comparatively, "like a flash of lightning."

"Felicia! Lady Felicia! Now, *are* you joking?"

"No, indeed, I am not."

"Well, but—oh,"—said Mr. Chubb, who felt incredulous still —"it seems—so—out of all character!"

"I readily believe it!" observed the chemist. "He's a fine, handsome fellow!"—a very handsome fellow! She saw him, fell in love with him, and married him! *That's* all natural enough!"

"Well, then, why don't you start off the bells?" said Mr. Chubb.

"Well, I don't know about *that*," replied Murray.

"Start them off, by all means! We must have a peal on such an occasion as this!—Start them off!"

"Well, I'll speak to Mrs. Murray about it."

"Start them off at once!"

"Shall *I* send to the ringers?" inquired the chemist.

"Well, do: I wish you would. It's nothing but right! We'll have a merry peal. *Now* will you believe me?"

They were satisfied then—quite satisfied then—and began to indulge in expressions of amazement mingled with warm congratulations.

"I suppose," said one, "they'll make *him* a lord!"

"Not a bit of it," returned Mr. Chubb: "he hasn't got bounce enough in him! When they make lords of them which are not kids of lords, they make them of them which bully the lords, and which, when they become lords themselves, grow very mild, and stick to their order!—But," he added, turning to Murray, "we must celebrate this, you know, in *some* way! What are you going to stand?"

"Anything you like;" replied Murray. "Go into the Crown, and we'll have a nice lunch. I'll be with you directly. My brother has just passed: I *must* go and have a word with him."

He accordingly left them, and found "uncle Cy" in a state of steaming perspiration.

" Gods in heaven !" said uncle Cy in his characteris-
tically deep, fat voice, as he blew out his cheeks and wiped
his brow, and adjusted his chins—of which he had three and
another coming—" Is the house on fire ?—Has the bank
stopped payment—or what ?"

" *Come* in," said Murray,—" Such news !—Come in !"   And
uncle Cy followed him into the room ; but the moment he
entered, the girls flocked round him, and all began to tell him
together.

" Let's have a solo," said uncle Cy : " a duet may do ; but
I can't stand a chorus."

Mrs. Murray then went to the point at once.   She announced the fact triumphantly ; and having done so, proceeded
with her embellishments, until uncle Cy, feeling slightly
bewildered, expressed a wish to look at the letter.

" Let's read the letter first," said he, "and then we can
have a fair start."

The letter was placed in his hands, and as he read it, his
happy face glowed with delight.

" Gods in heaven !" he exclaimed.   " There's a boy !   Ha—
ha—ha !—There's a boy !—Why, they'll make him a magistrate !
Ha, ha, ha !"

" Hark ! mamma," cried the eldest girl, as the church bells
struck up merrily.   " Oh ! how delightful !   How sweetly they
sound !   They are ringing for Alfred !—I know that they are.
Oh ! how I do long to kiss him !"

They listened to the joyous peal, and tears began to sparkle
in their eyes.   Those bells !—They never sounded so before !
The effect was thrilling !   Mrs. Murray wept aloud : Murray
himself stood motionless ; the girls were entwined in each
other's arms, and uncle Cy exclaimed, " God bless him !"

" I started them," said Murray, at length ; and the girls
ran up and kissed him ; and then they kissed uncle Cy, who,
wiping the tears ineffectually from his eyes, cried, " Out with

the wine! My heart is full: it swells with warmth and gladness! Out with the wine!—*There's* a boy!—Ha—ha—ha—ha—ha.

The wine was brought; and when uncle Cy felt sufficiently recovered—for while he laughed, the tears flowed freely—he said, with an air of solemnity, and in tones which proclaimed deep emotion, " May Heaven shower blessings upon them! May they be happy—God bless them!"

He put down his glass: he could't drink then: he said that he'd drink it presently.: he wanted to go to the window to think!—and he turned to the window; and gave vent to his " thoughts," which rolled down his cheeks unperceived.

" How often," said the eldest girl, " how often have we heard those bells, and thought them an annoyance: yet now they seem to speak of love, and trusting hearts, and hope, and joy!"

Uncle Cy— having become somewhat calm again—turned to that household god, *the* Bible, in which were registered the births and deaths of the family, from time immemorial; and, having ascertained the respective ages of the girls, he drew out his check-book—which proved to be another source of amazement to Murray, who never before knew that he had one—and wrote five cheques—giving to each of the girls guineas for years —and told them to get new dresses by Sunday, when he'd come and look at them, and kiss them, and dine with them, and thus duly celebrate the happy event."

The girls loved uncle Cy before!— they always *did* love uncle Cy!—he had such a warm heart, was so merry, so kind! but, albeit their love had been disinterested and pure, they then appeared to love him more than ever. How they did kiss him! The younger ones were especially enthusiastic, and felt that the world could not produce another uncle comparable with uncle Cy.

Murray then thought of his friends at the Crown,

and explained to Mrs. Murray the nature of his engagement.

"Cyrus," he added, "you'll join us? We are just going to have a bit of lunch, and a glass of wine: of course, you'll join us."

"I'm ready for anything," Cyrus replied. "But, I long to see that boy!"

"William, dear," said Mrs. Murray, privately. "You'll not remain long?"

"No, my love, no," replied Murray, "I'll not."

"Sometimes, dear," she added, with a smile, "when the heart is full of joy, wine makes love to the head."

"I'll be careful," said Murray, and giving Cyrus his arm, proceeded at a rapid rate—for Cyrus—to the Crown.

As they entered, they found their friends already uproarious, for, having drank the health of the bride, they were giving their celebrated three-times-three-with-one-cheer-more-and-a little-one-in!

"Who said he wouldn't come?" they exclaimed, having accomplished this feat to their entire satisfaction. "Here he is!"

"Now then," said Chubb, addressing Murray, "here you are. We've just drunk the bride's health—*go* in."

"All right," returned Murray, "let's sit down, and be comfortable.—Gentlemen," he added, "with far more pleasure than I'll venture to express, I join you in drinking the health of the bride!"

"Bravo! Bravo!" cried the guests.

"And I join you too!" said uncle Cy, who was hailed with corresponding expressions of approbation. "I don't know the lady," he added, "but this I know—she has taste!"

"I know her," said the chemist. "She's small, but very beautiful, and appears to be exceedingly amiable and mild."

"Is she anything like the Marquis?" inquired Mr. Chubb. "Because he, you know, *appears* to be particularly mild, even while he is letting you know the difference! He reminds me of the old judge which came round last year: *he* was one of your remarkably mild men: indeed, so mild, that when he was about to pass sentence upon a criminal, he'd make the fellow believe that he was going to upset the verdict, and get him off, until the blow came, and then *he* knew the difference!—like my old schoolmaster, Rumble: he was another mild man: he'd be so mild if you did anything wrong, that you thought he must mean to forgive you: he was so sorry—no one knew how sorry he was—he hoped it would never occur again, he sincerely hoped you'd know better in future, only, for this time you had to take *that!* and he'd give you such a *winder*, you hardly knew you lived!—It's the same with the Marquis · only get under his lash, and you'll feel it: the more he means to give you, the milder he becomes."

"*I've* seen him in a passion," observed the chemist.

"Very likely!—but not with a man which he means to crush. I've seen him in a passion too! and I've heard he can swear, pretty tidily!—but when he means to crush a man, he'll be as mild as milk."

"Well," said the chemist, "it may be so; and if it be, I hope the lady is *not* like the Marquis. But, gentlemen," he added, rising, "an observation fell from our friend Cyrus Murray, which reminds me that we have only drunk the health of the bride. He said that 'he hadn't the pleasure of knowing her, but he knew that she had *taste*,' and I agree with him: she *has* taste, and has displayed it conspicuously, in choosing him whose health I am about to propose. We all know Alfred Murray: we all know what he is: we all know him to be amiable and intelligent, and, therefore, I need not dwell upon the qualities of his heart and mind before you. He is married: he has married into a noble family, and a brilliant prospect opens before him. Under such auspices, his career may be glorious!—he may become one of the first men of the age! —Wealth and distinction are now within his grasp, and if compassed by him, I shall heartily rejoice. I therefore give you—Health, happiness, and prosperity, to Alfred Murray!— May his marriage be the source of domestic felicity, and world-wide renown."

This brief speech was hailed with enthusiastic cheers: and when the toast had been drunk, with all the honours, Mr. Murray rose and said, with some emotion, " In the name of my son, I thank you."

" Now look you here," said Mr. Chubb, rising, "I ain't nothing much at a speech, because it's right out of my latitude; but I rise on this occasion to do myself the privilege of proposing the health of the father of the son which we drank his good health just now. Gentlemen: you know what I am; you know my politics, and all about me; and although I'm not going to lug in politics here, I must say that this marriage betwixt the daughter of one which is a lord, and the son of one which is one of ourselves, only proves that a sort of a revolution is about to take place, in which them which are lords, and them which are not lords, will mix together more than they ever did before. Now, gentlemen, look here: they begin to see the madness of things; they begin to see it's no go to fling away their daughters upon them which are old men before they want shaving: they begin to see that rank is not rapture; that titles are but toys; that coronets *are* curses to them which wed them, and that pride is but poverty of *some* sort in disguise: they begin to see that their children won't stand it!—that they won't marry foozles because they are rich, nor idiots because they are lords:—they see this, and say to their daughters, 'Look here—you've got the affections and sentiments of Nature, which is the great card after all: you've got eyes to see, ears to hear, and hearts to feel in the regular way—look about you;—if you meet with a fine young fellow you fancy and feel you'll be happy with, *have* him!—never mind whether he's a lord, or not—have him!'—and this, it's quite clear to my mind, has been the go in this case; and I glory in it!—I like to see them mix!—they've got their sensibilities as well as we have!—and as such, I give you the health of our friend—and may he live to be the grandfather of forty!' "

When the cheering which followed this speech had subsided, Mr. Murray again rose and said, " Gentlemen : I appreciate the compliment you have paid me. I don't know whether our eloquent friend Chubb—who ought, after this, to be one of our members—[*Hear, hear, hear*]—is, or is not, right in his conjecture having reference to the way in which this happy marriage was brought about, because I've not yet received the particulars; but whether he be correct or not—whether the aristocracy, I may say the glorious aristocracy, take the same view of the matter as our clear-headed friend does—I beg most respectfully, and with heart-felt sincerity, to give you the health of the noble Marquis!' "

This was warmly responded to by all but Chubb, who said quietly, " Blow him : I know him!' " And as the waiter at this juncture entered the room to announce that the lunch was all ready in No. 2, they were about to adjourn, when Mr. Chubb rose and said, " Hold hard a bit : look here, gentlemen. Before we go to lunch, we can't do less than drink the health of one which is one of the family—one which is not more respectable than respected—one which we know to be a capital sort—which is one of ourselves, right up and down straight, just and jonnick, and no mistake about him; and, as such, I'll give you the jovial good health of the bridegroom's merry-hearted uncle.'"

In the midst of cheers, which were loud and protracted, notwithstanding lunch was ready in No. 2, uncle Cy slowly rose, and having blown out his cheeks as if to get up the steam, spoke in a rich, deep voice as follows :

"I glory in meeting you on such an occasion, and thank you for the compliment you have paid me. I feel proud of my nephew: and why? Because I know him to be a noble-hearted boy. I am no advocate for unequal matches; nor do I consider this an unequal match. He has had the education of a gentleman—an excellent education; he was at a boarding school for seven years, and his master, Mr. Montague, has frequently told me that he is one of the best classical and mathematical scholars he ever had. He is, moreover, an honourable boy: his moral principles are sound. Handsome, well-formed, highspirited, full of energy, with a happy disposition and a fine constitution, can you wonder that Lady Felicia should fall in love with him? Gods in heaven, if I were a woman I should fall in love with the boy myself! All that can be said against him is, that he was not born a lord; but if a title will weigh against the qualities I have mentioned, a title must be valuable indeed! But it will not!—and therefore I contend that the match is not unequal."

"Certainly not!" they all exclaimed. "Decidedly not! Unequal? No!" and finding, after a pause, that uncle Cy had no intention to proceed, they instinctively rose and repaired to No. 2.

Here they had lunch—oysters *au naturel*, broiled ham, devilled chickens, maccaroni, veal cutlets, rump steaks, collared eels, lobsters, wine, and cold punch—to which they did ample justice; and shortly afterwards, Murray, recollecting the mild suggestion of his amiable and truly happy wife, rose, and having intimated to the jovial party that he should look in again, retired.

On reaching the street, however, he suddenly found himself in the midst of another jovial party, who hailed his appearance with enthusiastic cheers, and hinted, with all the delicacy at their command—which wasn't much—that the health of the happy couple, was the object of their solicitude.

"Well, my good people," said Mr. Murray, "go and drink their health, and wish them joy. Here's a guinea for you: let it be fairly divided."

This inspired the "good people" with additional enthusiasm, during the manifestation of which Murray bowed, and passed on, and having reached home, found the parlour full of Mrs. Murray's female friends, who had flocked in to have the news confirmed, and to offer their warm congratulations.

Heavens! what a grand event it was! Their anticipations were brilliant in the extreme. In *their* gentle judgment, the foundation of the fortune of the whole family was laid. Alfred would be created a baronet, at least! Julia would be at once presented at court, and in all probability marry an earl: and when she became a countess, what might she not do for her sisters!—they might all marry lords!—while Bob—or rather Master Robert—instead of sticking to the shop, would receive some excessively lucrative appointment. They traced the whole family's future career with surpassing ingenuity. Their vivid imagination ran absolutely wild! They had, however, one request to make—one earnest request—which was, that when the lovely bride honoured the family with a visit—which her ladyship would do of course, immediately after the dear delicious honeymoon—they might have the delightful privilege of being presented. They *presumed* that Mr. Murray would now shortly retire: of course he couldn't think of remaining in business!—They *presumed*, that at least the younger girls would be sent to one of the most fashionable seminaries, to be prepared to fill with grace the stations to which they were destined! — they *presumed*, in short, a thousand things, calculated to inspire, not only Mrs. Murray, but the girls—who thought nothing impossible—with the most lofty notions; and left, full of hope that their intimate acquaintance with the family—whose friendship they meant to cultivate more assiduously than ever—might be highly advantageous to themselves.

The bells rang merrily still, and throughout the town nothing but "The Marriage" was thought of. The ladies were especially eloquent on the subject—this, however, need not have been recorded—and had privately heard from the most authentic sources, a conflicting variety of deeply interesting particulars. Some of them knew how the bride was dressed, how lovely she looked, and what diamonds she wore; while others knew how many bridesmaids she had, and how brilliantly *they* were attired; but they all agreed in this; that as Alfred, whom they knew and esteemed—would be sure to distinguish himself; and as Lady Felicia, whom they also knew and admired, was blessed with "the sweetest disposition in the world," their marriage could not fail to be the source of unmingled joy.

And now a fresh rumour arose; a rumour that Mr. Murray was treating everybody—absolutely scrambling his money away—in order that all might rejoice. The guinea which he had given to the enthusiasts outside the Crown was magnified into an indefinite amount; which no sooner reached the ears of a highly distinguished coterie of immaculate freemen—who were at all times prepared to do anything for beer, and who principally lived by the undoubted exercise of their sound constitutional privileges as freemen—than they loyally enlisted a glorious and independent band of musicians of their own peculiar caste in the cause, and proceeded to the house of "The jolly good Trump!—the true-born Briton!—the liberalest fellow in the world!"—for the nonce—Mr. Murray.

As they struck up "Haste to the Wedding" before the door, and shouted "Murray for ever! Joy to the Weddiners! Long may they never want noth'n. Hooray!" Mr. Murray called Simon Kibble—whom he knew to be one of the ringleaders—

in, and expostulated with him on the extreme impropriety of the proceeding—telling him that he had no objection to give them a guinea to enable them to drink his son's health and that of the bride, and explaining to him emphatically that, although he had caused the bells to ring, he by no means approved of such a popular demonstration as *that;* whereupon Simon Kibble, promising to remove the "jolly nuisance," and slipping the guinea into his own personal pocket, returned to the Sons of Harmony, and having told them that " Murray would'nt stand noth'n, and would'nt have em play," they, inspired with indignation, proclaimed him to be " a muck!"   He allus was a muck!—they knew him to be a muck!—he was never noth'n *but* a muck! and, despite Simon's efforts to induce them to leave, they struck up " The Rogue's March" furiously.

" Now really," said Mr. Murray, going out and addressing the trombone, " this *is* not kind.   Having given you a guinea to leave quietly"—

" A guinea!" exclaimed the trombone, " who to?"

" Simon Kibble," replied Mr. Murray.

The signal was given! They saw Simon pelting up the street, and away they went after him, full cry, with the view of tearing him limb from limb.

Shortly after they had started on this benevolent expedition, the local paper—which, although bearing Wednesday's date, was published on the Tuesday—came in, and Mrs. Murray, by whom it had all been arranged, having called the family into the parlour, read the following felicitous announcement:—

" MARRIAGE IN HIGH LIFE.—It is with peculiar gratification that we have to announce the marriage of Alfred Murray, Esq., of London, eldest son of William Murray, Esq., of Sudbury, and godson of the late noble Marquis of Kingsborough, to the beautiful and highly accomplished Lady

Felicia Jocelyn, third daughter of the present Noble Marquis of Kingsborough, by Florence Adeliza Elizabeth, only daughter of Rupert, tenth Earl of Fitzgall."

" The marriage was solemnized on the 27th inst., and soon after the interesting ceremony the happy pair, having had a magnificent *déjeûner*, left town to pass the honeymoon at Brighton."

" There ! " — said Mrs. Murray, triumphantly. — " There, William, what do you think of that !"

" It reads very well," replied Murray. " But why call me an esquire ?"

" Mr. Howe, whom I consulted on the subject, assured me that under the circumstances it was not only correct but indispensable !"

" Well, but what do you say they had—a *déjeûner ?*—What's that ? "

" Breakfast, pa, of course ! replied Julia.

" Then why not say breakfast?"

" Oh! *déjeûner* is more elegant—more fashionable !"

" Oh: that's it, is it? Well! Then in future, I suppose, when I want my breakfast I must say that I want my *déjeûner !*"

Mrs. Murray smiled, and playfully patted his cheek, and then proceeded to make out a list of the friends to whom she intended to send papers, soon after which, Murray—business having no charms for him then—rejoined his jovial companions at the Crown, with whom he spent a long and merry evening ; and when he returned, Mrs. Murray—although too happy to say anything severe—discovered that she had been quite correct in stating that, when the heart was full of joy wine made love to the head.

CHAPTER XII.

REVENGE.

WHEN the Marquis—who as usual received the local paper
in the morning—saw the marriage of Alfred and Felicia thus
paraded, he was furious!—he groaned with rage, and ferociously
swore that he would bring down destruction upon the Murrays.

He consulted no one. Acting solely upon his own judgment
—which was not a very safe guide then—he sent to order post
horses immediately—resolved on counteracting the effect of
the announcement, at least among those whom he held to be
"his own."

The preparations for the journey were but slight—his intention being to return as soon as possible—he did not even take
his valet with him: he started with James and his powerful
groom, and sought congenial amusement on the road by darkly
brooding over the "indelible disgrace," and fiercely invoking
the spirit of revenge.

On his arrival he put up at the Rose and Crown, and
immediately sent for his agent—he being the only man whom
he wished to see—but as the landlord of the Crown—as the
house was then more commonly called—conceived that his
friend Murray might like, under the circumstances, to pay his
respects, he went to him and told him that the Marquis had
arrived.

"Indeed!" exclaimed Murray, whom the announcement
somewhat startled. "I wonder what he's come down for."

"To arrange some business with his agent, I should say: he's
just sent for him."

" He didn't send for me ?"

" No," replied the landlord ; " but you'll go just to pay your respects, of course ?"

" I don't know about that," said Murray, doubtfully. " He might not like it."

"Nonsense, man! These great ones will take all the homage you can pay them. I don't see how you can do less than go!— I wouldn't show a want of respect to him now !"

" No, but that's not the thing! I should be indeed sorry to show any want of respect ; but the question is, wouldn't he consider it presumptuous ?"

" Presumptuous !"

" I mean—the question is—does he want me to call ?—and if so, wouldn't he have sent for me ?"

" *They* never make the first advances : it isn't likely. I should say myself, that you are bound to go! If you don't expect intimate friendship to follow, it *may* promote a good understanding between you !"

" Well, I'll go and speak to Mrs. Murray about it. I'll hear what she says. I should *like* to see him !—but I'll hear what she says."

He then went to consult Mrs. Murray, who, delighted with the prospect of promoting " a good understanding," advised him to go by all means !—and Murray, although he felt nervous, accordingly went.

" Now," said the landlord, on reaching the Crown, " do you remain here, in this room, and I'll go and announce you myself."

" Aye, do. You can say you know "—

" Now, don't at all trouble your head about what I'm to say I'll go in and do it like print."

Having been admitted to the room occupied by the Marquis, the landlord, bowing profoundly, said, " I beg your lordship's pardon ; but, Mr. Murray, having heard of your 'lordship's arrival, is anxious to pay his respects "

A dark frown clouded the brow of the Marquis, when he heard the detested name of Murray announced, but, having re-assumed an air of perfect tranquillity, he said in a calm tone, " admit him."

" Now then," said the landlord, on his return. " All right : come along. All you have to do is to mind your stops. Didn't I *tell* you he'd like it ?—come on."

Murray followed, of course, and, on being introduced, bowed respectfully, as the landlord withdrew.

" Well, Mr. Murray," said the Marquis, with an expression of the most perfect calmness, " you have, of course, heard of your son's marriage ?"

" I have, my lord, and rejoice exceedingly. I hope that he will be all your lordship can wish "

" What property has he ?'

" Property, my lord ? He has no property."

" What have you to give him ?"

" I have a large family, my lord, and what capital I have is locked up in my business."

" Then you can give him nothing ?"

" I must, of course, be just to the rest of my children."

" You mean, that you depend *entirely* upon your business, the profits of which are not more than sufficient to support them."

" I do, my lord."

" Then how does he mean to live ?"

" I really have no knowledge of his views, my lord; but I venture to hope that your lordship's influence will be exerted in his favour."

" I know nothing of him : I have never even seen him."

" Indeed, my lord !"

" Were you not before aware of that fact ?"

"I really had no conception of it. But I hope, my lord, that they did not marry without your lordship's consent?"

"They certainly did not marry with it."

"Dear me! I am sorry to hear that.

"No doubt."

"But I nevertheless hope that your lordship will forgive them."

"She was of age: she felt that she had a right to choose for herself, and has chosen. What's done cannot be undone: —they must do the best they can. I have nothing more to say on the subject."

"Still, my lord," said Murray, as the Marquis rang the bell, "I do most sincerely hope that your lordship, taking into consideration"—

"The fact is," interrupted the Marquis, "I have scarcely had time to think about it. I happen to have some business of importance on hand—business which has brought me down here—and—hasn't Mr. Slane arrived yet?" he inquired, as the servant at this moment opened the door.

"Just come, my lord," replied the servant.

"Then show him in immediately! — Good morning, Mr. Murray."

Well! Murray most certainly wished to say more—much more—with the view of propitiating the Marquis; but as that was entirely out of the question then, he respectfully bowed, and withdrew.

On his return to the bar-parlour he found his friend Chubb, who having heard that he had sought and obtained an interview with the Marquis, was anxious of course to hear how he got on.

"All right?" he inquired.

"Well," replied Murray with a doubtful expression; "I, hope so: I think so: I think it's all right."

"Only *think* so?"

" Well, the fact is, they married without his consent."

" Oh, that's it! I see! Well, was he in a passion?"

" Not at all! On the contrary, he doesn't seem to care much about it. He mentioned the fact, it is true: but then, he said —'What's done can't be undone! They must make the best of it! *I* have nothing more to say on the subject!' "

" Then he was calm?"

" Quite so! He seemed to view it as a matter of no consé-quence at all! I never saw a man *more* calm."

" Blow him, I know him of old," said Chubb. " He¹ *means* something! Mark my words, he *means* something! I know I'm right! I know it! When he means something he's always calm."

" Well, but what can he mean?"

" Here—sit down and have a glass of wine."

" No, I want to be off: Mrs. Murray will be anxious."

" Sit down, I tell you! We shan't be a month over a pint! —Now, look here," he added, having ordered the wine. " In the first place, who's your landlord?"

" Thompson. But I have a lease, of which five years are unexpired!"

" It wouldn't matter if you hadn't: Thompson's all right. Do you do much business up at the Hall?"

" Nothing very considerable! But I don't believe he means anything of *that* sort! Why should he go against *me*? *I* did nothing to promote the marriage! I knew nothing of it until it was over, and therefore if he were ever so angry, he couldn't be angry with me! But I don't believe that he's angry at all! —'The fact is,' said he, 'I have scarcely had time to think about it!' *He's* not angry—not to say angry!—the fact of their having married without his consent may nettle him a little, and very naturally; but that'll soon wear off: I feel convinced of it!"

" Oh; he'd scarcely had time to *think* about it."

" He has some important business on hand—business which

has brought him down here—and that, it seems, has engrossed all his thoughts."

" Yes, it may seem."

" He said as much."

" And thus confessed himself to be an unnatural scoundrel! His daughter has married without his consent—that is to say, she has run away—and he hasn't had time yet to think about it ! Murray, I know him; and if I were under his lash I should fear him."

" But *I* am not under his lash. How can he injure me ? If even I lose the Hall it will be of no *very* great importance. Besides, why should he injure me ? why should he wish to try to do so ? *I* had nothing to do with the marriage. But I don't believe that he has any such object. I feel, in fact, sure that he has not."

" Well," said Mr. Chubb, " we shall see; I hope I may be wrong—of course I hope I may be wrong, but when he means mischief he's always so calm."

"That may be too ; but surely he may be calm without meaning mischief ?"

" He may be—it's possible—he may be—but the fact of the matter is, he's a man which I *don't* like, and that's all about it."

This confession of prejudice Murray held to be sufficient to account for his friend's apprehensions, and when he had taken a second glass of wine he returned to Mrs. Murray, and communicated all.

" Dear me !" she exclaimed, having heard that the marriage had taken place without the consent of the Marquis. " What a pity ! I am very, very sorry to hear it. And yet it proves that she dearly loves him. But," she added, " the girls must know nothing of this ; it must, of course, be concealed from them, for if either of them were to follow the example I should never be happy again. And yet you say he doesn't appear to

care much about it.   Why, I should go out of my senses.
What a lamentable want of feeling these great men must have!
I should like to see Alfred a great man, certainly—it would be
my pride to see him great, but I'd rather he should move in
a less exalted sphere, than see him destitute of feeling.   I
suppose that, having the affairs of state on their minds, great
men cannot feel like other people, and yet I have a perfect
conviction, that as far as Alfred's feelings are concerned, no
affairs of state, however mighty, could destroy them "

Murray was thoughtful; he could not at all understand
what the Marquis had in view when the asked him how Alfred
meant to live!   Of course Lady Felicia had property! of
course she had!   In his judgment there *could* be no doubt
about that!   Perhaps she had not a very brilliant fortune!
Well, that was very likely, and that was doubtless what the
Marquis meant when he said, ".They must do the best they
can."   And yet, even assuming that she had *not* a brilliant
fortune, why should he have inquired how Alfred meant to
live?   Of course they must live within their income whatever
that income might be, and therefore it appeared clear to him,
that the only reply to the question, of *how* they meant to live,
must be, that *that* was how they meant to live!   Still the
question puzzled him; it also puzzled Mrs. Murray; they both
dwelt upon it most anxiously, and endeavoured to fathom the
meaning involved, but in vain.   " How does he mean to live?"
still rang in their ears, and inspired them with apprehension.

Having been with his agent in close consultation for nearly
two hours, the Marquis had some slight refreshment, and
immediately afterwards took his departure.   The important
business on which they had been engaged did not, of course,
transpire, but some idea of its nature may be formed by a
careful perusal of the following address, which, in the shape of
a hand-bill, was, during the evening, freely distributed throughout the town :—

"TO THE INHABITANTS OF SUDBURY.

" The announcement paraded in the paper you patronize, of a certain marriage, between Alfred Murray, Esq., of London, son of William Murray, Esq., of Sudbury, and godson of the late Noble Marquis of Kingsborough, to the beautiful and highly accomplished Lady Felicia Jocelyn, third daughter of the present Noble Marquis of Kingsborough, &c., &c., &c., must, on reflection, create feelings of the most intense disgust!

" It is unhappily true, that the vulgar man Murray—the junior esquire—aided by a French woman, and prompted by the senior esquire—the one esquire being a common shopman, and the other, as you are aware, a draper in this town:—it is, I say, unhappily true, that this profligate has by some foul means succeeded in seducing the inexperienced and unsuspecting Lady Felicia, from the bosom of her noble and affectionate family, from wealth and magnificence, from all the luxuries and elegancies of life, from peace and happiness, innocence and joy, to plunge her into an inextricable abyss of poverty, shame, and despair: all this is *true!*—it is also true that the highly *respectable* journalist, whom you patronize, announces the fact with ' peculiar gratification!'

" But what is the prospect—the ' gratifying' prospect—which opens before this beautiful but most unhappy girl! She has not a shilling—*prize* as the profligate thought he had secured!—nor is he worth a shilling—nor is the respectable senior esquire in a position to support them! What then are they to do? How are they to live? Is it to be expected, that the noble Marquis—after having had his very heart-strings torn—his paternal authority set at defiance, and his ancient and illustrious family disgraced—is it reasonable, I ask, to expect that *he* will support the vile adventurer? No!—and if *not!*—the unhappy lady has but to choose between absolute infamy and utter starvation!

"But the *godson*—forsooth!—of the late noble Marquis! *De mortuis nil nisi bonum;* but can the mother of this godson explain how he became the godson of the Marquis, without a *blush?* Fathers! who have daughters whom you love and would protect, whose virtues are your pride—your household gods!—Mothers! whom truth and *honour* guide!—who have *no* cause to blush!—whose children have *no* noble godfathers!—can you associate with, countenance, or even tolerate, those who are connected with practices so vile? Prove that you are true to the principles of virtue—prove your appreciation of all that is pure!—denounce such wretches by all the means at your command, for they merit your severest condemnation.

"AN OLD INHABITANT."

The effect of this address—delivered in every part of the town simultaneously—was electric! It appeared, *prima facie*, to be the most cruel case of seduction on record. The ladies were peculiarly appalled! Poor Lady Felicia! Poor dear young lady, what must her feelings be? And that shocking French woman! They all knew what French women were!—the unscrupulous, disgusting creatures! The foul means used were drugs, no doubt! And all because they believed her to be a prize! They pitied the *lady*—they did pity *her*—but they were very glad indeed that she hadn't a shilling. The Murray's had been, at all events, in *that* respect foiled, but that was not a single tithe of what they deserved!—nothing could be too bad for *them!*—in short, the prevailing impression was, that the father and son were ogres.

And then that dreadful Mrs. Murray! What a truly shameless woman she must be! And her husband had, no doubt, encouraged her in it. They always thought there was something; and now that they came to recollect, the late Marquis *had* the reputation of being gay? Why should he have stood godfather to a child of *hers?* That was the question: why? They didn't want an answer: they only asked why!—

That was quite enough for them! Good heavens! why this marriage was a species of spiritual incest! And yet that very Mrs. Murray had been held up as a pattern of purity and piety, and went with her family every Sunday to church! It was absolutely awful to contemplate!—They had *never* heard of anything more truly appalling!

Now, when Uncle Cy received one of these startling bills he was walking in his garden, and conceiving that it related to parish affairs—for there *had* been some talk about adding to the rates, for which he thought there was no necessity, and was, indeed, prepared to contend that there must be some sort of mismanagement somewhere!—he was about to return it to his housekeeper, that she might place it on the table to be read another time; but as on glancing at it he perceived the name of " Murray," he read a few words, and then called for a chair.

Before, however, the chair could be brought, he had hurriedly run through the whole; and when the chair came he at once sank upon it as if exhausted, and faintly said, " Bring me some brandy."

" Dear bless me!" exclaimed the housekeeper, as she perceived the big drops of perspiration on his brow. " Why, what on earth is the matter?"

" Some brandy," he repeated, and she rushed into the house.

" Now let me be calm," said he; " let me be calm: this is indeed dreadful—but let me be calm."

" Come," said the housekeeper, on her return, " drink this. —Do you feel any better?"

" I shall, I hope, presently. Leave me. I wish to be alone."

She obeyed him; but with an expression of anxiety, and had no sooner left than he burst into tears.

" All my fond hopes," he exclaimed bitterly, having wept 'for some time like a child, " are thus withered. But," he added, in tones of indignation, "it's false!—every word of it!"

I'll not believe a word!—*no* foul means were used! You *know* all about poor Louisa to be false, and that's a fair sample of the sack. But who is this savage?—This cowardly savage? I'll find him out! *He* shall not escape me!—The villain!"

He rose with the view of calling upon his brother, and as he passed through the passage he met his housekeeper, who was about to speak, when he exclaimed, "Don't believe it!"—

"Don't believe what?" she inquired.

"It's false!—every word of it!—Don't believe a word!" he continued, and left her to wonder.

He had not proceeded far when he saw a fellow flitting about with these bills, and, going up to him, immediately caught him by the throat.

"You scoundrel!" he exclaimed. "Tell me at once who employed you!—Speak the truth, and I'll forgive you: if *not* —I'll transport you, as sure as you're alive! Who gave you those infamous bills?"

The man was alarmed, and spoke somewhat incoherently still it might be gathered that *he* didn't know!—He didn't know noth'n about the bills!—He couldn't even *read* the bills; and, what was more, he didn't want to!—Blow the bills!

"By whom, sir, were you employed?"

He didn't know!—It was *some* gent!—He never seed the gent afore!—He came in the Tap and gave 'em all a crown a-piece to do it, and said he give 'em another crown if he found they did it well!—That's all *he* knew!

"Where did you leave him?"

"In the Tap"

"Which Tap?"

"The Dragon."

"Then come with me."

They accordingly went to the Dragon Tap, but found that the bird had flown.

"He's safe to come back," observed the man; " 'cos in course he's got to give us t'other crown!"

"I fear not," said Uncle Cy. "But do you remain here, and if he *should* come, let the landlord know. *I'll* pay you."

He then spoke to the landlord, and having explained what he wished him to do in the event of this "gent" re-appearing, he proceeded to his brother's, and there beheld a scene of appalling affliction.

The shop was closed, and in the parlour, Mrs. Murray was lying on the sofa, insensible, while the poor girls were shrieking around her.

"Cyrus," said Murray, as he grasped his brother's hand, with an expression of despair, "we are ruined, Cyrus!—for ever ruined!"

"No," exclaimed Cyrus. "No, William! No! We shall find out the cowardly scoundrel yet!"

"Find him! I know him already, too well."

"Who is he?"

"The Marquis."

"The Marquis!—That'll do.—I'll *trounce* him! If he had fifty coronets, I'd trounce him!—But we'll talk about that by and by."

"Are we *not* ruined, Uncle?" cried Julia, weeping bitterly.

"Ruined, my love! No! It's a blow!—It's certainly a *blow!*—but, fear nothing: there is a God in heaven, my love, who'll so manage it that truth will be triumphant. See," he added, as Mrs. Murray gave signs of re-animation, "she revives."

"William," said Mrs. Murray, faintly, having looked round the room, "William—Cyrus—my poor dear children!"

"Louisa," said Cyrus, soothingly. "Why, why is this?"

"Have you not seen that dreadful paper?"

"What, the squib! Why, you're *not* going to be wholly struck down by a squib? *You* live in Sudbury, and allow a squib to alarm you! Pooh, pooh—Gods in heaven! havn't we seen squibs enough to despise them! Havn't we, in times of excitement, known the very best amongst us charged with every possible crime, from kidnapping to murder? And it's not only here, but everywhere else. In the city of London—the very centre of civilization—I've seen on the walls, as large as life, 'WOTE FOR WENABLES THE ASSASSIN!'—and when I came to look closely at it, I found added, in the smallest of all small letters, the words—'of the King's English.' There are small letters in this!—but we'll have those small letters made larger!—well have them made so that people *shall* see them, and understand the drift of the whole "

" But, look at this," said Mrs. Murray, pointing tremulously to the last paragraph. "Look at *this!* "

" Well, I see! But don't we know it's all wrong!—don't we know it's all false! There, go to bed—go to bed—and sleep it all away. I'll send for the doctor presently, and then you'll think you really *have* something to fret about! Go to bed: go to bed: good night: God bless you!—but," he added, with an effort to conceal his emotion, " Louisa, *don't* be a fool!"

Assisted by her weeping daughters, Mrs. Murray, whose feelings were those of deep anguish, retired; but, as she again fainted on reaching her chamber, the family doctor was sent for at once.

" I feared this," said Cyrus, " I feared that the shock would be too great for *her;* but, let us hope—let us hope for the best. William," he added, with an expression of solemnity, " this is a rough look out: I have treated it lightly before them; but it really is a serious affair. Now, you say that you *know* the Marquis to be the villain. In the first place, how do you know that?"

Murray explained to him all that had occurred during his interview with the Marquis, and added, " therefore there can be no doubt."

" No," returned Cyrus, " there can be no doubt; but, unfortunately, all this affords no proof — I mean, of course, no legal proof—of his connection with these infamous bills. We cannot prove that he is the author: we cannot prove that he ordered them to be printed; nor do we know where or by whom they were printed, no printer's name being attached. We are, therefore, in a position to prove legally nothing; but we can, and will, make it quite clear that the Marquis is the man."

"But," said Murray, "if even we could prove it legally, we are not able to go to law with him."

"Are we not?" returned Cyrus, significantly—"Are we not? My boy, you don't know all. Place me in a position to prove that he ordered these bills to be printed, or had even the slightest connection with them, and we'll see what we're able to do!—we'll see! We shall not have to stand still for money. But pen and ink!" he added, "come, let's go to work!—No time shall be lost!—We'll do it right off!—We'll let him know, at least, what we mean!"

Having had the desk placed before him, he commenced, with a triumphant flourish of the pen; and as Murray shortly afterwards left him to accompany the doctor up stairs, he proceeded without interruption.

He was not a ready writer in general; but on this particular occasion he wrote away as if he felt inspired: indeed, the rapidity with which the pen travelled, amazed him; he had never written half so fast before.

"Well," said he, when Murray, having been for some considerable time absent, returned—"I'm getting on; I'm getting on!—But how is poor Louisa?"

"Very faint," replied Murray, "and very much distressed. The doctor says that she must be kept quite quiet. He's going to send her something which he hopes will soothe her."

" Well, I hope it will—I hope it will. And now let me go on with this—I've nearly finished—don't interrupt." '   '   "

At this moment Mr. Chubb was announced.

" Shall we have him in ?" inquired Murray.

" By all means—yes :" replied Cyrus; " only talk to yourselves "

Mr. Chubb was shown into the room, and grasping Murray's hand, said, "Never mind this ; never *mind* it, old fellow ! But was'nt I right ? Why, I knew I was right ! I knew it !—I knew he meant something, although I didn't think that he'd go and attack a woman in such a cruel, cold-blooded manner as this. If he'd let Mrs. Murray alone, I shouldn't have thought so much about it—all the rest might have been winked at, and treated with contempt ; but the idea of cutting against her, and that in such a vicious style of virtuous' indignation, is rotten ! He talks about fathers' 'household gods,' as if we didn't know him ! I wonder how many of these 'household gods' *he's* smashed the prospects of ! Look at Mary Ann Jones, which is now in the workhouse ! Look at Lydia Johnson, whose heart he broke ! Look at the girl Cole, which, although so mild and gentle once, has become, through him, a tigress. And yet he talks about honour and virtue ! But what do you mean to do ?—how do you mean to work him ?"

" Stop a bit," said Cyrus; " *I'll* show you presently."

" I'm afraid," observed Murray, " of getting into a law-suit with *him !*"

" Don't you be a mite afraid about that," returned Chubb, "he can't stand the racket; for a Marquis, I know he's as poor as a mouse. I know it !—and so does your brother. Everything's dipped that can be dipped, and dipped pretty tidily deep."

" Now, then," said Cyrus, having thrown down his pen, " this is what we mean to do, to begin with; I'll read it. Now, then :—

"ONE HUNDRED POUNDS REWARD!

"Whereas, some evil-minded, cowardly wretch, signing himself 'An Old Inhabitant,' has caused to be printed and distributed, certain handbills, reflecting upon the character of my family: Notice is hereby given, that the above reward of one hundred pounds will be paid to any person who will give such information as may lead to the conviction of the author or even the printer thereof!

"Signed,

"WILLIAM MURRAY."

"Well," said Mr. Chubb. "Well! that'll do, as far as it goes; but why not go into the matter more at large?"

"I have done so here," replied Cyrus, who then read as follows:

"TO THE INHABITANTS OF SUDBURY.

"An infamous handbill, designed by one who styles himself 'An Old Inhabitant,' has been issued with the view of denouncing the family of Mr. William Murray of this town.

"It appears that Mr. Alfred Murray has been guilty of the crime of marrying the object of his affections—the beautiful and amiable Lady Felicia Jocelyn—without the consent of the Marquis of Kingsborough. This is, 'the very head and front of his offending.' Loving her with all the ardour of a pure and noble heart, he married her without the consent of him whose consent he well knew—not being a *lord*—it would be useless for him to solicit; and for this crime—for a crime it appears to be considered—not only is *he* denounced by this 'Old Inhabitant,' but his mother—as virtuous and as amiable a woman as ever breathed—is assailed with the vilest and most cowardly insinuations.

"'Can the mother of this godson,' inquires this 'Old Inhabitant,' 'explain how he became the godson of the Marquis without a blush ?' I answer, yes! and will briefly explain for her. Many of my fellow townsmen remember the contest between Lord Charles Jocelyn and Captain Coleraine, when Lord Charles gained the election by one vote only. That vote was given by Mr. William Murray, and the late Marquis promised to stand godfather to his next child. Mrs. Murray had never spoken to the Marquis before; but he, in due time, performed his promise, and for this, it appears, she is expected to blush!

" But who is this ' Old Inhabitant ?' The statement of a few simple facts will enable you at all events to *guess!*

" The Marquis yesterday came down post-haste: he arrived at the Rose and Crown at two o'clock, and immediately sent for his agent, Mr. Slane: at a quarter past two Mr. William Murray had a private interview with him: at half past two Mr. Slane arrived, and remained with him, in close consultation, for nearly two hours: at half past four the Marquis left the town, and at seven o'clock these infamous bills were issued!

" Who then is this ' Old Inhabitant ?' Can there be a doubt about who he is ? No ! there can be no *moral* doubt on the subject; but we want the *legal* proof!—the legal proof is all that we require, and whoever will give such information as may enable us to get at that legal proof, shall receive from me one hundred pounds, in addition to the reward which has been offered by my brother.

" I sign my name—which the pitiful coward dared not do and am,

" Fellow Townsmen,

" CYRUS MURRAY.

Bravo!" exclaimed Mr. Chubb, "That'll do. That'll show him what you really mean! It'll also show, that if the boy himself hasn't a shilling, he's got them connected with him, which has. But I don't *believe* she has got no property! I know the old Marquis was very fond of her, and I don't think he'd leave her destitute, because he *could*, you know, leave her a little. We can, however, get at his will, and see."

"I don't care," said Cyrus, "so much about that. If she *hasn't* a shilling, that will not afflict me. If she be what I believe she is, he'll rise in spite of their teeth. Marry a girl above you, and she'll pull you up; marry a girl below you, and she'll drag you down—she'll bring you at least to her own level somehow. I have no fear of him."

"Nor have I," said Chubb. "But when do you mean to have these bills printed?"

"As soon as possible. I'll give these papers to Jackson to-night; he'll be at the Crown; if not I can send for him, so that he can have them printed early in the morning."

"Well," said Murray, "I must leave it all to you."

"Do so, my boy. We'll stick to you."

"That we will," interposed Chubb, "to the last. But come, let us be off."

"Stop a moment," said Cyrus, "we'll just hear how Mrs. Murray is before we go;" and Murray went up with the view of ascertaining, and when he had announced that she was much more calm, the friends took their leave for the night.

For some time after they had left Murray sat alone, wondering what Cyrus meant, by saying that he did'nt know all. He had never imagined that Cyrus was a rich man; he knew, of course, that he had *some* property; but the way in which he had acted in this affair, coupled with what his friend Chubb had said, convinced him that Cyrus in saying, that he did'nt know all was quite right. This, however, although highly gratifying, did not engross his thoughts long; they soon reverted to the position in which he then stood. What had he done to deserve censure? No charge had ever been brought against him before, and this was of course unmerited. He had been just to all—honourable in his dealings—steady, industrious, quiet and respectable through life—and yet he and his family were now the objects of persecution, and might be thenceforward despised by those who had theretofore esteemed them. This he thought cruel, and dwelt upon it mournfully, until it was announced that Mrs. Murray had expressed a wish to see him, when, following the example of Cyrus, he made an effort to look comparatively cheerful.

As he entered the chamber as noiselessly as possible, Mrs. Murray, who was sitting up supported by pillows, extended her hand, and with a tranquil expression, intimated a wish for him to sit on the bed beside her.

" William," she said calmly, yet faintly, " I may never recover from this cruel blow."

" My love," said Murray soothingly, "you must not talk thus ; although severe, we must not allow it to crush us. You feel faint and ill, of course, now ; but you'll very soon revive."

" I fear not, love ; but hear me : I have been indirectly accused of a crime"—

" What of that ? Do we not know the accusation to be false ?"

" *I* do, William. That I have ever been faithful"—

" Why, why is this ? "

" Still hear me. If my heart *should* break, I shall die in the sweet consciousness of innocence, and when we meet in heaven, William, you will hear the pure angels proclaim "

" Louisa, do not wound my feelings. I have no more doubt of your truth than I have of the purity of those angels. Let this consciousness of innocence sustain you : let it inspire you with fortitude."

" William ! " she exclaimed, as she fondly embraced him : " I already feel relieved. Accusations, my love, are the germs of doubt "—

" Not when they are known to be false !—Louisa, I never had

a doubt of your purity. But let us say no more on that subject. I have much to tell you—much that will relieve you. Listen, my love. I do not say that all your apprehensions will vanish at once: but listen, and they will be, at least, subdued."

He then calmly proceeded to explain to her the substance of all that had passed below, and having placed every point in the most favourable light, succeeded in rendering her comparatively happy.

CHAPTER XIII.

A POPULAR DEMONSTRATION.

WHEN the bills composed by Cyrus had been distributed a
fresh outcry was raised against Murray—an outcry proceeding
from the purely independent and peculiarly immaculate freemen, who had from time immemorial considered their votes
private property, of which it was their duty, as well as their
"eternal principle" and "sound constitutional privilege," to
make all they could.

Here was a man—if a man he could be called—who had
pretended to despise that fine old English practice of buying
up and paying for independent votes, which, by virtue of a legal
fiction, had been pronounced bribery—who had done all he
could to discountenance that practice, to bring it into contempt, and thus to take the very bread out of their mouths—
publicly proclaiming that he had voted for Lord Charles· in
consideration of the late Marquis standing godfather to his
son! Could anything in their judgment be more disgusting!
To do that in secret which it was their practice and their pride
to do openly, and for which he had so frequently denounced
them, appeared to them to be monstrous in the extreme·
Nothing could surpass it in turpitude : nothing was too bad
for such a man : he ought to have his house pulled about his
ears, the hypocrite !

They thus viewed it as a personal affair between him and
themselves ; and, knowing them too well not to know that the
explanation on this point would incense them, the agent to
whom the cause of the Marquis had been entrusted sent round

to the various public-houses certain confidential satellites, with a view of feeling the pulse of the indignant party, and getting up a popular demonstration of disgust.

The achievement of this object, however, was known to be impossible until that party had been well filled with beer · they were, therefore, well supplied by those "jolly good fellows" who never "dropped in" without treating them, because they "dropped in" only when they wanted something done; and who "calculated" that towards the evening their jovial friends would be pretty well primed.

But this was not the only party whose indignation the efforts of Cyrus increased. The ladies connected with that interesting borough deeply felt that, as far as the marriage was concerned, the matter had been made worse by that which appeared to them to be a defence of Alfred's conduct. Cyrus Murray didn't deny that foul means had been used; he didn't deny that the sole object was wealth; nor did he deny that Alfred had been infamously assisted by that odious French woman—the wretch! They therefore felt justified in assuming that these accusations, at least, were true; and as to that which had reference to Mrs. Murray's character, it was quite clear to them that there must be something in it!

It was all very well for her to get Cyrus Murray to *say* that it was solely in consequence of her husband having voted for Lord Charles: but how were they to know that it was solely in consequence of that? It was all very natural for her to make an *attempt* to get over it; but was there anything to prove that she had not been guilty of the conduct ascribed to her? No! They therefore couldn't think of associating with her, or with any one who even appeared to countenance such truly disgraceful doings.

Besides, Cyrus Murray seemed to think that the fact of a young lady marrying without the consent of her parents was nothing of any consequence!—nay, he absolutely appeared to

them to *justify* the frightful example !   Were they to have the
anxiety of bringing up their daughters—were they to have
them educated with the utmost care—were they to have them
taught music, dancing, drawing, and the rest of it, and dress them
like the daughters of the aristocracy—for no other purpose
than to see them, when they became sufficiently accomplished
to move in a higher sphere, throw themselves away upon
persons beneath them ?   The idea was dreadful !—and all who
attempted to justify the dangerous example which Cyrus
Murray had attempted to justify, ought to be not only avoided,
but denounced.   They would not have *their* girls associate
with such creatures for worlds !—and the girls were accordingly
enjoined to shun the Murrays with as much care as if they had
been lepers.

Meanwhile, Cyrus and his friend were anxiously endeavouring to glean the opinions of those with whom *they* had been in
the habit of associating ; and although Cyrus picked up nothing
but praise for the bold and manly spirit he had displayed, his
friend Chubb, before whom they were not quite so anxious to
conceal their real feelings, discovered that, in their view, the
Murrays were " no better than they should be."

Even the chemist, who had been so eloquent in Alfred's
favour, had had his opinion changed by the ladies.

"You can't, after all," said he to Chubb, who undertook
to defend the whole proceeding, " You can't, after all, much
wonder at the Marquis being angry."

"Certainly not," returned Chubb.   "And as I can't, I
don't.   I don't wonder at all at the Marquis being angry."

"Then why do you assail him ?"

" Because he has assailed a virtuous woman, the coward !
I don't assail him because he is angry! I should, doubtless,
under similar circumstances, be angry myself.   But, does it
follow that because he is angry, he should thus endeavour to
crush the spirit, to break the heart, and to blast the reputation

of an innocent woman? Had he attacked Alfred *alone*, I should have thought nothing of it: he might even have called the young dog a villain, and I should'nt have been at all amazed; but the fact of his having spit his venom upon the fair reputation of an unprotected woman—for a woman upon this point is always unprotected: neither the shield of virtue, nor the breast-plate of prudence, can protect her from *this* vile species of cowardly scoundrelism!—the very fact, I say, of his having thus endeavoured to deprive a virtuous woman of that which she holds dearer than life, proves him to be at heart a ruffian!"

"Well," said the chemist, "on that point he may have gone a little too far."

"A *little* too far!"

"Well, we'll say he might have left Mrs. Murray out of the question; but that which the women complain of most, is the fact of Cyrus having attempted to *justify* clandestine marriages!"

"Well, the women will talk: poor things, they must talk: it's their privilege to talk: and if it was'nt, they'd talk. But Cyrus does nothing of the kind!—he merely states the fact of its being a run-away match."

"Which they hold to be a very bad example."

"Of course! and I agree with them—it is a bad example an example which certainly ought not to be followed; for I believe that, in nineteen cases out of twenty, such marriages are the source of unhappiness: it therefore is a bad example; especially to set girls, who thus frequently become the victims of unprincipled men. But what would they say if one of their *sons* were to marry a lady of title clandestinely? Would any one of them, being the mother of that son, have any particular objection to that? I think not. I may be wrong; but it strikes me that she would'nt say a great deal against it. Why, then, should they be so inveterate against Alfred? Is there one of their sons who, if he'd had the chance, would not have done what Alfred has done? If there be, I would'nt give twopence for his spirit. But thus it is. If the son of our parson, or of any other parson, were to run away with the daughter of an earl, the reverend gentleman would endure it with due humility; but if his daughter were to follow suit with his miller, his humility and the miller would'nt mix. And it seems to be natural. Ambition is the universal prompter. It enjoins us to rise in the social scale:—rise!—rise!—keep continually rising! and we obey the injunction: we keep on struggling to get up—up—up! toiling and panting to rise one above another!—climbing—climbing—climbing still!— until Death just beckons us down into the grave, and then we're all level again."

" Certainly," said the chemist, " ambition is our prompter. But is it not well that we are ambitious? should we have made the progress in the arts and sciences we have made, if we had *not* been ambitious? Are not all our wonderful discoveries—those in chemistry, for example—ascribable to the struggles of ambitious men?"

" Then why denounce Alfred for being ambitious?"

" *I* don't denounce him! his ambition, no doubt, is to be great, and notwithstanding the opposing influence of the Marquis, he *may* achieve greatness. *I* don't denounce him!— I merely alluded to the impressions of the women!"

" Well, the women, God bless them, must have their own way; they wouldn't be happy if they hadn't. What they say is orthodox—they believe it's heterodox, of course, to contradict them; they are right in the long run—sometimes. But isn't there a little spice of *envy* at the bottom of all this?"

" If the prospect portrayed by the Marquis be correct, there isn't much in it to envy!"

" True: but that prospect—in which we see his fond paternal *hopes!*—has yet to be realized. We shall see all about this ' infamy' on the one hand, and ' absolute starvation' on the other: we shall see how calmly they'll steer between them! If they *haven't* a shilling they'll not be lost. We shall see!—we shall see."

" Well," said the chemist, " I *hope* he'll get on!"

" Hope seldom paints desperate doubts," returned Chubb, who, conceiving this to be sufficiently severe, left him to call upon Murray, whom he found sitting in a thoughtful mood with Cyrus.

" Well, "said he, as he entered, " how are you by this time ?"

Murray shook his head.

" What now ?" inquired Chubb.

" It will ruin me," said Murray. " I know it will ruin me!"

" Is that what you've made up your mind to ?"

" I see it!"

" Of course! Its wonderful how quickly a man can see ruin! If it were the brightest luminary in the universe he could'nt see it with greater facility. No sooner does anything happen to a man than up rises ruin to stare him in the face."

" I haven't had a soul in the shop to-day!"

" What of that? Are you going to be ruined in a day ? You *must* have the rickets to be ruined all at once! I didn't expect that you'd do much to-day! People haven't yet made up their minds as to whether they ought to come or not."

" I tell him so," said Cyrus. " It will be all right again by and by."

" Why, of course! Suppose they don't come for a week ? You can bear the sight of ruin for one week—*can't* you ? I know men who have seen it every day for the last thirty years: they have looked at it through a glass which has the peculiar property of making it appear nearer the farther it's off: they look at it still with astronomical regularity, and will continue to look at it as if they had a relish for the sight, until—whether it be far or near—the sight can no longer affect them. It's not a bad sign for a man to see ruin: it proves, at least, that he's on the look out."

"Well," said Murray, "it won't do to go on so long: I can't stand it long, that's quite clear."

"Nor will you be called upon to stand it long. People are very soon tired of wondering; they seldom wonder more than four or five days together; and when they cease to wonder, things go on as usual. But how is Mrs. Murray?"

"Calm," replied Murray—"comparatively calm, but she feels it more acutely than ever."

"Indeed! Why how is that?"

"Not a friend has been near her!—not one of them has either called, or even sent, to inquire how she is!"

"Then let them keep away! You are just as well without such friends, as with them."

"*I* don't want them!—only you see, the fact of their keeping aloof proves to her, that they believe the imputation cast upon her to be true."

"That's the mischief of it. I shouldn't have cared for anything but that. Had he left her alone—the unfeeling scoundrel!—all the rest might have been winked at; but he knew what effect it would have upon her, and therefore the coward couldn't spare it. This, however, must be met with fortitude: her grief must give place to indignation. I know what it is when a woman's attacked—I know well what it is!—but she mustn't be struck down, because, if she is, her 'friends' will ascribe it to conscious guilt. But it'll come home to him—mark my words: it *shall* come home to him, in one way, at least! I know what I know, and you'll see what I'll do! I *can* do a little, and all I can do I will! But come," he added, having delivered these words with a mysterious expression, which Cyrus, however, appeared to understand, "it's of no use to sit moping here! Come to my house, and we'll have a glass of wine."

"I'd rather not," said Murray. "Indeed, you must excuse me."

"Why excuse you?"

"Because," replied Murray, "if I go out, Mrs. Murray will know there's nothing doing, and that will distress her still more."

"Very good! Then we'll stop and have a glass of wine here. Keep up your spirits, my boy! Make up your mind to it! Don't be struck down. We'll let the noble Marquis into a secret before we've done with him!"

Here Mr. Chubb winked mysteriously at Cyrus, and Cyrus winked mysteriously at him, while Murray—who didn't wink at all, for he really saw nothing to wink at—thoughtfully got out the wine.

As evening approached, the indignant freemen—having been well supplied with beer—had become nearly ripe for action; and knowing from experience that a glass or two of rum upon the beer would be likely to have the desired effect, the sub-agents had arranged, that at eight o'clock their tools should assemble at one public house, ostensibly in order to drink the health of the Marquis.

Accordingly at the time appointed they met, and as there was no room large enough in the house, they adjourned to the yard, where they found one of their own bands of music, and of course a fair sprinkling of women and children; and when silence had been obtained by those who could make the most noise, one of their "friends" mounted a table and said:—

"Gentlemen! I rise to propose to you the health of the Marquis; for, although he is a Marquis, a better-hearted fellow never breathed—[cheers]. Gentlemen, I think that on an occasion like this, when we find that his heart has been almost broken, in consequence of his having lost, not by the hand of death, but by the hand of a profligate, one of his beautiful daughters; when we find that his feelings have been wounded,.

his high spirit crushed, and his authority as a father basely trampled upon; I say that when we find all this, gentlemen, we ought not to let the occasion pass without showing that we can feel for him as fathers and as men, and take up his cause like true-born Britons—[*loud cheers.*] Gentlemen, his beautiful child has been stolen!—Stolen " he continued, amid the groans of the freemen, and the shrieks of their wives—" stolen from the bosom of her family and her once happy home, to become an outcast of society for ever—[*vehement groans*]. Gentlemen, I will not harrow up your feelings by describing the misery to which an outcast of society is exposed, because that would touch a heart of stone; nor will I name him by whom she has been stolen, because that might excite your indignation to somewhat too high a pitch; I'll simply propose to you the health of the Marquis, and to show that we mean it we'll drink it in rum!"

Enthusiastic cheers at once followed this announcement. The idea of rum inspired them with rapture, and when after an interesting scramble the rum had been distributed, while the band played "Drops of Brandy," Joe Braywell, one of their spokesmen, rose and delivered the following speech indignantly :—

" Brother freemem! We have just drunk the health of the Marquis, and I'll add, may he have his revenge!—[*Bravo! So he ought to !*] Brother freemen, we know what it is to have children. We've some on us got too many perhaps, but we don't like to have 'em *stole !*—[*Loud groans.*] Now, this poor young lady *has* been stole! — stole from her friends, and her happy home—and who's the villain ?—who's the thief? Why one the late Marquis stood godfather to, and who, to show his gratitude, stole away his grandchild !—[*Yells, hisses, and groans.*] But why did the Marquis stand godfather to him ? That's the point!—Why ? Brother freemen, I'll tell you. There's a man in this town named Murray [*Down with*

him!] which has allus pretended that them which sold their
votes didn't ought!—[*Renewed groans.*] Why, what's the
good, I ask, of being freemen, if we haven't the privileges of
freemen?—and what's the good of having the privileges of
freemen if we don't use those privileges like freemen, and make
the most out of 'em we can? I say, every freeman's vote is
his property, as much his property as the bed he lies
on, and he which gives his property away is a rogue and
a fool.—[*So he is!*] Well, now it comes out, that this man
Murray, who's been saying all he could to deprive us of our
property—or, what's the same thing, to make it worth nothing
to us —[*Down with him.*]—now it comes out that this very
man sold his vote for this godsonship to the Marquis, and for
this very son, which has stole away she which is now to be
an outcast for ever!—[*Shame! Shame!*] Can anything be too
bad for such a man? Don't he ought to be scouted from the
Borough? Isn't he a rank disgrace to us?—and don't we
ought to let him know it?—[*We will! We will!*] I mean to
say he's a black sheep among us: a snake in the grass—a
viper in the bosom—a wolf in sheep's clothing—a monstrous
muck! and, as such, I propose three cheers for the Marquis—
whose cause is our cause—and three glorious groans for the
Murrays!"

When the groans had been given for the Marquis—for they
were all so impatient to groan, that they couldn't wait—and
then, by particular desire, transferred to the Murrays, it was
proposed that, in order to prove that the cause of the Marquis
was really their own, they should march round the town with
their band. This was agreed to unanimously: the procession
was formed, and they started with shouts of "The Marquis for
ever!"—"No child stealing!"—"Down with the kidnappers!"
—and so on; when the agents, conceiving that they had done
their duty, left them as usual to themselves.

They had, however, no sooner started, than old Sam Craybrook, one of their elect—having a brilliant eye to business, and believing that there would be, at least, " a crown hanging to it,"— conceived the idea of warning the Murrays of their approach, and accordingly ran round to the house on the instant.

" Mr. Murray," he cried, rushing into the shop. " Shut up, sir ! Shut up, if you vally your life !"

" What's the matter ?" cried Murray, darting out of the parlour, quickly followed by Cyrus and Chubb. " What's the matter ?"

" A mob's coming round, sir !—a drunken mob ! They'll pull the house down sir !—they'll smash all your windows at the lessest !"

" What for ?"

" They've been drinking the Marquis in rum !"

" Gods in heaven !" cried Cyrus.

" Where are they, Sam ?" inquired Chubb. " Where are they ?"

" They'll be round here directly ; I thought it my duty to come and tell you."

" You're a good fellow, Sam ; you shall not go unrewarded ; leave this to me," he added, turning to Murray, who stood pale and trembling. " Shut up, but leave it to me ; I'll manage it. Come along, Sam, I want you."

" But I marnt be seen in it," cried Sam. " They marnt know I told you."

" Nor need they," said Chubb, " come along. Now," he added, having got Sam out of the shop, " you go round to the band—don't say that I am in favour of the Murrays—but tell them that if they'll play up to the Dragon, I'll stand half a barrel of beer."

" All right," said Sam, " that's an-out-and-out move." And away he started and met the band, and when he had communicated the pleasing intelligence, they struck up of course with additional vigour and marched to the Dragon direct.

Here Mr. Chubb met them, and was instantly hailed with enthusiastic shouts of "Chubb for ever!" during which he gleaned from Sam a slight idea of what had previously occurred, and then went in to order the beer.

But how was it that *Chubb* was so liberal? They never before thought that he was *half* such a jolly good fellow. What was the meaning of it? They could'nt tell, nor did they much want to know: they wanted the beer, of which they felt more than ever in need, for they were really very warm and very thirsty.

"Now then," said Mr. Chubb, on his return to the yard, "I've got a double health to propose to you!—[*Bravo!*] It isn't often we have a mug of ale together; but as you all seem so happy, I don't see why, as a brother freeman, I shouldn't be happy with you.—[*Loud cheers.*] But this *is* about the happiest town in England! Go where you will about it, the people look happy! And so they ought, for although I say it, the freemen of Sudbury are about the best and jolliest fellows alive!—[*Enthusiastic cheers.*] The bells were ringing the other day—we were so happy! But that was for a wedding—[*Hisses*]—and a rare noise there's been made about it. Now, I know the whole particulars! I've got to the bottom of it all! We are not exactly *fools*, you know, brother freemen!—[*Cries of—No! not exactly.*] We are not to be led by the nose, you know! We can find out things and form our own opinions; and, having found this out, I will say —what you'll all say when you hear it—that the young man is not to be blamed.—[*Well, but didn't he steal the young lady?*] Steal her! I'll tell you how he stole her. They loved each other; they made up their minds to have each other; and as they couldn't get the consent of the Marquis, they met one morning and married without it.—[*Was that all?*] That's the sum and substance of the matter; and how many of us, brother freemen, when we were young dogs—how many of us are there who wouldn't have done the same ? I speak to you, you know, as men of the world—as men of sound, sterling, common sense—and as men who are not to be gulled by a sham tale of woe. All this hubbub has been made because she didn't marry a lord, as if lords, brother freemen, were better than ourselves,—[*cheers and laughter*]. And as to her being an outcast of society, reduced to starvation, and the rest of it, it's all perfect rubbish. *You'll* see them when they come down : *you'll* have a frolic then—[*cheers*]. *He'll* give you all a glorious jollification—[*vehement cheers*]. Instead of a profligate, as he's been called, you'll find him, and no mistake, a prince — [*enthusiastic applause*]. He's one of us, brother freemen, and as he rises we shall feel the benefit of it. He's worth fifty lords—I say fifty of them—because he's a regular trump—[*loud cheers*]. And then as to his father, there's so much talk about ; he knew nothing of the matter before it was over.—[*But he did sell his vote for the godsonship.*] —What of that ? Don't we all sell our votes ? Don't we consider it our privilege to do so ? What's the use of having votes ? What's the use of being freemen ? [*But hasn't he allus cut against us?*] No ! Whoever tells you that, tells you that which is false. *He* cut against you ? cut against his brother freemen he so highly respects ? It is'nt likely ! I speak to you, you know, as sound rational men—as men who *won't* be led away by a parcel of tales, although they *do* appear in the shape of a handbill. All in that handbill is nothing but nonsense—sheer, spiteful, miserable nonsense—and more especially that which speaks of their poverty. *They* in poverty ! Wait till they come down ; you'll see them then ; you'll see the style they'll live in, and as I know you'll like him, while your wives will like her. I'll give you, brother freemen, the ' Health of the happy couple !' "

The toast was hailed with enthusiastic cheers, and drunk with infinite alacrity. There were no cries heard against

"child stealing" then—the "kidnappers" had been completely
metamorphosed—he had taken the exact length of their ears,
and had filled them to their entire satisfaction. But he didn't
leave them! No: he sent Sam to let Murray know that all
was right, and remained to "enjoy their society." And
interesting society it was—of the sort: but that which interested
Mr. Chubb most, towards the latter part of the evening, when
the majority of them had left with their wives, was the phrensied
eye—he had but one—of a man of genius, whom he knew—
one Mr. Bob Bradley, a celebrated weaver, who had been
honoured with the sobriquet of the Lushingtonian Poet, and
whose pride it was to "compose a song" upon every subject of
local importance. Mr. Chubb, having watched him for some
considerable time, at length approached him—respectfully
of course!—and said to him, "Bob, what are you up to?"

"Only stringing a few lines together," replied the poet, who
was, even then, rather "far gone."

"What about, Bob?" inquired Mr. Chubb.

The poet, with all that innate modesty which is said to be
inseparable from genius, quietly handed the paper to Mr.
Chubb, who read the following refined freak of fancy :—

THE HAND-BILL BATTLE.

Have you heard of the hand-bill battle,
  'Twixt one with a thirty stone carcass
And him which drives his slaves like cattle,
  The regular lath of a Marquis ?

This Marquis, he had a fair daughter
  Which wasn't too young for to marry;,
And which the son of a draper sought her,,
  And she didn't much want to tarry.   ·

Says she, " I can go to a levee,
  And pick from the friends of the Marquis ;
But, oh! I do *love* that 'ere nevy
  Of him with the thirty stone carcass."'

So he rose and went to her running,
　　And as his love wasn't a *tame* thing,
Says he, "My life! I love you stunning!
　　I wish now you'd just say the same thing."

"Well," says she, "then, if that's the caper,
　　And you'll promise to make me right happy,
I'll rather have you, my illustrious draper,
　　Than be tied to a titled sappy."

Then they went off to church together,
　　Flying rage, and prepared to defy it.
And the knot was tied, round hearts light as a feather—
　　May they never once wish to untie it!

When the Marquis heard of the business
　　He flew into a furious passion,
Which brought on a sort of a dizziness,
　　Cause the match wasn't after his fashion.

So down he came post-haste, like lightning,
　　And issued a handbill severe enough,
And gave all the Murrays a tight'ning,
　　Which the thirty stone man saw through clear enough.

"Then," said he with the four or five fat chins,
　　"If that's what you mean, I'll just show you,
I'll—

　　　　　　　　—blow you!"

"Well," said Mr. Chubb, "but you haven't yet finished it."

"Oh, dear me, no," returned the poet, "I have a number of verses to add. Would you like to have it, when finished? Stand a quartern of rum, and it's yours."

Well! Mr. Chubb had no *objection* to become a patron of literature! He purchased the copyright for a quartern of rum—full half a quartern more than it was worth, it is true!—but he wanted to show it to Cyrus.

When, however, the copyright was sold, and the quartern of rum had been drunk, the poet couldn't possibly do any more to it! Instead of being mounted on his Pegasus, he found that he was on "a dead horse," and shortly afterwards performed the celebrated feat of "dropping into the arms of Morpheus."

Under these untoward circumstances, Mr. Chubb—viewing the matter in a philosophic light—took the manuscript as it was; and having no desire to prolong his stay—all danger then being at an end—he bade those with whom he had been conversing, good night, and left the house with a "glorious" reputation indeed!

CHAPTER XIV.

THE HONEYMOON.

UNCONSCIOUS of the course pursued by the Marquis, Alfred and his beautiful bride were entranced! Rapture the most thrilling, joy the most intense, happiness the most pure and perfect, were theirs! To them nature never before looked so lovely. They felt as if they had for ever escaped from a world of envy and ambition: for whom could they envy then?—of what could they then be ambitious—having attained the very apex of delight? Their world was within themselves — a paradise!—they held the artificial "world" they had left to be a chaos of folly and pride, and hoped for nothing more on earth than to live together thus in simplicity and peace.

Whether, fondly locked in each other's arms, gazing from the window calmly on the sea, or walking on the Downs like children, hand in hand, occasionally stopping to look into each other's eyes, which drank fresh draughts of bliss while contemplating perfection—for while Felicia was, in his view, perfection, he was perfection in hers—every hour teemed with sweet sensations which endeared them to each other more and more, and inspired them with love and gratitude to Him who had strung their hearts with those ethereal chords which rendered them susceptible of so much felicity.

Felicia would sometimes calmly review the brilliant scenes in which she had been an actress, and in which, as on the mimic stage, happiness was often represented by those who were perfect strangers to it, she sometimes reflected upon the stately establishments in which a hundred were engaged to supply the wants of one—upon the gorgeous halls, the splendid liveries, the magnificent equipages, and the dazzling entertainments at which smiles were wreathed when the heart was racked, and glittering tiaras proudly worn encircled the cells of convict thoughts, and' bosoms, though blazing with brilliants without, were dreary, and ;dark, and cold within : but instead of once wishing to *return* to those scenes, she would not have sacrificed the *joy* she then experienced for all the wealth and splendour in the world!

She was happy, most happy, and her own dear Alfred was happy too ; what more could she desire ? She desired nothing more, nor did Alfred—to whom Felicia appeared to be angelic ; still, although in a delirium of love—the thought of his position in a pecuniary point of view, would sometimes intrude itself for a moment. He saw no fear, however,—not the slightest ; and therefore deferred for a time, with the most perfect confidence, the full consideration of what was to be done.

Fidèle had undertaken the domestic arrangements, which, seeing that they were at an hotel, were but slight; still she had undertaken them ; but she did not think more of those domestic arrangements than she did of Mr. Wilkins.

She did'nt know how it was, exactly; but she had serious thoughts, and extraordinary dreams, and felt peculiar pleasure in being alone; not because she perceived that Felicia and Alfred were enamoured of retirement, but because she felt happier in solitude, and dearly loved to wander on the beach, and to watch the snowy spray, and to listen as if she expected to hear some voice she had somewhere heard before. She, moreover, thought it a very long week, whereas Alfred and Felicia considered it a short one, which was very remarkable : she really could'nt account for it: she could'nt, of course, pretend to account for it: but she actually appeared to wish for Sunday. She had nothing particular on her mind to cause her to wish to go to church so earnestly ; and yet Sunday was the day to which throughout the week she had anxiously looked forward. It could'nt be because Mr. Wilkins had intimated his intention to visit them on Sunday? Oh no!—and yet—well, she would wait until Sunday, and see; she might know more about it then. And she did know more about it then; for when on Sunday Mr. Wilkins arrived, her heart explained the whole matter to her.

Mr. Wilkins had started the previous evening by the mail, and having slept a few hours at the inn, at which it stopped, reached Alfred's hotel before they sat down to breakfast; and no man was ever received more cordially, not only by Fidèle, but by Alfred and Felicia, who shook him warmly by the hand, and expressed to him the pleasure his arrival imparted.

This reception, indeed, somewhat touched him; it was so cordial; but having gracefully congratulated Felicia on her appearance—which really proclaimed the existence of happiness—he very soon recovered his self-possession, and began to chat gaily with Fidèle.

Fidèle, however—although it was impossible for her not to manifest delight—did not talk to him so *playfully* as before: she felt as if his presence imposed some restraint; and when their eyes met she blushed, and seemed slightly embarrassed, and laughed considerably less than she did the previous Sunday. She wasn't sad!—not at all!—but then she wasn't merry! Her cup was full of gladness, but she couldn't pour it out.

Mr. Wilkins, nevertheless, rattled on; but Alfred noticed a great improvement, both in his language and his manners—the former being much less inflated, while the latter were much more refined—the true secret of which was, that he had admired the easy eloquence and gentle bearing of Felicia so much, that he had resolved on adopting her as his model. She was in his view a superior being, and he studied her with profound admiration; and as she was much more communicative then, he was enabled to "pick up something extra" every minute!

With this view he constantly addressed her—but always with the most respectful deference—and felt that a few more lessons from her and Fidèle, would "positively polish him up to such a pitch," that he should be able to shine in the highest sphere, to which his ambition could rationally point, and to prove when he got there, to all around, that he had moved in the best society.

He discovered that he had theretofore made a mistake—that magniloquence was not eloquence, nor stiffness grace: he could then duly appreciate Alfred's quietude, as well in dress as in language and deportment: he saw clearly then, that to be pompous was to be vulgar, and that a quiet, easy, graceful bearing was, in reality, the very acme of elegance, and regarded the opportunity of studying "the real thing," as one of the most fortunate events of his life.

After breakfast, Felicia retired with Fidèle, with the view of preparing for church; and Mr. Wilkins, grasping Alfred by the hand, said, "My boy: I need not ask whether you are happy or not, because I know that you are: I can see it!—I can also see that Lady Felicia is happy, and I rejoice at it—most sincerely rejoice. But have you heard from the Marquis?"

Alfred drew from his pocket-book an envelope, bearing the seal and signature of the Marquis.

"This envelope," said he, contained a letter which Felicia had sent to him, and which he returned, unopened. It is, you perceive, addressed to 'Mrs. Murray;' but look inside."

Mr. Wilkins did so, and read as follows:—

"Lady Florence desires that Mrs. Murray will not presume to write to *her*.
"Kingsborough House."

"Lady Augusta announces—in order to avoid the annoyance

of any attempt to effect a reconciliation—that she will neither correspond with, nor own Mistress Murray.

"Kingsborough House."

"Rather short of paper, at Kingsborough House," said Mr. Wilkins, sarcastically. "They might have enclosed two notes instead of writing on the inside of an envelope. But what effect had all this upon Lady Felicia?"

"Tears sprang into her eyes, but she instantly recalled them, and assumed an expression of firmness."

"Admirable!" exclaimed Mr. Wilkins. "That's the style of creature! All soul! Rather spitfiery though, on their part," he added, "rather serpentified and splenetic! I don't know what I should do with one of those girls. I should'nt be safe in bed."

"I am rather pleased," said Alfred, "that they made no attempt to conceal their real feelings."

"I understand. Any manifestation of kindness might and doubtless would have affected her more. But how are such girls to be tamed? What are you to do with them when you have got them? How are you to manage them? What sort of harness are you to put them into? You could'nt live in the same house with them, if even you ventured to live in the same street?"

"They are very imperious," said Alfred.

"Imperious! Heaven help their husbands, whoever they may be! But is this all that you have heard?"

"From them," replied Alfred. "Here's a note from my uncle—my old uncle Cy—one of the warmest-hearted fellows that ever breathed. Look at that."

Mr. Wilkins read the note, which ran thus:—

"MY BOY,

"Do you want any money to go on with?

"Only one word—Yes, or No.

                              "CYRUS MURRAY.

"That's the style of correspondence," he exclaimed. "There's no beating about the bush here! Do you want any money? Only say!—yes, or no. Well, and what did you say? 'my boy.'"

"No."

"That's right. Don't have any of them yet. It will bring their ideas down from heaven to earth. There's no poetry in money: there's nothing poetic in the sound. But how are you off for that article now?"

"I have the note which you sent me! I have not yet broken into that."

"Not broken into it yet?"

"Oh, no: I'm not permitted to be extravagant. Unnecessary expenses are not allowed."

"What, not by Lady Felicia?"

"Certainly not."

"Have you then an economist as well as an angel."

"I have! She will not cause a pound to be spent unnecessarily."

"That'll do," said Mr. Wilkins, "That'll do. The style in which she would expect to live was the only thing I feared."

"The style in which she hopes to live is that of pure simplicity. The carriage you left here has not been used once. I have proposed a trip to Lewes, and another to Worthing; but the Downs were so delightful; and a walk was so very beneficial to health! That there were other considerations I *suspect!*"

"But there's no necessity for going on so! You must do a *little* to it! You must, you know, enjoy yourselves now!"

"We do," returned Alfred, with a tranquil smile. "We have the purest enjoyment. I believe that Felicia is one of the happiest beings upon earth, while I—I cannot express to you how I feel, but imagine every sense I have, charmed by the great Creator, with the view of testing the amount of rapture of which His creatures are capable, and you may form some idea of the ecstacy of which this marriage has been the germ."

"The operation of those senses is a mystery"—said Mr.
Wilkins—"a mystery as inscrutable as that of the soul. How
they are worked is marvellous: the very machinery is inconceivable; we perceive the effect, and we sometimes know the
cause; but there is a refined something between the cause and
the effect, the contemplation of which makes a man feel little.
But do we all go to church? Does Miss Legrange go with us?"

"Of course!" replied Alfred.

"Well, but I thought the French were Catholics—I mean
Roman Catholics."

"The great majority of them are, but she is a Protestant."

"But how is that?"

"I suppose because her parents were Protestants."

"Well!—there's a great deal in that. If mine had been
Jews or Muggletonians, I might have been a Jew or a Muggle-
tonian: if Pythagoras had been my father, I might have been
one of the Metempsychi. I suppose it's a matter of chance,
chiefly. But who were her parents?"

"Do you recollect speaking to me about a shawl which you
thought would sell, as the favourite shawl of the unfortunate
Queen of Louis XVI., which, just before she was dragged to
the guillotine, she gave to one of her maids of honour, who,
being short of money"—

"Keep out of the shop:" said Mr. Wilkins. "It isn't fair:
keep out of the shop."

"But you recollect it?"

"I do."

'Well then, at the period to which you referred, Fidèle was
connected with one of the first families in France, whose wealth
and influence excited the vengeance of Robespierre."

"Indeed! I must get up the history of that sanguinary
period."

"To amuse her?"

"No, but just to show that one knows something about it."

" You would not, I know, willingly wound her feelings."

" Indeed I would not for the world."

" Then never, in her presence, refer to that period. The slightest word having reference to it has, I understand, a most frightful effect upon her. Her sorrows have not been common sorrows. She has seen her mother, father, uncles, all whom she held dear on earth, lying headless !"

" Heaven and earth ! Is it possible ? Oh ! how glad I am that you told me of this."

" I'll tell you all one of these days. But you have something to tell *me*, have you not ?"

" Something to tell you ?"

" You stated in your letter that you had something to communicate."

" Oh — yes — exactly — I remember. But that's of no immediate importance. We'll talk about that another time."

" Has it reference to the Marquis ?"

" Well—it has. We shall have, however, plenty of time to talk about that. I shall not leave until to-morrow night."

" Indeed ! I am very glad of that.—Felicia, my love," he added, as she entered the room at this moment with Fidèle, " I have news for you ! Mr. Wilkins does not leave us until to-morrow night !"

" That is indeed kind," said Felicia.

" Nay," said Mr. Wilkins, " do not call it kind. My object is of a selfish character. It is to enjoy your delightful society."

Fidèle looked at him, as Felicia slightly bowed, and thought that if that compliment had been addressed pointedly to her, its effect upon her might have been more pleasing. She soon, however, found that she had but little reason to complain, for as they walked to church together he lavished upon her, as pointedly as she could desire, a series of the most graceful compliments he ever thought of. Some of them were, in his judgment, strikingly elegant; but they all hit the mark at which they were aimed, with sufficient force to make an indelible impression.

But truth now prompts the disclosure of that which will not reflect credit upon Mr. Wilkins.—He very seldom went to church !

He had been in the habit of spending his Sundays by no means in accordance with canonical prescription. He would rise in the morning and dress for breakfast, over which he would read the weekly journals, picking out murders and monstrosities of all kinds, breaches of promise, and other "legal" diablerie, theatrical critiques, romances in high life, and facetiæ in low ; after which he would dress for the day, and if he had no engagement to dine at Richmond, Twickenham, Hampstead, or Greenwich, he would have a French dinner and go to Rotten Row ; he would then proceed to some suburban tea-gardens, and having chatted, quizzed, drank, and smoked sufficiently there, he would finish the evening at his favourite tavern with jokes, devilled kidneys, bottled stout, and cigars.

All this was, of course, incorrect: there was not, at that period, a bishop on the bench who would not have told him so distinctly : and the only palliation for the pursuit of such a line of conduct was, that, it being the usual practice of those with whom he associated, he had no one with sufficient influence over him to tempt him to follow a more correct example.

It must, however, in justice here be added that, having on this occasion been attentive to all that passed—having been touched by the impressive chanting of the *Te Deum* and *Jubilate* and reminded by a hymn which he had often sung in childhood that he had still religious feelings with in him— he felt so much relieved, so much lighter, so much more satisfied with himself, that he made up his mind, on leaving the church, not only to attend more frequently in future, but to go every Sunday, at least once !

Fidèle knew that he had been moved to tears, because she saw one of them fall upon the hymn-book. She, of course, took no apparent notice; but as it proved to her that, however gay he might appear, he had a heart susceptible of sweet emotions, the incident was pleasing.

Having returned to the hotel, the feelings of solemnity which the service had inspired, gave way to others of a more lively caste. They had lunch: and then a walk was proposed, and as the proposition met the views of all, they started,— Alfred and Felicia leading the way—and it may as well at once be recorded, that when they reached one of their favorite spots, they were allowed to have a very considerable lead! Whether Mr. Wilkins had tight boots on, or fancied that the shoes of Fidèle were not in fine walking condition, was never minutely explained; but, certain it is, that he hung back in a very extraordinary style, and equally certain is it, that Fidèle made no effort to hurry him on.

But that which struck Fidèle as being most extraordinary at this period, was the fact of his being silent! It was very mysterious! He had scarcely spoken a word for ten minutes Why was he so silent? What could he be thinking of? He could not be unconscious of her presence, because *her* right hand, which she had gracefully passed through his left arm, had got by some means into his right hand, which was very remarkable; and, what was more remarkable still, she made no attempt to withdraw it! He was, moreover, pressing that right hand of hers, and, therefore, he *couldn't* be unconscious of her presence. Why, then, was he silent?

She had seen his four asterisks, which she conceived represented four letters; and as neither "respects" nor "compliments," could by any possibility be spelt with four letters, she had an idea of asking what letters they were really intended to represent; but she found that she hadn't the courage to do it.

At length, having rejected one stepping stone after another,

Mr. Wilkins boldly made up his mind to say something. He had been thinking profoundly of an appropriate exordium, but, as he eventually felt that nothing formal would do, he said, " Well, what think you *now* of this marriage ?"

" What I have always thought," replied Fidèle, " that it will be a source of mutual happiness."

" They appear to be very happy !"

" They are very happy, and I have not the slightest doubt of their happiness being permanent."

" Nor have I," said Mr. Wilkins. " But," he added, mysteriously, " how very delightful the marriage state must be !"

Fidèle had nothing to say to this extraordinary observation, but she felt that it would *do*, that it would lead to *something*.

" Really," continued Mr. Wilkins, " my impression is, that it must be delightful in the extreme."

Fidèle had precisely the same impression ; but she thought it right not to tell *him* so.

" Upon my word," he added, " I should have no objection to try it myself."

Fidèle could say nothing at all to it. What could she say ? The style was so *very* extraordinary ; it did'nt give her a chance of saying anything.

" I have often thought," he resumed, " that marriage—that is to say the marriage state—must be enchanting."

Fidèle was determined to say something this time : she would'nt be silent any longer : it was so tiresome—she therefore said, " Have you ?"

A pause ensued, and Mr. Wilkins felt that if he could'nt improve upon this he had better leave off. Still " Have you ?" had to be answered, and he therefore said, " I have."

Well, there was an end of it. There was nothing more absolutely demanded ; but Mr. Wilkins was by no means satisfied. He never before felt so much confused, but he had no idea of letting it drop so. · He, therefore, having recovered himself a little, resolved on adopting a more playful style, and said eventually, " What do you think of Lady Florence ? "

" Lady Florence ! " echoed Fidèle, quite unable to conceive what Lady Florence had to do with it. " What do I think of Lady Florence ? "

" Would *she* suit me, think you ? Do you think she would *do?* Can you recommend her strongly, as a mild and gentle creature, calculated to make a steady, tranquil style of wife ? "

Fidèle looked at him and smiled.

" What think you ? " he continued ; " is she, in your view, sufficiently lamb-like ? Would she, in your judgment, suit my taste ? "

" Admirably," replied Fidèle, " if indeed you have a taste for the display of spirit."

" Spirit ! spirit is the very thing I like to see displayed. I admire spirit, and more especially in a woman : the spirit of love, the spirit of hope, the spirit of gentleness, when she is cherished, and the spirit of resistance when oppressed. The spirit of pride, the spirit of revenge, and all the other evil spirits, I leave out of the question, of course, because no one *can* admire them; but gentleness and amiability, combined with firmness and self-respect, are the germs of all I care to cultivate."

" But if the spirit you had to encounter were not that of gentleness ? "

" Well, then, that spirit must be subdued. She is, of course, to be tamed ? "

· " It strikes me that you would have to set her the example : you would have to go through the process first."

" Would that be the most effectual way ? If she were to tame me first, would that teach me how to tame her ? "

" If tamed at all, it must be by the force of example; I really know of no other force that would do. One must yield. If both held out you'd set fire to each other in a very short time."

" But what sort of a husband do you think she would like? "

" Either a nice quiet elderly Duke, with immense possessions and brilliant establishments, who would leave the entire management of everything—himself included—to her; or a very young Earl, with magnificent estates, and just sufficient intellect to avoid a commission of lunacy."

" Well, I don't like to flatter myself," said Mr. Wilkins, " but as I am neither of these interesting characters, suppose I, as I am, were to attempt to woo her, how should I have to go to work? Should I have to compare her eyes to fire, her teeth to pearl, her lips to the rose, and her cheeks to sun-illumined peaches?"

" If you were to do so it would have but slight effect. She hasn't a charm of which she is unconscious. The only way to woo her with any chance of success, would be to show her a splendid rent-roll, with the sketch of a brilliant settlement, and offer to place unlimited means at her command. I have no wish to dishearten you," she added, with a smile, " but I know of no other way to woo and to win her."

" Then I'll give her up at once," said Mr. Wilkins; " I'll think no more of her; I'll turn my attention to *one*," he added, and as he pronounced that little word, he pressed the hand he held emphatically, " who is as elegant as she is interesting, who has proved her appreciation of pure happiness —who has inspired me with feelings which I never before experienced; who has, in fine, taught me to love."

He said no more. He looked at Fidèle, who averted her eyes and blushed, and felt somewhat tremulous; when, finding that she was silent, and that he had, in reality, no inclination to say anything more then, they gradually drew nearer to Alfred and Felicia, who appeared to understand the very object which had kept Mr. Wilkins and Fidèle so far behind.

A smile from Felicia, and a playful remark from Alfred, on the great inconvenience of having corns, were, however, the only intimations then given of that object being understood: they pursued their walk, conversing upon topics of general interest, and in due time returned to the Hotel.

While at dinner, Mr. Wilkins—who was really relieved—for although he had made no direct declaration, he had, in his judgment, said enough to begin with—felt unusually gay: he chatted to Fidèle—who, however, said but little—addressed Felicia, and rallied Alfred, with so much success, that he fairly established the reputation he had acquired, of being one of the most agreeable persons they had ever had the pleasure to meet.

Nor, when they had retired from the table to have the dessert, as before, near the window, did he cease to amuse them. He was full of anecdote, and every one "told:" there was not a single failure amongst them—a fact which "polished up" his lively recollection "to such a pitch," that it absolutely teemed with facetiæ.

Towards the evening, at the suggestion of Alfred, Fidèle went to the piano, and very soon electrified Mr. Wilkins. She was, indeed, a brilliant pianist — perhaps one of the most brilliant out of the profession—but nothing could surpass the ecstacy with which she succeeded in thrilling Mr. Wilkins. He looked at her with an expression of amazement, watched the lightning-like rapidity with which her delicate fingers moved, and listened to the startling music she produced, with feelings of intense admiration. He was "struck." He felt bewildered. His veins tingled with rapture. He had never heard such music before! It was, indeed, in his view, enchanting.

Having accomplished the brilliant finale, she rose, and Mr. Wilkins really didn't know at all what to say. He felt as if he were under the influence of some magic spell, and instead of exclaiming "bravo," "excellent," or "beautiful "—

which, under ordinary circumstances, he would have felt
himself bound to exclaim—he looked at her and marvelled,
but made no effort to express the admiration with which he
had been inspired.

"Favour us with one more, dear," said Felicia; and Fidèle
at once returned to the piano with a hymn-book, and played
and sang in the most impressive style the very hymn which
had touched Mr. Wilkins in the morning!

This turned the current of his feelings on the instant, and
tears again sparkled in his eyes: nor could he check them : he
endeavoured to do so, but they were not to be controlled: they
continued to flow more and more as she proceeded; and it is,
indeed, questionable whether she could ever before have sung
that hymn with so much feeling.

As twilight approached, Mr. Wilkins mysteriously wandered
to the other window, to which he almost as mysteriously
attracted Fidèle; and, while Felicia was hanging fondly upon
Alfred's arm, and watching the horizon serenely, he set himself
a most extraordinary task, namely, that of arranging and
smoothing Fidèle's hair.

Now, it will be as well here to state that Fidèle's hair was
not out of order. It was, on the contrary, as well arranged
and as smooth as the most fastidious could desire. But
Mr. Wilkins, nevertheless, endeavoured to improve it: he
was amazingly particular about this hair; and smoothed it
first on the right side and then on the left, and then on both
sides at the same time! Of course, Fidèle thought this a
remarkable proceeding! She was unconscious of having
neglected her hair! Still she thought that an improvement
might possibly be made!—and immediately after this thought
had been conceived, an improvement *was* made—in her view, a
very decided improvement—for while he was thus smoothing
both sides at once, he absolutely bent forward and boldly
kissed her brow!

And Fidèle endured this? Yes!—she endured it ˌwith all the fortitude at her command. She blushed, but she didn't feel angry!—she didn't exactly know how to feel angry!—nor did she particularly wish to feel angry. It certainly was a bold proceeding; she couldn't conceal that fact from herself; but having taken all the circumstances into consideration, she eventually made up her mind to forgive him.

Her hair went very well indeed after that. Mr. Wilkins was perfectly satisfied with it; and he drew her arm in his and took her hand as before, and remained at the window until lights were produced, when they rejoined Alfred and Felicia.

It was then extremely questionable which was the happiest of the four. They were all happy then, truly happy, and enjoyed each other's delightful society until they retired to rest.

Having arranged with Alfred to have a walk before breakfast in the morning, Mr. Wilkins rose early, and when Alfred appeared they went together down to the beach.

The tide was low, and as they walked on the sands, Alfred again calmly inquired of Mr. Wilkins what it was that he had to communicate. "You may as well tell me at once," he added, "it will do away with all conjecture."

"When I assure you," said Mr. Wilkins, "that it is of no immediate consequence, let that for the present be sufficient. Let us defer it till the month is up, and then we'll calmly talk the matter over."

"I'd rather know it now!" urged Alfred. "Why not calmly talk it over now?"

"Well, we certainly *can* do so! My only objection is, that it may in some slight degree interfere with your present enjoyment!—and yet, I don't see why it ought to do so!"

"Then be sure that it *will* not. If it ought not, it shall not! What is it?"

"Well, I'll tell you! Last Monday, the Marquis called to

see the governor, with whom he in private conversed for some time, and when he left I was informed that Lady Felicia had no property."

" I am aware of it," said Alfred. " She will, I understand, be entitled to some on the death of Lady Loftus, her aunt; but at present she has none. Is that all?"

" That is the chief point," replied Mr. Wilkins. " The other is merely the declaration of the Marquis, that she shall have nothing from him."

" I don't *expect* anything from him," said Alfred, " nor does Felicia; but I am satisfied! I know, of course, that something must be done, and I feel assured that something will be done, to render us at least independent of him."

" I have not the slightest doubt of it. I have no fear whatever. I felt, when I heard that she had no property, that the fact would arouse all your energies. My only fear was, that you might perhaps live a little too fast at first, and thus create some slight dissatisfaction, when the time came to pull in; but that fear vanished at once, when you told me that economy—at her suggestion—was the order of the day. But how old is this aunt?"

" About seventy, I believe."

" An old maid?"

" No, a dowager."

" Ah: then *that's* settled. It's of no use to calculate at all upon *her*. An old maid might fidget herself to death, and so might a widow of fifty; but, directly she gets above sixty, regard her as one of the immortals. Widows above that age won't die. They live as if they meant to be immortal. Their whole proceedings smell of immortality. They'll talk about death, and live all the longer for it: the very exertion of talking about it, tends to promote longevity. They'll sometimes drop off, if you happen to be rich; but the poorer you are, the longer they'll live. They *are* the most obstinate people upon earth

They'll do nothing to kill themselves when above sixty! They settle themselves down, and begin life again: it is their spring of immortality. Life insurances then, are a bad speculation: you *literally* insure their lives then; for, if they know it, they won't die at all! We may well call old age second childhood. It is then, that these knowing ones start off afresh, and begin the world again with a better chance than ever. Every child born in the family gives them new life. Children are the dolls of second childhood, with which the old children play with as much delight as they played with the dolls of their *earlier* infancy. You can't by any means persuade them to die! They know better! They have a life's experience to guide them! Now, I've an immortal old grandmother," he continued, " I don't want her to die; but if I did, she wouldn't! She's been reckoned immortal for the last thirty years, and seems more immortal now than when I first knew her. She goes like a clock; and knows, not only how to wind herself up, but how to keep the machinery in order. I'm her favourite grandson: but what of that? When I have a son, he'll be sure to cut me out; and when he has a son, he'll be cut out himself, as a natural matter of retributive justice! If she doesn't go off in fifty years or *so*, I shall really begin to entertain the belief that she has discovered perpetual motion. I mention these things," he added, " in order to show that it is not only useless, but worse than useless, to calculate upon the death of this aunt."

"I should not think of *calculating* upon it," said Alfred; " still it may come eventually."

"It may. She may die to-morrow, and she may live to see you out. Don't depend upon that; depend upon yourself. I've no fear of you. *You'll* get on!"

"I hope so," said Alfred. "But, by the way, do you think of following my example?"

"Do I think of following your example? In what respect?—

Oh! with Fidèle, you mean! Ah. Well! I should'nt be in the slightest degree astonished! The fact is, I admired her before: that which you told me about her family rendered her, in my view, more interesting still; and that which subsequently passed between us convinced me that, if we were to make a match of it, I should'nt be at all amazed."

"But, I thought that there was a young lady in town, for whom you had an affection."

"Pooh! If I had married her it would have been merely as a matter of business; and as a mere matter of business she would have married me. That was understood. It was to have been a mere commercial partnership. I was to manage the shop below, and she was to manage her show-rooms above. The firm was to have been that of 'Wilkins and Co.,' and she of course was to have been the 'Co.' But this is a very, *very* different affair—an affair not of the shop but of the heart."

"But suppose this affair of the heart were to involve you in an action for breach of promise to the shop?"

"Breach of promise! We used to meet on a Sunday, and talk the matter over in a purely commercial spirit, just to ascertain how the speculation would answer, but no promise of the kind was ever made. Besides, this was by mutual consent broken off long ago. She has now another commercial lover, and I believe the deed of partnership between them is all but signed. Such a cold-hearted, calculating matter of business, however, ought not even to be thought of now. The amiable and interesting Fidèle has created within me feelings which I never before experienced, and which prompt me to believe that the example to which you allude will at no remote period be followed."

"Well," said Alfred, "I congratulate you on the progress you have made. She is a very superior girl, and the fact of your having won her affections alone proves that you are a very superior fellow."

Mr. Wilkins raised his hat, and when Alfred had explained to him all that he had heard of Fidèle from Felicia, they left the sands light-hearted and refreshed, and returned to the hotel to breakfast.

"What *have* you been laughing at?" inquired Felicia. "Fidèle and I have been watching you on the sands, and you really made *us* laugh, you were so merry."

"Mr. Wilkins," replied Alfred, "has been introducing a dear friend—his grandmother—to me. But could you see me laughing at that distance?"

"Through the telescope, distinctly!"

"The telescope!—Oh!—it will not do to walk on the sands, then, I find."

"But have you really a grandmamma living?" inquired Fidèle.

"Oh, yes," replied Mr. Wilkins, "and likely to have for the next half century."

"Indeed! She must be very aged?"

"Aged! Juvenile—comparatively juvenile—she has just commenced a new era of existence."

This was a fine opening for Mr. Wilkins—an opening of which he felt bound to take advantage: he therefore amused them while at breakfast, with a series of anecdotes, having reference to this immortal grandmother of his, and succeeded in throwing them into convulsions.

Having thus had their appetite taken away—for neither Felicia, Fidèle, nor Alfred could be said to have the power of making a fair breakfast—they prepared to accompany Mr. Wilkins—to whose sole direction the proceedings of the day had been confided—and shortly afterwards the happy party started for Worthing.

Worthing—which is not a very lively place now—was, at that period, dull in the extreme. But this suited them all the better! It tended to enhance their enjoyment. Surrounded by attractions, their attention would have been diverted from themselves. They required no amusement but that which they could afford—no "life" but that which was within them: they, in short, wanted nothing to excite their admiration, they were so well content to admire each other.

Now, the first thing which Mr. Wilkins thought of on his arrival was lunch; which he ordered, and which they all highly enjoyed: the next thing of which he thought was dinner; which he also ordered—privately, and in his own peculiar style: he then thought of a walk—a thought which especially delighted Fidèle—and in order to avoid telescopic observation, he proposed to abandon the beach for a time, and seek scenery of a character more rural than marine.

There were at that time some very delightful walks about Worthing, and to one of the most delightful Mr. Wilkins led the way. He did not, however, maintain the lead long: having reached a lane sufficiently secluded, he and Fidèle stopped to gather a variety of wild flowers, when Alfred and Felicia—as if they really understood all about it—went in advance.

Their admiration of these wild flowers, however—lovely as they were with their "quaint, enamelled eyes" — was but transient: for Mr. Wilkins gently drew Fidèle's arm within his own, and while pressing her hand, led her forward.

"Fidèle," said he, at length—and it being the first time he had thus addressed her, the very sound of her name was delightful—"Fidèle, do you remember what I said to you yesterday?"

"On what subject?" inquired Fidèle, who well knew, but it had had so sweet an effect upon her that she wished it to be repeated.

"The subject was *love*, Fidèle," he replied. "I alluded to one who had *taught* me to love. You remember?"

"I do."

"How wonderful is memory!—how inscrutable its machinery!

—-how mysteriously it works! If I knew how impressions were created and retained, as if the mind kept an everlasting record, I might have some idea of the mystic workings of the equally marvellous machinery of love. Love!"—he continued with an expression of tenderness, mingled with estacy—" Love! The very name is a sweet one, while its sound is suggestive of the most delightful feelings of which we are susceptible. But they who really love I find communicate their thoughts without giving them utterance. Their senses are charged with love's electricity for the conveyance of feelings from heart to heart. For example : I have never *said* that I love *you*, and yet you know that I do. You have never said that you love *me*, and yet I know that you love me! I need not *declare* that I love you; nor do I need any declaration from you. We have communicated the interesting fact to each other fifty times at least, even within the last few minutes. Our hearts have done the business—our hearts which have become dear friends— confiding, sympathetic friends : separate them ten thousand miles, and they'll communicate fondly with each other still. Nor is it through the eyes alone that this mysterious communication is kept up. Every touch produces an electric thrill. That kiss which I stole last evening, it was *but* a kiss, and yet what a *marvellous* sensation it created. Now all this is very mysterious, Fidèle. But our hearts, my love, are the engineers. They manage it : *they* understand each other well, and as they perceive no 'just cause or impediment' why they should not be for ever united, they glory in keeping up the mystic correspondence. Independently of which, Fidèle, mine will prompt me now to write to you every evening, and yours will prompt you, to write every evening to me. I shall, moreover, every evening, precisely at eleven, be induced Fidèle to kiss your signature, and you will find yourself induced at the same time exactly to kiss mine. I shall come down as often as I can ·to kiss *you*. And as soon as I am able to leave the house in which

I am engaged, without behaving unhandsomely, we'll commence, my love, that career of happiness of which we have the fore-taste now. Fidèle," he added, "you are indeed very dear to me. And now, as I have nothing more at present to say, as I don't expect you to say anything, and as Alfred and Lady Felicia are far in advance of us, I think that we may as well walk a little faster."

Well, certainly Fidèle thought this a strange address. The style was not in itself displeasing, but it was in her view so extraordinary! He had assumed that she loved him; he had assumed that she would marry him; he had, in short, assumed all he *could* assume. But then, was not all that he had assumed true? She knew that it was—quite true: and knowing this, she felt happy. Why, he had simplified the whole matter! He had not only thus declared himself; he had decided upon the whole course of wooing at once! But could this be called wooing? There had been no entreaty—no solicitation —everything had been taken for granted. Could that be called wooing? She *did* think that there might have been a *little* importunity! And yet, to what would it have amounted? But then, might he not imagine that she had been much too easily won? But in what had she acquiesced? She had said nothing to it!—she had not been won yet! The letters which were to pass between them would afford her ample oppor-tunities of showing that she expected to be wooed a *little*. Why, of course they would! and doubtless it was with this view that that course of correspondence had been proposed. Besides, what was the substance of all that he had done? He had embraced the very earliest opportunity of declaring that she was indeed dear to him, and, without expecting any reply, had left her to think the matter over. Why that was precisely what she had wished him to do: and although the style in which it was done still struck her as being extraordinary, she felt it—she could not but feel it—to be at the same time peculiarly pleasing.

Having rejoined Alfred and Felicia, Mr. Wilkins re-assumed an air of gaiety, and fondly urged Fidèle, who was still thoughtful, to throw off all restraint; and when they had had a delightful round, they returned to the hotel to dine.

The dinner was delicious; and when it had been by all highly enjoyed, Mr. Wilkins came out with a long string of anecdotes having reference to another relation of his—an interesting hypochondriacal individual, who had been in the habit of fancying himself transformed into all sorts of animals, from the lion to the lamb; and as he gave imitations of each animal as he proceeded, the effect was particularly comic.

Having thus been kept in a state of merriment until the evening, the party gaily returned to Brighton; and although Mr. Wilkins bade them all adieu that night—having to start by the coach at six o'clock the next morning—he was quite unexpectedly summoned at five to have breakfast alone with Fidèle.

CHAPTER XV.

In the course of the ensuing week, Sudbury was visited again by the Marquis. He came down as before, post-haste, and his arrival was announced, as before, to Murray, before whose imagination fresh handbills flitted, and who felt, in consequence, dreadfully alarmed. But the object of the Marquis *was* business this time, and business, too, "of some importance." He had business with his agent, business with his steward, and business with his attorney; but his principal business was with Mr. Chubb.

All this business, however, was conducted in a most mysterious manner. None but the parties immediately concerned knew anything of its nature—a fact which teemed with a thousand conjectures, based upon "the best authority." All that was really known of this business was gathered from one of the waiters, who heard Mr. Chubb mysteriously say, "My lord, what I have done I mean to stick to;" and when the Marquis asked, "Why?" he replied, "That, my lord, is *my* business."

This was, of course, *something* to build upon: but what had Mr. Chubb really done? They didn't blame him for sticking to it!—No; they by no means blamed him for sticking to it; but what, in reality, was it? Their utter inability to ascertain that was felt by the community at large to be galling.

During the progress of this business, Cyrus—who knew all about it, he being one of the "parties immediately concerned," although he studiously kept aloof—was visited by Murray,

whose object was to suggest to him the propriety of his seeing
the Marquis, in order to expostulate with him, and to show
that, having committed an act of injustice, it was his duty
to make all the reparation in his power; but Cyrus, who knew
that such an appeal to the feelings of the Marquis would be
useless, if not worse than useless, of course refused to adopt
the suggestion.

"What," said he, "do such men care about justice? Might
is right, with them, and justice a scarecrow. Had he been
acting under any erroneous impression—had he been on any
point misinformed—I would go to him without the slightest
hesitation; but as he knew at the time that he was acting
unjustly, an interview would only add fuel to the fire."

"My impression was," urged Murray, "that if it were
calmly explained to him, that I really had no knowledge of
Alfred's intention, and that all which relates to Mrs. Murray
has no foundation whatever, he might be induced, as a matter
of justice, to retract those portions at least."

"Retract! Would he admit his connection with any part
of it? No: he would at once deny all participation in the
matter. Suppose I were to go to him—it is questionable
whether he would allow me to be admitted—but suppose that
he did, and I were to point out to him what a cowardly
scoundrel he was, to assail an innocent woman, what would be
the effect? In the first place, he'd say that he had nothing to
do with it; and in the next, he'd want to know how I dared to
assume that it was done through his instrumentality"

"Nay, but you might go more calmly to work."

"Calmly! Gods in heaven! Who could speak of such a
libel to its cowardly author, calmly? No: we had better not
go near him: we had better leave the matter as it is. An
interview could have no good effect; but it might have a bad
one: it might incense him still more; not that *I* either care
about his rage, or expect that he will ever do anything for

Alfred : but it might induce the coward to inflict an additional wound upon the feelings of Lady Felicia. No : let it rest as it is."

"Cyrus," said Murray, with a mournful expression, "*something* must be done. If things go on much longer so, I shall be a ruined man. Having lost all my trade, what *am* I to do ?"

" Have patience," said Cyrus. " It will not be always thus. How much more would you have taken if this had not occurred ? Thirty or forty pounds, perhaps."

" Aye, sixty."

" Say sixty ; and say the profit would have been five and twenty per cent. ; that's fifteen : an awful loss, certainly, to conjure up ruin ! You have proved to me that you're in a *fair* position ! You have nothing immediately pressing upon you ! Have patience. Things will come round again by and by ! I see nothing desperate yet : when I do, I'll recommend you to give up business entirely."

" Well, but what am I to do in that case ? How am I to support my family, then ?"

" Oh, you'll not be lost. *We'll* find something for you to do."

" Cyrus," said Murray, " this mysterious 'we' puzzles me more than any thing else. You say *we'll* do so and so : *we'll* see about it. What is it you mean by *we* ? "

" Ah," replied Cyrus, with a smile, " you'll know more by and by. We have not been doing nothing for the last twenty years."

" But what have you been doing ? I have no knowledge of your having done anything !"

" Very few have, my boy ; very few have ! They who do the most business don't make the most noise ! Business is to be done very quietly sometimes !"

" Certainly, business is to be done quietly ; but yours must be a quiet business indeed."

"You'll know all about it, my boy, by and by. In the meantime have patience, and don't be alarmed."

Mr. Chubb was now announced, and as he entered the room Cyrus inquired if the Marquis had left.

"No," replied Mr. Chubb, "he's there still."

"All right?"

"Oh, yes. He did'nt like it much though."

"I suppose not. Slane there?"

"Yes!"

This was, of course, unintelligible to Murray, and as he really had a wish then to bring Chubb out, he ventured to inquire if he had seen the Marquis.

"Yes," replied Chubb. "Oh, how is Mrs. Murray?"

"Thank you," said Murray. "Pretty well in health, but her spirits are of course still very much depressed."

"Why, of course? Pooh! nonsense: why, of course? She ought to have got over that by this time."

"Is the Marquis still angry?"

"I don't know what he may be in his heart! There may be a storm there; but he's quite calm outside."

"He didn't say anything about me, did he?"

"Not a word."

"Then I hope there'll be no more handbills?"

"He has something else to think about now."

"I heard that he had come down on business. Is it anything very important?

"It isn't settled yet."

Well, as his friend Chubb would *not* be "drawn out," and as he felt that his absence would not be disagreeable, Murray rose, and, with a look which seemed to intimate that he *hoped* to know a little more about it by and by, left the close ones together.

"I feel more satisfied than ever," said Cyrus, that we have pursued the right course. As a mere speculation it will be a

good one. The thing will pay; it will build him up, and create
no little sensation."

"It'll stun a few of 'em, it strikes me," said Chubb. "But
the thing must be kept, you know, dark as night. If he has
the slightest notion that we want it, he'll make any sacrifice
rather than let us have it."

"Quite right," returned Cyrus. "We have only to keep
quiet. We shall get it; I feel quite sure that we shall get it.
The thing can't pay as they manage it now. We have but to
keep it to ourselves. We'll not even give the boy the slightest
notion of it. I want to see what he'll do. He'll do something;
but I want to know what. He has six months before him; and in
that time, unless I am greatly mistaken, he'll make a spring of
some sort. Does the Marquis seem to care *much* about it?"

"Well, he does'nt *seem* to care a great deal about it. But
then who can tell what he means? He cares more than he
seems to care; if he did'nt, he would'nt have come down. But
that may wear off. When he comes to look into the management of it, and finds that it is'nt worth *his* while to make any
sacrifice in order to keep it, the loss of it will not annoy him
much until he ascertains what we mean."

They then went into a variety of calculations, the whole of
which tended to prove that they were right; and having arrived
at this highly satisfactory conclusion, they went to have a pint
of wine together at the Crown.

As they passed through the gateway of the hotel, they saw
James standing stiffly with folded arms, and looking charac-
teristically majestic. They had no personal knowledge of
James — not the slightest; but as his gorgeous livery
proclaimed that he was one of the servants of the Marquis,
they felt more deeply interested in his appearance than if he
had been one of the private servants of the King.

"I'd give a five pound note," said Cyrus, "to have five
minutes' private conversation with that fellow."

"You can have it cheaper than that," returned Chubb. "But it won't do for *me* to be seen with him."

"Of course not; nor will it do for me to be seen with him publicly. You go into the bar, I'll see if I can manage it."

Having ascertained where the landlord was, Cyrus went to him, and said, "Greene, do me a favour. There's one of the servants of the Marquis outside; now I'm anxious, of course, to learn a little, and with that view I should like to have some talk with him about Alfred—*you* understand? Can't you manage to get him into some private room with me?"

"Oh! yes," replied Greene, "I'll soon manage that. Step in here; I'll bring him."

"Send a bottle of wine in first, and then you can ask him to have a glass with *you*."

"All right," said Greene, who sent in the wine and immediately afterwards re-appeared with James.

As he entered the room James bowed to Cyrus, and Cyrus said, "How are you, sir?" and when James had taken his seat at the table, Cyrus passed the wine.

"I should like to be just your size, sir," said Cyrus.

"I should just like, sir, to be *yours*," said James.

"Ah," returned Cyrus, "Thus it is; we are never content to be what we are."

"Never content, sir! Why you look the very picture of content! A man of your size, sir, always looks jolly! I like the size, sir! It looks so Shakesperian!"

"Was Shakespeare stout, sir?"

"Falstaff was, sir; and he's a Shakesperian character. I always think that a man of your capacity and bodily dimensions, sir, looks so aldermanic, the model of justice, with nothing to do but to eat, drink, laugh, and be jovial. He is also the model of substantial respectability!—none of the sort ever come to the workhouse."

S

"Good health to you, sir! You're a very pleasant fellow. You must have seen a great deal of life!"

"Life, sir! I've lived all my life in life!"

"Have you been with the Marquis long?" inquired Cyrus as the landlord rose to leave the room.

"Well," replied James, "a few years."

"You have lately had a marriage in the family?"

"Well, we've had a marriage in the family, but not, you know, what I call a family marriage."

"A run-away match, I understand?"

"Yes."

"What sort of person is this Lady Felicia?"

"A regular angel, and no mistake!—a regular angel, sir! Her *sisters* —belong to another parish."

"Is she *very* amiable?"

"I believe you! I don't think there's another in life like her! I only wish her husband was a little more nobby; but he only wants a lift to be as big as the best of 'em!"

"You know him, then?"

'Know him! What Murray! *I* know him well!—And, between you and me, I don't care a button about what they say; they may call him what they like; he's a fine, high-spirited, gentlemanly fellow! But this is, of course, between *us!*"

"Whatever you say to me," observed Cyrus, "I shall regard as being strictly confidential; and I may as well tell you at once that I am the uncle of Alfred Murray."

"You are!" exclaimed James, with an expression of amazement, I'm proud to know you; and I'll say again—though you *are* his uncle, and perhaps may not exactly approve of what he's done, that a better-hearted fellow than Mr. Murray doesn't breathe!"

"I believe it," said Cyrus, "I firmly believe it. But in what manner was the thing managed?"

"I'll tell you. He came with some silks, and she fell in

love with him; he came again, and he fell in love with her: and—I don't mind telling *you*, because, of course, it'll go no further—that through me they were speedily married. Had it not been for me, and my—what I may call—*vigilance*, they wouldn't have been married so soon, if at all: I was, sir, in fact, what another Shaksperian character calls the instrument of their pleasures!"

" There was no under-hand work, I hope ?" said Cyrus.

" Under-hand work! The Marquis was kept in the dark, of course !"

" But the lady was not tempted to leave her home by any unfair means ?"

" Certainly not ! She went off in the cool of the morning, like a lamb with all her intellects about her."

" Alone ?"

" No, her maid was with her—the lady's maid."

" A French woman ?"

" Yes : a Miss Legrange."

" What sort of a person is she ?"

" A capital sort: speaks forty or fifty languages; crammed with accomplishments: got 'em wholesale, sir; and, as she retails 'em, increases the stock: an out-and-out sort: good and amiable: something like Lady Felicia, and just about as much of a maid to Lady Felicia, as a maid of honour is to a Queen."

" Is she with Lady Felicia now ?"

" Safe ! They're like sisters. I'll warrant they're together. Her boxes went away only yesterday. They wanted to detain 'em: they wouldn't give 'em up: not a bit of it ! But the gentleman who called—a Mr. Wilkins—soon let 'em know the difference: he went before a magistrate, and soon settled that !"

" Does the Marquis *say* much about the marriage at home ?"

" Well, he doesn't say much before us, of course; but he's been in a rage ever since !"

"Is he, then, a very passionate man ?"

"Don't mention it! Isn't he ? *Can't* he go in ? See him out, and see him at home, and you'd hardly know him to be the same individual. People often say to me, 'what a very nice man the Marquis is !—so quiet, so mild, so remarkable pleasant!' They praise him clean up to the skies! But, as Shakespeare says, 'All the world's a stage,' and the best actors get the most applause. He's now in a rage—an awful rage—about something. He and his steward can't hit it at all. He *will* have this account, and *will* have the other. I wouldn't be his steward for a trifle. But, about this affair, our ladies are the worst : *they* say most about it : they're always at it, they are. They'd skin poor Lady Felicia if they could, and excruciate her afterwards, *they* would. According to them, she's to beg from door to door in about a fortnight, and I'll warrant they'd like to see her do it."

"But they won't !" said Cyrus. "They won't !"

"I hope not."

"If they see her at all, they'll see her happy !"

"*That'll* gall 'em !"

"Then, they shall be galled."

"As for that Lady Florence—do you know Lady Florence?"

"I may have seen her."

"You can't have seen her at all, if you don't know her. You've only got to see her once : you'll know her for ever after that. She's a tigress. You've only got to look at her eyes ; they'll tell you what she is—they're as big as coat buttons and such awful blazers—they come down upon you like a flash of forked lightning. She's the worst—she's ten to *one* worse than Lady Augusta. *She'd* have Lady Felicia burnt alive. I do believe that if she were to see her she'd pretty well tear her eyes out."

"Let her touch her, if she *dare*," cried Cyrus indignantly. "Let her lay a *finger* upon her, if she dare."

"I am glad to hear you say that,'' said James. "It proves you haven't taken a dislike to her, although she has married in this way. But who that has a heart *can* take a dislike to her? Such a man as you *can't* dislike her. She'll make you like her. The first time you see her you'll love her, and when you come to know what she really is—how amiable, affectionate, and good, she'll be just as much to *you* as if she were your own child."

"I feel that I love her already," said Cyrus. "I *feel* that I love her already, and if"—

At this moment Greene entered the room, and announced that the Marquis was just about to leave, when James started up on the instant, and said, "Nothing could have given me greater pleasure than the privilege of spending the evening with *you*, but I must go."

"Stop," said Cyrus, as he drew a five-pound note from his pocket-book. "Take this; buy a ring or something when you get to town. Good bye—success to you—good bye—but not a word about your having seen me to a soul."

James, who felt this last proof of affection deeply, gave the necessary promise, and took his leave, when the kind-hearted Cyrus, delighted with the information he had obtained, gaily rejoined his friend Chubb in the bar.

CHAPTER XVI.

ARISTOCRATIC PATRONAGE.

HAVING prepared themselves for the performance of those duties, which true love converts into pleasures, by intertwining their affections, studying each other's characteristics, and testing the sources of mutual delight, with the view of rendering the sweetness of the honey-moon permament, Alfred and Felicia returned to town.

Fidèle accompanied them of course, and Mr. Wilkins engaged furnished apartments for them; Felicia having stipulated for only *one* week, to enable her to procure an appointment for Alfred, before they went to visit his friends.

Her first task, however, was to write to her aunt, for whom she had ever cherished a warm affection, and this task she performed in a style, which she imagined well calculated to remove any unfavourable impression rumour might have created. She therefore sent the letter off at once, and directed the messenger to wait at Richmond for an answer, and being pleased with the manner in which she had succeeded in portraying the happiness of which her marriage had been the germ, she was not only sanguine of success, in so far as a reconciliation was concerned, but felt sure that her dear aunt would send for her and Alfred without delay, in order to promote, by her advice and assistance, the object they had immediately in view.

Anxiously, but without apprehension—she was too full of hope to be apprehensive then—Felicia awaited the messenger's return, and when he did return, and that too with an answer, she joyously opened the note, which ran thus :—

"Lady Loftus sends her love to Lady Felicia. She sends her love, but begs to state that, as the accounts she has received are of a character so afflicting, she is not yet prepared to receive her.

"Lady Loftus is not indisposed to pity Lady Felicia: she is not indisposed to make every allowance for her youth and inexperience; nor is she indisposed to believe, that when Lady Felicia degraded herself and disgraced her family, she was labouring under an aberratiou of intellect—seeing that to nothing but a species of insanity can such a monstrous proceeding, in her judgment, be ascribed; but although Lady Loftus feels disposed to view the lamentable affair in this charitable light, she cannot consent to receive Lady Felicia, until she has repudiated utterly the despicable set with whom she is now unhappily associated.

"Lady Loftus—notwithstanding Lady Felicia is cast off by all whom she ought to have held dear—notwithstanding she is, in the view of the world, lost and degraded—will, in that case, afford her an asylum; but she values her own reputation too highly, to venture to do even this, until Lady Felicia's connection with her present low associates shall have ceased.

"Lady Felicia may yet be restored to society, and Lady Loftus is willing to assist in restoring her—notwithstanding the expense of a divorce is great!—but she cannot consent to render her the slightest assistance, until she has washed her hands for ever of the vulgar set with whom she is now unhappily connected.

"When this has been done, the fact may be communicated to Lady Loftus; but unless it be expressly to announce that fact, any farther communication from Lady Felicia must be deemed by Lady Loftus obtrusive."

"Felicia," said Alfred, who had watched her while she read this malicious epistle, and who perceived by the convulsive curling of her lip, which expressed the most intense indignation, that it was galling—"Felicia! If you have been unsuccessful, let it not distress you! Your aunt, I presume, is not willing to receive you!"

"Not yet," replied Felicia, with an effort to conceal her feelings, "not yet. She sends her love; but she is not yet *prepared* to receive me."

"Well, my dear!—thus let it rest for a time. She writes then in an affectionate strain?"

"She sends her *love!* The very first sentence is, 'Lady Loftus sends her *love* to Lady Felicia!'"

"To *Lady* Felicia! *So* distant!"

Felicia wept.

"My sweet girl!" he added. "Be firm, my love! Come, come, be firm!"

"It is so cruel," said Felicia. "I cannot but feel it."

"If it be cruel, despise it, as cruelty in every shape ought to be despised. Among men, none but cowards are cruel: among women, none but the vile. Cruelty is accursed by God and man!—it demands scorn, not tears. But come," he added tenderly, "this will *never* do. What! Are you my own Felicia, and weep because an aunt, either actuated by malice or prompted by calumny, refuses to receive you! Is it the mere fact of her having refused, that you consider so cruel?"

"No, dear: not the fact alone; but the bitter terms in which that refusal has been conveyed."

"Well, but what does she say?"

"You had better not know, my love."

"Why not?"

"It will but annoy you."

"It will annoy me much more, my sweet girl, to see you annoyed, while I have no knowledge of the cause! Besides unless I know how she attempts to justify her refusal, I *may* judge her motives too severely! Let me see the style in which she writes: I like to see different styles!"

"I am really ashamed to let you see it: it is so gross."

"Gross! Oh! if it be gross, its effect will be but slight!—nay, in that case, it will not annoy me at all! *Now*, if you do not allow me to see it, I shall really begin to think that your amiable aunt is a somewhat indelicate person! Are you afraid that the style will corrupt me?"

Felicia tremulously gave him the note which he read, while she anxiously watched its effect; but the only effect developed by him was a smile.

"Well," said he, having read it attentively, "all this is very amusing! It would not have been nearly so amusing had it contained any particle of truth! 'The accounts she has received are of a character so afflicting.' Well, they must have been afflicting, if true! It strikes me that, if she knew the truth, nothing would afflict her more! Still, she is not indisposed to pity. Oh! no. Pity, however, is a sentiment she does'nt understand. But that appalling 'aberration of intellect,' Felicia! That is, indeed, dreadful! And what an exceedingly *charitable* view to take of such an awful state of things! The 'despicable set' has one merit at least!—if despicable, it is very select. But the 'asylum!' Think of that, my love! If even the worst should come to the worst, she *will* afford you an 'asylum,' and an asylum is a perfectly proper place for the insane! But the way in which you are to be restored to society is the richest and most amusing feature of all, seeing that your restoration to 'society' is to be effected by a divorce! The expense of a divorce would be great, she says. It would be, in this case, great indeed! We cannot be divorced without grounds, my sweet one, and therefore these grounds, this pure and amiable creature—she must be pure as well as amiable—would *have*—which not only proves her affectionate solicitude, but proclaims the extreme delicacy of her feelings! It has been said that, 'to the pure all things are pure.' This is your aunt's illustration of its truth. Really, my love, we ought to feel exceedingly obliged to her! *I* do! This has had the effect of making me feel thankful that she cannot consent to receive you; for with such gross ideas, such low and corrupt sentiments, such despicable feelings and impure thoughts, she is not a fit associate for you. The fact of your being shut out from such pure society, may well induce tears!"

" Alfred," exclaimed Felicia, with thrilling intensity, " it is not—believe me—it is not that!"

" I know it, my love; I was speaking ironically. I was merely endeavouring to prove to you, Felicia, how little, in reality, you have to regret the loss of such impure society. As for the grossness contained in this note, smile at it, my love, as I do, with contempt; and as it will be deemed ' obtrusive' to write to her again, until I shall have become the heartless villain she contemplates, you must wait for that interesting event with becoming patience! It is certainly fortunate," he added, with a smile, " that you have friends willing to assist you in obtaining a divorce! "

" Heaven forbid that such assistance should ever be required!"

" Then would you not be divorced?"

" Not for worlds," she exclaimed, clinging fondly to him, with an expression of the most unbounded confidence and love:—" Not for worlds! "

Alfred tenderly embraced her, and a compact was sealed, that not another word should be said on the subject.

Well! the " advice and assistance" of Lady Loftus being now, of course, entirely out of the question, Felicia—who had a list of highly influential persons, the whole of whom, she felt sure, would do all in their power to promote the object she had in view—set to work to prepare her applications.

In the sphere to which she had been accustomed, she had heard appointments spoken of as matters of course: they had, indeed, in her presence been claimed as a right, while anything in the shape of a refusal had been considered a species of personal insult. She had, therefore, no conception of there being the slightest difficulty about the matter; she, on the contrary, felt, that mere courtesy would prompt them to send an appointment at once, and, accordingly, wrote with the utmost confidence.

The first person to whom she applied was Lord Lough. She selected him, not because he stood the highest on her list in official importance, but because, having always been extremely attentive to her, he might, she imagined, feel somewhat annoyed if she omitted to apply to him first; and she was, of course, very unwilling to show him the slightest disrespect.

In her letter she was eloquent in Alfred's praise. She knew not what appointment to ask for: that she would leave to his lordship, of course: she only knew that Alfred was highly intelligent, and would distinguish himself in any position to which he might have the honour to be appointed.

His lordship was evidently pleased with this letter, and in order to show how highly he appreciated the courtesy which had prompted her to apply to him first, he sent the following answer by one of his private servants:—

"Lord Lough presents his compliments to Lady Felicia Murray.

"Had Lady Felicia's application been made a few days earlier, Lord Lough might have been of some service to Mr. Murray; but he exceedingly regrets that there is, at present, no vacancy either in his immediate department, or in any department over which he has the slightest control."

"Dear me!" exclaimed Felicia, having read this note. "How very unfortunate! Only a few days earlier: what a pity: is it not?"

"If true," replied Alfred.

"*True*, my love: oh! it is perfectly true!. He would, I know, have been delighted to oblige us. However, I'll write now to Lord Delolme. He knows me well, and is, moreover, one of the most influential men in the cabinet."

She accordingly wrote to Lord Delolme, and by post next day received the following reply:—

" Downing Street.

"MADAM,

"I am directed by Lord Delolme to acknowledge the receipt of your letter of the 4th instant, and to state that, in consequence of the numerous claims on the patronage at his lordship's disposal, and the reductions in progress in the public departments, his lordship can hold out no hope whatever of an appointment.

"I am, Madam,
" Your obedient servant,
" G. P. C. W. R. FOXE."

This was somewhat disheartening, certainly; and more especially coming, as it did, from so important a person as Lord Delolme! What could be the meaning of it? He had spoken, through his secretary, of the public departments in the aggregate, and could "hold out no hope." The "reductions in progress" she ascribed to the Whigs, and she had a vague notion that the Whigs were the enemies of the country, because she had often heard the friends of the Marquis thus denounce them; but how it was that appointments, which had been just before so plentiful, should become all at once so remarkably scarce, she was utterly unable to conceive.

But although in some slight degree discouraged, she was

not by any means dismayed. The next on her list was Sir Nicholas Byrne, and conceiving that a personal interview would have more effect than a letter, she called upon Sir Nicholas, who received her with due courtesy, and listened to her warm introduction of Alfred with the most polite attention.

"But," said he, "you forget that our party is not in power!"

"Upon my word," said Felicia, "I knew not to which party you belonged!"

"Oh! we are in opposition, and consequently have *no* patronage! You should apply to some one connected with the government!"

"To whom would you advise me to apply?"

"Well, let me see. You know Sir James Joliffe?"

"Perfectly well."

"Apply to him, *He'll* do something for you. He has the power: I have not. I should feel great pleasure in promoting your views; but, as I have explained to you, being in opposition, it is perfectly impossible for me to do so."

Having expressed her sense of the politeness with which Sir Nicholas had received her, Felicia took her leave, and the next morning called upon Sir James, whose manners were equally courteous.

"Well," said he, when the object of her visit had been explained. "I hope that Mr. Murray will be successful, and I regret that it is not in my power to promote his success; I should be, of course, delighted with the opportunity of doing so, if it were practicable; but, at present, it really is not. I, at all events, have not the power to procure him an appointment: nor do I think that my colleagues have an appointment to spare; for the fact is, the present state of parties is so precarious, that every vote is an object. Let me not, however, dishearten you. Why not apply to Lord Delolme?"

"I have done so," replied Felicia.

" Well, and what did *he* say ?"

" He said that the claims on his patronage were so numerous that he could hold out no hope."

"Exactly: I, therefore, see no chance for Mr. Murray, unless, indeed, an application were made through the Marquis. —*he* might manage it—but that, I presume, you wish to avoid. What has Mr. Murray been accustomed to ?"

" Mercantile affairs," replied Felicia.

" Ah: why doesn't he go to America ? There's plenty of room there for young men of activity and enterprise. He's sure to get on there: here there's no chance for him, unless he can secure the most powerful interest. I am sorry," he added, as Felicia rose somewhat abruptly—the idea of Alfred going to America being distasteful—" I am very sorry that it is not at present in my power to do anything—because, I should be, indeed, delighted to oblige you—still, if anything within the sphere of my influence *should* occur—if any office should become vacant, to which I have the power to appoint him— you shall certainly hear from me."

Felicia bowed, and withdrew; discouraged, of course; but she did not despair even then. There were other influential men to whom she could apply, and among them was the Earl of Elfin, whom she had frequently met, and of whom she had for some time considered herself a favourite.

Finding, however, that her week was fast wearing away, she wrote to several of these influential persons at once, and was perfectly astonished when she found that all their answers were unfavourable, save one ! She couldn't account for it at all ! People whom she had heard speak of appointments, had spoken of them as things for which they had but to ask, and yet she had applied to more than a dozen persons—the whole of whom were highly influential—and all their answers had been unfavourable, save one ! What the meaning of it could be, she was unable to conjecture ! It appeared to be so *very* extraordinary! Still, this one might possibly make up for all.

It was from Sir Percival Potts, who had stated that he would see what could be done: that he would use all the influence at his command, and that he had not the smallest doubt of being able to do *something*: which was certainly satisfactory as far as it went.

Two days elapsed, and Felicia's impatience began to resolve itself into despair; but on the third day she received a second note from Sir Percival, which she opened with avidity, and read as follows :—

"Sir Percival Potts presents his compliments to Lady Felicia Murray, and has the pleasure to announce that he has succeeded in procuring through the postmaster-general, an appointment for Mr. Murray, which he hopes Mr. Murray, by strict attention to his duties, will be enabled to retain.

" Sir Percival has enclosed the necessary letter of introduction to the postmaster-general, which Mr. Murray will have but to deliver in person, in order to be set on at once.

"The appointment is not very lucrative, although it is one which hundreds are anxious to obtain. It is that of one of his Majesty's postmen, and the salary is nominally a guinea per week; but Sir Percival is informed that there are many perquisites receivable principally at Christmas."

Having read this note, Felicia's bosom swelled with indignation! This then was the result of all her exertions! It awakened a spirit which she could not control, and which prompted her at once to write the following reply :—

" Lady Felicia Murray, with feelings of scorn, acknowledges the receipt of Sir Percival's studied insult.

"Lady Felicia had imagined that Sir Percival was a gentleman; she is sorry to find that he is not. She returns the enclosed letter, with all the contempt at her command, and recommends

Sir Percival to bestow his distinguished patronage upon one who has the honour to wear his livery."

This note she immediately dispatched; and expecting the return of Alfred, who happened—fortunately as she imagined—to be from home at the time, she endeavoured to recover that tranquillity with which this "appointment" had so seriously interfered.

She paced the room, and anxiously endeavoured to imagine the cause of Sir Percival's conduct. She was unconscious of having in any way offended him. He had always been exceedingly attentive and agreeable, while she had always appreciated his politeness too highly to treat him with the slightest disrespect. What then could have prompted him thus to insult her? What could be his motive? What could he mean?

While she was endeavouring to answer these questions, and before the return of Alfred, a carriage drew up, from which Sir Percival alighted, apparently in a state of trepidation.

Felicia, who although pale, was firm, at once prepared to receive him, and desired the servant who brought up his card to admit him.

"My dear lady," said he, having entered the room, "there must be some mistake; I am quite at a loss—I don't understand your note to me at all."

"Why have you insulted me?" demanded Felicia. "In what way, Sir Percival, have I offended *you*?"

"In no way. But *how* have I insulted you?"

"Mr. Murray, Sir Percival, although not a man of high birth, is in every true sense of the term a gentleman, and yet you offer him an appointment like that. The insult is gross, sir—the animus brutal."

"My dear lady, *my* motives were pure. Is he not in a state of destitution?"

" Do we look as if we were ?"

" No; and that has amazed me since I have been here. I expected to find you in miserable lodgings."

" By whom were you led to expect that ?"

" I'll explain. I have been the *cat's paw* in this business, I find; and therefore in order to justify myself, I'll explain that which was to have been kept a secret. Now do me the favour to listen one moment. Having received your first note I called upon the Marquis, in order to ascertain what could be done. I expressed my regret that I was not in a position to do anything just then, and urged him to exercise *his* influence. He replied that he would not directly do anything himself, but suggested that if I would procure the appointment in question I should be the means of saving you both from starvation. I *hinted* that such an appointment as that would not be likely to suit Mr. Murray, but he replied, ' you don't *know* him; he'll be glad of anything; he is but a shopman out of place, and bitter experience has taught him, that beggars must not be choosers.' "

" Beggars !" exclaimed Felicia, contemptuously. " If it be beggary to apply for an appointment, the whole of the aristocracy are beggars—importunate, perpetual beggars ! Through ignorance of the matter I have erred, I perceive. But if I have been a beggar, Mr. Murray has not been one. My applications were not made at *his* suggestion."

" The Marquis said that you had made several; that all whom you had written to had spoken to him, and that he had been the cause of your being unsuccessful; still, in order, as he said, to save you from *utter* destitution, he urged me to pro- cure this appointment, and so did your sister, Lady Florence; and being thus led to believe that the case was indeed despe- rate, I applied to the Postmaster-general at once. This is the only *insult* I have offered; but I think that you will now acquit me of the intention to insult you."

"I do," replied Felicia; "and have to apologize to you for the warmth I displayed."

"No apology is needed: I can well understand your feelings; and can no longer wonder at your being indignant. I shall certainly tell both the Marquis and Lady Florence that when next they want a tool, they had better not select me. And now, as regards a suitable appointment for Mr. Murray, ministers cannot act independently at present. It is a very close run between them and the opposition. Every vote is important, and if they offend a man like the Marquis, they offend twenty others. Every trimmer and every waverer must now be secured: all the patronage at the disposal of the Government is now claimed by such men; for personal interests have become the only spurs to public duty. Mr. Murray must therefore wait. Let him wait until things are a little more secure, and I pledge you my honour that something shall be done. Meanwhile, if you *should* require any assistance, let your first application be to me."

Felicia was about to thank him, but Sir Percival checked her: nor would he hear a word of an apology: he declared that he felt disgusted with the conduct of the Marquis, and having re-assured her that something should be done, left her comparatively tranquil.

She then perceived that she had done too much; that she had written to too many persons; and that her very anxiety had induced the belief that they were in reality destitute. She felt sorry for this; but then who had been the cause? Why the Marquis! The Marquis, aided by her sister Florence,— how could she cherish feelings of affection for either?—had rendered so many applications necessary. It was cruel— unnatural!—still, knowing that their object was to humiliate and annoy her, if not absolutely to break her heart, she felt it incumbent upon her to be firm.

Soon after the departure of Sir Percival, Alfred returned,

and perceiving at a glance that Felicia had been excited, he inquired if anything had occurred.

"I have had a visitor," replied Felicia, "who has explained to me why I have not been successful. I thought it very strange; but he has accounted for all."

"By pointing to the adverse influence of the Marquis, I presume."

"Exactly."

"No matter, my love. We shall be beyond the pale of his influence soon. You have had your week, and now it is my turn."

"But Sir Percival—he it is whom I have had here—has pledged me his honour that something shall be done!"

"It will not do to wait for that something, my love. I have no faith whatever in the promises of great men, unless, indeed, they promise to annoy you. He said before that something should be done; that he had not the smallest doubt of being able to do *something*! No matter. It is, perhaps, all for the best!"

He then proceeded to explain to her the purport of a letter which he had had just received from his uncle Cyrus; and having shown her how anxiously they were expected, they decided on leaving town on the following Monday.

CHAPTER XVII.

THE MARRIAGE OF MR. WILKINS.

IF ever two persons could with truth be said to possess a perfect knowledge of each other, those two persons were Fidèle and Mr. Wilkins. They absolutely knew each other's thoughts! —which was very remarkable.

Words with them were supererogatory. If Fidèle wanted anything, Mr. Wilkins—by virtue of some extremely occult species of necromancy—knew what it was: if Mr. Wilkins wanted anything, it was known to Fidèle. This may to some appear incredible! It is, notwithstanding, well worthy of belief, as subsequent events will show.

Now, in the first place, it had been arranged that they were to accompany Alfred and Felicia : it had also been arranged that they were at the earliest convenient period to be married; and as the week for which Felicia had stipulated, and the month prescribed by Mr. Wilkins—for the election of a new member of that establishment, of which he had been so distinguished an ornament—would both expire on the same day, it occurred to Fidèle that *one* of these arrangements would not be satisfactorily carried into effect. This *occurred* to her. She did not breathe a syllable on the subject to a soul! How could she ? The point was delicate. It merely occurred to her; and yet Mr. Wilkins—when he came that evening and heard that Alfred and Felicia had decided on leaving town on Monday—looked at Fidèle and read her thoughts!

" Fidèle," said he, " you are perfectly right."

"In what, dear?" inquired Fidèle, who, by some means, had taught herself thus to address him.

"I quite agree with you," replied Mr. Wilkins. "I think as you think. It must be so. Do me the favour to lend me that ring. Is it sufficiently tight for that finger?"

"This finger, dear?"

Fidèle knew which finger! Let it not be imagined for a moment that she didn't! But she, of course, very correctly pointed to the wrong one.

Mr. Wilkins tried the ring on the right finger, and then inquired if it were really a fit.

"Yes, dear; but what *do* you mean?"

Fidèle made this inquiry obviously because she loved to hear him give expression to his meaning.

"I mean," he replied, "that I have a little article to purchase, and an interesting document to obtain, to-morrow, without which our arrangements cannot be completed. You have been thinking of this; and, very fortunately, seeing that you have just communicated that thought to me: you have just caused a glowing idea to strike me, that if these things be not procured to-morrow, we shall be for three weeks, in the eye of the law, vagabonds upon the face of the earth. I shall leave my present habitation to-morrow, and unless I get the licence before I leave, we shall have to endure a species of excommunication. I'll therefore give you fourteen hours to decide."

"Upon what, dear?" inquired Fidèle.

"Whether we are to be married on Monday morning, or wait another month."

"My love, you know that I am in no haste!"

"Nor am I! But I don't like the idea of being excommunicated."

"But why on Monday morning?"

"Because we start on Monday morning. We can't be

married at Sudbury; nor can we be married here—if I omit to procure the licence to-morrow—until we have ceased to be in the eye of law *vagabonds*, having no recognized place of abode. To-morrow, therefore, at eleven o'clock, I shall expect your decision. And now about the bridesmaid. It is too late now to send for one of my sisters: it is also too late to send for one of Alfred Murray's: shall we have Lady Florence?"

" Lady Florence!" exclaimed Fidèle, whom the idea amused. " I wonder what she *would* say, if she were to be asked?"

" Would she not regard it as a compliment? I want to *know* that gentle young lady: I should like to have the honour of her company for a few agreeable days. Would you like to call and ask her?"

" Not at present," replied Fidèle. " Nor is it necessary. Lady Felicia will act."

" Oh! then you have settled it between you! Very good: and Alfred, of course, will give me away."

" Give *you* away?"

" You, I mean: it's all the same. But Fidèle," he added, with a serious expression, " I need not, however, be at all apprehensive; still, any one else—hearing me talk thus of marriage — would imagine that I treated the subject with levity; but you know me better. By the way, have you preserved my letters?"

" I have, dear, the whole of them."

" And I have preserved the whole of yours. Be therefore cross with me at any time, if you dare! If you be, I'll on the instant produce one of those letters, and convict you of inconsistency! I think of having them published."

" I hope not," said Fidèle.

" They would make a very nice little volume, and I'm not quite sure that it wouldn't become popular! What could we call it? ' *The Loves of the Angels*,' ' *The Young Ladies' Best Companion*,' or ' *The True Course of Courtship?* ' We couldn't call it ' *The Course of True Love*,' because, according to Shakespeare, that 'never did run smooth,' whereas ours has been without a ripple !—perhaps ' *Letters of Lovers* ' would be the best title ?   We'll speak to Lady Felicia, and get her to edit it; 'Edited by Lady Felicia Murray,' would look well. But, as I was saying, some people might imagine that I regard the subject of marriage with levity, but I feel convinced that those letters of mine have sufficiently proved that I really do do not.   We marry to be happy.   Very good.   Stop !—Here's a point for profound consideration.   Look at Alfred, and look at me.   When Alfred is happy, he's perfectly calm : when I am happy, I must be gay !   Now I wonder which enjoys the state of happiness most.   We cannot but be happy, it is true ; but which is the happier man—he who gives expression to all his happiness, or he by whom it is quietly cherished ?   Now there's a job for a philosopher !"

" Could a philosopher decide the point ?" inquired Fidèle.

" He might try," replied Mr. Wilkins.

" Would he be the proper person to make the attempt ?"

" He would think so."

" Can philosophers understand gaiety ?"

" They who do not are no philosophers."

" But are philosophers ever gay ?"

" Gaiety is part of their philosophy !   A recluse is not a philosopher !   Philosophy is not austere and ascetic.   Philosophy loves a glass of wine : philosophy loves to marry !   Philosophy has its amenities as well as its severities !   But which do *you* think is the happier man ?"

" I feel scarcely competent to form a judgment," replied Fidèle; " but I should *say* that if they be equally happy, *neither* is the happier man !"

" Very good," said Mr. Wilkins.   " That isn't so much amiss. But which enjoys happiness most ?"

" As far as the *show* of happiness is concerned, the difference,

I apprehend, may be ascribed to temperament! Certainly," added Fidèle, as Mr. Wilkins began to feel that he shouldn't get over it; " Certainly, he who expresses all his happiness does more to inspire those around him with gaiety, than he who keeps it within his own breast ; but is he not more likely to depress them, by giving full expression to his sorrow or his anger? Mr. Murray is happy; and although he is calm, he makes us all feel that he is happy. But can he who is habitually calm, and he who is habitually gay endure troubles with an equal amount of fortitude ?"

" There's something in that," replied Mr. Wilkins, who felt that it was all over with him on that point. " There certainly is something in that: not that I can pretend to know anything about it, because I never had any troubles."

" Heaven grant that you never may have!" exclaimed Fidèle. " I have known "—

" That is to say," interrupted Mr. Wilkins, perceiving that her thoughts had reverted to the period of which Alfred had spoken, and to which she had touchingly referred in one of her letters. " That is to say, I never had but *one*, and that was through a servile thief of a Scotchman."

He then proceeded rapidly to relate to her how this "vagabond" had served him, and thus amused her until Alfred and Felicia —who had been to a concert—returned, when he playfully charged Alfred with a malicious intention to put his marriage off for three weeks, and having spent, as usual, a merry hour with them, he bade them adieu for the night.

Fidèle failed not, of course, to embrace the earliest opportunity of communicating to Felicia the grand point at issue. This was done shortly after the departure of Mr. Wilkins. The consultation was but short, and the result of it was that, precisely at eleven o'clock the next morning, Felicia—Fidèle could'nt do it herself—informed Mr. Wilkins that, if he really were anxious for the marriage to take place on the Monday, Fidèle did'nt see how she *could*—offer any objection.

The ring and the licence were therefore procured, and due preparations were made for the event; and on Monday morning, at half-past eight, Fidèle became Mrs. Bartholomew Wilkins!

The whole of the arrangements for the day were left to Alfred; and as there was, of course, no necessity, as in his case, for haste, they returned to his lodgings to breakfast. It is however worthy of remark, that Mr. Wilkins was not so merry that morning: nor did he eat as if he enjoyed his breakfast: everything on the table was tempting, but his appetite was not particularly keen. He looked at Fidèle—who, although calm, was happy, and whom he had never so much admired before— as if he had'nt become exactly reconciled to the novelty of the position in which he had been placed. He smiled, it is true, but did'nt laugh: nor did he " come out" with any anecdotes of a strictly comic character: he certainly said that he had not the slightest doubt that the moon—the honeymoon he meant— would be as bright at Sudbury as it had been at Brighton; but beyond this he did'nt say much.

Alfred was, on the contrary, remarkably gay, and so indeed was Felicia. They enjoyed the novel position of Mr. Wilkins highly, and didn't fail to rally both him and Fidèle—but to very little purpose—during the progress of breakfast. After breakfast Mr. Wilkins felt a little more buoyant, and when they had started he became lighter still, and continued to improve upon it gradually, until they reached Chelmsford, when he threw off all restraint and was ' " himself again!"

Here they had lunch, and Mr. Wilkins both laughed and ate heartily: he very soon made up for the loss of his breakfast: nor did Fidèle fail to enjoy herself here, although her countenance still wore a certain thoughtful expression, which none but those who are conversant with these matters can understand.

They had then twenty-five miles to go, and as Alfred was anxious to arrive at Sudbury at the time appointed—having commissioned his uncle Cyrus to order dinner at the Crown— they almost immediately after lunch pursued their journey.

The time appointed for their arrival was four o'clock; but Mrs. Murray became so exceedingly anxious, that she couldn't wait till four!—nor could Cyrus. They therefore ordered a carriage at the Crown, and at two o'clock started to meet " the boy!"

They reached the George, at Halstead, about three, and shortly afterwards Alfred and his party approached; and— having changed at the White Hart, at Braintree—were about to pass through, but, were stopped by one of the postboys, who knew Alfred well, and who informed him that his mother and his uncle were there to meet him. Alfred therefore instantly alighted, and rushed into the room in which they were.

" My boy!—my boy!" exclaimed Mrs. Murray, in tones of thrilling ecstacy, as she fell upon his neck, " God bless you ! *God* bless you !" she added, and kissed him, with rapture, again and again.

" Ha, ha, ha, ha!" exclaimed Cyrus, as he grasped his hand, convulsively, " *Welcome*, my dear boy ! Ha, ha, ha, ha!"

" Mother," said Alfred, with deep emotion, " Mother!" He could say no more. Still clinging fondly to him, and looking at him, as a dear mother only *can* look, she unmanned him.

Cyrus went to the window. There was something in his throat : something which continued to swell!—he *couldn't* keep it down, and, therefore, drew forth his handkerchief privately.

At length he made a desperate effort, and turned. " The bride, my dear boy," said he ; " I want to see the bride. Come along. — Gods in heaven!" he added, as he felt the tears rolling down his cheeks, "this'll *never* do: she'll think we're not happy to see her. Louisa: come, come: now, compose yourself. There!— I say, my boy, go and bring her in: I want to fall in love; bring them all in. Here, here, a glass of wine, and then go and bring them in."

Alfred, having led his fond mother to the sofa, left the room, and soon returned with Felicia, who no sooner saw Mrs. Murray, than she flew to embrace her.

The beauty of Felicia struck Cyrus with amazement, and as she lingered in the arms of Mrs. Murray, he stood for a moment as if bewildered.

"Uncle," said Alfred, "Mr. and Mrs. Wilkins."

Cyrus seized them both by the hand, and exclaimed, "I'm glad to see you!—proud to know you! I have heard of you both! God bless you both! May you be—as you deserve to be—*happy!*"

He then turned to Felicia, and having looked at her earnestly, while pressing her hand, said, "I haven't exactly my faculties now. You have taken them away. When I have *recovered* them—I'll tell you what I mean."

Fidèle and Mr. Wilkins were then presented to Mrs. Murray, while Cyrus rang the bell, and ordered champagne. "Now, sit down," said he, "for *five* minutes. We have plenty of time. We have but eight miles to go. But," he added, how are we to do that eight miles? How are we to be divided?"

"The ladies," suggested Alfred, "perhaps, would like to go together?"

"I don't think," said Cyrus, "that the ladies would like to deprive us of their society! I don't think that they have the hearts to do it! Will you do me the favour to accompany *me?*" he added, addressing Felicia, who still nestled near Mrs. Murray.

Felicia bowed.

"And so will you," said Cyrus, turning to Mrs. Murray. "There, you see, I've won two already! You young dogs are not to have it *all* your own way! I must not, of course, *to-day* attempt to win Mrs. Wilkins; but two will be sufficient for me."

This was held to be a very good arrangement; and when the champagne had been twice round, they started. On the road, however, Cyrus had but little to say. He had enough to do to look at Felicia, who conversed almost incessantly with Mrs. Murray. He had quite enough to do to admire *her*, for in his view it was perfectly impossible for any one to be more intelligent, or more beautiful. She eclipsed all that he had conceived her to be, and his conceptions had been of a very high caste: she was the only one who had ever approached his ideas of perfect loveliness, and he thought of the words of James: "The very first time you see her, you'll love her; and when you come to know what she really is—how amiable, affectionate, and good—she'll be just as much to you as if she were your own child."

On their arrival at the Crown, they were joyfully received by Murray and his eldest daughter, Julia; and when warm congratulations had been again and again repeated, the ladies retired to dress for dinner.

Cyrus had invited Mr. Chubb, as one of Alfred's warmest friends; but Mr. Chubb had declined the invitation on the ground of his not being one of the family. When, however, it was known that Mr. Chubb was in the house, Cyrus *would* have him up; and when he did come up, he was not permitted to go down again. Nor, after the first five minutes, did he wish to go down, for he took so deep an interest in all that concerned Alfred, and found Mr. Wilkins so exceedingly agreeable, that although he was *not*, as he said, one of the family, he felt quite as much at home as if he had been.

The ladies having rejoined them, dinner was announced, and a really sumptuous dinner it was. Cyrus had told Greene to spare no expense, and Greene was proud of showing what he *could* do. The most delicious things that he could think of were produced, and he knew—he didn't want to be told, he *knew*—that there was no man in the eastern counties capable of getting a dinner up like him!

During dinner, however, delicious as it was, Felicia was the centre of attraction. Her grace, her beauty, her amiable attentions, and easy elegance charmed them. Cyrus shed tears, he was so delighted with her; and Chubb said privately, and of course in strict confidence, that if "when he was young he ha' happened of her, he'd ha' fallen right dead in love himself." Fidèle, they admitted, was very elegant and very beautiful—*she* was exceedingly lady-like and pleasing; but Felicia! "They may well call her an angel," whispered Cyrus. "True," returned Chubb, "and they may well call the Marquis —no matter."

After dinner Alfred's sweet little sisters arrived to "kiss dear Lady Felicia," who was delighted with them, and had them all near her, and supplied them with the choicest fruits on the table, and chatted with them all so familiarly, that they very soon became the best friends in the world. They felt that they loved her before they saw her, but then they loved her dearly, while Felicia, in the bosom of so amiable a family, whose affection was so genuine, felt happy indeed.

In consequence of a little freemasonry between Mrs. Murray, Felicia, and Fidèle, which Cyrus, however, appeared to understand, the ladies retired unusually early, when Alfred, who in his letters had spoken of Mr. Wilkins in very high terms, proposed in a speech of much eloquence and tact, the "health of the bride and the bridegroom."

This was received with much warmth, and when they had not only cheered him, but shaken him by the hand with the utmost cordiality, he rose to acknowledge the compliment, amid silence the most profound.

"Gentlemen," said he, "when hearts are all right, how soon perfect strangers are converted into friends! I have a great idea of the knowledge of the heart. I believe that hearts become acquainted with each other, and fall in love with each other: that by virtue of some mysterious species of electricity, they communicate with each other; that they teach themselves to cling to each other, and nothing clings to that which it abhors. We say that our hearts *tell* us to like such and such men, and to dislike such and such others; and when we say this, depend upon it, there is more in what we say than human reason can define. Gentlemen! you are strangers to me; I never saw you before; and yet I feel that I *know* that you have warm and generous hearts. My own heart *tells* me that you have; your hearts have communicated the fact to mine, and prompted me to respect you. Gentlemen! I appreciate your friendship, which is the more pleasing to me, because you are connected with one for whom I have a *brother's* love, and of whose friendship any man, whether he be a merchant *or* a marquis, might be proud. You, sir, are his father: there is no man in Europe, sir, blessed with a more noble-hearted son. You are his uncle; and of all the affection which I *know* that you have for him, he is worthy; while you, sir, who are his *friend*, possess in that name, sir, a title as honourable to you as if it were that of an earl. [Here Mr. Chubb seized the hand of Cyrus, and, with a mysterious expression, shook it heartily.] Gentlemen!" continued Mr. Wilkins, "we are all men of business, and therefore can speak as men of business. This is not a thoughtless, extravagant creature, whom Alfred Murray has married! She is not one who will squander away every shilling she is able to get hold of—not one of those who can think of nothing but drawing-rooms, dress, and dancing!—She is a wife who will take care of number one, and who will not spend a pound unnecessarily! This has been *proved*, and the proof, considering the style in which she has lived, not only delighted but amazed me. In society you have seen what she is, you saw how attentive she was to us all, and how delighted she was with those beautiful children! Amiable, affectionate, elegant, and pure—she must command the admiration of all but the vicious. This is one of Nature's matches, gentlemen!—Nature made *this* match!—and I have a large idea of Nature. I feel that when Nature becomes the study not of the few but of the mass, we shall, in the aggre. gate, act more in conformity with her laws. She is, or ought to be, in all things our guide. We go to her for instruction, and she imparts it: we have but to study to adore her. We talk of our inventions, and think much of them; but what are they but copies from Nature! Genius is a flash of Nature's light- ning! she is *the* universal genius. Go through the whole of our professions and our trades, and we shall find that Nature is the genius of them all. She is the finest doctor, the finest lawyer, the finest preacher, the finest machinist, the finest chemist, and the finest mathematician: she is the finest weaver, look at her webs; the finest joiner, look at her joints: the finest tailor, look at her bears: the finest draper, look at her birds: the finest tanner, look at her hides. Over all creation Nature presides. We see her in the valleys, and we see her on the mountains; we see her on the ocean, and we see her in the stars; we see her in the wonderful trunk of an elephant, and we see her in the very hind quarters of a flea. Look at a flea, we're all after him; but he who catches one of those fellows catches one of the finest works of Nature. Look at his hind quarters, look at his spring. If *we* could leap as far in proportion to our size, a leap and a half would take us over Europe. I mention these matters in order to show that in all Nature's works there is much to admire; and as this match, gentlemen, is one of Na- ture's works, it is worthy of all admiration. Lady Felicia is·a

wonderful work of nature, and I am happy to say, that through
Alfred—I should never have known her but for him—I have a
wife of the same pattern. They have been companions for
years, and will be I hope for years to come. I hope that we
shall all be companions. I don't know where I may be settled,
but this I know, gentlemen, that I have so high an appreciation
of the kindness of your hearts, that if I live ten thousand miles
away, I shall ever cherish a fond recollection of you all."

The hand of Mr. Wilkins was again in requisition; they
really felt as if they couldn't shake it enough. They did,
however, eventually allow him to sit down; but he had no
sooner done so than he rose again, and in a brief speech proposed to them the health of Mr. Murray.

This toast was hailed with great pleasure, and after a pause,
Mr. Murray slowly rose, and said, in tremulous accents—
" Gentlemen : I thank you for the compliment you have paid
me. My heart is too full to allow me to express what I feel,
but if the theory of Mr. Wilkins be sound—and I believe that
to a great extent it is—the expression of my feelings on this
occasion, may be dispensed with. Gentlemen, I am glad to
see you all. May we long enjoy each other's society in this
world, and meet again hereafter."

Cyrus then left the room—he had evidently something on his
mind—and during his absence his health was proposed by Alfred,
when Mr. Wilkins, who was listened to with the most profound
attention, began to explain the characteristics of various
domestic animals—including the dog, the cat, the rat, and the
mouse—and eventually gave an elaborate definition of the line
which separates instinct from reason.

To Murray, and his friend Chubb, this was amusing, but
Alfred wondered what detained his uncle, seeing that he
had been absent then more than half an hour ! Presently,
however, he heard carriages start, and Cyrus re-entered the
room.

The interesting fact of his having had his health drunk, with all the honours, during his absence, was then communicated to him, with due propriety; and when he had had a glass of wine, with the view of doing full justice to the toast by drinking his own health, he rose and said, in tones of peculiar depth and "fatness:"—"Gentlemen: I'm a stout man— a very stout man—I weigh no-matter-how-many stone; but were I twice the size—which Heaven forbid!—I shouldn't have a breast half big enough to hold the joyous feelings which this happy meeting has inspired. I have seen so much beauty, witnessed so much affection, proved the existence of so much manly friendship, and heard so many generous sentiments expressed, that were I to call this the happiest day of my life, I shouldn't be very far wrong. I am delighted with Lady Felicia. I'm delighted with you all. I'm delighted with everybody and everything, and all I can say is, God bless you all, and may you always feel as happy as I do now."

Murray then proposed the health of Mr. Chubb, and when that gentleman had very appropriately explained, that he agreed with all that had been said by those who had spoken before him, and that he had never enjoyed himself so much since he was born, Cyrus gave them, "The Ladies," and added with much *gusto*, "When we've drunk their health—God bless them!—we'll rejoin them."

The toast was drunk with enthusiasm, and Alfred then inquired in which room they were.

"In which room?" returned Cyrus. "They're in no room in this house! They're off, bag and baggage!"

"Off! Where?"

"Home, of course!"

"What! father's?"

"No, your own home! Do you think you hav'nt got a home to go to?"

"Well, but where is it?"

U

"Not far," replied Cyrus. "One of Mr. Wilkins's *fleas* would leap the distance in no time. Come along."

Alfred couldn't understand this at all! He nevertheless followed his uncle, and found a carriage ready to convey them.

"Now," said Cyrus, "you are the youngest; mount that horse: we can't all get in here."

Alfred accordingly mounted the horse, while Cyrus, Murray, Chubb, and Mr. Wilkins, entered the carriage, when Greene the landlord, who had all his men—and many more who did'nt belong to him—ready, gave Alfred nine enthusiastic cheers, in the midst of which the happy party started.

They had but three miles to go, and Cyrus explained to Mr. Wilkins on the road that, in order to promote the comfort of all, he had furnished a house at Melford. "You'll feel more at home there," he added; "you'll be more to yourselves, more quiet, more retired than you could be by any possibility at an inn."

Mr. Wilkins, of course, highly appreciated this, and expressed his sense of the obligation warmly.

"How far have we to go?" inquired Alfred, riding up to the carriage when within half a mile of the *town* of Melford.

"To the first house on the left," replied Cyrus; and Alfred, perceiving Felicia and her friends on the lawn, galloped off on the instant.

"Oh! Alfred," exclaimed Felicia, before he dismounted, "What a beautiful place!—so handsomely furnished, and such a sweet garden!"

"I'm glad that you like it, my love," returned Alfred. "I had no idea of this."

The carriage now arrived, and when Cyrus had alighted, Felicia said: "I know not how to thank you," and—kissed him!

Mr. Wilkins then rallied his "run-away wife." It was a fine theme for him, and he made the most of it; and when they had all walked round the garden together, admiring everything they saw, and seeing everything to admire, they had coffee in what was pronounced to be "one of the sweetest little rooms they had ever seen."

Certainly Cyrus had displayed great taste: there could be no doubt about that. Everything was—on a small scale—splendid; and everything had been admirably arranged. Felicia knew not how to express her delight: she knew that all had been done to delight her, and felt more happy than ever!

But they all felt happy—truly happy—and happily they passed the evening together, until at the time appointed the carriages arrived, when after the most affectionate expressions of endearment, and infinitely more kissing than ever took place on any occasion in *that* house before, Cyrus and Chubb, with Mr. and Mrs. Murray and their beautiful girls, left their happy friends for the night.

CHAPTER XVIII.

NOVEL VIEWS.

FIDÈLE and Felicia were now more like sisters than ever. There never had been any display of superiority on the part of Felicia; nor would it have been at any time felt, but for the deferential conduct of Fidèle ; but now, although she assumed no more, Fidèle ceased to feel that conventional inequality by which she had been almost unconsciously influenced, and, loving Felicia fondly as she did, she regarded her as a sister indeed.

Nor did Alfred and Mr. Wilkins—to whose manners example had given a refined tone, and whom Fidèle now called " Barley" —and he admitted that "Bartholomew" was "a mouthful"— appear less like brothers.   They consulted each other on every point, and drew out a variety of plans for the future, the chief of which was that of going into partnership, and " carrying all before them ;" but the whole of these well-conceived plans were set aside by a singular observation of Mr. Wilkins.

" Alfred," said Felicia, having dwelt upon the idea which this observation had engendered, "I have been thinking of the playful proposition of Mr. Wilkins to publish that volume of correspondence which passed between him and Fidèle."

" A good speculation !" said Alfred, with a smile. " I'll certainly be one of the subscribers !"

" Yes, dear; but that jest of his has been the germ of a thought which may tend to supersede the necessity for your going into business."

" Indeed !"

" You are an excellent scholar," pursued Felicia. " You

write with great purity of expression: you are studious, reflective, persevering, and patient!—Could you not write a novel?"

"A novel?" echoed Alfred, thoughtfully.

"I feel *sure* that you could!"

"I fear that I have not sufficient knowledge of the world."

"Younger men than you have written novels, my love!—And I feel quite convinced, dear, that you could. I know that you can write with great spirit and feeling, both of which, in a novel, are delightful."

"But *I* have not been a novel reader!"

"So much the better, my love! You will be likely to write with more originality."

"But what description of novel?—Not a fashionable novel?"

"Why not?"

"I have not moved in fashionable circles!"

"You mean in what is falsely called the best society. But *I* have, dear! and I could suggest to you *such* a host of incidents!—all drawn from real life: and *such* a variety of singular characters! Oh! I feel perfectly sure that you could do it!"

"Well," returned Alfred, "I am certainly not quite sure that I could not! I like the idea much, and would adopt it with pleasure, if I felt that I could do so successfully."

"My love, have confidence. *Feel* sure that you could. I have heard that, 'They can conquer who believe they can.' Now, do oblige me, dear, by inspiring this belief. I'll give you such a number of kisses!—I'll be kissing you all the time that you are writing."

"I shall be able to get on then, no doubt!"

"But seriously, dear, will you try?"

"Certainly I will, and that with infinite pleasure, although I still feel afraid"—

"Fear nothing!—You have but to try, to succeed."

"I am not quite so sanguine, my sweet girl! However, I am pleased with the suggestion, and will endeavour to adopt it, although I am unconscious of having the necessary talent."

"I know that you have tact, my love, and I have heard that tact is the highest order of talent!"

"They may co-exist, my dear: certainly, a man possessing the highest order of talent may have tact; but I apprehend that tact and the highest order of talent are by no means convertible terms. There can be no doubt that he who has tact is enabled to get on *faster* than he who possesses the highest order of talent, seeing that the highest order of talent generally struggles against the stream, while tact is content to glide smoothly with the tide. There are some men who will not go with the current: there are others who have not the power to stem it: still, although, of course, conscious of not having the highest order of talent, and perfectly unconscious of having the necessary tact, I'll try what I can do, and shall not be entirely struck down if I should fail."

"*You* will not fail: I'll not dream of a failure; and if I once know that you do, I'll awake you. I have, of course, no idea of how long it will take; but we hear of such sums being given for novels, that were you to write only one in a year, it would enable us to live in a style of independence."

"Those sums, my love, are, of course, given only to men who have become popular—men who are well known, and whose works are extensively appreciated!"

"Still, every one of them had a beginning. Besides! what a delightful place this is to write in!—so quiet, so retired, so suggestive of thought! Now, which room, dear, shall we convert into a study?—this which overlooks the garden?"

"I'll leave that entirely to you; I don't know how I shall get on, but"—

"*I* do! I know that you will get on excellently well! And what a pleasing occupation it is!—so intellectual and so independent! You will sit down immediately after breakfast, and when I fancy that you have written sufficient we'll go out for a walk, and then towards the evening you can do a little more, and when I think that you are tired we'll go out again, or in the winter we can sit together, and while I am reading to you some suggestive work, you can take notes and reflect upon what you have written, and think over what you have still to write. It will be so delightful! And then I can read what you have written, and soon become sufficiently bold to make observations and to offer suggestions, and tell you how I like it, and that which pleases me, dear, may please many more!"

"If you were to be my only critic," said Alfred, "I should not be much alarmed!"

"But if the thing be really good, my dear, you need not fear even professional critics!"

"In the works of some men critics look for the beauties: in the works of others, they look for faults."

"But we'll be before them? If there be any faults we'll find them ourselves, and not let the critics see them! Of course, a thing of this kind, although light, requires thought: it is not to be dashed off and done with like a letter!—you will require some little preparation—some training!"

"Well, including this necessary training, how long do you imagine that I should be about it!"

"I have really no idea: we shall be better able to judge when you have made a beginning; but suppose that it should occupy six months?"

"That's a long time to speculate upon," said Alfred thoughtfully.

"I am aware of it. And I know what you are thinking of: but we can manage: I can manage it myself! The question with you is, how are we to live in the interim without the assistance of friends? Now leave that entirely to me, my dear. Don't give it a thought. I know exactly how much we shall require. I've made all my calculations. Let us say six months. It may not require so much time; nor do I believe that it will, but we'll say six months; I can manage."

" But how, my love ?"

" Be kind enough to leave that to *me*," replied Felicia, playfully. " Now when will you commence ?"

" When you please !"

" Then begin to-morrow morning. I'll have the room ready. I'll allow you two hours to draw out a sketch: you must not do too much to begin with."

" Very good. Now, what tone am I to take ? Am I to write severely ?"

" For a fashionable novel, the truth is at all times sufficiently severe. It has often been remarked, that they who have moved in aristocratic circles, portray aristocratic manners and feelings most severely. This is merely because they know the truth and tell it. Real characters will do, my dear : caricatures are not at all required."

" Well," said Alfred, thoughtfully, " we shall see."

" I'll ascertain what uncle Cyrus thinks of the plan : he'll be here by and by. But you have made me *so* happy, by falling so readily into my views, and I feel *so* sure of your being successful !"

He embraced her, and she left him; and the subject at once engrossed all his thoughts. It opened to him quite a new field for contemplation—a field too, which he contemplated with pleasure. The idea was, in his view, excellent; and although he had no lofty opinion of his own powers, and *could* have no knowledge of their extent, he saw nothing insuperable !—nothing which perseverance might not enable him to accomplish. Hence, instead of waiting until the morning to commence, he began to work at once; and when Cyrus called, as usual, to take Felicia for a drive, he found him in his appointed " study," deep in thought.

"My boy," exclaimed Cyrus, as he entered the room, "what's the matter? Lost your spirits? What's the matter?"

"I'm endeavouring to work out an idea," replied Alfred, "an idea which pleases me much."

"You don't appear to be particularly pleased!" observed Cyrus.

"I am, uncle, nevertheless, But Felicia will explain the matter to you. I'm busy."

"Very good!" returned Cyrus, who didn't, of course, pretend to understand it; but, as Felicia, who was then dressing, would explain all to him, he said no more, but went to wait for her in the garden.

Cyrus, who was not only delighted with Felicia, but almost beyond conception proud of her, visited them daily. He had purchased a horse and phaeton, expressly for the purpose of driving over to Melford, and taking her out, sometimes accompanied by Fidèle and her "Barley," but generally alone; and nothing pleased him more than to drive her into Sudbury, that all there might see that the Lady Felicia was yet some distance from starvation point.

Nor was she the only attraction on these occasions: *his* personal appearance created a sensation. He had previously paid but slight attention to dress: a suit of black put on "anyhow," and a hat of which the shape was anything but *distingué*, formed the chief characteristics of his daily "turn out;" but now with his broad-brimmed beaver, turned up at the sides, his blue coat studded with brilliant metal buttons, his primrose waistcoat ample enough to envelope *three* men, his cassimere "smalls," as they were called in those days, and his black silk stockings and polished silver buckles—he looked like "a squire of high degree," and absolutely felt as if he were one!

"My love," said he, when Felicia had joined him in the garden, "You have to explain to me the cause of Alfred's thoughtfulness this morning. He says that he is pleased, but he does not appear to be particularly gay! What is it all about?"

Felicia explained, and while doing so praised Alfred's talents so highly, and spoke with so much confidence of his success, that Cyrus, whose latent views it suited precisely—was perfectly charmed with the idea.

"That will do," said he. "The very thing! That will just do. You may have noticed, my love, that when he and Mr. Wilkins—whom I highly respect—have spoken about entering into partnership, I have been silent : not because it might not or could not be managed, but because I've no desire to see him established in business—a fact which you will both understand by and by. Now this—if he can do it, and you appear to be very sanguine on the subject—is the very thing that I should like to see him do!—it will, at all events, enlarge his views, and train him to habits of reflection and application. Encourage him, therefore, by all the means of which you are capable—your encouragement will go a great way — and although I don't pretend to understand much about it, I shall, for your sake, glory in his success."

"He'll succeed, dear uncle!—I know that he will. And now," she added, archly, "I want you to do me a favour—a favour which involves a secret, which must not—at all events at present—be revealed."

"Well, my love! let us go into the arbour.—Now then," he added, having led her to a seat, and sat beside her, "what is it?"

"I have no idea," replied Felicia, "how long it will take him to write this novel; perhaps three or four months; perhaps five or six; but to be safe we had better say six months; and during that time I am anxious for him not to be troubled with matters of a pecuniary nature : in fact, I have undertaken to manage this without him, and hence it is that I want your assistance."

"You shall certainly have it, my love! I'll lend you whatever sum you may require. How much will you want?"

"Nay! I do not wish to borrow; nor will I do so: I'll not tax your kindness in that way: I appreciate your affection: I'll not tax your purse. The favour I wish you to do for me is not to lend me money: it is certainly to get me some, and that in a way which, as I have said, involves a secret. Now, I have a few diamonds, the value of which I don't know, but which I shall never again want to wear."

"How is it possible for you to know that?" said Cyrus. "*How* is it possible for you to know that?"

"Well, it certainly is impossible for me to know, but I should say that, in all *probability*, I never shall! Now, some of these diamonds were given to me by a dear, kind soul, whom you knew."

"The late Marquis, I presume."

"Exactly: and those—if even I never again wear them— I am anxious to retain; but there are some to which I attach no value beyond their intrinsic worth, and those I wish you to sell for me."

"Do you wish to have a desperate quarrel with me? Because if you sell any one of them, or say another word about selling any one of them, we shall have a very desperate quarrel indeed! Where are these diamonds?"

"Shall I go and bring them to you?"

"Do so, my love. I should like to see them."

Felicia accordingly left the arbour, while he thought of a plan to supply their wants without letting either of them know "too much."

"These," said Felicia, on her return, "are the jewels I wish to preserve. To those I attach no importance."

"Very pretty," said Cyrus, having examined them; "very— very pretty indeed; and I think that they would look quite as pretty upon you as they would upon any one else; indeed,

I know that they would!—and if you don't wear them, or some of them, every time I dine with you, I shall regard it as a want of courtesy. Wear them, by all means! I like to see you look like what you are! Everything which tends to enhance your natural beauty delights me! Wear them, my dear! Don't say another word about parting with one of them! What money you want, from time to time, you shall have; but if you say another word about parting with your jewels, you will give me great pain, which I know that you would not do wantonly. These, however, are not the only jewels you have, or *will* have. Lady Loftus has in her possession a suite of brilliants which will, at her death, revert to you."

"Indeed! I was not aware of that."

"I have had the will of the late Marquis examined, and in that will those brilliants are named."

"Can you then tell me what property I shall have in the event of my aunt's death?"

"Yes: five thousand pounds."

"Has my aunt the power of bequeathing that sum to any one else?"

"Certainly not. Both the money and the jewels are left in trust for her use during her life, and at her death they become absolutely yours. Her death, however, must not be calculated upon. It is, of course, as well for you to know these things. I have *heard* of Lady Loftus! But we'll not talk about anything disagreeable now. You preserve your jewels, my love, and—if it be only to delight *me*—wear them. And now," he added, "we'll go for a drive. As Mr. and Mrs. Wilkins are at my brother's, shall we go, my dear, and meet them?"

Felicia, of course, with pleasure consented, and as Alfred, who was still "busy," wished to remain at home, they left him, and started for Sudbury.

Mr. Wilkins and Mr. Murray had become great friends, and this morning had been appointed for Mr. Murray to explain to Mr. Wilkins the true cause of his trade having fallen off.

While, therefore, Fidèle was engaged with the girls—the whole of whom she had set to work, one to learn French, another drawing, another embroidery, and so on—Mr. Murray produced the hand-bills, and with an expression of solemnity proceeded with his sad explanation.

At first, Mr. Wilkins was exceedingly thoughtful, and shook his head very severely at that which was, of course, understood to be the hand-bill of the Marquis.

"Does Lady Felicia know of this?" he inquired.

"No," replied Murray, "nor does Alfred."

"That's right. Better keep it from them both if you can. It would only distress them. But," he added, having read the bill issued and signed by Cyrus : "this upsets that altogether!"

"But look at the effect it has had upon my business!"

"Oh! you'll soon get over that."

"I fear not," returned Murray. "The trade appears to be irrecoverably lost!"

"And will be, doubtless, if *you* appear to be irrecoverably lost! Make a stir, and bring it back, sir! There's nothing in life like a stir."

"But what stir can I make?—what sort of a stir?"

"I'll tell you what sort of a stir *I* should make!—I'd renovate the whole establishment. I'd send to London for a man whom I know, and get his estimate for a splendid new front.—You have a lease, I suppose?"

"Yes, with five years unexpired."

"Well then, in the first place, stick in a new front, and in the next, make a brilliant show, and advertise well. Let it be the cheapest, as well as the most attractive shop in the town. Look more to returns, and less to large profits. Five per cent. upon large returns, will give a man a splendid income: fifty per cent. upon small returns, will hardly enable him to live.

Thus the big ones swallow the little ones up! The little ones can't compete with them in either agriculture or commerce! Look, therefore, principally to the returns, and with a renovated establishment, you'll soon get your trade back, and twice as much to it; but if you go on in this dull despairing way, people will begin to think that you can't last long, and then, of course, the thing will dwindle down to nothing. Everybody goes where everybody goes: but where nobody goes, sir, nobody *will* go. Rats abandon a falling house, and in this respect men and women are like them. Let a house have the appearance of prosperity, and people will make it in reality prosperous; but let it have the appearance of poverty, and they'll make it, by keeping away, poor indeed. People don't like the look of poverty; they can't bear the sight of it, and the poorer they are, the more they admire splendour! Therefore, stick in a splendid shop front to begin with, and have your name emblazoned as if you were proud of it. Let it be in letters of gold, six feet high!"

"But a new front would cost a deal of money, would it not?"

"Not so much as you might imagine. But look at the speculation!—never mind a little expense! Suppose it cost eighty or a hundred pounds!—it would soon clear itself! Attraction is the great point, and such a front as that which I mean, would, in a town like this, be of itself a great attraction; and that, combined with cheapness, would inevitably bring them. They *would* come. They couldn't keep away. They don't deal with a man to oblige him!—they do it to accommodate themselves. They'll not give him a great price because they respect him!—they'll go to the cheapest market as we do. The more they believe that a man wants support, the less they'll give him; but the less he appears to want it, the more he'll have. The appearance is the thing! Now, just think the matter over. Send for this man—he'll be glad to come down on speculation, and you can't get it properly done by any one here—send for him: he'll give to the place an appearance of prosperity, whereas it looks now like the abode of despair. Now, *do* think the matter over. *Will* you?"

Murray not only promised that he would do so, but was so highly pleased with the suggestion that he went into a variety of calculations with Mr. Wilkins, who continued to illustrate the expediency of a "grand stir," until Fidèle rejoined him, when, unconscious of Cyrus and Felicia having started to meet them, they left with the view of walking home.

"Barley, dear," said Fidèle, as they passed through the town, "don't you think that if I were to open a school, I should have a fair number of pupils?"

"Yes," replied Mr. Wilkins; "I have not the slightest doubt of it."

"Well, I'm very fond of children, and I'm very fond of teaching; and Mrs. Murray has just informed me that there is, at the present time, a very excellent opening here!"

"Well, my love?"

"Well, dear, suppose I *were* to open a school."

"There is no *necessity* for it, Fidèle!"

"Necessity?"

"No one, except as a matter of necessity, would, I apprehend, think of keeping a school!"

"But teaching, to me, is a pleasure!"

"It may be, my love, on a small scale; but it strikes me that, if you had twenty or thirty pupils, you would not find it quite so pleasurable!"

"I feel sure that I could manage them."

"No doubt of that!"

"Well, then, calculate how much in the course of the year I should receive for the instruction of twenty or thirty pupils!"

"Why, what are you dreaming about, Fidèle! Do you imagine that I would allow you to be pestered"—

"Nay, dear! Still, I might render some assistance."

"When I can't support a respectable establishment without your assistance—except, indeed, in so far as affairs of a purely domestic character are concerned—I'll consent, my love, to think the matter over; but I shall have, even then, to think a very long time before I consent to have you troubled with a school. I don't, of course, know yet where I may settle; but let me settle where I may, Fidèle, I shall always be able to support you, I hope, without bringing your accomplishments to market. But look," he added, as Cyrus and Felicia approached. "What a fine-hearted, splendid old fellow he is!"

"Well, my boy," said Cyrus, "I thought we should meet you. Jump up."

"Are you going to your brother's?" inquired Mr. Wilkins.

"No: I think not. We haven't time. I have an invitation to dine with you to-day, and I don't want to hurry the horse."

Having entered the phaeton, Fidèle began to chat with Felicia; and as Cyrus knew why the appointment that morning had been made, Mr. Wilkins proceeded to explain to him the substance of all that had passed.

"Ah," said Cyrus, "he wants a man like *you* to join him! I like your views much, and he shall adopt them, too, if I have any influence over him; but he wants a little spirit infused into him, and *you* are the very man to do it!"

"I have endeavoured to do so this morning!"

"Ah! but he wants a man like you to be constantly with him! and I'm not quite sure that it would'nt answer your purpose!"

"I don't know that it would *not*," returned Mr. Wilkins.

"There's a very fine trade to be done!—a capital trade—an excellent trade. I think it would answer the purpose of both: but that we can talk about, of course, another time."

Well, this idea pleased Mr. Wilkins. Feeling, with Cyrus, that an excellent trade might be done, he thought that it would indeed answer his purpose. But then what was Alfred to do?

' They had not proceeded far before Cyrus explained to him what Alfred not only thought of doing, but was even then anxiously preparing to do, which induced Mr. Wilkins to think still more seriously of entering into partnership with Murray. He however said no more on the subject then; but resolved on embracing the first opportunity of going fully into the matter.

On their arrival they were gaily received by Alfred, who with a smile of confidence whispered to Felicia, "I can do it!" and while the ladies were dressing for dinner, he drew Cyrus and Mr. Wilkins into the garden, and there explained to them how easily it was, in his judgment, to be done. They said all they could to encourage him, of course, and he really was in excellent spirts; but when Felicia and Fidèle appeared, to be led in to dinner, his countenance instantly changed.

Felicia, solely in order to please Cyrus, wore her best suite of diamonds, and Alfred in consequence became apprehensive that she was, after all, really fond of display. He was therefore during dinner, exceedingly thoughtful, and began to dread the consequences of that which appeared to him to be the revival of a passion for the splendour she had sacrificed. But when Cyrus—having been urged by Felicia—had explained to him why she on that occasion wore them, Alfred recovered his spirits, smiled at his fears, and playfully congratulated her on her appearance.

Cyrus, having read Alfred's thoughts, enjoyed this, and quietly expostulated with him when Felicia had retired with Fidèle for believing that a creature so pure, and so fond of simplicity, could ever regret the loss of that of which she knew the moral worthlessness. But all this was soon set aside by Mr. Wilkins, who reverted to his contemplated partnership with Murray, and as this was a subject which interested not only Cyrus and Alfred, but Felicia and Fidèle, nothing else was talked of the whole of the evening.

CHAPTER XIX.

BUSINESS.

"BUSINESS is business." The author of this celebrated apothegm is supposed to have been buried for ages in oblivion; but the apothegm itself is immortal.

He might have been the author of "eggs is eggs;" he might have been the antediluvian Whig, who first called for "the bill, the whole bill, and nothing but the bill;" or the legist, who originally enjoined "the truth, the whole truth, and nothing but the truth;" or the ancient chartist, who started "the hog, the whole hog, and nothing but the hog:" but certain it is that he was a man of business, who wished to impress upon the minds of men of business, that business is business, and nothing but business; and equally certain is it, that Mr. Wilkins was one of his disciples; for, after daily consultations and hourly calculations, within a month from the time that Cyrus offered his suggestion, a new front had been "stuck" into Murray's establishment; the parlour, and even the garden had been "thrown" into the shop, and on a board of Brobdingnagian dimensions, and in letters of gold, the very largest under heaven, stood proudly forth "MURRAY AND WILKINS."

Nor was the presiding genius in his calculations "out!"— The attraction of splendour *was* " immense :"—the appearance of prosperity *did* " draw :"—the " big ones" *did* " swallow the little ones up;" and " everybody" *did* go where " everybody" went: for they had no sooner opened than they had a " roaring trade ;" and in less than three months they were " carrying all before them !"

Meanwhile Alfred—delighted with his new occupation—charmed by Felicia, and panting for fame—pursued his task with surpassing diligence. At first his progress was but slow; he wrote tremulously; he was afraid to give expression to his conceptions, and when he had done so, the erasures, the interlineations, and restorations confused him; but as he proceeded be wrote with more confidence, and was able, in a very short time, to dash through a scene with facility. Felicia, however, having watched him with the most anxious solicitude—soon became alarmed. He looked pale! She therefore feared that a sedentary occupation must undermine his fine constitution; she felt sure that the necessary application was too severe, and frequently declared a fortnight's rest to be absolutely essential to the preservation of his health; but Alfred, being anxious to get on, did all in his power to allay her apprehensions: he assured her that, although he looked pale, he never felt better —that although he seemed thoughtful, his spirits were high! Still she feared that he studied too much. Well, then, he wouldn't work so hard; he wouldn't devote so much thought to it; he wouldn't sit so long at one time; he'd begin an hour later in the morning; he'd leave off an hour earlier in the evening; he'd promise anything to calm her fears, and by virtue of these promises he was permitted, without having *one* " fortnight's rest," to finish the work.

It then had to be carefully read. Felicia had read it again and again; but it had to be read as a whole. And it really read well! There were many very beautiful passages in it— many beautiful thoughts well expressed! It was very good— very good indeed! They felt sure that the critics would like it, and if they liked it, everybody else would, of course! But who was to publish it? That was the question. They consulted Mr. Wilkins on this important point; and in doing so, consulted the very man!

Mr. Wilkins had the honour of knowing Mr. Douall, the

celebrated publisher of fashionable novels—he had known him for years : he knew him when he was one of the first men in one of the first publishing houses in town: he had had, in fact, "many a glass of grog" with him : independently of which, he knew that he had published several novels in the course of that year; the whole of which had been spoken of highly. Mr. Douall was, therefore, the very man! He would see justice done to it: he would advertise it well: he would, in one word, "push" it into circulation.

Accordingly, Alfred and Felicia accompanied Mr. Wilkins to town—it was deemed by all, of course, extremely fortunate that Mr. Wilkins happened to know such a publisher—and the next morning Alfred was introduced to Mr. Douall, whom he found to be the very quintessence of politeness. His courtesy was indeed of an *affectionate* caste. Had Alfred been his own son, he could'nt have received him more warmly : he was such a very nice man.

Having introduced Alfred as a man of sterling talent, the husband of Lady Felicia, and so on; Mr. Wilkins proceeded to introduce the novel, which he said was "a really magnificent thing," and when Mr. Douall—having received it with delight —had succeeded in inspiring Alfred with a high appreciation of his importance as a publisher, and general amiability as a man, he promised to "peruse it with infinite pleasure," and to give him a final answer in a week.

Well, this was held to be an excellent beginning. Alfred was perfectly delighted with the interview, and congratulated Mr. Wilkins on his knowledge of such a man.

"He is one of the right sort," said Mr. Wilkins ; "a gentleman and a man of the world. *He'll* have it: I feel sure that he'll have it: and if he should, he'll give you a rattling price. There are things in it which I have seen myself worth the money. It requires but to be pushed, and he's the very man to push it: he is, in fact, *the* man! Of course, you can't expect to get so much now as you will by and by, when your name is up! But *he'll* make it answer your purpose: I feel convinced of it! you see what he is! He doesn't look like a niggardly man. I never had any transactions with him, but you can see that he is straightforward, candid, and liberal." ↲

"I like his appearance much," returned Alfred, "and shall feel quite proud of his friendship."

Having reached the hotel at which they stopped, Felicia— who had been anxiously awaiting their return—perceived at a glance that they were both highly pleased, and felt, therefore, elated; but when Alfred had explained to her how warmly he, had been received, and how courteous, encouraging, and friendly, Mr. Douall had been throughout the interview, she was quite overjoyed.

"Oh!" she exclaimed, "how I *should* like to see him! I know that he is a dear good soul, and I almost love him for being so kind to you."

Business! business again interposed: Mr. Wilkins had business in the city. He had to purchase a lot of goods which were wanted at home, and wished to return to Sudbury that night. He, therefore—having again and again expressed his conviction that Alfred would be eminently successful—left them, full of hope mingled with joy.

The week was before them. How were they to spend it? What were they to do? They would visit all the places of public amusement—Alfred might have to describe them: they would read all the papers, and all the magazines, and all the new novels, in order to ascertain whether any one of them were comparable with Alfred's. They would go —no, they would not go—into the Park. They would go—yes! they'd go down to Brighton—that sweet place!—they *must* spend a day or two there. Should they go down at once, and put up at the hotel where they had passed so *many* delightful hours together? Yes!—they'd start in the morning; remain there

two days—only two days—and then return to London. And
they did start for Brighton; but, instead of two days, they
remained the whole week — their reminiscences were so
enchanting.

With heads full of visions and hearts full of gladness, they
then returned to town, and on the following morning, Alfred
called upon Mr. Douall, who received him with even more
warmth than before.

"Well," said he, having made a few preliminary observations, "I have perused your very interesting novel, and like it
much."

"I am happy to hear it," said Alfred.

"I think that it will do!—that it will be likely to create a
sensation, and make a hit!—provided Lady Felicia's name be
attached."

"Attached?—in what way?" inquired Alfred.

"As the authoress, my dear sir, of course! It would take
like wild fire!—it would be, in a word, *the* novel of the
season."

Alfred was thoughtful, he knew not what to say.

"You see, my dear sir," resumed Mr. Donall, "the very
title will tell! that alone will give it an impetus!—an impetus
that will impart a velocity to the sale. Authorize me, therefore, to announce Lady Felicia as the authoress, and I shall be
able to treat with you liberally."

"But," said Alfred, "I should, in that case, be authorizing
the announcement of that which is not really true."

"My dear sir," returned Mr. Douall, with a most playful
smile, "we view these things as mere matters of business. It
is, after all, merely nominal. We place on the title page her
ladyship's name instead of yours, that's all! What possible
difference — yes, it will make a difference: it will make a
difference of a hundred pounds to *you*—but, in other respects,
what difference can it make? You and Lady Felicia are one

—legally, morally, religiously one!—bone of one bone, you know, and flesh of one flesh!"—he added, laughing very merrily. "Don't you see! The work belongs to the firm! We are all fond of our children; and our works are our children; but your children, I *hope*, are Lady Felicia's also! What possible objection, therefore, can you have to our calling this *her* child?"

"She," replied Alfred, "would have a very great objection to it, I know."

"But my dear sir, why should she have? The publication of a work like this, with her name, would do honour to the aristocracy to which she belongs. She would play the sun to the aristocracy's moon: she would give it light, life, and glory. The aristocracy would regard it as an honour, and seize it with avidity. 'Here,' they would say, with an air of triumph, 'you talk of rank and talent being inimical,—look here!' It would sell like wildfire."

"I have no doubt that her name would give an impetus to the sale," observed Alfred, "but she would'nt consent to be announced as the authoress, seeing that she really is not."

"I am aware," said Mr. Douall, very blandly, "that these high-souled people are scrupulous. I am, of course, perfectly well aware of that. But let's see if we can't overcome these scruples; let's see whether we can't announce her ladyship's name with a strictly religious adherence to truth. Has her ladyship perused any portion of this novel?"

"Oh, yes; she has read the whole of it."

"Very good. Did she, while perusing it, suggest alterations?"

"Yes, several."

"And those alterations were made, I presume?"

"In most cases they *were*."

"Then she at least *edited* the work?"

"Well, if you call that editing"—

"It is more, much more, than *some* editors do. She, by
perusing it and suggesting alterations, to all intents and
purposes edited the work."

"Well, she suggested the work itself."

"Then she is absolutely the *authoress* of the work. But as
I perceive that there may be some difficulty in inducing her to
consent to be thus announced, suppose we adhere to the gospel
truth, and say 'Edited by Lady Felicia Murray.' She *can* have
no objection to that."

"That certainly would not be so objectionable. But I must,
of course, consult her on the subject."

"By all means; certainly; consult her, of course. And let
me see," he added thoughtfully, "are you particularly engaged
to day? If not, come and dine with me. Say you'll come."

"I shall be most happy to do so," said Alfred.

"That's right. I shall be indeed delighted to see you. We
poor publishers, you know, don't live in a very grand style.
But *you'll* not care much about that; men of sterling talent
seldom care much about grandeur. Say six, and in the interim
you can speak to Lady Felicia. By the way," he added with some
hesitation, "would her ladyship condescend to honour us with
her company?"

"She will come with great pleasure, I am sure," replied
Alfred.

"We shall feel indeed proud to receive her."

Having had his hand pressed and shaken with really unexampled energy, Alfred left him; and on his return to Felicia,
explained to her what Mr. Donall had proposed.

At first Felicia was silent and thoughtful: she felt apprehensive that unless her name appeared, the work would not
be published at all."

"Did he," she at length inquired, "Did he distinctly say
that he could publish it on this condition only?"

"No, my love, no!" replied Alfred; "he merely intimated

that if your name were attached, he could give us a hundred pounds *more*—clearly meaning that it was not a *sine qua non*—that it was not absolutely indispensable!"

"Then I think, my dear, that we had better make the sacrifice. I would, love—as you are aware—consent readily to anything which might tend to promote your views: but I don't think that eventually this *would* do so: on the contrary, I think that its tendency would be to defeat them.—Your object is, to become popular; and irrespective of all pecuniary considerations, I should glory in your success. But how is it possible for you to become popular if you thus remain unknown? Besides, my love, there is one point—pray do not allow it to influence you unduly—still let me name it :· I will at once consent, if you wish me to do so; but the point that I would mention is this :—If my name were to appear, it would be said at once by those who would, I fear, rejoice at our downfall :—'He cannot support *her*: she therefore writes to support *him!*'—which would place you, my love, in a position, the very appearance of which would give me intense pain. All the credit would then attach to *me* : whereas I am anxious for it all to attach to you. I would have them know that you possess talent of which they little dream, and that the exercise of that talent enables us to live in a style of independence. I, of course, my love, merely suggest this point."—

"Felicia! how can I fail to feel its force!"

"It would be not only unjust to you; it would give them apparently a triumph! Still, if you wish me to consent"—

"I do *not*, my love: no; when it was proposed I hesitated only because I was unwilling to give a flat refusal, and without doing so, I really knew not what to say."

They then began to talk of the invitation, with which Felicia was highly pleased—conceiving that it might tend to establish a lasting friendship between Alfred and Mr. Douall—and at the appointed time they were received by that gentleman and his lady with much ceremony, and many expressions of delight.

Mrs. Douall—who had been a handsome woman, and whose manners were courteous, if not indeed refined—had invited two ladies whom she was anxious to provoke—to meet "Lady Felicia, the lovely and accomplished daughter of the noble Marquis of Kingsborough"—to whom they were of course very formally presented—and when dinner had been announced by a servant, whose livery proclaimed a startling struggle with the gorgeous, Mr. Douall—who profoundly bent himself nearly double while offering Felicia his arm—led the way into a room which struck Alfred as being, for a "poor publisher," sufficiently magnificent.

Nor was the dinner at all unworthy of the highest consideration of any "poor publisher" who happened to have an appetite!—everything was done with a view to the superb, and the failure was by no means conspicuous.

During the ceremony the gentle elegance of Felicia excited admiration: had she dined with them fifty times before she could not have appeared more at ease. Nor were the graceful and pleasing manners of Alfred unattractive; but as a pure "piece of acting," the performance of Mr. Douall surpassed all!

Business, however, was still business; and that gentleman— when the ladies had retired—was not long before he was in it.

"Charming lady," said he, "charming lady, Mr. Murray: a very, very, very charming lady: I never had the honour o conversing with a more delightful person. But you can always sir, tell the true stock! There is always a certain sort o something about them which stamps them—I may say absolutely *stamps* them—with an air of aristocratic superiority! By the way, have you spoken to Lady Felicia on that little point?"

"I have," replied Alfred; "but there are certain strictly private consider.tions which render the announcement of her name inexpedient."

"I am very sorry for it—very, very sorry for it. Her name would have sent the work flying through the world. Can *nothing* induce her to allow us to say, ' *Edited* by Lady Felicia Murray ? ' "

" She is unwilling to have her name in any way announced."

" But it might *ooze* out that you are her husband ?"

" Well, I've no objection to that, if it be not paraded."

"Oh, there need be no parade. It might be done in a paragragh, as an *on dit*, for example. ' It is *said* in the highest circles, that the gifted author of the forthcoming novel is connected by marriage,' and so on. There need be no parade."

"Well, if you think that it would assist the sale, let it be done so."

" Very good. Well, then the next point is, how are we to arrange ? *My* system—the liberality of which I am proud to say has been highly appreciated—is to give an author the full benefit of his first production—to give him the whole of the advantage of the sale—that is to say, to publish it for him on his own account; advertise it well, get it well reviewed, push it by all possible means into circulation, get his name up, establish his fame—in short to manage the whole matter for him, charging him a mere ten per cent. upon the proceeds. This is *my* system, and I am happy to say that it has given universal satisfaction. I have, of course, as you are aware, facilities for establishing an author which no other publisher has. I don't say this in any boasting spirit—the fact is universally known; and I may add that, although many of them have left me, for gratitude forms no part of the composition of some men—there is not in literature a popular man who does . not owe his introduction to me. I brought them all out. They are all

my literary children; and although some of them have been
ungrateful children—running away as soon as they found they
could run alone—I am proud of them still, and that pride
prompts me to wish for many more. The money that I have
spent in order to get authors' names up is beyond calculation.
I have given them the full benefit of their first productions
without imposing any condition; but I have at length resolved
on giving this advantage to an author no more, unless he
pledges me his honour as a gentleman, that he will let me
have, for at least *two* years, the first offer of every work that
he may write. Do you blame me?"

"I should say, that an author studies his own interests by
entering into such an agreement."

"Of course he does. But there really are some who will *not*
stick to one man. They will run to different publishers in
order, I presume, to show their independence."

"Well, it certainly strikes me as being unfair, if indeed you
are willing to give as much"—

"My dear sir, I can give 'more. It answers my purpose
to give more: for who has the facilities for pushing a work
that I have? I have of late required a written agreement to
this effect, but your word will be quite sufficient. Pledge me
your honour that you will let me have the offer of every work
that you produce within the next two years, and I shall be
happy to publish this, your first production, and give you—
minus ten per cent.—the full advantage of the sale."

"As far as the pledge is concerned," said Alfred, "I will,
of course, willingly give it; but suppose, instead of publishing
the work on *my* account, you give me a certain sum for
the copyright, and do the best you can with it on your
own"

"That would not be fair towards you. No: I wish to take
no advantage: nor will I. I value your friendship too highly.
I am satisfied with my ten per cent. Sometimes it yields me

two hundred pounds, and sometimes not so much; but, if I take one with the other, it pays me sufficiently well."

"Two hundred pounds!", exclaimed Alfred. "That's ten per cent. on two thousand."

"Oh, that might be almost taken as the average. I don't mean to say that namby-pamby things will do it; but a work written in your dashing style, is perfectly certain to pay."

"Well," said Alfred, who scarcely knew what to think of it, "I can't be expected to know much about the matter, but I thought that you would have purchased the copyright."

"You take my advice," returned Mr. Douall. "I have had some experience, of course, and I don't for a moment hesitate to give you the benefit of it, because you are no common man. Let it be published on your own account. I'll take care that justice is done to it—and you'll see how much better it will answer your purpose."

"Well then," said Alfred, "let it be so. I place it entirely in your hands, with a feeling of the utmost confidence, and all I can say is, do the best you can."

"Depend upon that. I'll announce it immediately, and raise the public mind to the highest pitch of expectation. It shall sell: I'll make it sell: I'll push it into every corner of the globe. And now, when do you think of returning?"

"I have nothing now to detain me in town."

"Then return at once, and commence another work, so that it may follow on the heels of this. I'll send you down the proofs to correct; but, get on with another. *I'll* keep you at work," he added, playfully. If you are idle, I'll haunt you! *Will* you commence immediately? Do, by all means; because, you see, when your name is up, it will be a thousand pities to let it go down. Therefore, set to work immediately on your return."

With golden visions floating before him, Alfred promised to do so; and when Mr. Douall had portrayed his impressions of the leading literary men of the day — which, under the

circumstances, deeply interested Alfred—they rejoined the
ladies, who were in excellent spirits, and with whom they
passed the evening very agreeably.

Having explained all to Felicia—who had been led to repose
the utmost confidence in the honour of Mr. Douall—Alfred,
anxious to begin work again, proposed that they should leave
town the following day, and as Felicia felt equally anxious for
every suggestion of Mr. Douall to be adopted, they started by
one of the early coaches in the morning.

The work was immediately put in hand, and the announce-
ments were certainly of a most attractive character, and
calculated to excite the very highest expectation. It didn't
"ooze" out; it came out at once, that "Alfred Murray, Esq."
was a "gifted writer," that that "gifted writer" was "allied to
Lady Felicia;" that Lady Felicia was "the young and lovely
daughter of the most noble the Marquis of Kingsborough; and
that the work would not only "create a startling sensation,"
but be "celebrated as one of the most true and trenchant
pictures of high life extant!"

It was published, and a rush was made to the libraries ·
"the last new novel" was considered "a great card." Felicia
ordered a dozen copies, and had them elegantly bound: one
for Fidèle, who still lived with her, one for Mrs. Murray,
one for Mr. Murray, one for each of the girls, one for uncle
Cyrus, one for Mr. Wilkins, one for Mr. Chubb—by whom she
was admired "above all other creatures under heaven!"—and
one for herself. Papers were sent down constantly, containing
very favourable reviews, and Mr. Wilkins, who was frequently
in town, ascertained that the work was well known in "the
trade;" that it was understood to have sold very well; that it
was to be found at all the libraries, and that the next, by the
same author would, in all probability, sell as well.

During the whole of this time Alfred worked very hard:
the road to fame was in his view clear, and he made up his
mind to pursue it with diligence. Still he was anxious to

know how he was going on: he wanted to *see* the realization of some of those " golden dreams" by which he had so long been enchanted. When, therefore, three months had expired, he wrote to Mr. Douall on the subject, and that gentleman very promptly, and with infinite politeness, appointed a day for " the settlement as far as the thing had gone."

Alfred accordingly went up to town, and was received by Mr. Douall with all his characteristic courtesy. He hoped that he was well: he hoped that the delightful Lady Felicia was well: he hoped everybody connected with him was well: he was particularly anxious to know if there had been any increase in the family, and was altogether very pleasing, playful, and affectionate.

" Well," said he, having fired a volley of civilities, " our novel didn't go off so well as I expected: I pushed it well too! but the public mind is flat: times are not what they used to be: pockets are not so well lined as they were: people haven't the money to spend. This Currency Bill has played vengeance with the circulation—pinched everything up. There's *nothing* stirring: all is spiritless and dull, and, therefore, in spite of every effort, it hangs fire. But you mustn't be disheartened! it was, you know, but a first production after all! *we* shall improve upon it; the next will tell the tale."

" But," said Alfred, " I understood that it sold very well!"

" I caused that to be understood by the public at large:—I made every earthly effort to induce them to believe it:—that was, of course, a mere matter of business. However, I don't know how we stand! I have directed my clerk to make out the account; he may have done it by this time: we'll ring and ascertain."

A dark veil fell between Alfred and his hopes, and all his bright visions became indistinct.

" Mr. Murray's account made out?" inquired Mr. Douall, of a sleek and obsequious, but very artful card.

" Yes, sir," replied the card in question, "just finished it."

"Bring it in."

The clerk went for the account, and during his absence Mr. Douall directed Alfred's attention to a painting, which had just been presented to him, he said, by one of the most celebrated artists of the day. The painting, however, had no charms for Alfred; he wanted to see the account.

"Well, how do we stand," inquired Mr Douall, when the clerk had returned."

"There's a balance, sir, of ninety odd pounds."

"Oh, said Mr. Douall, as he perused the account, while Alfred thought ninety odd pounds would be *something*. "But," he added, "you have put the balance here on the wrong side."

"No sir; the balance is against Mr. Murray."

"Against Mr. Murray!" said Mr. Douall, with a well-defined expression of amazement. Haven't you made some mistake?"

"No sir; it's all correct."

"Go and bring the books, bills, vouchers, and all. Dear me," he added, as the clerk left the room, "I made so *sure* that it would sell, that I advertised it more than I otherwise should have done; but I certainly had no idea of this."

Alfred was silent; the books were produced, and when Mr. Douall had examined them as minutely as if the whole thing had been new to him, he directed the clerk to leave the room.

"Well," said he, "certainly this is correct. It struck me when I found that it hung fire, that it would'nt be a *very* great card, but I did think that it would, at any rate, have cleared itself. It's a sad job, certainly—a very poor beginning. But I'll tell you what I must do: I must give you two hundred for the next."

"But I don't understand *this*," said Alfred. "You said that you would give me the full benefit of the first production, and you bring me nearly a hundred pounds in debt. This surely is not what you *meant* by the full benefit."

" My *dear* sir, if I had dreamt that the thing would'nt pay —and that handsomely too—I would'nt have published it, either on your account or on that of any other man alive. But these things are, after all, speculations. We can't expect them *always* to succeed. They will, in spite of you, *sometimes* fail. I'm of course sorry for it—very sorry for it. I feel, nevertheless, conscious of having done all I *could* to make it pay. However, as I said before, in order to meet the thing as far as I can, I'll give you two hundred for the next."

Alfred took no apparent notice of this; his eyes were wandering through a labyrinth of charges for composing, correcting, printing, binding, advertising, and a host of *et ceteras*, which he did'nt understand, and therefore could'nt dispute. The only thing which he understood distinctly was that " the balance of ninety odd pounds was against him." But then what could he say? He knew what he thought, but how could he prove that what he thought was correct?

Mr. Douall endeavoured, with the most affectionate solicitude, to raise his spirits. He playfully alluded to the difficulties and struggles of " other great men," and assured him that his were over—that his name was up—that he was already popular, and that all he had to do was to achieve immortality.

" Now think no more of it," he added, at length. " Don't allow it to depress you for a moment. Finish the work you have nearly completed, bring it to me, and there's your money. You'll dine with me to-day?"

Dine with him! Alfred *thought* not. He didn't feel disposed to dine with any one then. Having left Mr. Douall—who up to the last moment laboured to assure him, that in *his* esteem he occupied a lofty position!—he had a savage dinne alone.

CHAPTER XX.

THE MYSTERY SOLVED.

ALFRED, on his return to Sudbury, was met at the inn by Cyrus and Mr. Wilkins, and when he had explained to them that instead of receiving, as he had expected, "five hundred pounds at least," he had been brought by Mr. Douall nearly a hundred in debt, they didn't fail to express their amazement.

"What!" exclaimed Mr. Wilkins indignantly—for he felt himself to some extent compromised—"Oh! it's a swindle!—it must be a swindle!—a dirty, disreputable, swindle! But how does he make it *out?*"

Alfred produced "the true and particular account," which Mr. Wilkins understood almost as much about as he did, and when he had sufficiently confused himself among the "ads" and the "pars," and the startling figures connected therewith, he said "Let me have this. *I'll* see about this. I shall be in town again in the course of the week. I'll see about it. Leave it to me."

"Why, my boy!" exclaimed Cyrus, with a smile, "this is a lucrative profession you've got into. After all your anxiety and care—after racking your brains from morning till night, and sticking to work like a leech for months—to be rewarded with a balance of a hundred pounds against you—a very, very lucrative profession indeed! We'll have no more of *this,* my boy! We'll see after something that will pay a *little* better. This is worse than *nothing* per cent. upon capital. But never mind: keep up your spirits; you'll know more before you're a week older. It doesn't much matter, after all."

"Not matter, uncle?" said Alfred, "not to have ones hopes blasted "—

"My boy," promptly interrupted Cyrus, don't give way to any bitter feeling. Do you mark my words. You'll know more before you're a week older! Before you are a week older, you'll care no more about this than I do, and that is but little. I am glad that you have done what you have done, because you have proved what you can do. I am proud of it, and you may be proud of it too; but had it turned out more profitable even than you expected, you would never have written another work!"

"Why not?"

"Because I have something better for you to do! As I have said, you'll know more in less than a week. Therefore don't fret at all about this. Keep up your spirits, my boy! and above all, say nothing about this failure to Felicia!"

"How is it possible for me to keep it from her?"

"You can say that the thing isn't settled: nor is it!—Mr. Wilkins will see about it when he goes to town."

"If I *live*!" exclaimed Mr. Wilkins, energetically. "I will, if I live! If it be possible to ascertain the truth, the truth shall be ascertained!"

"But," said Alfred, "had I not better complete what I am now about first? I shall have, at all events, a hundred pounds to receive then!"

"Have nothing more to do with such a man," returned Cyrus. "Besides, you haven't time to do anything more for this 'celebrated' individual now. But come," he added, "let us be off. Felicia will be anxious."

Having left Mr. Wilkins, who was still most indignant, they started for Melford; and notwithstanding Alfred's efforts to look cheerful when he arrived, Felicia, at a glance, saw that all was not right.

"I fear," she observed, after the first affectionate greeting, "that you have not been so successful as you expected, love—have you?"

"Well," replied Alfred, "the thing is not settled. The account was made out, but not satisfactorily."

"Then have you to go up again, dear?"

"Not at present."

"Dear me! that is very, very tiresome. He said, distinctly, that he would settle as far as he could. If he were not prepared to do so, he ought not to have sent for you. What did he say, dear?"

"He said, that for the next he was willing to give me two hundred pounds."

"*Two* hundred! Not more than that! And did you say that you would accept it?"

"Not distinctly. But we shall hear from him again, by and by, I've no doubt."

Felicia at once perceived that he wished to avoid the subject, and therefore would not press it then; but having, during dinner, watched him anxiously, she felt quite certain that something was wrong. While, however, she was watching Alfred, Cyrus was watching her; and as he saw clearly that Alfred had failed to satisfy her natural curiosity, and that she was in consequence full of apprehension, he made up his mind to relieve them at once, by revealing to them that "profound secret," which he had intended to conceal another week.

Accordingly, after dinner—Fidèle being absent—he assumed an expression of deep mystery, and said, "I have something of great importance to communicate—something, indeed, so important, that it involves the prosperity and the happiness of the remainder of your lives."

He drew nearer to the table, while Alfred and Felicia—whom this startling and mysterious exordium amazed—looked at each other and marvelled.

"The Hall," he resumed, with emphatic deliberation, "has

been, as you are, of course, aware, for some time advertised for sale. It is mortgaged, deeply mortgaged, and has been for years : it is mortgaged for more than it will fetch—seeing that it has of late been sadly neglected—but not for so much as it is absolutely worth. That mortgage was six months ago called in, and various attempts have been made to get another, but as no one could be found to invest more than two-thirds of the present estimated value of the estate, it must come to the hammer — nominally, in consequence of the Marquis having purchased a larger estate; but virtually, because he cannot find the money, even with that two-thirds, to clear off the old mortgage. Very well. Now, on Wednesday next, the estate is to be sold at Garraway's, and—you shall buy it !"

"I !" exclaimed Alfred, with a look of amazement. "I!—I buy it !"

"Yes! You shall buy it, my boy! Ha, ha, ha! We are not at starvation's door yet."

Again, Alfred and Felicia, in a state of amazement, looked at each other, and wondered what he really meant.

"My dear," resumed Cyrus, addressing Felicia, "you were born at the Hall : you passed the greater part of your early youth there : you shall pass the greater part of your life there, my love :—you shall be, as you deserve to be, its mistress."

"But," said Alfred, "tell me distinctly what you mean."

"I mean," replied Cyrus, "that you shall buy the estate; I mean that you shall reside at the Hall in which Felicia was born, and which is dear to her, I know. I have told you that it is mortgaged : I have now to tell you, that we hold that mortgage !—and when I say *we*, I mean Chubb and myself— although my name does not appear. We hold the mortgage ! We have been working together, quietly, for years! You don't know all, my boy !—although you *are* a "very popular" man, you don't know all !—nor does your justly "celebrated" publisher. I don't mean to tell you, that when you have purchased the estate, it will be at once absolutely yours! But the thing can be *managed*, my boy!—it can be *managed!*—and let that, for the present, be sufficient. It has been of late very much neglected: I know that it has: the Marquis must have lost, through neglect, a deal of money; but, if you, with a view to its improvement, will but work half as hard as you have worked in that lucrative profession, from which you'll now happily retire, it will pay. And now give me a glass of wine, and I'll tell you a little more."

Both Alfred and Felicia looked as if bewildered, and when Cyrus had had a glass of wine, he thus continued:—

"Now in the first place, don't say a word about this to mortal; not a word; if you do, you will, in all probability, spoil all. There may, nay, there doubtless will be, two or three bidders, whose surveyors have of late been hard at work, but if we keep the thing secret we shall have it. Certain reasons will prompt me to go a little farther than it will answer the purpose of most men to go; but if we strictly keep what we mean to ourselves, we shall have it, and that without much competition. Understand, that in buying this estate, you can't be said to go against the Marquis. It is publicly advertised; it is open to be purchased by any one; and when you have purchased it, my boy, you will not appear to be quite so near starvation point, as some people predicted you would be."

"Who were they?" inquired Alfred.

"No matter for the present; you'll in all probability know by and by. All I wish to observe having reference to the Marquis is, that in purchasing this estate you will not appear to be actuated by any desire to injure him. And now," he continued, "I'll tell you why I have kept this from you so long. In the first place, as the old adage says, 'There's many a slip 'twixt the cup and the lip,' and as I know that you would feel very seriously disappointed, in the event of the estate passing into other hands, I would not in this respect raise your expectations. In the second place, I thought that if I told you what I intended, it might possibly 'ooze' out, as your celebrated publisher would say; in which case I knew that any sacrifice would be made to keep it from us. And in the third place, I wished, my boy, to see what you would do, and although the profession you adopted has, in your case, been amazingly *lucrative*, I am proud of what you have done, for it proves beyond doubt that you have energy, talent, and perseverance. Nor should I have told you even now," he added, turning to Felicia, " had I not perceived, my dear, that you were full of apprehension, in consequenee of Alfred's inability to satisfy you that all was right in town."

" All then is *not* right ?"

" Certainly not. This young gentleman has been struggling all this time to get a hundred pounds in debt to his celebrated publisher."

" Indeed !" exclaimed Felicia.

" Oh ! it's a fact. He has been working hard for a celebrated balance of ninety odd pounds against him."

" But I don't understand."

" Nor do I, my dear ; nor does Alfred ; nor indeed does Mr. Wilkins, who has taken the matter in hand ; the celebrated publisher alone understands it ; all that we understand is the interesting fact, that when the nominal proceeds of the sale are deducted from the nominal expenses of publication, there is not only a nominal, but an actual balance of ninety odd pounds left for Alfred to pay."

" Dear me," exclaimed Felicia, " it was very wrong indeed of Mr. Douall to mislead us."

" What does Mr. Douall, my love, care about that ? What would he care, my dear, if even he *knew* that you had absolutely no other resource ? Nothing. Nor need we care much about it.   Feeling, however, that when it came to your knowledge you would not only care but fret about the matter, and knowing that while you were kept in the dark, you would continue to be tortured with apprehensions, I made up my mind to impart that secret which I certainly intended to conceal another week."

"You are, as you ever have been, kind and considerate.   I should have felt indeed distressed, had I known this *alone*."

"Of course you would!   But let us say no more about the courteous Mr. Douall: let us fix our attention upon the one grand point, and remember, that the slightest hint may have the effect of frustrating the object we have in view."

He then proceeded to enter into a variety of calculations, in order to prove to Alfred that the estate, if well managed, would yield a very splendid revenue; and having remained with them—explaining his connexion with the Bank and various other matters, of which they had no previous know-ledge—until Fidèle and the indignant Mr. Wilkins came home; he privately gave them one more serious caution, and left them in a state of amazement the most intense.

It really appeared to them to be a dream.   This accounted for his quiet display of conscious independence.   It accounted for the extraordinary willingness on the part of the Bank to afford the firm of Murray and Wilkins the "accommodation" of which they had spoken so highly.   It accounted, in short, for numberless things which had always appeared to be mysteries.

Well!   The "writing" was set aside of course.   Alfred had got his lovely heroine into an appalling dilemma, and there he left her.   He never got her out.   She is in it to this very day. There she and the "perfidious one" stand.   He had no time to see after either.   His time was devoted to Uncle Cy and Mr. Chubb, with whom he was engaged in calculations on and off the estate, until the day before the sale, when they went up to town, where they met Mr. Wilkins, who informed them that Mr. Douall's *clerk* had " made a mistake."

At the time appointed for the sale to commence there were several persons present, who looked like purchasers, and when an hour had been allowed for conversation, business began, and the sale proceeded slowly. Chubb, being known to the agents of the Marquis, kept studiously aloof from Cyrus and Alfred, until the auctioneer, notwithstanding the offers made were insufficient to cover the mortgage, appeared to be really in earnest, when he promptly gave the pre-concerted signal, and Alfred made an offer. This put one of the bidders, who was accompanied by his surveyor, and who appeared to be determined to have it, upon his mettle, and a somewhat severe competition ensued, but Alfred, urged by Chubb and Cyrus, out-bid him, and to Alfred the estate was eventually " knocked down."

Chubb then introduced him to the Marquis's solicitor, who promised that no time should be lost in preparing the conveyance; and when all the necessary arrangements had been made, Alfred took possession of the estate.

CHAPTER XXI.

THE CONCLUSION.

THE expansive powers of a social circle, of which wealth is the centre, are known; but those powers in the case of Alfred and Felicia were not tested.

They had no sooner taken possession of the estate with the reputation of being almost inconceivably rich, a reputation which Conjecture, with Rumour, his wife, can at all times with infinite facility establish, than the neighbouring "gentry"— the butterflies who are seen only where the sun shines— fluttered round them with fascinating smiles, and expressions of intense admiration; but Felicia, who loved tranquillity still, and who well knew the value of these conventionalities, gave them no encouragement whatever to persevere in their efforts to "draw her out." She knew the constitution of society, and looked beneath its surface. She knew that if hearts were open, and feelings were material things conspicuously developed, circles of "friends" would be but small; and therefore pursued her gentle course—was courteous and kind to all around her, and enjoyed that sweet tranquillity of soul which purity only can impart, and which social hypocrisy tends to destroy.

But the greatest sensation prevailed in the town. Where had Alfred procured the money to purchase the estate? How had it been done? Who had made him so rich all at once? There had been no death in the family of Lady Felicia, because she was not in mourning! and if the Marquis had made them a present of the estate, why had it been advertised and publicly sold? Had it been done for a blind? It might have been; and yet the Marquis was not the man to conceal his generosity. Perhaps one of Lady Felicia's rich relations had taken pity upon her! It must have been so: and yet why *must* it? Had they not been living in a style of independence ever since they came down? Had he not been writing novels? Who could tell what they had realized? And yet—he couldn't have written a sufficient number in the time. No: it wasn't that—they were sure that it wasn't that: *what* it was they couldn't tell!—nor was it necessary for them to know. The tradesmen's wives who once *had* a chance of being introduced to Lady Felicia, now reproached themselves bitterly, while the tradesmen—who had waited with the utmost impatience, to see Alfred and Felicia wandering about the streets in a state of starvation, for the express purpose of fulfilling the prediction of the Marquis—humbly solicited their patronage and support.

Meanwhile, Alfred was full of energy. He had procured the advice and assistance of the most eminent practical agriculturists of the day: he broke up two-thirds of the park, which had never before yielded a shilling: in short he made every possible effort with a view to the improvement of the estate, and his success was beyond even the most sanguine expectations of uncle Cyrus and Mr. Chubb.

About twelve months after they had taken possession, Felicia received a letter from Richmond, stating that Lady Loftus felt exceedingly ill, and was anxious to see her once more. She accordingly, accompanied by Alfred, went to Richmond, and saw her aunt, whose death was then daily expected, and who received her most affectionately: she begged to be forgiven for all the pain she had inflicted, and explained with much emotion, that the accounts which she had heard from Florence and Augusta—the whole of which she had proved to be false—were of a character so shocking, that she felt it her duty to act as she had done. " Do not leave me, my love," she added, at length. " This house is yours. Do not leave me. I shall not be here long."

Nor was she. She died the next day, and left all she possessed to Felicia.

This incensed the Ladies Florence and Augusta still more; for they had been led to expect that all beyond the five thousand pounds, which reverted to Felicia, would be divided between them. They were frantic with rage when the fact became known to them, and charged Felicia with having "wheedled" her aunt on her death bed, not because she *wanted* the property, but in order to be revenged upon them. No robbery was ever, in their judgment, committed with more consummate impudence! They wouldn't go while they knew that she was there, nor would the Marquis: they only wished they had gone! It would have been, however, quite useless: the will was made before Felicia arrived.

Florence, about six months after this, married: she married Lord Delorme, who had a spirit as imperious, and a temper as violent, as her own; and having spent the "honeymoon" with him—"a honeymoon," characterized by the most furious efforts on both sides to obtain the mastery!—she returned to Kingsborough house, disgusted with *him;* and he left England declaring that he would not even live in the same land with *her!*

This, however, did by no means intimidate Augusta. She was not to be daunted, not she! She married the Earl of Ellesmere; and in a few weeks they arrived at a point of indifference, which prompted them to enter into a compact to keep up "appearances" as man and wife, but not to interfere *at all* with each other's pleasures.

Mr. Chubb about this time wrote to the Marquis on the subject of an account which was still between them, and which ought long before to have been settled; and as the Marquis, who had then no agent in Sudbury, was anxious to have "more time," he went down himself, and saw Mr. Chubb; and when an arrangement had been made—for Mr. Chubb had no desire to be severe so long as the thing was arranged in *some* way— the Marquis inquired "how those people got on at the Hall?"

"Excellently well," replied Mr. Chubb. "It is impossible for any man to get on better. Active, intelligent, full of energy, and spirit; that young man is *coining* money fast.".

"I was robbed," said the Marquis, "I see it now—daily and hourly *robbed*."

"Very likely, my lord," returned Mr. Chubb coolly. "I think it very likely, indeed. But Alfred Murray is not above attending to his own business! You should see the estate *now*, my lord. You'd scarcely know it. It would be worth your lordship's while to ride up and have a look at it. Let me recommend you to do so, my lord. Just go over it."

"What, I?"

"Why not, my lord? You will find Mr. Murray as gentlemanly a man as you ever spoke to, while his amiable lady is an angel, my lord, if there ever were one upon earth."

"Do you forget, Mr. Chubb?"

"No, my lord; but I think that it's high time for *you* to forget, or at all events, my lord, to forgive."

"To forgive in such a case, is to countenance an example, which is in itself pernicious. *No* girl ought to marry without the consent of her parents."

"I admit it—I admit that the example is bad, and therefore one which ought not to be countenanced; but do you countenance an act of disobedience, by forgiving the child who has committed it? Does nature, or even common justice, prompt a father to crush such a child? Must he labour to crush her, or hope to see her crushed, in order to prove that he cannot countenance her fault? What becomes of our paternal affection—what becomes of Christianity itself, if such a doctrine be admitted? The practice is a bad one; and in the great majority of such cases, lasting misery is the result; it is seldom, indeed, that true happiness springs from a clandestine marriage: but is it our duty to mark our disapprobation by rendering that misery more acute, or by wishing that our children *may* be miserable—that they *may* become outcasts of society—that they *may*, to use the words of a certain handbill, have to choose between infamy and utter starvation?"

"I know what you allude to," said the Marquis; "but that did not emanate from me."

"I don't know, my lord, whom it emanated from; I only know that it must have emanated from a coward. But, as I was saying, ought we to wish for destruction to alight upon our children because we have neglected to inspire them with that love for us which is the very germ of obedience? Who ever heard of an instance of a child, whose parents had properly taught her to love them, being in this grand respect disobedient? Disobedience springs almost invariably from neglect. When I point to the happiness of Lady Felicia, I do not point to it as the result of a clandestine marriage; because her case on that point is one out of a thousand—no, I point to it merely as the result of a combination of purity, energy, and honour. It must, my lord, be remembered that if there ever were a case in which an act of disobedience—it may more properly be called an act of independence, seeing that as your lordship had no knowledge whatever of its being contemplated, you could'nt have forbidden it—I say if ever such a case could be held to be venial, *that* case is Lady Felicia's. She had no dear mother to guide her—she never felt the sweet influence of a fond mother's love —which I, old and rough as I am, my lord, *have* felt, and still feel—although she is gone—and shall continue to feel until the heart over which it ever reigns shall cease to throb. She had no dear mother, my lord: *you* could'nt attend to her; and her sisters—to say the least—were unkind. *Ought* she not therefore, my lord, to be forgiven? I speak irrespective of her present prosperity, because that is, of course, adventitious; but I say, that a father, possessing the heart and the feelings of a father, can't in his own breast, my lord—in his own *breast!* —justify himself in refusing to forgive her."

"Does she ever mention me?" inquired the Marquis, with some emotion.

" Frequently; and I know that if she had but your forgiveness, her happiness would be indeed perfect."

" Then, I'll go and speak to her."

" You *will*, my lord!"

" Yes: I'll go and see her. Will you accompany me?"

" With much more pleasure than I am able to express."

The Marquis rang the bell and ordered his carriage at once, and when it was ready they started for the Hall.

Felicia, who was at the window with Alfred playing with their beautiful boy, no sooner saw the carriage approach, than she clung to him as if for protection.

" My love!" said he, " why so tremulous?"

He had, however, scarcely spoken, when he recognized James, and then, of course, knew the cause.

" Be firm," he added. " Be firm, my love!"

The carriage stopped, and when Chubb alighted with the Marquis, Alfred felt that the visit was not hostile. He did not, however, go out to receive them: the Marquis was shown into one of the rooms, and Chubb went to announce his arrival.

" The Marquis," said he, addressing Felicia, with an expression of gladness. " The Marquis! It's all right! He has come in the most friendly spirit! He has come to make you happy! Go to him, my dear!"

Felicia, still instinctively clinging to Alfred—fear, not love, being the lesson which the Marquis had taught her—trembled with increased violence. Alfred, however, tenderly led her to the room, and when he found that the Marquis embraced her, retired.

" Felicia!" said the Marquis, as he held her in his arms, " I am much pleased to see you. A feeling has been awakened which has long lain dormant. Let all that has passed be, if possible, forgotten. Be happy. God bless you. Where is your husband?"

Felicia rushed from the room, and clinging to Alfred, drew him in.

"Mr. Murray," said the Marquis, as he took Alfred's hand, "I have been wrong — very wrong. Be prosperous and happy."

"I am delighted, my lord, to see you here!" said Alfred. "But you will not leave us yet?"

"I called, but for a moment," replied the Marquis. "Felicia," he added, "write to me: call upon me when you come to town. God bless you—God bless you both."

He embraced her once more, and having again shaken Alfred by the hand, he returned with friend Chubb to the carriage.

Felicia now felt completely happy. The presence of the Marquis had overpowered her, and rendered her unable to utter a word—the fond name of father she had never been taught to utter—still, the fact of his having called was, in her view, sufficient, and when Cyrus heard of it, every feeling of resentment vanished. He always spoke of the Marquis respectfully after that, and he had constant opportunities of doing so, seeing that he then resided entirely at the Hall, and there continued to reside until his death, when the estate became Alfred's own.

Friend Chubb soon followed his warm hearted "brother:" the loss was too great for him to bear: he saw him in his grave, and wept bitterly, but came out of his house alive no more. His manners were rough, but his nature was kind; and his pride was to love Felicia, who was, indeed, beloved by all who could appreciate purity, and whose life was that of a gentle spirit, inspired with tranquil joy.

J. HADDON, PRINTER, CASTLE STREET, FINSBURY.